CAERPHILLY COUNTY BOROUGH
3 8030 09411 5121
D0581588

Also by Jan Newton and available from Honno Press

DS Kite novels
Remember No More

RATHER TO BE PITIED

by

Jan Newton

HONNO MODERN FICTION

First published in 2019 by Honno Press, 'Ailsa Craig', Heol y Cawl, Dinas Powys, Vale of Glamorgan, Wales, CF64 4AH

1 2 3 4 5 6 7 8 9 10

A catalogue record for this book is available from the British Library.

Published with the financial support of the Welsh Books Council.

ISBN (paperback)
978-1-909983-86-1

ISBN (ebook)
978-1-909983-87-8

Cover design: Graham Preston
Text design: Elaine Sharples
Printed in Great Britain by Gomer Press, Llandysul, Ceredigion SA44 4JL

For Merv, always

As always, there are so many people who have encouraged me in th writing of this book. I have been gratified and humbled by the response to *Remember No More*, the first book in the Julie Kite series, which made it so much easier to embark on this, the second. The wonderful people of mid Wales and beyond have taken Julie Kite to their hearts, and I'm truly grateful for their continued support and feedback.

Grateful thanks to Chris Kinsey, who motivates me constantly, to write and to improve.

To Kevin Robinson, retired West Yorkshire Police Inspector, once again huge thanks for his support in ensuring that my facts were factual, and for painstaking proof reading with a forensic eye. As usual, any mistakes in any aspect of this novel are, of course, my own.

Thanks to everyone at Honno for their help and support, especially Caroline Oakley, my editor, for accommodating all the recent ups and downs away from the writing side of life.

Lastly, but most importantly of all, my gratitude to Mervyn, without whom none of this would have been possible. For over thirty years, he has supported everything I have ever wanted to do with insight, patience and pride. I will always be grateful.

CHAPTER ONE

Day One

Mark Robinson sat down on a dry tussock of grass in the shelter of a slab of rock. If it hadn't been for the breeze, this would have been a perfect July day. There was barely a cloud in the china-blue sky and from somewhere nearby, the cry of a curlew stirred long-forgotten memories of his own childhood. One more hour and he could finally drop the kids off at the school gates and head for home.

Mark sighed. He'd always prided himself on his patience, on the fact that he would always take the time to listen to his pupils and would never ever give up on them, no matter how trying they were. And yet, after three days under canvas with this lot, traipsing around in circles in the middle of nowhere, he was beginning to appreciate the attitudes of some of his battle-weary colleagues. He counted his charges yet again. God knows what would happen to them when they did the expedition on their own in three weeks' time. He pushed his water bottle back into his rucksack and stood up.

'Right, where is he?'

'Who, Sir?'

'Very funny, David, as if we couldn't guess who might be missing.' Mark clambered onto the rock he had been sitting on and scanned the moorland. 'Where is he this time?'

'I've got him, Sir. Look, he's over there by that sheep.'

'Could you be a bit more specific in the sheep department, Sasha, help to pinpoint it a little.'

'The dead one, Sir, there.'

Mark looked to where the girl was pointing. Three hundred yards away, Owen Lloyd was approaching the carcass of a black sheep with unaccustomed alacrity. Entirely appropriate. As they watched, the boy suddenly took a step backwards, then another, still staring at the sheep, before turning back towards the group and breaking into a run. Mark watched him stumble over the clumps of reed and the tufts of tough moorland grass, but it wasn't until the boy stopped suddenly and bent forward with his hands on his knees that Mark set off towards where Owen was stooped.

'Stay there,' he shouted over his shoulder. 'Sasha, you're in charge of keeping everyone here, OK? Don't let them move.'

By the time Mark reached him, Owen was retching up his packed lunch into the peat.

'What is it? What's the matter?'

Owen wiped his mouth on his sleeve and pointed in the direction of the sheep. 'Over there, Sir.'

'It's all right, it's just a dead sheep. I know it's sad, but it happens all the time out here. It's difficult to get to. It's hard for the farmers to cover such a vast, boggy area.'

Owen shook his head and stared at his teacher. His eyes looked huge and dark in his pale face and Mark realised, perhaps for the first time, that Owen Lloyd was still just a child.

'It's not a sheep, Sir.' Owen's bottom lip trembled and he closed his eyes.

'Stay here,' said Mark. 'I'll go and have a look.'

'Don't, Sir, it's horrible.'

'You stay here. I'll go and check it out, it might just be injured.'

'It's a body, Sir,' Owen blurted, 'and it's covered in maggots.'

Owen Lloyd's description was all too accurate. The skin on the man's face was dark and peeling. Flies buzzed lazily around him. Mark tried to look away. The smell caught in his throat like the sickly-sweet whiff of something decomposing gently in the bottom of a hedgerow, but far, far worse. He stood up and struggled to swallow the bile that burnt his throat. Against his better judgement, he glanced back at the corpse. One of the man's hands appeared to be missing; the cuff of his black denim jacket rested in the mud and several fingers, a couple of small bones and a gold ring lay scattered next to him. The bones could have been sheep bones, couldn't they? But the ragged flesh which covered some of them looked far too human. Sheep didn't bite their fingernails either, did they? His stomach lurched. He lifted his phone from his pocket. No signal. He backed away as if retreating from something sacred, then turned, took a deep breath and returned swiftly to where Owen was sitting with his head in his hands on a clump of grass.

'Have you got your phone on you, Lloydy?' he asked, as casually as he could.

The boy looked up at him. 'But you said we couldn't bring phones, Sir.'

'And we both know that would make no difference at all, don't we?' Mark forced a grin. 'Could you check to see whether you've got a signal?'

'Honest, Sir, I haven't got my phone.'

'OK.' Mark took him gently by the elbow and led him back towards where Sasha was standing high on the rock, hands on hips, attempting to keep the group in order. 'Listen, Owen, I'd appreciate it if you didn't tell them what you saw. There's no need for them to have nightmares too, is there?'

Owen nodded. 'Do you think... well, could he have been murdered, Sir?'

'Out here?' Mark shrugged. 'There's not much chance of that is there? It's far more likely that he was out walking and was taken ill, I'd have thought. Anyway,' he put his hand on the boy's shoulder, 'let's not worry about that now shall we, let's just get you all to the minibus.'

'What is it, Lloydy?' David was running out to meet them. 'You all right?'

'Yep, I'm fine.' Despite the wobble in his voice, Owen managed a nonchalant shrug. He looked up at Mark. 'It was just a sheep.'

CHAPTER TWO

Day One

Julie Kite watched DI Craig Swift scuttle across the office towards her. He only ever moved as quickly as this when there was something really important to impart. She was already reaching for her jacket when he approached her desk.

'A group of school kids have found a body,' he said, slightly breathless from his exertions.

'Where?'

'Above Pont ar Elan, on the Monks' Trod.'

Julie frowned. 'On the what?'

'Follow me, I'll fill you in on the way.'

She smiled. So much for him being office-based these days. Rhys Williams rolled his eyes as she passed his desk. One of these days, Swift would let the two of them out together without him. Julie followed Swift down the stairs and through the reception area. Brian Hughes, the desk sergeant, grinned at her as she whizzed past him in an attempt to keep up with Swift. It was amazing how quickly he could shift if he wanted to.

Swift strode across the car park, dropped into the driver's seat of his Volvo, waited for Julie to clamber in and fasten her seatbelt and crunched the gear lever into reverse.

'Right, so where are we headed, Sir?'

'Pont ar Elan. Bridge on the River Elan.'

'And that's where, exactly?'

'It's up above Rhayader on the old Aberystwyth Road.' Swift steered the nose of the car out of the car park and into the school traffic – the only sort of rush hour Julie had encountered since her ıove from Manchester Metropolitan Police, three months before. She smiled to herself as she watched drivers politely giving way to each other at a tricky junction, as they did every day.

'So, what's this Trod thing all about then?'

'The Monks' Trod,' said Swift. 'That's one for your Adam. He probably knows more about it than I do already.' He swerved round a campervan which had stopped suddenly. Its occupants appeared to be arguing over a map.

'It's an ancient route up in the hills.' He nodded towards the north. 'Apparently the monks used to use it to travel from Strata Florida Abbey in Pontrhydfendigaid to the sister house at Abbeycwmhir.'

Julie blew out her cheeks. She would never manage these Welsh names with their convoluted vowels. 'Yeah, he's already mentioned something about drovers' roads. Would that be similar?'

Swift laughed. 'He doesn't hang around does he now? How's he getting on at the High School? Has he settled into the new job by now?'

'Oh God, he loves it, and the kids, the countryside, the lack of traffic, having no neighbours, the whole bit. It's as though he was always meant to be here. He's got huge plans for the summer holidays.' She grimaced. 'But almost all of them involve running and cycling.' She turned to Swift. 'I don't suppose you know of anywhere he could practise his open water swimming, do you?

Swift glanced at her. 'Do I look as though I would have the inclination or the ability to squash myself into a wetsuit, Sergeant?

Julie stifled a smile. 'Maybe you have a point there, Sir.'

Swift slowed to allow an oncoming lorry to squeeze past and then he accelerated away round the tight bend, bringing the solid stone walls of the cathedral into view on their right. 'Strangely enough, I can't say I've ever heard of anyone wanting to do open water swimming.'

'What about up at the reservoirs, Sir?'

'The Elan Valley?' Swift shook his head. 'No swimming, sailing or otherwise larking about up there. Not on the water anyway.'

'Oh well, it was worth a try.'

'And what about you, Julie? Are you feeling a bit more settled here now?'

Julie watched through the side window as the houses petered out and the car headed into open countryside. 'I'm getting there, Sir. I love the way everybody knows everyone else and the fact that it's completely silent at night. I love the views and the rivers and the way people calculate journeys in minutes rather than miles.' She thought of home, of the centre of Manchester, the bustle and drive of the place, the fact that everyone was a comedian. 'I'm a townie at heart though. I think it may take a little while longer for me to feel like a total country bump– er, person, Sir.' She gazed over fields full of sheep and ever-growing lambs. It was a very long way from the concrete and tarmac maze she had been used to. 'Would I be right in thinking that this location's going to be muddy, wet and covered in sheep shit?'

'See, you've cracked it. Spoken like a true local that was. I don't suppose you remembered to bring your wellies?'

'Actually, Sir, I didn't. Give me time, it's not quite a reflex reaction yet.'

Swift laughed. 'You're in luck, Sergeant. Apparently this one's not too far off the road.'

*

Dr Kay Greenhalgh's black Alfa Romeo was in the tiny car park at Pont ar Elan. Next to it was a marked patrol car and a gleaming black van with chillingly dark tinted windows. Swift slid the Volvo to a halt. Just up the lane, a white Mountain Rescue Land Rover was tucked into the bank, from which a pair of deep and grass-filled vehicle tracks led sharply uphill.

'Who found the body?' Julie asked, as Swift pulled on a pair of battered black wellingtons. He slammed the boot lid, hitched up his suit trousers and set off up the lane towards the Land Rover.

'It was a school kid on a practice run for a Duke of Edinburgh expedition.'

'Kids? Out here on their own?'

'They had a teacher with them, thank God. He phoned it in from the bus, but he insisted on taking them back to school once he knew we were on our way. They had parents waiting to collect them, so he thought it would be better to get them out of the way. He said he didn't want them to see anything they shouldn't.' Swift's breathing became more laboured with the gradient of the hill and he waved Julie past him as they drew level with the Land Rover. 'Up that slope and turn right at the top.'

Julie followed the line of the track as it disappeared round the curve of the hill. Away to her left, the river Elan bent left and right then broadened into the beginnings of what looked like a lake. Bog cotton waved in the breeze, the white heads reminding her of enthusiastic and exhausting trips to Hayfield and Edale with Adam. At the top, she waited for him to catch her up.

'It's a godforsaken spot, Sir. He probably died of hypothermia.'

'In July, Sergeant?'

Julie laughed. 'It's July, Sir, but it feels like February in Urmston.' Despite the heat of the sun, the wind felt as though it came straight from the Arctic. Overhead, a buzzard circled and she shivered. 'Do we know who he is?'

'Not yet, but no doubt the good doctor will have a theory.

Despite Swift's assurances, Kay Greenhalgh was a good ten-minute muddy walk from the road. As they climbed over the brow of a rock-strewn bank, they saw her and her entourage of Scene of Crime Officers, starkly obvious against the unrelenting greens and browns of moorland, in their light blue paper suits. Outside the locus, there were two uniformed PCs, and two men dressed in black who stood motionless, their hands clasped and heads slightly bowed. Four members of the Mountain Rescue team, in their bright orange suits and white helmets, waited on the other side of the cordoned-off rectangle, with a sled-like stretcher on the ground between them.

The scene beneath her reminded Julie of watching a play from the front circle, with the brightly coloured costumes of the actors brilliantly lit in the dark theatre. This production needed no words.

Julie squelched on down the track through puddles with their iridescent surface indicative of peat. She attempted to wipe the worst of the mud from her shoes on a tussock of reeds. 'I thought you said it wasn't far off the road, Sir.'

'It could have been worse, Julie, this track goes on for miles.'

The doctor greeted Swift with her stock opening line. 'Good afternoon, Inspector. Nice of you to join us.' Kay Greenhalgh smiled at Swift. 'I've almost finished here. I need to get him on the slab before I'll be able to tell you anything useful. It looks as though he's been dead for five or six days at most, judging by the maggot activity. There's no rigor and apart from the head, the skin has a marked green tinge. He also has a catastrophic head injury, but that's all I can say for now.'

The bloodstains on the rock showed that the man had probably been in a sitting position originally, with his back leaning against the rock and his legs straight out in front of him. Now he was slumped forward into a dark tidy heap. Dr Greenhalgh lifted the shoulders. The skin on his face was dark – almost black – and there were maggots weaving their way in and out of every facial orifice.

'Why is the skin on the face at a different stage of decomposition to the rest of him?' Julie asked.

'Well observed, Sergeant. Unfortunately, I have absolutely no idea. I'll know more once I've done some testing.'

'This is probably a daft question, but do you think he could have been a rambler?' Julie asked.

'It's not a daft question. In my experience, there are very few daft questions. He was wearing boots and they were fairly old ones by the looks of the sole pattern, though he didn't have a rucksack.'

Greenhalgh leaned back and took a long look at the body. A frown flitted across her face. 'He didn't have a map or satnav either. Would you walk out here without bringing anything with you?'

'Did the head injury kill him do you think, or could he just have fallen and then been caught out by the weather?' Swift leaned over the blue and white incident tape to get a closer look at the face and grimaced.

Greenhalgh gently released the shoulders. 'He could have died of exposure of course, but it's unlikely at this time of year, even up here.' She turned to gather up a sheaf of evidence bags. 'And I'm not even sure yet that he died in situ. Those boots are a pretty common make but there are a surprisingly large number of other types of boot print on the ground for such a godforsaken spot.' Kay stepped under the tape. 'Although I'd not fancy carrying a body so far from the road, even one this slight.' She crouched suddenly, beside her bag, and looked at the corpse from her new location. She shook her head, filed the evidence bags and snapped her briefcase shut.

'Could he have been dumped from a vehicle?' asked Julie.

Swift shook his head. 'They've banned vehicles up here, blocked off the access with boulders. The illegal off-roaders have caused so much damage it's made it impassable in places.'

Kay Greenhalgh raised her head and then her eyebrows. 'Are you really saying there's no way to get out here in a vehicle now that the path's blocked?' She snorted quietly. 'The weekend warriors might not manage it, even the ones with upswept exhausts and impressive sticker collections, but a good quad bike or tractor driver with local knowledge would get you out here, no problem, wouldn't you say?' She looked back at the corpse. 'Or what about a pony? There's nothing of him, you could easily sling someone that size over a pony's withers.'

Julie also raised an eyebrow. Every time she met the pathologist, she was impressed by the breadth of her knowledge.

'Fair point.' Swift tugged at his ear. 'Can we tell if he *was* dumped?'

Greenhalgh shrugged. 'It's too sodden for there to be any tyre tracks, but the position of the body would suggest he'd been carefully placed, leaning against the rock.' She looked at Swift. 'Or he could have just banged his head on the rock, managed to right himself and then expired of course.'

Julie noticed the suspicion of disappointment cross Swift's face at this possibility. 'Do we know who he is?' she asked the doctor.

'There's absolutely nothing to identify him. Nothing at all in his pockets, and he wasn't even wearing a watch. There's a signet ring but there's nothing inscribed on it, no initials.' Greenhalgh jiggled a plastic bag. 'At least we think it must be his, although it's not very big and it's not actually attached to a digit. Could be a pinkie ring?'

'Had the hand dropped off?' Julie took the bag from Kay and examined the grisly contents. Along with the ring were several small bones.

'Nope, too soon for that, and judging by the marks on the bones in the wrist, it looks as though a fox has had a go at it. Most of it was down there on the ground next to him.' Greenhalgh retrieved the bag and held it up for Swift to see. There were several pieces of finger in the clear plastic bag. Flaccid skin still clung to the bones and the nails that were visible were bitten down to the quick. 'I'm guessing the damage was post mortem.'

'Thank goodness for small mercies,' muttered Swift, dabbing his mouth with a large white handkerchief. 'When do you think you'll be able to fit him in for your ministrations?'

'Seeing as it's you, Craig, I'll get it started first thing tomorrow morning. I'll let you know as soon as I've got anything – unless you'd rather be there for the main event? I know you like a hands-on approach.' She jiggled the evidence bag and Julie laughed

'I could go, Sir?'

'Ah yes, you and your gruesome penchant for a good PM, Sergeant.'

'It beats paperwork, Sir.'

'There's nothing wrong with being interested in watching science at work, Craig.' Greenhalgh stepped well away from the locus and removed the shoe covers from her wellingtons. She dropped them into a large evidence bag, which was being held open by one of the uniformed constables. 'You might even learn something.'

'I think I'll leave it to the sergeant, if it's all the same to you. It's a relief to finally have a member of the team who enjoys all the blood and guts.'

Greenhalgh shook her head and began to walk away from them. 'Oh,' she said, turning back to face them. 'There was one odd thing. His good hand is twisted slightly as though he'd been holding something. It might be nothing, it could have happened as he died – some sort of reflex action or spasm – or it could have been caused by a pre-existing condition. Anyway,' she pushed back the hood of her SOCO suit, 'Sergeant Kite and I can discuss it in more detail tomorrow.'

Swift and Julie watched Greenhalgh walk away.

'So where does this bewildering love of necrotising flesh come from eh, Sergeant?'

Julie shook her head. 'It's not that ghoulish, Sir. I just find the whole forensic pathology thing fascinating. You can find out so much more about some people after they're dead than when they were alive. There's nowhere to hide anything, is there, on a slab?'

'That's far too much information for my liking.' Swift curled his lip.

The two dark-coated men zipped the corpse into a black body bag and slid it onto the stretcher, and the Mountain Rescue team lifted it carefully between them. The entourage was moving en masse off the hill now, leaving the two uniformed PCs to carry out a final check and remove the tapes. A huddle of mountain sheep watched them approach. All but one fled. She looked up briefly, considered them carefully then put her head down and carried on grazing.

'Given what we've got to go on, it might be an idea,' said Swift, nodding towards the sheep, 'to bring her in and take her hoof-prints.'

CHAPTER THREE

Day One

Julie's first impression, as she slowly crossed the reception area towards Owen Lloyd, was that he had, outwardly at least, recovered from his ordeal out on the moors. He wore what looked like brand new and expensive white trainers but his grey skinny jeans were still mud-spattered from his rural exertions. His chin was buried in the folds of a red hoody and he sprawled untidily on the low reception seating, typing frenetically into his phone. Beside him, a dark-suited man wearing a sober shirt, navy tie and a pained expression, hissed urgently.

'Can you try to look as though you've just found something shocking and not as though you're lolling on a sun lounger?'

Owen groaned with his eyebrows but there was no deceleration of his thumbs stabbing at the screen.

'Owen, are you listening? You'd better not be broadcasting this to all and sundry on that thing.'

'No.'

'No, you're not listening?'

'No, I'm not saying anything.' Owen glanced sideways. 'Not about that anyway. Mr Robinson asked me not to.'

'Oh, so how can Mr Robinson get you to do as he wants?'

Owen stopped typing and sighed theatrically. 'Because *he* treats me as though I'm a person and not just one gigantic disappointment.'

The boy's body was angled away from his father; the father's face was becoming increasingly flushed as the boy spoke. Julie held out her hand first to the younger Mr Lloyd and then accepted the limp handshake offered by his father.

'Owen. Mr Lloyd. It's good of you to come in this evening. Hopefully things will still be clear in your mind.' Owen grimaced, but didn't reply. 'We've just a couple of questions, it's nothing to worry about.' She smiled at the father. 'We'll try not to take up too much of your time.'

In the interview room, Owen hurled himself into the plastic chair in the same position he had favoured in the reception area. His words were almost glib to begin with and each sentence was punctuated with shrugs as he told Julie about the expedition. No, he couldn't remember where they had walked or what they had seen. When she asked if he had enjoyed the trip, he looked at her as though she had suggested he might like to give up social media and read a good book, but when she asked about what he'd found, out there up in the peat, he couldn't hide his emotions.

'I thought it was just a sheep. A black sheep.' He looked up at her. 'But then I got closer, and I could see it was a person.' He took a jerky breath. 'From the way it... he was sitting, I knew he would probably be dead, but I didn't expect it to be like that.'

Owen's father moved towards his son, but Owen shifted in his chair, edging away. 'His skin, the skin on his face, it was gross. Bits of it were flaking off.' He swallowed and sniffed quietly. Both adults pretended they hadn't heard, but then Owen caught his breath in a half-sob.

'Do you want to take a break? Should we stop and let you get a drink?' Julie ducked her head so she could see under the hood. 'Or we could do this tomorrow if you'd prefer?'

Owen shook his head. 'Let's get it over with now, and then I can forget about it.'

His father shot Julie a look which confirmed they were both aware that for Owen to forget what he had seen might take far longer than the boy realised.

'Well just say if you do want to stop. OK?' Julie waited for the small nod before moving on.

'Did you touch anything?'

'Why would I want to do that?'

'I just need to know whether you might have dislodged anything, can you remember?'

Owen shook his head. 'I didn't touch it or anything near it. It was all totally gross.'

'And you weren't wearing those trainers earlier this afternoon?'

'Obviously not, Sergeant.' Mr Lloyd was controlling his contempt with difficulty.

'Well, would it be all right if we had a look at the boots you were wearing, just so that we can eliminate any marks you may have made at the location from the results of our forensic examination.' She turned to the father. 'Perhaps you could bring them in first thing tomorrow. If you could put them in a clean plastic bag that would be a big help.' Mr Lloyd suddenly looked less confident and Owen's eyes widened.

'I didn't do anything, I swear.'

Julie smiled at him. 'It's OK, don't worry. You're doing great. I'm not saying you would have touched anything, Owen, and if you did, that's understandable, given what you experienced out there. We just have to know if everything was in the same place as when we saw it, that's all.'

'I didn't move anything. I didn't want to touch it, any of it.'

'That's fine. So there was nothing with the... there were no belongings?'

Owen stuck his chin out and Julie waited for the defiant response, but instead, out of nowhere, he began to sob. 'It... there were flies and maggots everywhere... it looked as though he was still moving.' He swiped his sleeve across his face. 'They were crawling all over his face, in his mouth, but he couldn't feel them.'

Owen's father was out of his chair now, holding on to his son, both arms wrapped tightly around him, his chin resting on the top of Owen's hooded head. Owen made no move to push him away. Julie waited until Mr Lloyd let go, until he had rubbed Owen's back self-consciously and sat back down in his chair.

'That's fine, Owen. You've been brilliant. If you think of anything else that might help us...' Julie paused in the face of a stare from Mr Lloyd. It was easy to see which parent Owen had inherited his impressive facial expressions from.

'I think I'm ready to take my son home now, Sergeant, if that's all right with you.'

Julie watched them walk out of the building. Mr Lloyd had an arm firmly round Owen's shoulders and the boy was leaning into his father. She realised Brian Hughes was watching her from behind the reception desk.

'All right, Julie?'

'I think I upset the poor lad. He'll have nightmares.'

'He'd have had nightmares anyway after seeing something like that.' Brian smiled. 'But I think you've just helped to improve a pretty dodgy father-son relationship. For a little while anyway.'

Swift was standing by the board and Rhys was writing down, in neat colour-coded sections, all the information they had so far. There was very little there. Julie watched Rhys stick a photograph of the body and a section of the local Ordnance Survey map on the board. A red dot marked the location where the body had been found.

'Sorry, Sarge,' Rhys said as she went to stand next to him.

'What for?'

'Well, I know you're not too keen on corpses on the board, are you?'

'We don't have much of an alternative this time, do we?' She grimaced at the photograph. 'Besides, it's not the gruesomeness I'm bothered about, although this one is pretty spectacular in that department.' She stepped back and looked at the photograph, the map and the rest of the sparse information. 'I'd just rather see the deceased as they were, as a living, smiling person. It makes it seem even more important that we find out what happened to them.'

'If you say so, Sergeant.' DI Swift gave her the slightly nonplussed look he'd bestowed on her at regular intervals since her arrival on his team as an eager, newly promoted detective sergeant. 'So, what do we think?'

'He could have been a walker.' Goronwy offered.

'Do people walk on their own in places like that?' Julie asked.

'There are all sorts of oddballs up in the hills,' Morgan Evans offered.

'You're doing your charitable human being thing again then, Morgan?' Julie laughed, still unsure of him, and whether he would see the joke, get her sense of humour.

'It's true though. Loads of people go walking on their own. What about your Adam?'

'So you're saying he's an oddball?'

Morgan cocked his head on one side. 'He does go out running on his own, Sarge.'

Julie couldn't tell from his deadpan expression whether *he* was joking now.

'Fair point.' Swift stepped between them. 'There could be lots of reasons why he was out there on his own. He could have been working out there or walking or any number of other things.'

'Maybe he was checking sheep.' Rhys said. 'Or looking at wildlife or something. Rhian's brother's into all that Iolo Williams nature stuff. He goes all over the place with his binoculars.'

'At least he says it's wildlife, eh?' Goronwy attempted to look innocent.

'He was drunk at that wedding, you know he was, boy.' Rhys wagged his whiteboard marker towards his annoying cousin.

'Thank you, children and just for your information, there were no binoculars or anything else found with the body.' Swift tapped the map on the board. 'So he could have been on his own, but if he wasn't, then who would have left him out there? Could he have been separated from a group and got lost?'

'He's not far enough off the path for that though, is he?' Julie watched Rhys write 'Why was he there?' on the board. 'Even if he'd had a heart attack or a fall or something, and was on the ground, they'd still have seen him if they came back to look for him. There's no cover up there at all. There's no way they'd have missed him.'

'So that leaves the possibility that someone left him there knowingly.' Swift shook his head. 'Or that he died of natural causes and bashed his head on his way down.' He pursed his lips. 'Although I'm not at all convinced about that idea. Well, we've absolutely nothing at all to go on so we'd better start with missing persons. Could you do that now, Goronwy, please.' Swift waited for Goronwy's acknowledgement before moving on. 'I'm not aware of anyone from the area having been reported missing, but we need to make sure. It's more likely he's from off, so you'd better make it fairly broad. If he was a tourist, then he could have been staying locally, so we'll need to start with hotels, B&Bs and campsites in and around Rhayader and work outwards.'

'There might be a car somewhere, Sir?' Julie said. 'He didn't get there on public transport, did he?'

'You're right, Julie. Morgan, see if anyone's reported an abandoned vehicle and try the car parks and the Visitors' Centre in the Elan Valley. And get Traffic to keep an eye out for anything that could have been abandoned in a layby.'

'He could have come from the other end though, from Pontrhydfendigaid, couldn't he?'

'Good point, Morgan, he could.' Swift checked the map again. 'So, Julie, first thing tomorrow, you're going to go and find out more about our corpse. Morgan can check out the towns at the other end of the Monks' Trod.' He scratched his ear. 'Rhys and Goronwy can tackle accommodation in Rhayader for a kick off, see if any of their guests didn't come home recently. I'll make a start on the hill farms and we'll compare notes later tomorrow morning, unless anything earth-shattering comes to light before that.' He ambled off towards his glass-fronted office. 'Sergeant Kite and I will touch base after the PM,' he shouted back at them. 'I think she and I may need to go and ask a few questions in Llandrindod.'

Morgan Evans rolled his eyes and Julie laughed.

CHAPTER FOUR

Day One

Julie chased the last grains of risotto rice round her plate and picked up her wine glass. 'You're getting better at this cooking thing,' she said. 'You'd never know that was veggie.'

Adam carried both plates to the sink. 'Thank you for the back-handed compliment,' he said, gazing at the pile of pans and chopping boards balanced on the draining board. 'And you'd never know that you'd agreed to do the washing up.' He sighed. 'There's nothing wrong with vegetarian food either. It's not all lentils and mushrooms, you know.'

'You have to admit though, you do get through the lentils. And the beans.'

'You like beans.'

'Only baked beans, preferably cold and straight from the can.'

'You're a heathen. And that rather splendid risotto you just devoured was actually vegan.'

'I've told you. You'll not convince me in a million years to go vegan. I need bacon butties and shepherd's pie, there's no way I can think on a diet of rabbit food.'

'Your little grey cells will be fine with plant-based sources of protein, believe me.' Adam dribbled washing up liquid onto the plates in the sink and turned on the tap. 'Your diet is horrendous.'

'There's nothing wrong with my diet. It's better than a lot of people's.'

'It's better than Helen's, I'll grant you that. God knows what she's eating now you're down here. At least you cured her of the Mars bar for breakfast habit. She'll be back on the kebabs and the stuffed-crust pizzas by now.'

'I should see if there's a job going at the station for you. You're like the food police. There must be nothing worse than a newly converted vegan. And just so you know, I absolutely refuse point blank to feel guilty about pizza.'

'It's your body, it's up to you whether you want to look after it.' Adam rinsed a plate under the tap and gave her his *you know I'm right* expression. God, he was positively angelic when he got going. It almost made her want to take up smoking.

'What can you tell me about the Monks' Trod?' she asked.

'Are you changing the subject by any chance?'

'Possibly.' She smiled as he pulled off bright orange rubber gloves and folded them carefully over the tap. 'But I'm serious. We were out there today and I'd love to know what made people totter about up there centuries ago, and why they still do. There's absolutely nothing for miles. Except mud and very smelly water.'

'So there's been foul play in the Cambrian Mountains.'

'Something like that.'

'Come on, Jules, you know I'll find out by this time tomorrow, anyway.'

'Even though you're in school tomorrow? Do you think the jungle drums will reach you that fast down in Builth then?'

'You never know. Anyway, I might feel the need to go for a long bike ride after school. For training purposes. There are some brilliant hills over that way.'

Julie shook her head, but she was smiling. 'OK. You win. Yes, there has been foul play in the Cambrian Mountains. Possibly. Up above Pont ar Elan. We don't know yet and it could quite easily be natural causes, although Swift is not chuffed at that idea, obviously. I'm off to the post mortem first thing, and the others are making a start asking questions in Rhayader and Pontreedsomething.'

'Do you know who it is?'

'It's probably just a walker who was taken ill out there on his own. Poor old thing.' She shrugged. 'Well, I say old, but there's nothing of him. He's probably much more likely to be a teenager.'

Adam poured more wine into Julie's glass, screwed the top back on the bottle, returned it to the fridge and sat back down at the table. 'Well I don't know a huge amount about it,' he said. 'I do know the track was part of a longer one, leading from the abbey at Strata Florida to the one at Abbeycwmhir, hence the Monks' Trod. I think it was Benedictine monks who used it originally, and then after the dissolution of the monasteries, it became more of a drovers' road.'

'And what did the drovers actually do?'

'They moved livestock for a living, cattle and sheep and even geese. On foot, can you believe that? They even took them as far as London. Can you imagine how hard that must have been? It's got to be two hundred miles from here.' Adam was suddenly animated, in teacher mode. 'They used dogs to help them – corgis a lot of the time – and when they got to London, they'd just send the dogs back. On their way home, the dogs would stay in the same lodgings they had stayed in with their masters on the way down.'

Julie laughed. The kids would love it, imagining corgis running about all over the country looking for digs. They'd love Adam's enthusiasm too. 'I'm glad you don't know very much about it.'

Adam looked hurt until he saw her face and he smiled. 'Yeah, all right, Sergeant Sarky, but I can find out more for you. I'll go to the reference library in Brecon tomorrow and check it out.'

'And there I was, wondering what you'd do with yourself all summer. You're loving this, aren't you?' She laughed, but Adam's features had rearranged themselves into a frown. She bent to get a better look at him but he moved his head away.

'Jules.' Adam picked at the corner of his place mat and looked away, out of the window to the hills beyond.

'Go on.'

'I don't want you to over-react. Promise me you'll stay calm.'

'What have you done, ordered yet another bike? Bought a new wetsuit? Told your mum and dad they can stay for a month?'

'Seriously, Jules, I need to tell you something important.'

Julie leaned back in her chair and folded her arms. Her stomach was suddenly doing somersaults.

'This sounds ominous.'

'No, honestly, it's really not that bad. The thing is... I just don't want you to find out any other way and get the wrong idea. You know what you're like with that imagination of yours.'

'Find out what, Adam?' There was no response, and he still refused to meet her gaze, so Julie bent forward, into his eye line. 'What is it?' Adam looked down at the table and fiddled with his mat until she slid it out of his reach. 'Tell me. Is there something wrong with you?'

He shook his head. 'It's fine. Everything's good, nothing to worry about, honestly. But you need to know in case there are phone calls.' He closed his eyes. 'Just in case she phones.'

Julie's hand tightened round her wine glass. 'She?'

'She's just being daft. It won't come to anything.'

'You're not trying to tell me that she's at it again? It's *her*, isn't it, it's bloody Tiffany.'

Adam nodded miserably. 'You know what I told her at the Christmas party. I couldn't have made it any clearer that it was over, could I? And there was no doubt she definitely got the message, given the names she shrieked at me as she left the pub. And that was months and months before we moved here. And I showed you the letter I sent her in January. For God's sake, you even edited it.' Adam stopped and took a much-needed breath, finally meeting her stare. 'And before you ask, yes, I did post it.'

Julie took a large gulp of wine. 'So, what's the barmy cow done now then?' She willed herself not to over-react, not to pick up the wine glass with its slender pale green stem and hurl it at the newly decorated wall.

'It's nothing much, honestly, she's just been texting again.'

'What did she say?'

Adam shrugged. 'She said she needed to talk to me.'

'And that was all?'

'She said she had something to tell me and that she would rathe do it face to face.'

Julie stared at him. 'And what do you think that could be, Adam?'

'I have no idea, but I'd lay odds it's not what you're thinking.'

'How do you know what I'm thinking?'

'I know you. And to be fair, I'd be thinking the same thing, except that I know it's not possible.'

Julie watched his face. 'But you said you'd changed your phone number.'

'I did change it. Don't be soft, Jules, you know I've got a different provider, a new number, everything.'

'So how has she got hold of your new number?' Julie wanted to reach for the glass again but instead she forced herself to sit still and breathe slowly and evenly. He'd promised he wouldn't ever stray again, hadn't he?

'Adam, how has she found you?'

Adam looked up at the ceiling. When he eventually faced her again, she knew from experience that he was telling her the truth. 'It was Fran.'

'Hadleigh High Fran?'

Adam nodded. 'Tiff was in doing some supply teaching, just after the May half term, and she persuaded Fran she needed Derek Jamieson's number to talk to him about a pupil of his. Fran said Tiff was worried about the girl, she thought she might be being abused at home. Fran says she just brought the staff phone book up on the computer with Tiff standing there and didn't think anything of it.'

Julie refolded her arms and leaned back in her chair. 'And what with your number being next on the list to good old Mr Jamieson's?'

'I knew you'd be able to work it out.' Adam gave a little smile and waited for Julie to reciprocate. She didn't. 'But what do I do about it?'

Julie unfolded her arms, rested both elbows on the table and gazed at him, using the blank stare she used to make suspects squirm in interview rooms. It had the desired effect. 'She doesn't know your address?'

Adam blushed and shook his head. 'Fran had only put the phone number on the list in case of any queries but she hadn't put our new address on the computer, thank God.' He traced the edge of the table with his finger. 'She said she couldn't spell it. So no, Tiffany doesn't know where we live.'

Julie nodded. 'Good. That's something, at least. Let's hope it stays that way. You'd have thought a school secretary would be a bit more cautious with personal details, wouldn't you?'

'Oh come on, Jules, that's not fair. You know Fran, she's so careful with any information about the kids. She was just trying to help. You'd never imagine that you'd have to keep a teacher's details private from a colleague, would you?'

'Wouldn't you?' Julie arched an eyebrow. 'So what did you do when you got the texts?'

'I didn't do anything.'

'You haven't replied to her?'

'Well, yeah, I did reply to the first couple, just to tell her to leave me alone, but I've not answered the rest. I promise.'

Julie stood up and walked to the fridge. She retrieved the wine bottle and filled her glass almost to the brim, leaving the chilled bottle on the table. She could see Adam resisting the urge to slide a coaster under it, but he stayed where he was.

'Say something, Jules.'

'What do you want me to say? You promised me before we even moved here that it was all over.' She shrugged. 'If I hadn't believed your promise, then I wouldn't be here would I? If you really haven't said anything to encourage her, then it's not going to be a problem, is it?' Julie watched Adam relax as though someone had released the stopper from a beach ball.

'Thank you.' He leaned across the table and gave her free hand a clumsy squeeze. 'I didn't know what you'd say.'

She shook her head and picked up her glass, sipping slowly. 'I wasn't too sure either, to be honest.'

Adam's lopsided grin was one of the things that had made her fall for him in the first place and he knew when to use it. 'So what can we do?'

'I don't think there's anything we can do, is there? If she's only sent a couple of texts and you've left her in no doubt as to where she stands, then we just have to hope she'll get the message. If she's no idea where you live, then what can she do?'

'Julie Kite, I don't deserve you.' Adam kissed the top of her head and then sank back down into his chair.

'You don't, Mr Kite. Now pass me the Pringles.'

CHAPTER FIVE

Day Two

Julie had set the alarm for 6am. Dr Greenhalgh wasn't one to hang around, whether she was driving her sporty Alfa Romeo or delving into the mysteries revealed by close examination of internal organs. Julie knew from experience that her meticulous ministrations would begin at eight o'clock sharp. Adam was already up, banging around in the kitchen, directly below their bedroom. From the clatter of cafétière and the gentle squeak of the fridge door, she gauged that breakfast would arrive in around two minutes. She lay back on the pillows and sighed. How on earth would they begin to find out what happened to the decomposing soul up there in the peat? Where would they start with all that empty land with no people to question? What were the chances of a witness having seen anything? What was he doing up there with no belongings? Where did he come from?

She could hear Adam bound up the stairs and flick the door latch. He plonked the breakfast tray on the bed and whipped the curtains open so that sunlight poured in, making Julie screw up her eyes.

'There's nothing like being woken up gradually, is there?' she said.

Adam sat down on the bed. 'I know how you hate to be late, I'm just speeding things up a bit for you.'

'I suppose you've been out on the bike already?'

'I have. And in less than a fortnight I won't need to get up at 5am. Not with six weeks of holiday stretching out in front of me. I'll have all day to play out.'

'Don't rub it in.' Julie reached for her mug of extremely dark black coffee while Adam sipped at a green tea and scraped hummus thinly onto wholegrain bread.

'How can you eat chick peas for breakfast?' She shuddered and bit into thick white toast, which Adam had, unusually, smothered in butter and a thick layer of strawberry jam for her. 'What are you planning to do today?'

Adam stretched and leaned back on his elbows, making the tray slant on the covers. 'I thought I might take myself off to Brecon after school and have a look at the Monks' Trod in the library for you.'

'So, you're not training yourself into oblivion for a change then?'

'I'll go on the bike.'

'But it's miles to Brecon.'

'It's not that far. I'll just nip over the Epynt.'

Julie sipped her coffee. 'You, Adam Kite, are absolutely barking mad.'

'But you wouldn't have me any other way.'

*

Julie pushed through the swing doors and breathed in the hospital smell. Why did she like it so much? It made Swift heave, she knew that, aware as he was of the horrors he'd seen down this corridor over the years. Maybe it was because she enjoyed that sense of cleanliness, of things being black and white, alive or dead, the hard facts provided by the victim's body and a skilled pathologist. She looked at her watch. 7.50am. She knocked on Kay Greenhalgh's door and was answered by a muffled *hang on a moment.*

The door opened and Dr Greenhalgh swept out past Julie into the corridor, her short white wellingtons squeaking gently on the polished lino.

'Nice to see you're an early riser too, Sergeant.' She turned sharp left without slowing her stride and backed through double doors, gesturing to another door on her left. 'I'll be with you in a minute, make yourself at home.'

Julie climbed the four steps up to the gallery and took a seat behind the full-length window. Beneath her were two stainless steel tables and banks of surgical instruments, buckets and weighing equipment, all beneath operating theatre-strength lighting. From the right hand side of this stage, a trolley appeared, pushed by a gowned and masked assistant. The body of the victim made only the slightest of contours in the white sheet. Only the peak of his feet and the rounded bump of his head gave away the fact that this had, very recently, been a person.

From the door on the left hand side, Kay Greenhalgh emerged, snapping on surgical gloves. She reached for the overhead handle, repositioned the brilliant light, flicked on her tape recorder and asked her assistant to remove the sheet. Carefully, she cut away the checked shirt, which was crusty from its contact with the peaty water. Even from a distance, Julie could see Kay's eyebrows raise, pushing up the unflattering blue headgear further into her hairline. 'Well, there's a turn up.' She glanced up to where Julie was sitting with her face as near to the glass as it could be. 'I must book an appointment with a good optician,' Kay said. Then, into the recorder, 'The body is that of an extremely emaciated *female* of perhaps eighteen to twenty-five years.'

*

By 9.30am, Julie was in Kay Greenhalgh's office, sipping her second caffeine-packed coffee of the day. Kay smiled. 'So, keen on pathology *and* iv caffeine. We could be related if it weren't for't fact that you're from the wrong side o't Pennines entirely.' Julie laughed at the deliberate accent slippage, which was rare from the doctor, but somehow made them feel like allies. Against what, she wasn't quite sure.

'So, what do you think? Was she murdered?'

'That's going to take me a bit longer to unravel. What I can't work out is what the odd smell was that she was giving off.'

Julie raised an eyebrow. 'How long have you been a pathologist? That smell when you open up a body is like nothing else.' She sniffed and shuddered, but only slightly.

Greenhalgh nodded. 'Even after generous application of the most expensive shampoo money can buy, I still think people will smell it on me when I'm in the queue at Costa at lunchtime.' She leaned back in her chair and looked up at the strip lighting above her desk. Two large and very dead bluebottles lay on the patterned plastic. 'But, apart from the familiar scent of putrefying internal organs there was something else. Something with a distinctly chemical whiff about it.' She glanced back at Julie. 'And it wasn't Estée Lauder, that's for sure.'

'And you've no idea what that might be? What are you thinking: could it be petrol or diesel? Something you'd find in the back of a vehicle, maybe?'

'Sergeant Kite, you should have been a scientist.' Greenhalgh clinked mugs with Julie. 'There are a few possibilities I'm toying with. I've taken samples and I'll send them off for testing today, but it may take a little while to sort out.' She set her mug back on her desk. 'Annoying though, because I recognise that smell. It takes me back to when I was a kid, but I just can't remember why.' She sighed. 'Anyway, as you heard in there, she was female, probably early- to mid-twenties, and she has, at some stage, given birth, although I can't tell you how long ago that might have been.'

'And the hand was definitely gnawed by something, rather than being removed?'

'Yes, the marks on the end of the radius and ulna are definitely consistent with striations made by teeth rather than a blade. There was no evidence of blood either in-situ or on the clothing, which would also suggest that the hand was detached post mortem.'

'Thank heavens for small mercies. So we've not a huge amount to go on.' Julie sighed. 'Where to start?'

'Well, we've got the signet ring. Despite what I said yesterday, once I got it under the microscope, I could see that there are in fact very faint initials on the ring – CRH, we think, and there's that fairly distinctive tattoo on the left shoulder.' Greenhalgh flipped through photographs on her screen. 'What do you think that could be?'

Julie stared at the screen. 'A four-leaf clover maybe? Or a shamrock, with a red rose. Could it be a Lancashire rose?'

'And it could be the red rose of England. You Lancastrians. What are you like? At least our Yorkshire rose is a little bit more distinctive.'

Julie laughed. 'Fair enough. Can't blame me for trying though.'

'Any excuse to drag the conversation back to Lancashire then, is it?' Greenhalgh smiled. 'Have you been back since you moved?'

Julie shook her head. 'I should do, my mum's been nagging on a regular basis. I've not seen them since we got here.'

'They're missing you?'

'She thinks there's something wrong with Dad. He's just taken early retirement and he's bored witless, but she thinks he's not quite himself.'

'She could be right. Will you go and see them?'

'I will, it's just...'

'So, at a guess, work's getting in the way?' Kay Greenhalgh drained her cup and stood up.

'You know what it's like.' Julie rolled her chair out from under the desk but remained seated. 'I will go back, once we've got this poor girl her answers.' She glanced at the photograph of the corpse on Kay's screen. 'What about the needle tracks? Was she a serious user?'

Greenhalgh handed Julie a selection of plastic evidence bags containing clothing. 'I would say that she was in the industrial usage bracket. There were even very faint tracks on her feet and neck, and some of them very recent. I'm still waiting for toxicology reports to come back, but I'll let you know as soon as they do. Despite the head injury we'd have to assume an overdose until we can prove otherwise, given the evidence.' She shook her head slowly. 'Why do they do it?'

Julie shrugged. 'I've never been able to understand drugs. I've never done anything more outrageous than ibuprofen.'

Kay grinned. 'Nor me. Her clothes don't give much away, cheap chain store stuff, all well-worn, but clean if you disregard the mud. There's a checked shirt, jeans, black denim jacket nothing distinctive.' She reached up onto a low shelf and brought down a bag containing the boots. 'These are interesting though.'

'Doc Martens?'

'They are DMs, but really old ones. The insides and the edges by the laces give it away, with the uncoloured leather. The newer ones are prettier, with neatly coloured innards. I'd have said 1970s or maybe eighties at a push. I had a pair just like these.'

'I'll defer to your judgement as an innards expert, Doctor.' Julie laughed. 'I didn't have you down as an aficionado of Northern Soul, Dr Greenhalgh.' Julie took the bag from her and twirled the boots in their plastic shroud to get a better look. 'Did you go for the long skirt and bomber jacket too?'

'Cheeky mare.' Kay Greenhalgh was laughing now and Julie thought it made her look years younger. 'For your information, young lady, I used to get over to Manchester as often as I could. Tony Wilson was a god.' She shook her head and gave a wistful little sigh. 'There's nowhere quite like the Haçienda was in the eighties.'

Julie smiled. The doctor was full of surprises. 'Nice to know you were the right side of the Pennines occasionally though, eh?' She grinned and hooked a stray strand of hair behind her ear. 'Thanks, Kay. We've got a lot more than we had yesterday. Now all we've got to do is find out who she is and what happened to her.' Julie stood up and Kay held the door open for her.

'Good luck with that one then,' Kay Greenhalgh said. 'Hopefully I'll be able to phone you in an hour or two with a bit more information.'

CHAPTER SIX

Day Two

Swift drove slowly, leaving a dust cloud in the Volvo's wake, which was coating the car in a thick grey film. The track ran alongside a small stream, and on either side, the valley soared almost vertically. It reminded him of the Westerns he'd watched as a kid with his dad. This would definitely have been classed as a gulch. Would that be the same as a *bwlch* in Welsh, he wondered. He slowed for a deep-set cattle grid with nettles and reeds growing through the metal and accelerated away once the car lurched back onto the scalpings. That was Julie Kite's influence, making him look at maps and signs and working out what names meant in English. Was it her age or her Manchester background that made her look at things so differently? Her sense of humour was certainly northern and he wasn't entirely sure that Morgan Evans would ever quite get the hang of that. He smiled to himself. Maybe it was healthy for the two of them to spar, now and again.

Where the track turned into a vast oblong of pale concrete by the farmhouse, Swift drove straight on, heading for a long stone building with a rusted, corrugated roof and tall wooden doors which were propped open. He parked the car and peered into the cool gloom of the shed.

'Hello, Mal, are you there?' He stepped inside, straining to see, and gingerly avoiding various piles of animal droppings. A sheep[illegible] stood up but lay down again in a rattle of chain as he passed. '[illegible] You about?'

'Well, if it isn't young Craig Swift. Where have you been hid[illegible] Mal turned the ewe between his knees back onto her transferred a fearsome pair of hoof clippers into his left hand and pumped Swift's hand vigorously. Only a small amount of the purple spray transferred itself to Swift's shirt cuff. 'Foot rot,' Mal said, attempting to wipe Swift's cuff and making things infinitely worse.

'Not to worry,' Swift said. 'Glad to see you're still on with the sheep.'

'What else would I do? You know me, I'm not one for sitting about indoors. Come on in, Sarah's been baking.'

'I'm on business, Mal, if I'm honest. I was wondering if you'd seen anyone hanging around over on the Monks' Trod, or anyone here or in town who looked...' Swift struggled to find a word which wouldn't immediately give the game away.

'As though they might be up to no good?' Mal frowned. 'We heard about that poor chap left out there. He was in a bit of a state, from what we heard. All maggoty.'

'Yes, Mal, as though they might be up to no good.' Swift shook his head benignly. 'And you heard right. Although goodness knows where you got it from.'

'You know me, Craig. I always say it pays to keep your ear to the ground, especially the way things are today. It's not like it used to be in the old days, is it?' Mal stepped outside the pen and clanged the hurdle shut. 'Come on in and see Sarah, have a *panad*. You can tell me more.'

'That's not quite how it works,' muttered Swift, following the old man out of the shed and across the yard. Despite Mal's observation, it seemed that this place had barely changed since the day it was built, maybe three hundred years ago. There were no cables into the house or the barn. The phone network hadn't yet reached this far up the valley, nor were Mal and Sarah linked to the National Grid. The faint hum of a generator and Mal's pristine red truck were the only signs that this valley wasn't trapped in a time warp.

Sarah had been busy. The kitchen table was loaded with fruit cakes and pies, and there were enough scones and bara brith to feed a family of ten. As the men came in and Mal removed his cap and his boots, Sarah pushed the enormous joint of meat she'd been basting back into the belly of the Rayburn and reached for the kettle.

'Still tea with two sugars, is it, Craig?'

'There's nothing wrong with your memory, Sarah.' Swift smiled. 'You cooking for the five thousand?'

Sarah beamed at him. 'Not quite. The boys from the Graig are going to be over before dinner. They're gathering the last of the hill sheep for us. We'd normally have had it done a couple of months ago, but when Mal broke his ankle we were a bit stuck for a while.'

'You're fussing, again.' Mal shook his head. 'Craig doesn't want to know about all this.'

'I do.' Swift sat down in the chair Sarah had pulled out for him at the table. 'What happened?'

'Stupid really. I was trying to catch that Herdwick tup that Mogs had lent me to take it back. They have a mind of their own those things. I thought Texels had a sense of humour until I saw this one.' Mal looked up at Sarah as she handed him his tea. 'It cleared the cattle grid.'

'And Mal didn't.' Sarah patted him on the shoulder. 'Bit like a man trap, that grid. We couldn't get him out. By the time I'd come out to see where he was and heard him shouting, well his ankle had swelled up like this.' She held out both hands, curving her gnarled fingers to the size of a small football.

'What did you do?' Swift went into incident mode, but was having trouble imagining a plan for this particular scenario.

'Frozen peas and Vet Wrap,' Mal said. 'Good job she was in the Girl Guides or I might still be there.' He smiled up at Sarah. 'She managed to get the swelling down and then bound my ankle so tight it made my eyes water. Still, it was the only way I was going to get out of there. If she'd left it until someone had got here, it would have been huge. We'd have had to cut the grid to get me out.' The way they looked at each other was something else which Craig thought might not have changed in the sixty years since the two of them had moved to Sŵn y Coed to begin married life together.

'Besides,' Sarah said, 'the ruddy truck was this side of the grid, wasn't it. I'd never have been able to get out to raise the alarm without running him over.

Swift managed to squeeze in two cups of tea, a slice of bara brith and a scone before he was allowed to talk about the real reason for his visit. Sarah was more forthcoming than Mal about sightings of strangers.

'He won't tell you because he thinks accepting any help is admitting he's past it.'

Swift laughed. 'There's no way he's past it, Sarah. He's a lot fitter than me, and half the lads on the force.' He waited for her to continue, which she did only after receiving an almost imperceptible nod from Mal.

'Well, someone's been mending our fences. We were going to have to replace most of the posts alongside the *wern* down in front of the house. They get wet down there, see, even if you creosote them, they rot pretty quick.'

'You need to be careful with that creosote,' Swift said, wiping crumbs from his hands with his handkerchief. 'They've banned it, haven't they? Isn't it carcinogenic or something?'

Mal laughed a deep rumbly laugh. 'We don't seem to be doing too bad on it, do we now? Besides, there's enough of the stuff in the shed to see us out. Can't waste it, can we?'

'So, who do you think is doing it? Is it your neighbour? Could they think it's their fence?'

Sarah tipped peeled potatoes into a huge pan and lifted it onto the stove before adding cold water in stages by means of a large pottery jug.

'It's them next door, it is. They've been here maybe ten years now. He was something legal maybe, and she was a social worker or a teacher or something. Anyway, they're nice enough, and they seem to have lots of help.'

'It's not just us,' Mal said. 'They sent some chap round with a chainsaw when a tree came down on the lane to Gwyneth's place. She didn't ask them to do it, they just turned up, or some boy who works there did.'

'But that's just being neighbourly isn't it?' Swift asked.

'Ah, but Gwyneth isn't too keen on people roaming around up there, is she. She's even more solitary than she was as a kid.' Sarah smiled. 'She was a funny little thing even then, but if anything, she's worse since she's been back in the valley.'

Swift drained his cup and Sarah applied the teapot even before he got it back to the saucer. 'They're good Samaritans then?'

Mal snorted. 'Some people just have a knack of taking over.'

Swift nodded. 'So, they have a lot of people working for them?'

'We reckon, apart from the office staff and the manager, there must be about four of them working out there on the farm, but it's hard to tell to be fair. They all look just about the same. And there's another funny thing.' Mal looked up at Sarah and then across at Swift. 'You never see any of them driving anywhere. We've seen them in town a few times, but they only seem to go in on market day and always with her, the wife.'

'But we're glad they're there, aren't we, Mal? We could call on them if we needed anything.'

Mal grunted. 'I'd be happier if I knew what was going on. It seems a bit odd to me like.'

Swift knew Mal would never be happy asking anyone for help, least of all people who weren't from the valley. He eyed the Welsh cakes, but decided to exercise unaccustomed self-control. Instead he stood up and pushed his chair back under the table. 'I'll go and have a word,' he said. 'I'm going to be asking around anyway, about the discovery on the Monks' Trod, so I'll let you know if I find out anything.'

'About the body?' asked Mal, rather too eagerly

'About the neighbours,' Swift said. 'I'll leave you to find out about the deceased.' He smiled. 'But do let me know if you come across any information in that department won't you?'

'You can rely on us, Craig, can't he, Mal?' Sarah patted Mal's shoulder.

'He can, *cariad*,' Mal said. 'That he can.'

CHAPTER SEVEN

Day Two

'So, we've had no luck with B&Bs or hotels in Rhayader.' Craig Swift plonked himself on the edge of Julie's desk and surveyed the board. 'We need to broaden it out then. I assume there's been no abandoned vehicle reported either?'

Goronwy shook his head. 'Nothing, Sir. No vehicle, and no sighting of anyone matching what we've got in the mortuary.'

Swift looked at the map. 'Right, Goronwy and Rhys, you can ask around in Pontrhydfendigaid. It won't hurt to be over there for a second time, just in case it manages to make someone feel uncomfortable enough to talk to us. Go over and talk to the B&Bs and campsites, ask around in town. Have a look at Tregaron too, while you're there. Morgan, you can have a run up to Llangurig and any of the villages between here and there and do the same.' Morgan Evans scowled at the prospect of another long and probably fruitless journey.

'Go on, Sergeant,' Swift said. 'Give us the gruesome detail.'

'Well, we do know that the victim is a young woman,' Julie said.

'No way.' Rhys stared at the photograph on the board. 'That can't be right. So we'll have to go and ask all the people we've already contacted about a missing man, and tell them that we're actually looking for a missing woman then is it?'

'Sorry, Rhys, it's true. And she's had a child at some stage, but the doctor couldn't say when. There was no identification on the body apart from a signet ring with the initials CRH engraved on it. But that doesn't mean it was hers. The only significant distinguishing feature, other than the impressive network of new and healed needle tracks, is a small tattoo on the left shoulder. We think it's a red rose and a shamrock or a four-leaf clover.' She handed Rhys a photograph, which he carefully Blu-tacked and stuck on the board. 'Dr Greenhalgh is waiting for dental records to be circulated. Apparently, the victim had absolutely terrible teeth and,' Julie flicked through her notebook, 'Dr Greenhalgh was concerned at the state of the rest of the body too.'

Goronwy frowned. 'It's not as bad as some we've seen, Sarge. What's the problem?'

Julie pointed at the photograph. 'She's taken X-rays which have revealed multiple fractures to both arms, legs and several ribs.' She looked up at the others. 'All the fractures have healed, apart from two. Apparently, the poor woman had recent fractures to her right arm, which, judging by the mis-alignment, had never been attended to. The doc thinks that was the reason for the odd shape her right hand was held in when she died.' Julie scanned her notes. 'There was also some recent blood spatter on her clothes. It wasn't her blood but it was human. Given where she was found, the doc checked it wasn't from a sheep or something.'

'Now that's more promising,' Swift said. 'Is she running tests on the blood?'

'She is, but nothing's come back immediately. She says there are other possibilities and she'll let us know when she hears anything.'

'How did we not notice she was a woman?' Swift was incredulous. 'Dear God, that was a bit of an oversight.'

Julie nodded. 'Don't beat yourself up, Sir, Dr Greenhalgh missed it too. But what she did say, which might help explain the slightness of the body, was that on examination of the intestines, she discovered absolutely flat villi which would have led to problems with the absorption of nutrients from her diet.'

'Villi?' Morgan Evans grimaced. 'You do like to get into the finer detail don't you?'

Julie ignored him and held up her hand, spreading her fingers wide. 'Your intestines are full of bumps, like this, which absorb the vitamins and minerals you need from the food you eat. If they're flat, there's a lot less surface area to do the job and you can end up seriously malnourished.'

Swift scratched his ear. 'And I have every confidence that you're going to tell us what causes this anomaly, Sergeant.'

'Of course she is,' Morgan muttered.

Julie ignored him. 'Coeliac disease, Sir. People who have coeliac disease can't eat gluten because that's what causes this sort of damage.'

'You're kidding.' Rhys whistled through his teeth. 'So that's bread and stuff, is it?' He rolled his eyes. 'Rhian's decided that bread's bad for you. She's bought some sort of celebrity cookbook and now I can't even get toast at home. Nerys does it for me when I get to work.' He shook his head. 'I don't know if I can bring myself to tell Rhi she's actually right.'

'So, what does the doctor think about the broken bones?' Swift slid off the desk and wandered over to the board and its scant information. 'Battered wife maybe?'

'She says she wants to run a Dexa scan, just to be sure, but she thinks maybe her bones were more brittle than usual due to the diet problems. Still,' Julie tapped her notebook on her teeth, 'she might have had a little bit of help sustaining the fractures, don't you think?'

'Well can we not just cross-check dental records with people with this disease then? If it can affect your bones and teeth then she could be pretty easy to track down, couldn't she?' Rhys was suddenly animated and Swift smiled.

'Good idea,' he said. 'And we need to chase up fingerprints too, don't forget.' He turned to Julie. 'I think you and I should go and have a wander round Llandrindod, Sergeant, and see what we can come up with, as that's about the only place we haven't covered yet. Besides,' he grinned, 'Brian Hughes has heard a rumour that our victim may have been seen hanging around outside the Metropole, just over a week ago.'

*

Julie still hadn't got used to the way Swift was greeted when he ventured out of the office. In every shop and on every street corner, there was someone who knew him and either waved or stopped to speak to him. She waited while he chatted with a woman in Middleton Street, and imagined Frank Parkinson and Helen in the back streets of Manchester, dodging insults, spit and far worse. The only mention of pigs or bacon since her relocation had been in the station canteen. Nerys produced the most amazing bacon and fried egg barmcakes, every Friday morning. Julie hadn't mentioned that to Adam, of course. That would have meant another lecture on the dangers of processed meats, saturated fats and choline consumption. Strangely enough, he hadn't yet ventured into gluten free territory.

Swift ended his conversation and they turned left and crossed the road by the bandstand. Several teenage girls were sitting on the steps, their ties and skirts as short as humanly possible.

'Hiya, Mr Swift.' One of the girls waved as they passed and Julie grinned.

'Is there anyone you don't know?'

'I don't know as many people in town as I used to, to be honest. What with all the movements in and out there must be a fair few I don't know by now.'

'But there can't be that much movement of people, surely?'

'There's more now than there used to be. Some of the kids go off to college and don't come back. Then there are those who come here to retire.' Swift waited for a sizeable gap in the sporadic traffic before ambling across the road to the Metropole Hotel. 'But I suppose I must know quite a number.'

'I can't get over how friendly everyone is.'

'Not everyone's pleased to see us, not by any means, but we don't do so badly, fair play. I'd say most people are glad to see us.'

'Well I've not been called a pig for over three months now, and that has to be a record.'

'Not that you've heard anyway, Sergeant.' Julie glanced at Swift. His expression betrayed little, but he couldn't hide the smile around his eyes. He held the door open for her and they entered the hotel to be greeted by the sound of laughter in the bar.

The manager was blessed with a good memory for faces. 'Sergeant Kite, how can we help you?' He held out his hand to Julie then Swift. 'Craig. Found another body have you?

'Actually, we have.'

Julie looked at Swift. 'Where was it again, Sir?'

'The body of a young woman was found yesterday above Pont ar Elan. We're just enquiring about guests who may have not returned when they were supposed to, say within the last week or so.'

The manager's face had paled and he shook his head slowly. 'I was joking. I never thought you really had found... I mean I didn't know. No, we've had nothing like that. All our visitors are accounted for.' He ran his finger down the register. 'I can't believe there's another one. That sort of thing never happens here and now we've had two in the space of a few months.'

'I'm beginning to think I'm a bad influence,' Julie said. 'I don't suppose you've heard of anyone in town misplacing a guest lately?'

'No, not that I know of. Unless... no, I'm sure there was a sensible explanation for it.'

'Go on,' said Swift.

'Well, I don't want to tell tales, get anyone into trouble or anything.'

'Please,' Julie said, 'if you know anything at all that might help us identify this person, tell us.'

'Well,' the manager looked from Julie to Swift and back again. 'There was a kid hanging about outside here one evening. Scruffy. Looked as though she could do with a good meal. Probably about a week ago now, but I'm not completely sure what day it was. She did come in eventually and asked if we had a cheap room for a couple of nights.' He smiled. 'When she said cheap I think she really meant free. I told her we were fully booked.'

'And were you?' Julie asked.

The manager gave Julie what her mother would have called an old-fashioned look. 'No, but I didn't want to embarrass her to be honest. But then she asked if I could point her in the direction of a reasonable B&B,' he paused and looked down at the register. 'The thing is, the lady who runs the B&B I told her about is the mother of a rugby mate of mine. She'd applied for all the right licences but it was taking a while to get the paperwork back. I probably shouldn't say this, but she was struggling a bit to make ends meet.'

'Go on,' Julie said.

'I'm sure it's nothing to do with this person in the Elan Valley.'

'We're not interested in whether the paperwork's in situ.' Swift scratched his ear. 'But we do need to find out who this poor soul was.'

'Yes.' The manager reached for a notepad and a pen. 'Of course. I think you'd better ask her yourself though, rather than me telling you tales.' He handed Julie the piece of hotel notepaper, which she read and passed to Swift. 'I don't know if the girl ever turned up, but that's the address. It's a Mrs Pritchard.'

*

The house wasn't what Julie had expected. It was at the centre of a sweeping Victorian terrace, red brick and sandstone. From the cellar, right up to the gabled window set high in the slate roof, the late afternoon sun reflected from gleaming glass. Three floors of tall windows were edged in heavy lined curtains, held in identical curved flounces. The front door with its gleaming black finish and its artfully arranged brass fittings wouldn't have been out of place in Downing Street.

'Are you sure this is the address, Sir?'

Swift looked up at the brass numbers and back at the paperwork. 'That's what it says.' He lifted the knocker just as the door opened.

'Mr and Mrs Simpson?' The woman who held the door open was

maybe in her early fifties and immaculately turned out, from the double row of pearls at her throat to the suede of her pale grey court shoes. Swift showed her his warrant card.

'DI Craig Swift and DS Julie Kite. Mid Wales Police.'

They watched the colour drain from the woman's face. 'So you've found him then.' She swayed slightly, despite holding firmly onto the door. 'So you've come to tell me that either he's dead or he's going to prison, have you?'

Julie exchanged a glance with Swift. 'Do you think we could come in, Mrs Pritchard. It is Mrs Pritchard?'

The woman nodded and stepped back, allowing them into the hallway. It was carpeted in plush pale blue, which led to wide, curving stairs, and the whole hallway was beautifully decorated in greys and creams. Julie couldn't help noticing empty hooks on the walls and the faint shadows of pictures no longer there. The sitting room was equally tasteful, but on the ornate side-table was a leather-bound folder bearing the legend *Information for Guests* in gold italics. Cardboard displays spilled colourful maps and brochures onto an inlaid sideboard, like wilting tulips discarding petals onto the dark wood.

Mrs Pritchard motioned for them to sit either side of the bay window, in pale blue winged chairs. She remained standing, the fingers of her left hand grasping her right wrist, as though she was attempting to anchor herself there.

'Who is it that you've lost?' Swift's voice was gentle, and Julie was reminded, yet again, of his compassion. How had he kept hold of that after everything he'd seen over the years? It took Mrs Pritchard several moments to reply.

'Mr Pritchard. James that is. My husband.'

'And what makes you think that Mr Pritchard deserves to be in prison?' Swift stood up, motioned for her to sit and drew up a straight-backed wooden chair for himself. 'Can you tell us about it?'

'I don't know. Not exactly, but there must have been something awful happening that he couldn't tell me about. He must have been in some sort of trouble. There's no other explanation for it.' She sat down and immediately looked away, out of the window and across the avenue, but Julie doubted she was seeing the parked cars, or the trees in the park beyond.

Mrs Pritchard turned back to Swift. 'He left me. Just like that, after thirty years.' She looked up at Swift. 'He didn't even leave a note. He just didn't come home from the office one night and when I finally thought to check, after phoning round friends and making a total fool of myself, all his clothes were gone.'

'It must be horrible,' Julie said, attempting to emulate Swift's easy style, 'to find out that someone has left you like that. But even so, it's not usually something that carries a prison sentence.'

Julie, it seemed, still had a way to go, and Mrs Pritchard's bottom lip began to tremble. 'But he's taken everything. He emptied all the bank accounts, except the current account, which had very little in it. He took the car and even his golf clubs.'

'And you've not heard anything from him?' Swift was frowning.

'Nothing. I thought something terrible must have happened to him. I phoned round all the hospitals I could think of and anybody who might know where he was. But then a neighbour said she thought she'd seen him on Anglesey, at a pub we used to go to when we were visiting friends who live in Bangor. Of course, I went straight up there. I was there for three weekends, searching all the old haunts. I even asked at every hospital between here and there too, just in case, but there's been was no sign of him.'

'And when did all this happen?' Julie asked.

'It was about a fortnight before Christmas. We were planning a huge family party, a great gathering of the clan.' She shook her head. 'He was supposed to bring home the invitation cards from the printers that night, so we could get them written and in the post in good time.'

Swift offered his handkerchief before she had even realised she was crying. 'Did you report it to the police?'

Mrs Pritchard nodded, dabbed her eyes, took a deep breath and handed the crumpled linen back to Swift. 'They were very nice about it, but said I should leave it a few days and then go back. As an adult, they said, he had every right to go away for a few days on his own.'

'So when you went back to the police,' Julie said, 'there was still no sign of him?'

'I didn't go back.' Mrs Pritchard turned towards her. 'By that time, I'd managed to work out that he'd emptied the bank accounts, and then his work phoned to say his P45 was ready to be picked up.'

'So he'd handed his notice in?' Julie frowned. 'And you had no idea?'

'None at all. The girl from HR joked about how lucky we were to be able to take a sabbatical in such a lovely warm place. It was all planned, you see. I didn't let on, couldn't even ask her where she thought he might have gone, but I went straight over there to collect the P45 and asked for his final pay by cheque rather than the normal transfer at the end of the month. I told her we were in the middle of changing banks. She probably shouldn't have done it, but thank goodness she did. At least that cheque gave me enough to keep going for a few months.'

'So what have you done since then? Do you work?' Swift asked.

'I had a little voluntary job at the charity shop, but apart from that I've not worked for years. I've no CV to speak of and even my office experience is years out of date.' She stood, abruptly. 'He didn't want me to work. He said he wanted to relax at weekends and not get involved in anything domestic.' She straightened the embroidered antimacassar on the chair back. 'Anyway,' she said. 'This isn't why you came to see me, is it? Shall I go and make us some tea?'

'No,' Swift said, standing himself and causing his bulk to block her exit. 'No, we're fine, but thank you. We just want to ask you about a guest who may have stayed with you lately. A young woman, probably in her early twenties, very slight in build and with rather short dark hair.'

Mrs Pritchard sank back into the chair. 'My other runaway. So she's turned up has she? What was her excuse?' She held up a hand. 'No, don't tell me, I think I'd rather not know. I thought she looked honest enough and I only let her stay as a favour.' She sighed. 'I felt sorry for her, but it's just further evidence of what a really awful judge of character I am, isn't it?'

'What is?' Swift asked.

'The fact that she disappeared too, without so much as a word. It was just like James all over again, except she owed me money.'

'Let's start at the beginning, shall we?' Julie turned to a new page in her notebook. 'So a young woman answering this description did stay with you about a week ago? And she was a paying guest?'

Mrs Pritchard frowned. 'Well, that was the idea, although as it turns out, it was probably better that she hadn't actually paid me anything. I'd taken a gamble letting her the room, you see. I wasn't properly licenced when she turned up. I should have waited for the paperwork, which turned up a couple of days later as it happens. But, as I said, I felt sorry for her.'

'And why was that?' Swift sat back down. 'What was the matter with her?'

'I was never completely sure, to tell the honest truth. She was distraught when she arrived. She looked as though she hadn't had a square meal for weeks and her clothes... well let's just say a charity shop wouldn't have accepted them.' Mrs Pritchard curled her lip at the memory. 'But once she'd had a good soak in the bath and I'd run up the road and got her some half decent stuff from Oxfam, she was actually quite a pretty little thing.'

Julie swallowed hard. Pretty was the last thing that would have come into her mind to describe the woman she'd seen up there on the Monks' Trod. 'Did she say why she was here in Llandrindod? Did she give a reason?' Julie's pencil was poised. 'Did she have any luggage?'

Mrs Pritchard shook her head. 'She didn't tell me anything. She had a tiny rucksack, one of those knapsack things that workmen used to carry their lunch in donkeys' years ago, and there was a big oblong carrier bag type thing. From a supermarket. I remember thinking how incongruous it looked, her in that state with a bag wider then she was, plastered with citrus fruits and pineapples and mangoes. But that was all she had with her.'

'And she took them with her when she left?' Julie asked.

'Well that's the odd thing.' Mrs Pritchard's tone was suddenly confidential. 'She left them both here. I was sure she'd taken the knapsack out with her, but she can't have done. I assumed at first that she'd be back of course, but after three days I realised I'd probably not see her again either.'

'Did you look inside the bags?'

Mrs Pritchard blushed. 'Well it was only because I thought I could send them on to her. I didn't want to be nosey, nothing like that. I didn't remove anything, Sergeant.'

'And did she leave any money in the bags?' Swift sounded innocent, but Mrs Pritchard read the question with precision.

'Yes, Inspector, she did. But there was nowhere near enough to cover the cost of the room and,' she offered a small smile, 'it's all still there, waiting for her to come back. Would you like to see the room?'

Swift and Julie exchanged a glance. 'Yes please, that would be very helpful,' Swift said. 'By the way, did she give you her name?'

'She did, but I wasn't sure it was her real name.' Mrs Pritchard gave the two officers a knowing look. 'In the circumstances.'

'And?' said Swift.

'Rosa.' Mrs Pritchard smiled. 'Rosa Quigley.'

The room had been let several times since Rosa left, Mrs Pritchard told them on the way up the curving staircase. There had been a teacher who had come all the way from Somerset for an interview, then an older couple who said they were looking for a house, fed up of the rat race and their noisy neighbours in Birmingham. Last night there was a very nice man from Germany who spoke only a smattering of English. He managed to tell her he was from Düsseldorf and he had been learning Welsh, but she had no idea why and as she had never mastered the language herself, that got them no further on.

'Where was Rosa from, Mrs Pritchard?' Julie asked.

Mrs Pritchard stopped abruptly on the stairs, which allowed Swift to catch them up. 'Now that would have been a good question to ask her, but it wasn't the first thing on my mind when I saw the state she was in.' She climbed the last few stairs and turned to the right.

'What about her accent, did she have a distinctive dialect?' Julie asked.

'Nothing obvious. I'm pretty good at accents, but only the more obvious ones – Birmingham, Liverpool, Scotland.' She pushed open the door to a bedroom at the front of the house and sunlight streamed out onto the landing. 'And Yorkshire, like yours.'

Julie said nothing, just concentrated on stifling the age-old retort related to points of the compass and the Pennines.

'How long did she stay?' Swift was examining the drawers in the bedside table, which were empty apart from a brand new hard-backed copy of the Gideon Bible and a small clothes brush.

'Two nights. Although she was very late back on the second night and she'd gone before I got up the next morning.'

Swift bent down and lifted the corner of the valence and peered under the bed.

'You won't find anything in here by now,' Mrs Pritchard said. 'I'm very fussy.'

Julie nodded to herself. That wasn't a surprise. 'What was her state of mind when she was here? Was there any indication of how she was feeling? Did she talk to you much?'

'She looked awful, to be honest with you. She was very pale, and when she arrived I thought she'd been crying.'

'She didn't tell you what that might have been about?'

Mrs Pritchard shook her head. 'That first day she barely spoke at all. She had a bath, as I said and I made her something to eat. It was only beans on toast but she was so grateful for it that I dug out the lemon cake I had in the freezer. I'd been saving it for my son, it's his favourite, but he's not called in for a while and she looked as though she needed looking after. I suppose you can't help it, once you've had kids, you just revert to mother mode.'

'I'll take your word for that,' Julie said. 'How old is your son, just out of interest?'

Mrs Pritchard blushed. 'Almost thirty-one.'

Swift smiled. 'So Rosa didn't tell you why she was here?' Mrs Pritchard shook her head. 'But you don't think she was on holiday?'

He walked over to the window and looked out across the narrow street. By the ornate brick wall that fronted the park, a young fair-haired woman was talking to an old man who leaned heavily on a stick. Swift couldn't see who had spoken, but suddenly the pair of them rocked with laughter.

'Well I didn't want to get involved.' Mrs Pritchard paused, and Swift turned and gave her a look over the top of his glasses. She sighed. 'The poor girl seemed agitated, but she didn't say why. One thing she did say which struck me as a bit strange, when I thought about it afterwards, was that she was looking for something. Someone had taken something really precious from her and she was going to get it back.'

'You don't know what that something might have been?' Julie joined Swift at the window. 'Was it money do you think, or could it have been some sort of property?'

'I'm sorry. I didn't ask. I suppose I didn't think it was any of my business. I'm new to this landlady thing and I'm finding it difficult to know what sort of tone to establish with the guests. Maybe I should have asked her. I'm assuming, if you're looking for her, that she's in a bit of trouble, is she?'

'In a manner of speaking.' Swift looked at her. 'We found a body in the Elan Valley yesterday afternoon.' He paused and watched the colour drain once more from Mrs Pritchard's face. 'We have reason to believe that it may be Rosa.'

'Oh God no, that poor girl.' Mrs Pritchard sank onto the edge of the bed. 'But you're not sure? Could you be mistaken?'

'We have no information which would allow us to make a formal identification as yet,' Julie said.

Mrs Pritchard closed her eyes. And you want me to tell you whether the body is her... Rosa?'

'It would help us if you could make an identification, Mrs Pritchard. Perhaps you would be kind enough to come to the police station as soon as you can,' Julie said, handing her a card.

Mrs Pritchard swallowed. 'She's at the police station?'

'No, she isn't, but if you could tell us whether you recognise the clothes we have, that would be sufficient, at the moment. It might not be possible for you to identify the body itself.'

Mrs Pritchard moved remarkable quickly as the inference struck home. They could hear her retching in the en-suite. When she came back into the room she was even more softly-spoken than before.

'I know exactly what she was wearing. Her own stuff wouldn't have survived the washer. I threw everything in the bin. She was wearing the clothes I got for her from Oxfam. Jeans and a checked shirt – the sort of thing farmers wear – in reds and blues, and a black denim jacket. Nearly new that was, it was a real bargain. And I let her have a pair of socks James left in his drawer, just ordinary black socks you'd wear for work.'

'So did he have tiny feet then?' Julie asked.

Mrs Pritchard offered a small smile. 'No, Sergeant, I shrank them in the tumble drier. I just hadn't got round to throwing them out.'

'Can you remember her shoes?' Julie asked. 'Would you recognise them?'

Mrs Pritchard's hand went to her neck and she threaded the lower string of pearls between her fingers. 'Yes, I would recognise the shoes.' She smiled. Her focus was not on her visitors but somewhere far away. 'They were my shoes, from another life.'

'Can you describe them for us?' Julie glanced at Swift. They both knew that this just might put the identification beyond doubt.

Mrs Pritchard let the pearls go and they settled back into position over the pale grey lambs' wool twinset. 'They were Doc Martens. Black. The sort that end about here.' She tapped her calf. 'The laces were yards long.' She shook her head. 'I sometimes think I might have been better following my instincts and sticking with the person I was then, when I wore those boots, rather than getting sucked into this Stepford Wives fantasy world.' She jerked her head, taking in the perfectly aligned curtain swags and the guests' tea tray with colourful sachets of herb teas and a small Kilner jar containing rounds of home-made shortbread. Her gaze settled on the tall, gilt-framed mirror above the dressing table. The reflection of her face reddened and her lips tightened into a grim line. 'When I think of what I've wasted with that...'

'Quite,' said Swift. 'So these boots were, er, shall we say they weren't new, then?'

Mrs Pritchard's face creased into a smile and she abandoned her reflection and twinkled at him. 'No, Inspector, they were pretty ancient.'

Swift smiled back and Julie sighed impatiently. 'So when you say she was back late on the second night, which would have been what, Thursday, did you see her come back?'

'Well, no, not exactly. I heard her though. My room is just next door and I heard her put her key in the lock at around 1.30am.'

'And you're sure it was her?'

'Well, who else would it be?' Mrs Pritchard raised her eyebrows in query, but Julie noticed that they descended rather swiftly into a frown. 'You mean the person who... her attacker... he could have been here?'

'We don't know yet if she was attacked, and we certainly don't know that a male was involved in any way in this lady's demise,' Julie said. 'We just want to be clear about the last time she was here and whether anything could have been taken from her belongings by anyone else.'

'Of course. Yes. I see.' Mrs Pritchard again fingered the pearls at her throat. 'But he could have been here?'

'I'm sure it will have been Rosa who came back late.' Swift's voice was soothing. 'Please don't worry about that now, but we would like to see her belongings, if that would be possible.'

'Yes, of course. They're in here.' Mrs Pritchard bustled out onto the landing and opened the door of a tall airing cupboard filled with neatly folded sheets and Witney blankets. She gestured to the two bags, which looked oddly out of place beside the folded white linen.

Julie snapped on blue latex gloves and picked up both items of Rosa's luggage and Mrs Pritchard shepherded them down the stairs and opened the front door.

'Thank you,' said Swift. 'We'll get these straight to forensics. Do you think it would be possible for you to leave us your fingerprints when you call into the station? It's just for elimination purposes, it will speed things up for us.'

Mrs Pritchard's mouth opened and closed a couple of times, but she obviously thought better of what she had been thinking of saying and remained mutinously silent.

Julie looked over her shoulder as she stepped onto the garden path. 'About Mr Pritchard,' she said. 'Do you want us to look for him?'

Mrs Pritchard paused, twiddled the pearls, looked down at her feet and slowly shook her head. I think, Sergeant, all things considered, I may well be better off without him.' She went to close the door, then opened it again, just a crack. 'But thank you for asking.'

CHAPTER EIGHT

Day Two

Back at the office, Julie and Rhys sifted through the meagre belongings in the knapsack. There was a small pink purse containing £25 and some change, but there were no credit cards, and there would have been no way of paying the bill at Mrs Pritchard's, let alone anything else. There was a Yale key with a key-ring bearing a green plastic fob with the name Bryn Awel and the number 3 picked out in white.

'Well, Mrs P was telling the truth. She didn't take anything from Rosa's bags. Not even her own door keys,' Julie observed.

'There's no phone.' Rhys was disappointed. Julie knew he harboured a particular fascination for trawling through other people's social media.

She relented. 'There could have been though, couldn't there? Why don't you get onto the providers and see if you can find her?' Julie picked up the supermarket bag with its colourful assortment of luscious fruits and improbably blue droplets of water emblazoned on front and back. 'If she did have a phone, chances are it was a pay as you go, but we wouldn't want to deprive you of your fun, would we?' Rhys smiled, and Julie tipped the contents of the bag onto her desk and spread them out. 'What does this lot tell you about her then?'

Rhys rolled his chair over to her desk. It was an odd jumble of objects. There was a Fair Isle cardigan, threadbare at the elbows, two rounded pebbles, a small dog-eared photograph of a glamorous-looking woman in a fur-trimmed coat, and various other items which bore no clues to the owner's identity or lifestyle. Rhys frowned and picked up a small blue teddy bear, which had definitely seen better days. One ear had been well chewed, and long frayed threads dangled towards its right eye. He handed it to Julie. The fabric round its middle was grubby and clumped, the way a ewe's wool goes when it needs shearing, Julie thought, which made her laugh out loud.

'Sarge?'

'Don't mind me.' She shook her head. 'I'm just going native, that's all. What do you make of the bear then, for starters?'

'Well, it's obviously a child's toy. Well-loved I'd have said. Rhi's sister has a little girl who must be about four by now, and she won't go to sleep without her camel.'

'Camel?' Julie snorted. 'That must be a bit lumpy to cart about.'

'Well it is. But it looks like that.' Rhys pointed at the bear's midriff. 'All its fur's matted like that, where she carries it around. Mind you,' he shook his head, 'there's hell to pay if she loses the thing. Left it in a café in Hereford a couple of weeks ago she did. Refused to go to bed when they couldn't find it.'

'So what happened?'

'Rhi's sister put out an APB on Facebook. Somebody she knows recognised it and they tracked it down within twenty-four hours.'

'I don't suppose Rhi's sister's got a week or so free just now, has she? We could do with all the help we can get.' She turned the blue bear over in her gloved hands. 'So, maybe it could belong to the child Dr Greenhalgh said the victim had given birth to.'

'Definite possibility, I'd say.'

'A boy then?'

'Maybe, Sarge.'

'One question that bothers me though,' Julie picked up the key to Room 3. 'Why didn't she take the key out with her? She didn't know she wouldn't be coming back, did she?'

'And why didn't she take her bag? Rhian never goes anywhere without her bag, or at least her purse.'

Julie nodded. 'That's a good point, too.' She tapped the key on her teeth. 'OK, what about the map?' She handed Rhys part of a battered Ordnance Survey map, which showed the area round the Elan Valley and another section, cut from a larger-scale map. This second map was obviously part of a city, but there was nothing at all to identify it. 'Can you tell where this is?'

Rhys picked up the city map. 'That could be anywhere, Sarge. Without the name of the place, we've got no way of identifying it, have we?' He held it up to the light. 'There's something circled on it here, look. Maybe it's a house or something. But it could be absolutely anywhere.' He put it back on the desk. 'This looks interesting, though.'

'What have you got?'

'It's some sort of token I think.' Despite his gloves, he picked it up carefully, by the edges. 'It looks like one of those bits of plastic you get in supermarkets, you know, to vote for local charities.' He turned it over and placed it carefully on his desk. 'Has it been checked by forensics?'

Julie nodded. 'There are only her fingerprints on any of this stuff. Apart from the purse which also seems to have been thoroughly checked by her landlady. She wasn't best pleased when we asked her to come in and have her prints taken.'

'And you're going to tell me we haven't got a match in the system for the victim's fingerprints, aren't you?'

'I am.' Julie sighed and poked at a box of orange Rennies with the end of a biro. 'There's nothing on the DNA either.' She glanced across at Rhys' desk. 'Let's have a look at the purse again.'

'I've done that already, but feel free.' Rhys grinned, wheeled his chair back to his desk, picked up the purse and wheeled himself back again. 'There's nothing in there.'

'I know. You said.' Julie unzipped the purse and tipped the change onto her desk. 'So what's this then, Scotch mist?'

'Eh?' Rhys frowned. 'It's a euro, I think, isn't it? Someone's just slid it into her change and diddled her out of a quid.'

'It is a euro, but why assume she was given it by mistake?'

'Well she wasn't globe-trotting with no luggage was she, Sarge?

And there's no passport is there?' He leaned back in his chair and watched her face.

'Good point. But with a name like Rosa Quigley, the dodgy shamrock tattoo and the lack of absolutely anything else at all,' she grinned at him. 'You will have observed that I'm totally clutching at straws.' She scooped everything back into the bag and snapped off her gloves.

'Let's call it a day, Rhys. I don't know about you, but I can't see the wood for the trees.'

Rhys needed no second bidding and reached up to turn off his computer. Julie crossed the office and stood, watching Swift through his window. He was deep in thought, leaning back in his chair with his hands laced behind his head. She knocked on his door and he rocked back to attention.

'Any thoughts, Sergeant?'

'For a second there, I did wonder if she had come over from Ireland, but that might have been a thought too far. And I suppose even the geographically challenged Mrs P might have noticed an Irish accent.'

Swift smiled. 'I spotted your displeasure at being accused of being from Yorkshire. I didn't realise it was such a big deal.'

'So, you don't remember the Wars of the Roses then, Sir? It was very big in some parts.' She laughed. 'They still call cricket matches between Lancashire and Yorkshire the Roses Matches.'

'I stand corrected,' Swift said. 'Do we have anything at all from her luggage?'

Julie shook her head. 'There's nothing in her belongings to suggest where she came from or where she was intending to go. Rhys is going to chase up to see if she had a mobile phone, and he's still waiting for his cross-matched dental records. For some reason there's a delay, but we're not sure why.'

'I'll have a play with this map and see if I can find out where this is.' Julie wafted the city fragment towards Swift. 'Can I take a copy of it to look at when I get home?'

Swift nodded. 'I don't have a problem with that, but you should make sure you have a bit of time away from it all too. I think Gwen's probably kept me sane over the years, insisting work stays at work.'

'I bet you don't stop thinking about it at home though, Sir?'

'Well there's not a lot she can do about that, is there?' Swift smiled. 'But she'd be unhappy if I took actual physical work home. She swears by recovery time, does Gwen. Thinks hobbies are a cure for work.'

'So what are your hobbies, Sir?' Julie grinned. She couldn't imagine Craig Swift doing anything remotely sporty or growing his own veg.

'There's nothing wrong with your interrogation technique, is there, Sergeant?'

'I'm just curious.'

'Well, as you ask, I sing in a male voice choir.'

'No women allowed then, Sir?'

'That's the idea.'

'Are you allowed to do that these days, keeping women out of your choir? Isn't that a bit non-PC?'

'I don't suppose the ladies' choir would be too happy if we asked to join them either.' Swift laughed. 'Don't tell me you've never heard of a male voice choir?'

'Nope.'

'Well that's disappointing, Julie. There are choirs all over your part of the world too. Mind you,' Swift smiled, 'they're not as good as ours here in Wales.' Julie missed Swift's gentle challenge and didn't reply. 'I was joking, Julie. I'm sure they're just as good in Manchester.'

'Sorry, Sir, I was just thinking about what you said about Gwen and work. Adam says I need a hobby.'

'So, what do you like doing in your spare time?' Swift closed the lid of his laptop and looked up at her. She was blushing.

'Well, I... er, I do a lot of reading.'

'I may be barking up completely the wrong tree here, but I suspect that may well be work-related research?'

'Well yes, that's some of it.'

Swift shook his head, pushed himself back from his desk and stood up. 'You need time away from all this,' he waved a chubby hand over the contents of his desk. 'You'd go mad if you didn't.'

Julie nodded. 'You sound just like Adam. He's a great believer in down time. Mind you, I wouldn't have the energy for his sort of down time.' She glanced at the fragment of map in her hand. 'It's hard to switch off though, Sir, when there's someone like Rosa lying there in the mortuary. There must be people out there somewhere, worrying about her.'

'I know, but all we can do is be methodical and determined, and not beat ourselves up too often. There's been nothing interesting from Llangurig or the western end of the Monks' Trod either.' Swift sighed. 'I think you and I should do a little detour round the reservoirs in the Elan Valley tomorrow. I think you need to take a look at the layout of the area and see if that helps put the place where she was found into perspective. We can call in on those neighbours of Mal's on the way back and see what they have to say for themselves. It's probably nothing, just Mal being touchy about his age, but it might be worth a little look.'

'Have we heard any more about cause of death from the doc yet, Sir?'

'We have, but I'm not entirely happy with it. She says that despite the evidence of a large amount of historic and recent heroin usage, now she's had the toxicology reports back, she thinks it was almost certainly the blow or blows to the head that actually killed her.'

'Oh great, the ambiguous blunt instrument.' Julie said. 'And you're not happy because what? That means it's more than likely that she was high as a kite and fell against that rock she was sitting next to when she was found?'

'Do I detect a note of your well-honed Manchester sarcasm there, Sergeant Kite?'

'Me, Sir? Sarcastic?' Julie laughed. 'Could be. I don't know I'm doing it. But go on, tell me why you think she couldn't have done it herself. She's riddled with track marks and despite the damage caused by the possible gluten problem, she has all the hallmarks of drug abuse.'

'So she hit her head twice in her stumblings by the rock?'

'It's possible.'

'And the fox that damaged her left hand ran away with the syringe and any other drug paraphernalia she may have had with her, did it? We didn't find anything in her belongings to indicate that she was using at the actual time of her death, did we? If she was so out of it how did she get up there in the first place?'

'True, but if it *was* her who went back to the B&B that night, she could have disposed of it then or the following morning. It doesn't prove she wasn't still using, does it?'

Swift tugged his ear, then took off his glasses and put them on his desk. 'No, but she didn't know anything was going to happen to her did she? Why should she have disposed of anything? Besides, Mrs Pritchard swears Rosa was right handed. She made her sign a registration card.' Swift rubbed his eyes and put his glasses back on. 'I phoned her just now. She said Rosa wouldn't leave an address, but she did sign the card, after a fashion, but she appeared to have trouble holding the pen properly. So, I phoned Kay Greenhalgh too.'

Swift was enjoying his moment but Julie could hide her impatience no longer. 'And the broken bones in her arm almost certainly meant that she wouldn't have been able to inject herself with her right hand. She wouldn't have been able to put enough pressure on the syringe's plunger to inject into her left arm, and no doubt that's where Kay thinks the most recent track marks are.'

Swift looked crestfallen, but only for a second. 'Got it in one, Julie. The doc says there's no way she could have done it herself. And she certainly couldn't have spirited away the evidence. Besides, she thinks the last time Rosa injected was a while before she died.'

'So, we know who she was and we have an idea of how she died.' Julie shook her head. 'But until we can work out the why, we're just pissing in the wind.'

'Sergeant Kite!' Swift looked shocked, but his features rapidly morphed into a grin. 'Can women do that then? In my experience, it's only us men who suffer from random vagueness which comes back to haunt us. Women seem to be very much more direct.'

Julie blushed. 'Sorry, Sir. That was one of my old sergeant's favourite expressions.'

'Don't apologise,' Swift laughed. 'Get yourself off home. I'll pick you up tomorrow morning and we'll go to the Elan Valley and have a nosey round. Let's say eight o'clock at the post office in Newbridge.'

CHAPTER NINE

Day Two

Julie drove along the single-track road between what passed as a main road in these parts and the cottage she now called home. The ground rose just as steeply skywards on the right and plummeted just as sharply down to the burbling little Chwefru river on her left as it had in April, but somehow, even in that short space of time, the topography had begun to seem more normal. There was even an additional, slightly less annoying gate across the road now that the weather was kinder and sheep were roaming on the hill, but she was already less impatient with the impediments of rural living.

In a small field by the second, less easy gate (which required dragging, scraping, swearing and lifting), Joe Morgan, their landlord, sat on his quad bike watching Julie's progress. Behind him, a black and white collie gazed down at the ewes, daring them to make a run for it.

'You still haven't got the knack, then?'

Julie clanged the heavy metal gate against the post, lifted it with difficulty and shot the bolt home into its horseshoe catch. 'It's nowt to do with knack and everything to do with someone not putting a decent set of hinges on this thing.'

'You're just too slow. Give it a good swing.'

Julie glared at him. 'I'll swing for you one of these days, Joe Morgan,' she muttered, just quietly enough for him not to hear over the rumble of the quad.

Joe grinned. 'What would I do for sport if I mended him, then?'

Julie shook her head. 'So, what's new? I suppose you know all about our latest local difficulty?'

'That I do.' Joe nodded sagely. 'Nasty business that, with a young girl too. They're saying she was killed.'

'Who are?' Julie raised an eyebrow. She knew full well that the local grapevine was better than anything she had encountered in Manchester. She was still surprised not to read all about their daily progress in the *Brecon and Radnor* or the *County Times.*

'Folk,' Joe said. 'They say you don't know who she is.'

'Do they? Well maybe if they find out first, they'd be good enough to let us know.'

'They will, be sure of it,' Joe said. He turned to pat the collie and the dog stared up at him, his mission to guard the sheep forgotten at the attention from his master. 'Menna tells me you might be thinking about going out riding with her.'

'I'm still just thinking. I'm thinking mostly that I'd be totally rubbish,' Julie said. 'But it must be nice to wander round the forestry tracks on a horse. It's so flipping steep to walk round here.'

'Well,' Joe smiled and kicked the quad into gear, 'the offer's still there, you're welcome to ride Cam any time. He could do with a bit of attention.' Then he was gone, bouncing across the field, his collie hanging on for grim death behind him and sheep scattering to all sides.

Julie watched him go and shook her head. She never knew when he was being serious. They had almost come to blows as soon as she had arrived after a misunderstanding about incomers and foreigners. At least now she knew that Joe considered her the 'right sort' of incomer. God help the others, she thought as she climbed back into the car.

Adam had his bike upside down on the drive. It stood balanced on handlebars and saddle, and both wheels were lying on the ground. Julie could tell before she even got out of the car that he was not best pleased.

'You had a puncture?'

'Well done, Sherlock.' Adam threw a tyre lever into his tool box and scowled. 'Both tyres are shot.'

'Right. That was unlucky, then, they're new aren't they? Were you far from home? You should have phoned me.'

'I was still at school. Andy gave me a lift home in his Land Rover. And there would have been no point phoning you, would there? Not with you working on a case.'

'Fair point. I would have probably been useless, as per.' Her face was serious.

Adam laughed. 'Sorry, Jules. It's not your fault, but it's damned annoying.'

'Still, it could have been worse. You could have had a blowout on your way back from Brecon. You wouldn't stand a chance coming down that gradient into Garth if your tyre went, would you?'

'I don't think this was wear and tear though, Jules, you're right, these tyres are practically new. I think someone did this deliberately.'

Julie frowned. 'Are you serious? You really think someone vandalised your tyres?' She prodded one of the tyres with the toe of her shoe.

'It looks that way. The holes are too big and too symmetrical to have been made by a nail or a thorn. It looks as though someone has stuck the tip of a knife into them.' Adam waved one of the offending articles under her nose. 'What do you think, Sergeant. Criminal damage?'

'Could be. Would it be one of the kids, maybe? Have you ticked any of them off lately?'

'I can't see it. They're a great bunch in Builth. If this never happened at a school in inner city Manchester it's even less likely that the kids here would do it.'

'So that leaves a member of staff or an irate passer-by with nothing better to do with his bread knife then?'

'I don't suppose you could –.'

'If you're going to say what I think you're going to say, then I'd say "on yer bike", Mr Kite, there's no way this is a police matter.'

'Fair enough.' Adam laughed. 'Come on, let's eat. I've done a lovely lentil dhal.'

Julie rolled her eyes. 'Oh my. What have I done to deserve this?'

'Don't say anything until you've tried it.'

'Hmm. You don't fancy a trip to Pontrhydfendigaid do you?'

'My, you've been practising your pronunciation. Why Pont?'

'Well, it's the other end of the Monks' Trod. I just thought it would be nice to get an idea of where everything is in relation to where the incident was.'

'Where the body was found?'

'Yes, all right, where the body was found.'

'Yep, we can do. But we'll eat first shall we, just in case you've decided it's an excuse to find a takeaway.'

Adam said he'd drive so she could take in the sights. They turned right onto the main road in the direction of Beulah.

'This is a pig of a hill on a bike,' Adam said.

'I can only imagine,' Julie said, calculating the odds of her ever finding out. The road plunged downhill in a series of bends and after three miles, Adam turned right into the village with its pub and petrol station and shop.

'Civilisation,' Julie said. 'And an A-road.'

'Don't get used to the idea,' Adam said, turning first right. They passed a handful of bungalows and drove over a bridge.

'Was that it?'

'You'll love this road.'

'How can you love a road, Adam?'

'Look on your map.'

'This isn't like any road I've ever been on,' Julie said, following the tiny yellow lane with its collection of crazy bends and gradients picked out with black arrowheads on the map. 'So this is on your list for a bike ride?'

'Just as soon as that bell goes a week on Friday.'

'From this map it looks as though there are one or two sections that even you could find a bit of a challenge.' Julie smiled. 'Though I'm sure a little thing like vertical tarmac won't put you off.'

The road took them past a small church and bent to the left, into trees. As the road swung sharply right and began to climb, Julie was forced to look up from the map. 'People pay good money for this sort of experience at Blackpool Pleasure Beach.'

'It gets even more interesting in a little while,' Adam said, squeezing his car tightly into the side of the road to let a van through and causing Julie to discover vertigo she never knew she had. She turned away from the chasm-like drop to her immediate left.

'Oh my God. I'll never complain about the Mancunian Way ever again.'

A road sign announced their arrival in Abergwesyn, but after turning right through a small gaggle of buildings, they were once again out on the open road.

The road swooped and dived into Abergwesyn Common, alongside the little Irfon River. After several miles of single-track wilderness, two bridges crossed and re-crossed the river by a solitary cottage.

'They're unusual,' Julie observed.

'Ah, now those are Irish bridges. Much cheaper than building a higher bridge, but completely useless when it rains a lot. They flood really easily.'

'You wouldn't want to traipse all this way and have to turn back would you?'

The road bent right into trees and rose spectacularly quickly.

'You'd have fun on a bike up this,' Julie said. 'I'm not sure I'll be coming with you when you do though.'

'It's impressive, I'll give you that, but you would be able to do it if you practised. It's all a state of mind.'

Julie looked at him, but said nothing. On the right, a metal crash barrier snaked up to a left hand hairpin bend and beyond it the road rose even more steeply. Beneath them the cottage and the bridges already looked minute. A second sharp bend, this time to the right, and the road climbed on, through clumps of tiny fir trees that had obviously been recently planted. The sawn-off trunks and brash of their predecessors was still visible among the new growth.

'You were saying?'

'Well, it could be a bit of a challenge, but you would be able to do it, eventually. If you want something badly enough you'll do anything to achieve it.'

'That's why you're a teacher and I'm a copper. You really believe that don't you?'

'I do. I have to, otherwise the kids I teach won't get the best mentoring I can manage.'

The road continued to climb, and with it Julie's conviction that there was no way on earth she would ever ride this road on a bike. She looked at Adam as he concentrated on the tiny strip of sinuous tarmac as it turned steeply downhill. He was enjoying every minute of this. Their move to Wales had certainly done something for his resolve. Maybe it was time she started to develop the kind of self-belief which he found so easy.

CHAPTER TEN

Day Three

The little post office-and-shop in Newbridge was busy. There were more vans and 4x4s than cars parked outside, and most of the customers were dressed for the outdoors in heavy boots and work shirts. Julie looked at her watch and decided she had time to investigate the shop. It must be the nearest retail outlet to the cottage at a mere five miles away, but she still hadn't been inside. She seemed to have lost the knack of shopping now that there wasn't a mega Sainsbury's on the doorstep. About now, her mum would be honing her list for the weekly shop at Booths Supermarket. It was her little extravagance in what she liked to think of as the northern version of Waitrose, way too posh for Julie's needs. She could say for certain that Morecambe Bay salt marsh lamb and artisanal Lancashire cheese had never made it to her shopping list. It wouldn't now either, not with himself doing the vegan thing. He wouldn't be happy until he'd persuaded her to join him on his bean and broccoli crusade, but then she had the Tiffany Sanderson ace up her sleeve to counter that one. For now. Maybe.

The shop was buzzing. Small but perfectly formed, it had everything you could ever run out of and more besides. She picked up a Twix and waited in the queue behind an old man whose basket contained a bottle of decent red wine, a swiss roll and a turnip.

'Do they know who it is yet?' The woman on the till counted change into Julie's hand. 'The body on the Monks' Trod,' she added by way of clarification. 'With you being in the police, you'd get to know before us, wouldn't you?'

'I wouldn't count on it,' Julie said, stuffing the chocolate into her bag. 'Let me know if you hear anything, won't you?' She left the shop and stood by her car in the sunshine, watching for Swift's Volvo. Menna hurtled past in her Land Rover, hooting and waving. Julie waved back, and thought, not for the first time, how amazing it was that the local people greeted her like a long-lost friend after such a short space of time.

Swift was in good spirits as she climbed into the Volvo, and they set off out of the village into the vista of hills which rose ahead of them. In two hundred yards they had passed the pub, the tiny carpet shop, and the turning towards Julie's new home, and they were already back into open countryside.

'Busy day today, Julie, and you'll get to take in a few more of the sights.'

'So where are we off to exactly?' Julie attempted to unfold her Ordnance Survey map in the limited space between herself, Swift and the dashboard. Typically, the map was two-sided and the other side was the one she needed.

'I thought you needed the guided tour of the Elan Valley. I know you saw some of it with the Collins case, but if you've not already done it, it will give you a good idea of where everything is. Besides,' he slowed to let a pheasant scuttle into the grass verge, 'with you living over this way, it gives me an excuse. I don't often get the chance to drive this road.'

'Why, what's so special about this road? And what is it about men and roads?'

'You'll see. It's a glorious piece of countryside and it goes right round the reservoirs and the area we're looking at. Why don't you just use the map book in the back, it's a lot easier to manage.'

'I need to see all the points of interest,' Julie said, finally managing to fold the map down into a manageable oblong. 'You can learn a huge amount from large-scale maps, Sir.'

The main road followed the broad River Wye, which ran alongside, but in the opposite direction to them.

'Where does the Wye end up, Sir?'

'Cas-gwent.'

'Where?'

'Chepstow, on the Severn Estuary and right on the border with England. You should go and have a look round, it's a lovely little town.'

'I'll put it on the list for if I ever get another day off, Sir.'

Swift grinned. 'The Wye and the Severn both have their source on Pumlumon Fawr, just up the road here, up in the hills west of Llangurig. Very wild and woolly it is up there.'

Julie gazed out of the windscreen at the steep, bracken-covered hills. 'How do you tell where the wild and woolly stops and the other bits start, Sir?'

Swift slowed into the speed limit outside Rhayader and stopped to let a gigantic logging wagon through the narrow piece of road between the buildings, then turned left into West Street.

'I've just realised the street names are the actual points of the compass.'

Swift smiled. 'Well done, Sergeant. Perfectly logical, when you think about it.'

The road wound past houses and up a small hill and suddenly the whole valley was spread out below them.

'You should go and look at the village down there, if you get a chance. It was built by the water company for its workers originally,' Swift said.

Above the Visitors' Centre, a small metal fence separated the road from what, to Julie, looked like an enormous drop down into the valley. She sought solace in the words on her map.

'So *bryn* means hill?'

'It does. I told you you'd get the hang of it.'

'What's Bryn Mawr, then, Sir?'

'Big Hill.'

'Imaginative names they have for hills round here. We saw some interesting ones last night. We went for a drive over to Pontrhydfendigaid.' She separated the five syllables into manageable chunks and smiled triumphantly.

Swift laughed. 'Well done, Sergeant.'

'It's just so frustrating that I can't even understand a map. I'd do better in France.'

'You'll get there. It's nice to know you're interested in the language.'

The road skirted reservoir after reservoir, and Swift named each one as they passed. Caban Coch, Garreg Ddu, Penygarreg and the last one with hills soaring ahead of it, Craig Goch.

'I didn't realise there were so many of them, Sir. Or that they went on for so many miles.'

'There's a lot more to Caban Coch than we've seen, and there's another one west of that called Claerwen. It's supposed to be almost as big as all the others put together. There's a stunning walk along its banks with all sorts of wildlife up there, even flesh-eating plants.'

Julie grimaced. 'No way.'

'Sundews they're called. They eat flies.' Swift laughed at the queasy look on Julie's face. There was supposed to be another reservoir, Dol y Mynach that one was, but they didn't finish it. Then there was Nant-y-Gro, where the Dambusters tested the bouncing bomb. They do say that Barnes Wallis came out to see it. It was built originally as a water supply for the workers who built the dams and the other reservoirs.'

'How come you know so much about it?

'We've been coming up to the Elan Valley for as long as I can remember. My dad used to bring me and my brother, and then when we had the kids we'd bring them up here on a Sunday afternoon. It's a great place to walk. We should do it more often, Gwen and me.'

Swift slowed the car and pointed to the hills on the left. 'And that's the Monks' Trod, just up there.'

'So, what are the chances of finding anyone or anything out here do you think?'

Swift considered the question. 'It's huge, I'll grant you that, and fairly remote too, but the local people are quick to spot anything different – a caravan in deepest woodland, holidaymakers, even fly tippers, and they're not afraid to share their information with us.'

‘So you think we’ll manage to work out what happened?’

‘Have faith, Sergeant. We always get there in the end.’

Julie shook her head. ‘It makes knocking on doors in Rochdale seem easy.’

‘And where’s the fun in that?’

‘Are we going to have a look round the Tregaron end today, too?’

Swift shook his head. ‘The lads assure me they’ve asked at every shop, hotel and B&B within a twenty-mile radius. Until we know more about how the poor girl found herself up on that track, we just have to cover all angles and let the locals over there know there’s a police presence.’ He glanced across at her. ‘Did you see the site of Strata Florida Abbey on your travels last night?’

Julie nodded. ‘It’s hard to believe how important it used to be. Adam said it was something to do with Benedictine monks and that the Monks’ Trod went from there to Abbey somewhere? I know you mentioned it but I’ve forgotten.’

‘Abbeycwmhir, or Abaty Cwm Hir, to be a bit more Welsh about it.’

‘So go on, I know *cwm* is valley, and *abaty* must be abbey, so Valley Abbey Something?’

‘*Da iawn.*’ Swift nodded his approval. ‘Abbey in the Long Valley. But, I think they were Cistercians, the monks. I have a picture in my mind that goes back to my schooldays of them trying to pick their way along that track in long white robes.’

They passed the little car park where Kay Greenhalgh had parked her car two days ago and rounded a tight bend up to the steep junction. Swift turned left and the car sped over the invisible county line between Powys and Ceredigion and the ground to the left of the road opened up as the contours on Julie’s map flattened. Rough tracks to left and right led to isolated farmhouses and a small bridge crossed a wide stream. Julie turned the map. ‘*Afon* is river, is it?’

Swift nodded. ‘Well done.’ He nodded towards the bridge. ‘It’s the Elan, and now we're just up from Pont ar Elan, where we were the other day.'

'But this track over the river, Sir, it runs almost parallel to the Monks' Trod. Someone could have driven the victim out along here.'

'They could, but they would still have had to get the body from the track up to where we found it.'

'Or made them walk up there.'

'Good point, but from what I remember, it's even muddier on this side and the victim was relatively mud-free. But it's a fair point, Sergeant, and well-observed. I'll make sure we get someone out there in a Land Rover to see if there's anything worth looking at, but I won't hold my breath.'

The Volvo passed the point on the Monks' Trod where the river bent round towards the road and Swift paused, so they could both take a long look.

'Needle in a haystack then, Sir?'

'I'd say the odds are rather worse than that, wouldn't you?' Swift turned the Volvo round and headed back towards Pont ar Elan.

'House to house could take some time.' Julie scanned the map. 'Are we going to start knocking on doors now?'

Swift shook his head. 'I'll get the local lads in Rhayader to ask around. They know everyone up here and it will give them a chance to tell the farmers to keep an eye open for anything or anyone that isn't usually here.'

'So what's the plan?'

'Well, after we've been to talk to Mal's neighbours, I want another word with that teacher this afternoon. What's his name?'

'Mark Robinson, Sir, but what do you think he can add?'

'I want to make absolutely sure that he didn't see young Owen or any of the other kids picking up anything from near the body, or that there was anything there originally which wasn't there by the time we arrived. It doesn't feel right that the poor girl had nothing with her.' Swift turned the car right, through rough stone gateposts, and onto a long, straight tarmacked drive with a closely mown verge.

At regular intervals, there were young saplings – oak, sycamore and hazel – which were supported by identical crossed stakes and circled by triangular cages of sheep netting.

'Wow. This isn't your usual hill farm, then?'

Swift smiled. 'Rumour has it they came into rather a lot of money. I'm not sure how they came by it, but you can imagine the speculation that goes on. And not just about the money either.'

'Go on, this is starting to sound interesting.'

'Well, since I spoke to Mal, I've been doing a bit of asking around, and there's more than a bit of concern about several men who work for them.'

'Why? What have they done?'

'Well, that's just it. They don't appear to have done anything, apart from help Mal with his fences.'

Julie raised an eyebrow. 'And that provokes concern around here does it? You'd have to do a bit more than that to get an ear-lagging in Harpurhey.' She shook her head. 'So, there has to be more to it than that.'

Swift reached a fork in the drive, and steered the Volvo down the left-hand side and on towards a sheer wall of rock which rose on the far side of a bubbling stream. 'These men don't speak to anyone, apparently. They've only ever been seen in town with one or other of the people who own the place, a Mr and Mrs Wilkins or Wilkinson. Mal wasn't entirely sure. They've only ever been seen in town on market day.'

'So do they sell stuff on the market? Do they have stalls or something?'

'It's not that sort of market. It's a livestock market every Tuesday. It's mostly sheep, but there are cattle too. This place is a little more *up*market. Look.' Swift pointed to a large group of bizarre-looking animals, which were watching the car from a pristine paddock, surrounded by white post and rail fences. As Swift drove past, about fifty pairs of eyes followed them and small heads swivelled on improbably long necks.'

'Good God.' Julie craned over her shoulder. 'What are they?'

'Alpacas. Not indigenous to these parts, it has to be said.'

'Aren't they more at home in the Andes?'

'Well done, Julie. You'll turn into a country girl if you're not careful.'

'Not me, Sir. Strictly a city lass, I am. I've never dealt with anything more exotic than a stray Chihuahua or an escaped parrot.'

'Well they'd be pretty exotic in the Cambrian Mountains,' Swift laughed. 'It's only what you're used to.'

'Do people eat alpacas then? Do these end up at the livestock market?'

'I'm not entirely sure, but these are mainly kept for their wool apparently. It's a sizeable business, from the little I've managed to find out about it.'

The valley widened out now, and the post-and-railed meadows were lush with wild flowers and grass which was so green it looked as though it had just been painted. To the left of the drive, just in front of the stream and the bare rock face stood a substantial stone house surrounded by immaculate gardens. The lawns were as manicured as anything Julie had seen in Alderley Edge or Wilmslow, and formal flowerbeds of red, white and blue flowers lined the winding path up to the front door. To one side of the house, a small orchard was bursting with fruit trees. To the other, a regimented vegetable plot harboured every shape and colour of leaf Julie had ever seen.

'How on earth do they manage to grow all this stuff so high up?'

'I have absolutely no idea, Sergeant. I have trouble keeping up with the grass, let alone the garden. That's Gwen's department.' He turned to Julie. 'One of her departments. If I'm honest, she does far too much.'

'That'll be the job, Sir. It doesn't leave much time for anything else, does it?' She grinned, pleased at the slight vindication of her obsession with work in the light of last night's discussion.

Swift parked the Volvo neatly in the designated place and pulled on the handbrake, rattling the ratchets and setting Julie's teeth on edge.

'I wasn't entirely fair with you last night,' he admitted. 'I made it sound as though I don't care enough about work. But sometimes I do wish I had a nine-to-five that I could forget about once the front door closed. A job that didn't wake you up thinking about the awful things people can do to each other.'

'No way, you'd miss it too much. We'd both be hopeless in a normal job.'

'I'm feeling more than a bit hopeless in this one too, just at the minute, Julie.'

'Give it time, Sir. So, what are you thinking about these mysterious blokes then? If the locals are to be believed and they only leave this place under some sort of supervision, could they be being held here against their will, maybe?'

Swift grunted. 'I wouldn't rule it out totally. There have been a couple of horrendous cases in rural areas in the past couple of years. People living in worse conditions than the animals and working for a pittance.'

'Are we talking about slaves here then?'

'Let's keep an open mind shall we, Julie. I can't really imagine that happening somewhere like this, can you? Besides,' he rocked himself out of the car, 'there could be all manner of innocent explanations for it, couldn't there?'

Mrs Wilkinson was charm personified. From the mass of silver-streaked curls which had been sculpted into a pristine bob, right down to the knee-length suede and leather stable boots in fetching shades of chestnut, Julie could tell that she was entirely happy with her recently improved financial fortune and the easy confidence which it bestowed

'Good morning. I'm afraid we don't buy anything on the doorstep, but if you'd like to leave your literature, I'm sure we'll get back to you if we –.'

'Mid Wales Police,' Swift said 'I wonder if we could have a few minutes of your time?'

Mrs Wilkinson inspected both warrant cards in turn. 'And how might I be able to help you, Inspector?'

'This is very impressive,' Julie said, her gaze taking in the full panorama of hill farm tamed to within an inch of its life. 'How long have you lived here?'

'We've been here almost ten years now. We inherited it from an ancient aunt of my husband's. It didn't look like this when she lived here though.' Mrs Wilkinson wrinkled her lightly freckled nose and grimaced delicately. 'It was almost derelict when I first set eyes on it.'

'You must have worked very hard on it after the old lady's death,' Swift said. Julie spotted the insinuation, but the lady of the house was, it seemed, oblivious. 'Indeed. My husband was made aware that I would only relocate from Hereford once the place was actually habitable.'

'It must have been quite a way to come and visit the old lady, from Hereford,' Swift mused – to himself, apparently.

'Have you made any progress at all in identifying the poor soul on the Monks' Trod?' Mrs Wilkinson smiled but it was, thought Julie, as cosmetic as the rest of this place. 'I hear you're still struggling.'

'How many staff do you have here, Mrs...' Julie consulted her notebook and looked up with a smile, 'Wilkinson?'

'We have a farm secretary of course, and there's a manager who is responsible for the herd.'

'Herd?'

'The alpacas.'

'Ah, right.' Julie wrote slowly and deliberately in her notebook. 'And there are others, of course. You must have an army of help with a place this size. How many acres do you own, Mrs Wilkinson?'

'I think it's around eight hundred hectares.'

'So what would that be in old money?' Swift asked.

'Two thousand acres, give or take,' Mrs Wilkinson supplied.

Julie whistled through her teeth. 'So who else do you have working here?'

Mrs Wilkinson paused, twisted her wedding ring a couple of times and sighed. 'Yes, we do have other staff.'

'How many?' Julie asked.

'It varies, but at the moment there are three of them.'

'And do they live here on site, or do they live locally?'

'The three men live here, the secretary and the manager live in Rhayader.' For the first time, Mrs Wilkinson seemed irritated by Julie's questions, which had obviously struck a nerve. 'And why exactly do you need to know our domestic arrangements, Sergeant? I wasn't aware you intended to question me. I think perhaps I need to phone my husband.'

'It's nothing to worry about, Mrs Wilkinson.' Swift's tone was courteous. 'We're asking everyone locally about what happened over on the Monks' Trod.' He smiled. 'I assume you've heard all the details?'

'Yes, of course.' Mrs Wilkinson appeared mollified. 'Terrible business. But I'm sure nobody here will be able to help you.'

'So the three men who live here with you, would it be possible for us to speak to them, just so that we can eliminate them from our enquiries?' Julie asked.

'You're not serious?'

'It's routine in a case like this.'

'Then I think I should phone my husband.' Mrs Wilkinson slid a mobile phone from her pocket.

'I'm surprised you have a signal up here,' Swift said. 'You don't have a landline, do you?'

Mrs Wilkinson gave a mirthless, brittle laugh. 'We don't get anything at all up here, Inspector. We have a generator and an array of solar panels for electricity, our water is pumped from a borehole and all communication uses satellite. So we have every piece of modern technology available to drag us into the twenty-first century.' She walked away from them and spoke quietly into her phone. Neither Swift nor Kite could make out what she said.

'She seems a bit edgy, wouldn't you say?' Julie watched as Mrs Wilkinson's body language became more animated, even from the back.

Swift shrugged. 'Maybe she's just not used to dealing with the police.'

Mrs Wilkinson thrust the phone back into her pocket and crossed the polished pale oak flooring back to where Swift and Kite were waiting. 'My husband says the men are out on the hill, shearing the last of the hoggs and are unlikely to be back on the yard until this evening.'

'Would it be possible to see their accommodation?' Julie's face was wide-eyed innocence, but Mrs Wilkinson frowned.

'So that's it, is it? You've heard the rumours circulating in the valley? No doubt our upstanding neighbours have delighted in imparting their thoughts about us.'

'What rumours would they be then, Mrs Wilkinson?' Swift's expression was bland, but Julie noticed that his gaze never left Mrs Wilkinson's face. 'We haven't heard anything have we, Sergeant?'

'I don't think so, Sir.'

'Well then,' Swift said. 'Perhaps you would be kind enough to show us where these men are living.'

Mrs Wilkinson blushed, turned on her heel and walked smartly from the room. Swift and Kite followed her out into the hallway, through the kitchen and out into a yard at the back of the house, which was hidden from the drive. By the stream and backing onto the rock wall stood a dilapidated caravan. Swift and Kite exchanged knowing looks.

'How long have the men been here?' Swift asked.

'It varies. Some stay longer than others, it just depends on how they get on.'

'So you have a high rate of staff turnover, then?'

'We can do, but then we see that as a positive, Inspector.'

Julie frowned. 'Surely you'd want them to stay for as long as possible?'

They walked past the caravan and turned into an even smaller yard, lined either side by a row of stables. At least, one side was still stables, but the right-hand building had been painted white, and the doors were no longer wide enough for equine occupants. There were six doors, painted in primary colours, which gave the low building a beach-hut feel. Mrs Wilkinson took a bunch of keys from her belt and, walking along the block as far as the fourth, royal blue door, she opened the Yale lock.

Julie stifled a gasp. The floors were the same light oak as the house, with brightly patterned woollen rugs. There was a living room with a small settee and coffee and dining table and chairs, a tiny kitchen and an equally tiny but beautifully fitted bathroom. The French doors at the back led onto a decking patio with views of the rock wall, the stream and away down the valley.

'I'm assuming this isn't quite what you were expecting?'

It was Julie's turn to blush. 'Not exactly.'

'This one isn't occupied, but the others are identical. I would have to ask permission before letting you see inside, obviously.'

'Obviously,' nodded Swift. 'So these men, the workers, they're free to come and go as they please?'

Mrs Wilkinson ushered them towards the door and locked it behind them. 'They are.' She hooked the keys back onto her belt. 'But many of them choose not to drive, if that's what you're asking.'

'Why on earth would you want to live all the way out here and choose not to drive?' Julie said.

Mrs Wilkinson smiled. 'I can see that you and I feel the same way about splendid isolation, Sergeant. I couldn't imagine not driving, but,' her smile faded and she shook her head, 'some people don't have the choice.' She gestured for them to walk back past the caravan and towards the house. 'We have always tried to protect them from gossip and tittle-tattle, but my husband is adamant that I should tell you why they are here.'

Swift and Kite stopped walking and turned back to look at her. 'Go on,' Swift said.

'The three of them are ex-servicemen. Two served in Afghanistan and the third, well, I'm not sure I'm at liberty to tell you where he served.'

'So your husband is a military man, is he?' Swift asked.

'He was. And he saw first-hand what can happen to soldiers who are no longer needed by the government. We've been doing this for years, making our own tiny contribution to the mess that is left behind after conflict.'

'What is it, exactly, that you do, Mrs Wilkinson?' Julie's tone was conciliatory and when Mrs Wilkinson replied, the superior edge had disappeared from her voice.

'It all began just as a favour for a friend, an ex-colleague from my husband's army days. Howard was in Swansea when he saw a man begging in the town centre. He was obviously homeless and starving, wrapped in layers and layers of putrid clothing, filthy and shivering with the cold. People were pretending they couldn't see him, as they do.' Mrs Wilkinson shook her head and sighed through her nose. Her lips were a tight line. 'They send money to all sorts of dubious charities they see advertised on afternoon television and there are people out there on our streets struggling to survive every day.' She took a deep breath. 'Sorry. It's a hobby horse of mine.' She laughed and her whole countenance was transformed. 'Or one of them. Anyway, Howard put a ten-pound note in the man's paper cup. The man didn't say anything, but it was as Howard bent down to pat the little dog beside him that he heard the man sobbing quietly. As Howard turned to him he realised that this old homeless man with tears running down his grimy cheeks was a thirty-two year old sergeant from his old battalion.' Mrs Wilkinson blinked and looked up at the ceiling.

'That must have been a shock for your husband,' Swift's hand hovered over the pocket containing his handkerchief, but it wasn't required. Mrs Wilkinson cleared her throat and shook her head as if to dispel the vision.

'What did he do?' Julie asked.

Mrs Wilkinson shrugged. 'What else could he do? Howard brought him home with him. He was in a terrible state, and not just physically. We cleaned him up and fed him and once he was stronger, he said he wanted to repay us for what we'd done for him. He worked for us here for three years, until he was back on his feet. He wouldn't accept any money from us, but we put his wages away for him in a bank account, and when he was ready to move on he had a little money behind him.'

Julie shook her head. 'How had he ended up like that? Was it PTSD?'

Mrs Wilkinson nodded. 'It's a terrible thing. Some of them never come to terms with what they've seen in combat, or the fact that they survived and others didn't. His family had tried so hard to understand and make allowances for his problems, but he had two small boys and his wife just couldn't cope with his mood swings and irrational behaviour around the children.

Julie's notebook was forgotten. 'So there have been others since, and you've managed to help them all?'

'Sadly not all of them, Sergeant. One or two are no longer with us. The second lad, Patrick, he came back from Afghanistan with PTSD. His best friend trod on an IED right in front of him. They managed to mend Patrick's wounds, but they didn't cure his mental health. He couldn't sleep because of the nightmares. He started drinking heavily and then progressed onto heroin. Gradually he lost his job, his wife and his home.'

'And you tried to help him?'

Mrs Wilkinson attempted to quell her tears once again, but admitted defeat, and Swift's handkerchief was accepted gratefully. 'We couldn't save him. We took him in, we tried to get help for him, but we failed him. Nobody wants to know, you see. And then one Friday night he walked in front of an InterCity express outside Doncaster, when his wife was too frightened of him to let him see his own children.'

'I'm so sorry,' Swift said. 'I can't imagine how you must have felt.'

'We still do, Inspector.' Mrs Wilkinson stopped outside the front door of the farmhouse and passed the handkerchief back to Swift.

'Can you vouch for them all?'

Mrs Wilkinson turned to Julie and shook her head. 'You really should be less cynical, Sergeant. Yes, I would swear that the three who are with us now know nothing about what happened out there. They would have told us. If you really must interview them, then could I suggest that you call back this evening when my husband and the men will be here?'

'Thank you for your time and your candour,' Swift said. 'If you think of anything which might be of interest to us in the meantime, then please let us know. Otherwise, shall we say we'll be back for a chat at seven o'clock this evening then?'

Mrs Wilkinson nodded and ushered them towards the winding path between the patriotic annuals, then she slipped through the front door and closed it rather firmly behind her.

They followed the path through the gate and headed for the Volvo.

'Well that was a bit bonkers, Sir, not what I was expecting at all.'

'It's not the word I would have chosen.'

'People never stop surprising you, do they?' Julie looked back at the immaculate garden and the pristine house. 'So what do we do about the three men?'

'I think, given that you live over this way, if you've nothing planned for this evening, you could come back and have a quick word with the husband and the three lads, just to see if there's anything we should be following up.' Swift scratched his ear. 'But at least now we know why the locals think they act a bit strangely.'

'I wonder why they don't drive?'

Swift dropped into the driver's seat and put his key in the ignition. 'Who knows, Julie. They could be on medication, I suppose, or maybe they just don't feel up to driving, one way or another. PTSD can be very debilitating.'

'So just the usual questions then?'

'For now, at least.'

'Names and home addresses?'

Swift paused with his hand on the Volvo's gear lever. 'See what they say first. We don't want them scurrying away anywhere. Keep it light.'

The road passed through the shade of tall trees and ended in an abrupt T-junction.

'So that's us back in Rhayader then, Sir.'

Swift drew a sharp intake of breath. 'Don't let the locals hear you say that, Julie. This is Cwm Deuddwr; Rhayader doesn't start until... here.' They crossed the bridge spanning the River Wye and up into the traffic on West Street. Swift indicated right and waited for the inevitable minuetting confusion caused by the congruence of four roads round a clock tower, which seemed to be causing the driver of an oil tanker considerable logistical difficulties.

'It's easy enough once you get used to it,' Swift said, in answer to Julie's look. The tanker reversed, and with much signalling of headlights to oncoming traffic, it rounded the clock tower on the wrong side of the road and headed away, honking thanks, along East Street.

'People are so patient,' Julie said. 'I'm not sure that would work in Manchester at all.'

'Not everyone's patient, Julie, truth be told. We have more than our fair share of fatal accidents on these roads, but on the whole I agree with you. I like to think we still know how to respect others, most of the time.'

CHAPTER ELEVEN

Day Three

Julie crossed the road from where Swift had dropped her, back to her parked car. The lady from the shop was outside, watering brightly coloured pots of bedding plants with an old-fashioned metal watering can. She waved as Julie got back into the Fiesta.

Resisting the urge to call in at home, Julie followed the Beulah road as far as its ski-run bends and slopes at Troedrhiwdalar, went left for Garth, and then headed for the steep and winding road which led up onto the Epynt. When she'd arrived, just a few months ago, this place had seemed so remote, so alien she'd thought she would never get used to it. Now it was a place she liked to sit, briefly, and contemplate the stunning view, which took in Llanafan and the foothills of the Cambrian Mountains beyond. It still seemed very strange to think of this lonely landscape as home.

The car rattled over the cattle grid and continued to climb until a sweeping series of bends and a huge red flag, hanging limply against its pole, heralded the summit. Julie glanced at the clock. She had a few minutes to spare. She turned the Fiesta into her usual parking slot, facing out over the expanse of countryside, hills and valleys, tiny white houses dotted here and there and the chapel on the road from Garth to Builth, and reached for her phone. The voice that answered her call was loud and cheery and Julie could picture Helen Mitchell at her desk in their old office.

'By heck, Julie, I thought you'd forgotten my number. How are you doing in the back of beyond?'

'Very funny. You could phone me, you know.'

'I'm fed up of trying. Have they not sorted out your mobile reception yet?'

'It's random. I don't think they're speeding things up just because I've arrived.'

'Well they should. It's like trying to phone the outback.' Helen laughed. 'What's happening there, then?'

'We've got another body.'

'What, another murder?'

'The boss would like to think so. So far all we know for sure is that it's just another suspicious death. I'm on my way to see the pathologist now, see if there's any more information she can give us.'

'You and your post mortems, you always were an odd bugger.'

'And I miss you too, DC Mitchell. There's nothing wrong with a good pm. You can learn a lot, and being there just makes it more... vivid.'

'God, you can say that again. I can never get that manky smell out of my nostrils. Not without extra strong mints, at any rate. It sticks to your clothes for hours.'

'You're still honing that legendary sympathy of yours, then?'

'There's nowt you can do for the poor buggers when it's got to that stage, is there?'

'You can find out what happened to them.' Julie sighed. 'Anyway the PM's already been done.'

'Aye, well, I'm happy to let someone else do the close work. So, what about the body. Where did you find this one?'

'Well, strangely enough, on open moorland.'

'What's wrong with them round there? Does nobody meet a sticky end in an urban setting?'

'Not so far. Anyway, there aren't many sticky ends at all, judging by the statistics, and urban settings aren't that common either.'

'You've just been lucky then?'

'Lucky?'

'In frequency of post mortem terms. Still, at least it's not all about cats and stolen bicycles, that would drive you mad.'

Julie laughed. 'Yeah, you're right there. So what's happening in Manchester then?'

Helen let out a breath. 'Let me think. We've got a possible gangland shooting, one missing child, some sort of siege going on at a petrol station in Bredbury and the usual other stuff. Why, are you missing it?'

'Of course I am. And nipping to the Roebuck after work. And the Arndale.'

'You're missing the Roebuck? And the Arndale? Dear God, things must be bad. Do they not have shops in Wales then?'

'Don't be daft, of course they do. But it's miles to proper shops from here.'

'I'm going to have to come and have a look at where you are, lady. I can't believe it's as grim as all that.'

'It's not grim, it's just different. Everything's so spread out. It takes ages to get things done.'

'Sorry, Jules, I've got to go, Parki's shaking his car keys at me. I'll phone you tonight, I promise.'

Julie tapped her phone on her teeth. She could imagine the dash down four flights of stairs to the car park, Frank Parkinson hurling his car into the maelstrom of traffic and weaving through cars, buses and trams far too fast, but somehow getting away with it. She pulled back out onto the narrow strip of tarmac.

*

Kay Greenhalgh was flustered, which was as disconcerting as it was unusual.

'I was just about to phone you, but I've not had a chance. We've got bodies coming in from upstairs faster than we can park them,' she said, as Julie peeped round the office door. 'God knows what they're doing up there.' She grinned. 'Come in and cheer me up. I'm so annoyed with myself.'

'Why, what's up?'

'Do you ever get the feeling that you're letting a victim down, that you've missed absolutely everything that you could have missed?'

'Are we talking about Rosa?'

'We are. Not only do I mistake the poor lass for a bloke, but it's taken me until now to work out that she was a Type 1 diabetic.' She gestured for Julie to sit down and pulled two mugs from the shelf. 'Other autoimmune diseases go hand in hand with coeliac disease. I would never have passed my finals if I'd been so dozy then.' She turned her laptop so Julie could read the screen. 'And then there's this.'

Julie read the words aloud. *Degraded compound of coal tar.* 'So what's that then, that grotty yellow soap?'

Kay shook her head. 'It's good old-fashioned creosote. Horrible stuff, totally carcinogenic and banned for domestic use years ago.' She stared at the screen. 'I should have known what it was from the smell. I'm annoyed with myself that I could have saved you time if I'd been more with it.'

'Well, we're only talking the day before yesterday, and we've confirmed who she is, so don't beat yourself up.' Julie smiled. 'You're worse than me at this perfectionist caper.'

Kay poured boiling water onto instant coffee, swished the liquid in both mugs and handed one to Julie. 'Do you ever wish it was in your nature to just shrug your shoulders and not worry about every precise little detail of a case?'

'I do, but I would. Worry, that is. Maybe I should phone you at three in the morning to discuss the finer points of bluebottle and maggot development rather than catching up with social media on the iPad.'

'And maybe your husband would think that was a bit strange,' Kay laughed. 'Does he understand the compulsion?'

Julie frowned, blew on her coffee and considered her reply. 'I'm not sure to be honest. He's happy to spend far more time than he should on his school stuff, but he can switch off once he's done his marking or come up with another fabulous project for the kids. I'm not sure he understands obsession *per se*. Not unless we're talking about the history of the downtrodden masses.'

'Mine didn't either,' Kay said, peering into her mug. 'That's why he's the ex Mr Greenhalgh.'

Julie spluttered coffee. 'You didn't?'

'Didn't what?'

'Persuade him to take your name?'

'Of course I did. I needed to keep mine because of continuity with the professional thing, and he insisted it would be too confusing if we had different names.' Kay shrugged. 'I did say he could hyphenate it, but he didn't seem too keen.'

'Why, what would he have been?'

'Whittingstall-Brown-Greenhalgh.' Kay snorted.

Julie laughed. 'Fair point. So, what do you think about this creosote?'

'Well, there was none in her lungs, so she hadn't drowned in it, but her head, and only her head, had definitely come into contact with it at some stage. I sent hair samples off for drug analysis and that's all they've come back with, that and a cocktail of agricultural chemicals. No drugs at all in the very recent past, so she definitely wasn't high. She could have had a hypo though.'

Julie nodded. 'There was no insulin in her belongings.'

'So that's a definite maybe then. I've been going through all the possibilities. She could have fallen when she hit her head and landed in water with an amount of creosote in it, but my particular favourite, and totally off the record, maybe someone put a bag, which contained residue from small amounts of the stuff, over her head. That might account for the differential putrefaction of the skin, given our sweltering summer temperatures, especially if the bag was some sort of heavy-duty plastic. Either way, I'd have said for there to be no evidence of drowning or suffocation, whatever it was is likely to have happened post mortem.'

'And this is off the record?'

'Totally. I'll need to work on it a bit more to be completely sure.'

'So it could still be accidental death. If she fell, due to a hypo or any other reason, and hit her head, picked up the creosote from where she fell but recovered enough to get out of the water, would that explain it?'

'It would, but we took samples of the water up there where she was found, and there's nothing in those samples that would indicate that's what happened. And then, of course, there was nothing like that in her lungs.'

'But she could have managed to stagger some distance from where she fell, if she fell?'

'I would have thought so, but I can't be definite about that.'

'And it could be murder?'

'That is just as likely. The main blow is a hefty head injury in its own right, and I would have expected her to be at least a little unsteady on her feet after that, but her clothes weren't muddy enough to suggest that she'd been tottering about in the bog up there.'

'So what are you thinking?'

'I honestly can't tell you, Julie. I wish I could, but if it were my job to speculate, I would put my money on someone having covered her head with something that had been in contact with these substances and moving her to where she was found after she was dead.'

'Swift will be pleased.' Julie smiled at the excitement this would provoke, but the pathologist's expression made Julie rapidly re-evaluate her facial expression.

'Craig Swift is one of the best I've ever worked with, to be fair,' Kay said. 'He's just as obsessive as we are, but he seems to be able to manage it far better than I do. He won't be happy until the case is solved and her relatives have closure.'

Julie nodded. 'You're right,' she said. 'At least we can do that for her.'

'And find her killer,' Kay said. 'If there is a killer.'

CHAPTER TWELVE

Day Three

Adam was feeding the cat when she got home. As soon as the food hit his bowl, the cat began wolfing it, gulping it down like a feline Labrador.

'He's definitely gone feral in the food department,' Julie put her bag on the table and peered into the oven. 'Rather like you.' She wrinkled her nose at the brown concoction on the middle shelf and closed the oven door. 'What is it?'

'That,' said Adam, 'is cauliflower korma.'

Julie's shoulders sagged. 'Really? What is it with ruddy cauliflower? Cauliflower mash, cauliflower pizza bases – it's just cauli squashed into submission. How can you call curried cauliflower a meal?'

'I've made bread to go with it.' Adam looked hurt and she was sorry for that, but this new food thing of his just wasn't normal. Was it?

'That's more like it.' She cut two large chunks from the still-warm granary cob and dolloped butter onto them, waiting as it melted into the bread. 'That'll do me,' she said, wiping butter from her chin. 'I've got to nip out again anyway.'

'Aw Jules, have they never heard of shift patterns in Wales? You never seem to have stopped since we've been here.'

'It's only to ask a few questions, and then we can get moving again first thing tomorrow.'

'How long will you be? Shall I keep your curry warm?'

'I'm not sure. Best not. I'll sort myself out when I get back'. She put the butter back in the fridge and watched Adam as he tasted his korma and added some sort of oddly lurid green herb. 'So have you heard any more from Tiffany?'

'Well, I'm not sure.' He dropped his spoon onto the draining board and turned to face her.

'Not sure? How does that work?'

'The school secretary handed me an envelope today. It was addressed to me and it was marked strictly private and confidential, so she didn't open it.'

'And?'

'Well that's just it. When I opened it, there was just a blank sheet of paper inside.'

'Was there a postmark?'

'It's a bit smudged, I can't make out where it's from.' He pulled the padded A5 envelope from his jacket pocket on the back of a chair, unfolded it and handed it to her. What do you think?'

'I think I've an aversion to padded envelopes at the best of times. It could have been much worse than a blank sheet of paper in here you know.' She smoothed the creases and nodded. 'Definitely illegible. I've not a clue where it's from. She turned it over and inspected the back. 'And you've not ordered anything online? They could have slipped up in the packing department.'

'I did order a second hand book about the Drovers' roads.' Adam grinned sheepishly, and Julie laughed.

'You always know what to say, don't you?'

'But if it is her, what do we do?'

'Tiffany you mean?' Julie shook her head. 'There's still nothing we can do, even if it is her. It's not an offence to send someone a blank sheet of paper, and it's not exactly as though we've a huge amount to go on, is it?' She sighed. 'Not unlike the situation with our poor lass in the Elan Valley.'

'Is that where you're off to now?' Julie nodded, and Adam took back the envelope and studied it carefully.

'Let's have a look at that again.' Julie opened the flap and retrieved the single sheet of white A4. She held it at an angle, checking both sides, then straight ahead of her, catching the light from the small window.

'Anything?' Adam crouched down to look over her shoulder.

'Nope. No indentations that I can see, no watermarks.' She picked up her bag, pecked him on the cheek and collected her car keys. 'Don't worry about it. I'll probably be a couple of hours.'

Looking back as he closed the door, she could see that her advice would definitely not be heeded.

*

The chicken in black bean sauce in the foil container on the dashboard was gently fogging the windscreen. One thing that working with Helen had taught her was to be prepared for any culinary eventuality. In a plastic box in the boot, she kept a spare plate, cutlery and packets of salt, pepper and a selection of little packets of sauces and mayonnaise from various pubs. The tomato ketchup that she added to the fried rice on her plate was from the Roebuck, the pub where they'd sometimes gone after work in Manchester. Without warning, a tear splashed onto the lurid red plastic and she sniffed. Had it been easier then, when Adam was always working late and she and Helen had eaten greasy chips and congealed beans in the pub after work? But he hadn't been working late, had he, and deep down she had known it, even then. She had just turned a blind eye and hoped she was wrong. She sniffed again and poured the chicken over the rice and ketchup. She ate it alone, in the empty car park on Dark Lane, watching the dog-walkers and wet-haired swimmers on their way home.

*

Mrs Wilkinson opened the door and looked past her. She seemed displeased, or possibly disconcerted that Julie was on her own, but she was civil, with none of the superiority they had seen earlier in the day.

'My husband is in here, Sergeant. We thought you ought to have a word with him on his own first, if you don't mind.' She glanced at the ketchup stain on Julie's blouse and smiled. 'Would you like a cup of tea?'

'Could I have coffee, please? The stronger the better.' Mrs Wilkinson scurried away and Julie turned to her husband, who thrust out his hand. She was surprised how hard the skin was and, although his hands were clean, she noticed that the creases around his knuckles were ingrained with regular contact with soil. So he didn't just direct operations then. He motioned for her to sit.

'Thank you for coming to see me, Sergeant,' he said. Julie raised an eyebrow at the subtle shift in their relative positions with this opening gambit.

'Not at all. I was hoping to be able to speak to your employees.' She chose the word carefully and noted that Howard Wilkinson bridled slightly before regaining total composure.

'As my wife said, I would prefer to set the scene for you before you speak to them. We are very careful not to force them into stressful situations. Two of them are still undergoing quite intensive treatment and we wouldn't want to undo all the good work, would we?'

'No, Mr Wilkinson, we wouldn't. But I do need to ask some routine questions to rule out any involvement in an extremely serious matter.' Julie opened her notebook and flicked to a blank page. 'So perhaps we could start with you.'

Wilkinson frowned. 'I can assure you, Sergeant, that I have absolutely no information about the deceased person, nor indeed of any involvement of any of our guests in that matter.'

'So you hadn't seen a young woman in the area at any time prior to the discovery of her body on the Monks' Trod?'

'Definitely not.'

'And you haven't noticed any strangers around the farm, vehicles parked for long periods of time, anything out of the ordinary?'

'No, nothing.'

'And you would have noticed if there was anything, would you? You're an observant sort of person?'

Wilkinson raised his eyebrows. 'Sergeant, I have had a very long and very distinguished military career. If my powers of observation were not outstanding, I doubt if I would still be here to answer your questions.'

'Quite, Sir.' Julie beamed at him. 'Jolly good.'

Mrs Wilkinson bustled in with cups and coffee pot on a tray and set them on the low table. Once coffee was poured and distributed, she perched on the arm of the sofa.

'Just for the record, Mrs Wilkinson, I have to ask whether you have noticed anything unusual around here in the last two or three weeks.' Julie smiled at her. 'Anything at all?'

'Nothing that I can think of, unless...' she turned to her husband, who gave the slightest shake of his head and continued the movement more obviously as he bent to pick up his cup.

'No, Sergeant,' he said. 'I think it must have been an errant rambler. We heard the sheep making rather a lot of noise late one evening recently, and we thought it might have been a fox, but the alpacas are extremely good guard dogs. If it *had* been a fox out there we would have heard them too.'

'And can you remember when this was, Mrs Wilkinson?'

Howard Wilkinson put his cup down in the saucer so forcibly that coffee slopped onto the woollen rug beneath. Mrs Wilkinson leapt to her feet and scurried into the kitchen.

'My wife tends to get a little confused about dates, Sergeant. It must have been at least two or three weeks ago now.'

'That's fine.' Julie stood up as Mrs Wilkinson reappeared with a cloth and sheets of kitchen roll. 'I'll talk to your employees now, if I may, and then I'll be out of your way.'

The three men were together in the first cottage. The bright red front door and pale oak and chrome interior were at complete odds with the men's appearance. All three were on the thin side of slim and dressed in black walking trousers and navy polo shirts with the legend 'H W Alpacas'. There was a small silver animal embroidered on the shirts, above the name, but it could have been a donkey or a large dog, for all Julie knew. The men stood in unison when Julie and Wilkinson entered the room.

'As you were,' Wilkinson said, as though speaking to one of the small silver animals on their chests, and the men sat, but they were, she noted, definitely not at ease.

'This is Detective Sergeant Kite. She has a few routine questions for you. Please be as accurate and truthful as you can.'

'Thank you, Sir, I won't be long here and I'll come and find you when I've finished.'

Wilkinson hesitated, but Julie held the door handle, looked out into the yard and waited for him to walk from the room. He didn't say a word, but the rising colour in his veined cheeks gave the game away. Julie shut the door firmly behind him and turned to the three men.

'There's nothing to worry about guys, and whatever is said in this room won't go any further unless it's pertinent to the case. Is that understood?' Two of the men nodded. The third stared steadfastly at his boots.

'All I want to know from you is if you've seen anyone or anything up here in the last couple of weeks that might be useful to our enquiries.' She pulled up a chair and sat facing them. 'What exactly is it that you do here?'

'We help out on the farm.' The tallest of the three smiled at her. 'It's not exactly rocket science, but it's out of doors and heavy duty, which helps you sleep sometimes.'

The second man, a good head shorter than his colleague and looking all of sixteen, nodded. 'And it's teaching us a lot about farming, growing, looking after animals. It's good, we'll be able to get a job when we leave.'

'And what about you?' Julie turned to the third man, who was still staring at the floor. Unlike the other two, he had long, lank hair, which provided a curtain protecting him from his questioner. 'Do you enjoy the work?'

The third man shrugged. 'It's OK.'

'And have any of you seen anything unusual around here lately?'

The tall man leaned forward and spoke to the other two, quietly but forcefully. 'We have to tell her, guys. It's all going to come out in the end, one way or another.'

The younger man nodded. 'Maybe the Sergeant won't have to tell Major Wilkinson.' He looked up at Julie and she wondered who had let this child go to war at all.

'Well, if he doesn't need to know, then I won't have to tell him, will I? What is it that's troubling you?' she said to the third man. She bent down to peer under the curtain of hair and was horrified to hear that he was weeping quietly. She fished a crumpled tissue from her bag, straightened it, gave it a quick visual check and handed it to him. Now she knew how Swift's clean linen hankie idiosyncrasy had developed.

'He'll throw me out.'

'Who will?'

'Wilkinson. It's in his rules and regulations.'

'What is?' Julie resisted the urge to part the curtain of hair and get a good look at the man's face, but he blew his nose and glanced up at her.

'No visitors and no overnight stays. But he was in a bad way. Upset. Had nowhere to go.' He sniffed. 'And it was only for a couple of nights. He was no trouble.'

'Let's not worry about that now.' Julie crouched next to the man and looked up at him. 'So who was this man, and why was he here?'

There was a shrug, and the hair fell back into place. 'He just said his name was Ard.'

'Would that be short for something?'

Another shrug. Julie looked at the other two men. The tall man grinned. 'Funny sort of name, I thought. He said he was Ardal. I only remembered it because it means *area* in Welsh.'

'So you speak Welsh?'

The man shook his head. 'I'm from Dorset, just a learner. I wanted to know what all the place names mean and how to pronounce them. It's like being abroad again and I felt bad that I couldn't even say the names.'

Julie nodded. 'I know that feeling.' She stood up slowly. 'Well, at least we have a name for him. So, Ardal what? Any idea?'

'Sorry.'

'Well, why was he here? Did he stay here with you?'

The curtain of hair moved again. 'We put him in one of the spare cottages. Well, I did. It was nothing to do with the others, it was all my idea. They just helped with a share of their food. He was out on his feet, starving. We didn't think Mrs W would mind.'

'Did you tell her?'

The three men exchanged glances and the tall man finally spoke. 'We don't want to get her into any bother. She's been very good to us. She'd never have known, but we were cleaning the place after he'd left and she came round with a cake she'd just baked.' He smiled. 'She caught us with the hoover out.'

'So you did tell her. But not the Major, is that about the size of it?'

The younger lad sighed. 'We only told her after he'd gone. She didn't know anything about him being here. We felt bad about not being straight with her.' He shrugged. 'But she made us promise not to tell him, the Major. He's a really good bloke, but he won't tolerate anyone breaking his rules.'

'OK, that's fine, I won't tell him either, not unless I have to, but I do need to know as much as you can remember about this man. How old was he, what colour was his hair, what was he wearing, were there any distinguishing features.'

'Whoah, Sergeant.' The tall man laughed. 'Steady on. One question at a time. Didn't anyone tell you're we're damaged goods?'

Julie laughed. 'Sorry, I do that. Put it down to being impatient. Go on then, what can you tell me?'

'Well I'd say he was probably late twenties, early thirties, blonde hair, blue eyes, leather jacket, jeans. Fancied himself a bit, but likeable all the same.'

Julie nodded. 'Did he have transport?'

The young lad shook his head. 'He said he'd walked from Ray... Where is it, Baz? You say it.'

'Rhayader. He'd walked from Rhayader. He was looking for someone. He said he'd been let down.'

'About what?'

'Dunno. Did he say anything to you, Mick?'

The hair moved again, but this time it parted, and Julie saw Mick's face for the first time. She had to stop herself staring. In all her years in the job, all the things she had seen and wished she hadn't, this face was one she would never be able to get out of her mind, especially at three am when her insomnia kicked in. It wasn't the puckered skin around his left eye or even the jagged scar, which ran from his nose to a point just below his jaw line. It went much deeper than that. His expression seemed devoid of anything at all, as though there was nothing beneath the flesh and bone. But it was his eyes that would haunt her. The only other time she had seen eyes like these, they had belonged to a young dog – a bearded collie – which her father had brought home when she was about seven. The dog had been badly beaten and her father had wrestled him away from the man who owned him. Julie had been so upset because the dog wouldn't even look at her, he just sat cowering by her father's chair. Weeks later, once the dog had been persuaded out of his new refuge under the kitchen table, he had looked at her with eyes just like these. Slowly, he'd learned to trust her, and for the next twelve years, until he died of old age, he was always by her side, protecting her. Would Mick ever trust anyone again? He spoke quietly, to a pattern on the rug at his feet.

'He said a woman had stolen his sister's son and he had come to find him.' Mick looked up at Julie 'He said he thought he knew where she was.'

Julie snapped the elastic band off her notebook and Mick flinched.

'Sorry. Did he tell you where he thought she was?'

Mick shook his head. 'Just somewhere not too far away was all he said.' He hooked hair behind his right ear and looked at her. 'Do you think he had something to do with what happened out there?' He nodded towards the moorland.

'It's possible,' Julie conceded eventually. 'But even if he wasn't involved, we'd like to speak to him, to eliminate him from our enquiries.' She tapped her notebook with her pencil. 'Did he give any indication of where he was going?'

The three men shook their heads.

'Any sort of accent or dialect? Do you think he was local?'

Baz laughed. 'He sounded a bit like you, Sarge. Up north was all he said when we asked him where he was from.'

'So no idea of where up north he was talking about? He didn't mention a town?'

The three of them shook their heads in unison. It was like trying to get information out of the three wise monkeys.

'And how long was he here?'

'Two nights,' Baz said.

'And can you tell me the dates?'

A shrug and two head shakes. 'Every day's pretty much the same up here.' The youngster spoke this time.

'But Mrs Wilkinson came up here the day after he'd left, bearing cake, didn't she?' Julie tapped her pencil on her teeth. 'She might remember when it was. And you said he was here for the two nights immediately before that?'

'Don't speak to her when he's there.' Mick suddenly flashed her a look that gave her hope that he might have fight left in him. 'Promise you won't drop her in it.'

Julie held up a hand and shook her head. 'I promise I won't drop her in it. But I do need to establish exactly when he was here, what time he arrived and what time he left.'

'That's fair enough, Mick.' Baz stood up. 'If you let us have a word with her while he's not around, we'll phone you tomorrow with dates and times.' He walked towards the door. 'Is that it, then?'

'Almost. Did you notice any distinguishing features? Scars, tattoos, anything else you can remember?'

'He had a tattoo.' Mick pointed to the inside of his wrist. 'Here. It was some sort of flower. It could have been a rose. A red rose.'

Julie closed her notebook, stood up and walked to where Baz was standing. 'I'll need one or all of you to come to the station tomorrow and we'll put together an impression of what this man looked like.'

Baz blushed. 'I'm not sure we can do that, Sarge. The Major doesn't like us to leave the farm without him or Mrs W. It might be difficult for us to get to you without causing problems. He'd need to know why wouldn't he?'

'I can draw him for you if you like.' Three heads turned towards Mick.

'I didn't know you could draw,' Baz laughed. 'You're a dark horse.'

'There's a lot about me you don't know,' Mick said. He walked over to the dresser and pulled out an artist's pad and a tin of drawing pencils and pastels. He smiled, almost imperceptibly. 'Make the Sarge a brew while I do this.'

CHAPTER THIRTEEN

Day Four

Julie was staring at her computer screen when Swift arrived in the office. She had uploaded and enlarged the little piece of city map from Rosa's bag, and was poring over the dense housing and unusually straight roads.

'Any joy with Mark Robinson, Sir? Did he come up with anything else?'

Swift walked over to her desk and glanced at the screen. 'No, nothing new, and I have to admit he seems pretty genuine to be honest with you. He said he'd made sure none of the kids had taken anything or found anything up there and he's sure only Owen saw the body.' He leaned further towards the screen and perched his glasses on his forehead. 'Well there's not much to go on there, is there?'

Julie shook her head. 'I can't believe there's so little on this map. There are five places of worship, one with a tower and one with a spire, minaret or dome, according to Ordnance Survey. Then there are six schools, two colleges, a library, a station and an Ice Dome, all within about a mile and a quarter.' She grimaced. 'But there are no road numbers, no rivers and nothing else that would be blindingly obvious.'

Swift let his glasses drop back into position. 'Even the railway station is anonymous.' He stood up and frowned. 'That bit to the west of the caravan site, the very top left-hand corner. Could that be beach?'

Julie clicked on the tiny pale orange triangle where Swift had been pointing and enlarged it. 'I think you could be right, Sir. So if that's beach, then this oblong job here could be part of a pier?'

'So that's narrowed it down then, Julie. All you need to find is a seaside town with a pier and well-educated, God-fearing ice-skaters.'

'Right, Sir. I'll get onto seaside Ice Domes then.'

Rhys, Goronwy and Morgan burst into the room, discussing a disputed high tackle in last night's rugby match, although Julie thought this might not have been the only explanation for Rhys grabbing Morgan round the neck and attempting to drop him to the floor. There were still occasions when she would like to attempt that move on him herself. The three of them sauntered over to the board, still shoving each other like schoolboys. Julie pinned an enlarged copy of the map onto the board and then reached under her desk and retrieved a large carrier bag. 'This might be altogether more enlightening, Sir.' She removed the bag and handed Mick's drawing of the stranger to Swift.

'Someone's talented then. You haven't done this, have you?'

'Not in a million years. I got thrown out of art lessons at school. I was so bad, the teacher thought I was taking the mickey,' Julie laughed. 'It was the best thing that ever happened to me. I got to do chemistry instead.'

'The detail on this is absolutely stunning,' Swift said. 'Look at the depth in that face.' He held it at arm's length. 'That's impressive, that is. Who is he?'

'It turns out the boys at the farm found a waif and stray up in the hills on the farm's land and took pity on him. They let him stay for a couple of nights in one of the cottages. He said he was looking for a woman.' Goronwy chuckled, which earned him a look from Swift. Julie dug her notebook out of her bag and flicked through the pages. 'They said, "a woman had stolen his sister's son and he had come to find him". And this is the best bit, Sir, they thought he knew where they both were.'

'That's excellent, Julie. Well done. And where were they?'

'Ah, well, that's the bit they didn't know.'

Morgan Evans tutted loudly. 'Well that's no use to anyone is it?'

Julie turned to glare at him, but Swift ignored him 'So why didn't Mrs Wilkinson tell us this?'

'I think they're all just a bit terrified of Major Wilkinson, to be honest. The lads didn't want him to know that they'd let the man stay, or that Mrs Wilkinson knew about it.'

Swift nodded. 'Fair enough, but let's make sure we keep an eye on them over there shall we? Now, Morgan, what have you got for us?'

'There's just a bit more, Sir.' Julie pulled a smaller drawing from the bag. 'It's the same rose.' She held up Mick's drawing of the tattoo on the man's wrist next to the photograph of Rosa's tattoo. 'See?'

'But that's not conclusive, is it?' Morgan shook his head. 'A rose is just a rose. It doesn't mean to say they were done by the same person. I think we're adding two and two and coming up with nine here, Sir.'

'Oh come on.' Julie rolled her eyes at Morgan Evans. 'There's more than a nod to an Irish connection here, with the Quigley thing and Rosa's shamrock tattoo. So maybe this guy, Ardal, is Rosa's brother and just maybe she was down here trying to find her son.'

'Everything is possible,' Swift said. 'Let's remember to keep an open mind shall we? It's not as though we're falling over ourselves with clues is it, Morgan? Now, how did you get on with the market in Builth yesterday? Does anybody know anything else we didn't already know?' Swift wandered over to join Julie at the board.

Morgan Evans shook his head. 'No, nothing interesting. One or two of the lads work a few of the markets, but they said they'd not heard anything from Builth or from anywhere else either.'

'Rhys, Goronwy, anything to report?' Swift asked.

'I'm expecting a call back now, this morning,' Rhys said. 'We think we might have got somewhere with dental records on the victim.' He dropped his bag on his chair and joined the others. 'She had terrible teeth, which made it pretty conclusive apparently. They phoned late last night. She *is* Rosa, but her surname isn't Quigley, it's Harding.'

'So where is she from?' Julie asked.

'Well, up until five years ago she was living in a place called Walton-le-Dale.'

'That's a posh part of Preston,' Goronwy said. 'We've contacted social services and the local GPs to see if she's known to them. Turns out she was known to social services, but only for serial truanting from school. She fell off their radar at the same time the GP last saw her. After that we've nothing.'

'Has someone contacted her last known address?' Swift asked.

'Not yet, Sir, we wondered if you might want the local police to visit, just in case it's her parents still living there. They wouldn't know what's happened to her yet, would they?'

'Good point, Goronwy.' Swift blew out a breath. 'I wonder if a little trip up to Preston might be an idea.'

'I could do that, Sir.' Morgan Evans pushed past the others to stand by Swift.

'How old would that make her now, Goronwy?' Swift asked. 'When was the last time social services had any contact with her?'

'She was sixteen.' Goronwy checked his notes. 'After that she seems to have got herself sorted out. But these reports mean that we now know she was twenty-three when she died. She did finish school, and without any further problems, according to social services. The woman I spoke to said she'd just got in with a rough crowd and she picked up a couple of warnings, but she was soon back on the straight and narrow. As far as she was concerned, Rosa was never a huge problem. She even did her A Levels and had a place at university.'

'So where did she go to uni?' Julie asked.

'She didn't. She was supposed to be going to Edinburgh to study veterinary science, according to the school, but she never showed up for registration.'

Swift sighed. 'We're going to have to talk to the parents then. She hasn't come up anywhere else on the radar? No hospital visits, A&E, benefits?'

'We only found out her real name late yesterday, Sir. We'll get onto that now, this morning.' Rhys headed back to his desk and Goronwy followed.

'We now know she was a Type 1 diabetic too,' Julie said.

Swift let the air escape from his mouth. 'She didn't have much going for her at all, did she, poor dab.' He stared at the board. 'OK, let's consolidate what we've got and we'll get together at three o'clock. Morgan, I'd like you to concentrate on this map. See if you can work out where it is and if you can get an address for the house circled here,' Swift pointed at Julie's map. Julie frowned but Swift handed her Mick's drawing of the blond man. 'And you can get this copied and circulated and see if you can work out who he is, Sergeant.'

'That won't be tricky, hardly at all, Sir.'

Julie collected the copies of the drawing of the missing man and mused, where on earth she should start? Goronwy had confirmed from social service reports and dental records that Rosa's former name was Harding and that there was no record of a Rosa Harding of the right sort of age having been married in the UK.

'Had she always been known as Rosa, do we know?' She stood by Goronwy's desk as he flicked through screens.

'Rosa was her middle name, apparently. According to the dental records she was Caroline Rosa Harding. And there's no record of a marriage in that name either.'

'So she dropped the Caroline.' Julie grimaced at the state of the dental X-ray on the screen. 'I suppose that would make her a bit harder to trace if her parents were looking for her?'

'So why did she run?' Julie asked.

Goronwy shrugged. 'Why does anyone do a runner?'

'Parent trouble?' Rhys grinned. 'I sometimes felt like doing a runner when my dad got going.'

'Your dad's really sound, soft lad. And you wouldn't have gone anywhere, not really. Your mum looked after you far too well for that.'

'Why else would you just disappear?' Julie tapped her biro on her teeth and Rhys cringed, as he always did. 'If I'd had a place at uni to study veterinary science nothing would have stopped me from going.'

'Maybe she was worried about going to university?' Rhys said. 'It's not easy for some kids to leave home, is it?'

'Easier to go to uni than to just run away though, surely?' Julie said. 'Unless...'

'Go on, Sarge.' Goronwy looked up at her.

'Well we know she had a baby, don't we? Kay Greenhalgh said she couldn't be sure when that was, but what if she was pregnant when she left school or soon after and by the time she was due to go to Edinburgh three months later...'

'She couldn't hide it any longer.' Rhys rolled his eyes. 'Maybe her parents didn't even know anything about the baby.' He nodded towards Morgan Evans who was bent over the fragment of map across the room and lowered his voice. 'Do you think the boss will send Morgan to see her parents?'

Julie shrugged. 'I think if there's a possibility that we may be right about her identity and provided we can find her parents, then maybe Lancashire Constabulary might be a better bet. The signet ring and the initials fit, but now we've got final confirmation from Kay Greenhalgh and the appalling teeth and your research that it is Rosa, or Caroline, then the parents will need local support.'

'Sarge.' Morgan Evans shouted across the office. 'Do they have trams in Blackpool?' When she got to his desk he was pointing at the very edge of the map at a faint black line with tiny cross-markings running between what they'd decided was a pier and the Ice Dome.

'They do, Morgan.' How the hell had she missed that? 'And if that *is* Blackpool, then the oval patch of sand with a star on it will be the Sandcastle and the scribbly mess just below the Ice Dome isn't an industrial estate. That must be the Pleasure Beach.' She shook her head. 'Stupid.'

'Call yourself a northerner, Sarge, fancy not spotting the tram track.' Morgan Evans laughed. 'It had to be somewhere on a west-facing coast with the beach over there didn't it?' He pointed to the pier. 'So how come you know all the sights of Blackpool then?'

Julie blushed 'It's not that far from Manchester you know.' She smiled, remembering girlie nights out, the Golden Mile, the cheesy illuminations and heart-stopping rides at the Pleasure Beach. 'I may have been for the odd visit.'

'So where's this house, then?'

'I've absolutely no idea, but it shouldn't be too hard to find out, should it?'

Morgan laughed. 'So I finally get to do some detecting, do I?'

Julie bit back a retort, which even by her standards of sarcasm would have seemed unkind.

To be fair to him, he had probably reacted in exactly the same way she would have done, if she'd failed her Sergeants' Exam, twice, and some foreigner from the big city had been foisted on her.

'Give me a minute,' she said, heading for Swift's office. Two minutes later she was back. 'Come on,' she said, handing him the pile of posters. 'Hand that over to Rhys. He can bung it into Google Street Map and have a virtual wander round the streets of Blackpool. Let's go and see if we can work out who this guy is and what he's been up to.'

CHAPTER FOURTEEN

Day Four

'Another day, another market.' Morgan indicated right, away from Smithfield and its trucks and trailers, and weaved his way onto the Dark Lane car park.

'Do they sell different types of livestock at the different markets?' Julie asked, wrinkling her nose at the smell from the sheds which wafted across the main road.

'To be honest, I've no idea about livestock.' Morgan felt in his pocket for change. 'We're not all welly-wearing hill farmers you know. Don't believe everything you hear about the Welsh and sheep.'

Julie laughed, remembering her leaving party in Manchester and the red Hunter wellies and the sheep wrapping-paper that had been part of her leaving present. She handed him change, and he dropped the coins into the ticket machine.

'So it's not just me then, who doesn't understand the black art of livestock management?' She watched him stick the ticket on the windscreen and slam the car door. He began to walk away. 'Aren't you going to lock it?'

'You worry too much, Sarge,' Morgan said, but he locked the door anyway. 'Right, where do we start?'

'You tell me, you're the local. If it were me, I think I might start with B&Bs, hotels, shops, caravan sites, the Leisure Centre?' She nodded across the street.

'Or maybe we could do North, South, East and West streets in order?'

'Ooo tidy mind, I like that.' Julie laughed, Morgan rolled his eyes and they headed into the Leisure Centre.

The pool had the usual damp smell in the air and squealing children behind the tall windows. The glass-fronted gym behind the desk was busy, the modern machines full of lycra-clad men and women, some of whom, Julie was relieved to note, had turned various shades, ranging from pale fuchsia to pickled beetroot.

'Wow, that's impressive.'

'So you expected our exercise classes to be along the lines of sheep shearing and bale tossing, did you?' Morgan was scowling.

'Well, no. I just –,' Julie frowned. 'No, it's not that at all. I'm just surprised at how modern it is, and how many people are in here during the day. Just wasn't expecting it to be so popular.'

Morgan shook his head, but she could tell he was trying not to smile. 'God, Sarge, you're going to have to ditch those prejudices of yours.'

She followed him down to the reception desk. Was that really what it was? She thought of herself as the least racist person on the face of the planet, but did he have a point?'

'What can I do for you?' The girl behind the desk smiled up at them. 'Are you looking to join the gym?'

Julie showed her warrant card. 'Well, I hadn't even considered it, but I might be persuaded to think about it.' She handed a poster to the girl. 'Have you seen this man anywhere recently, either here or just around Rhayader?'

The girl studied it carefully. 'He's so striking. No, I'd have definitely remembered him. Why, what's he done?'

'We'd just like to speak to him in connection with a current investigation, that's all,' Julie said.

'That poor girl up at Pont ar Elan is it?'

'Could we put one of these on your notice board?' Morgan asked. 'Just in case it jogs someone's memory.'

'No problem. I'll put him on the board now, and I can stare at him from here.'

The girl took the poster and handed Julie a flyer and an application form. 'All the information you need to join the gym is on there. You can pay monthly and it's very reasonable.'

It was the same story everywhere they went. Nobody had seen the man and most were sure they would have remembered him if they had. At quarter to one, Julie dragged Morgan into the café by the clock tower.

'I'm starving, and I have to make sure of a decent meal at lunchtime, because it will be beans and bloody lentils again tonight.' She took out her purse and dropped her bag on a chair by the window. 'There's only so much beige food I can take. What do you fancy?' She ordered food and brought their coffees back to the table.

Morgan blew at the froth on his latte. 'How did he get there?'

'How did he get where?'

'The farm. How did he get from wherever he was to there? We've not found a car, there's no public transport and we've asked every taxi company within a fifty mile radius.'

'He could have hitched a lift.' Julie nodded. 'But that's a really good point, Morgan. He could have even walked or cycled.'

'And it could have been from anywhere at all, to be honest, couldn't it?'

One of the girls from behind the counter slapped knives, forks and serviettes onto the table. 'You forgot to pick these up,' she said, pointing with her head towards the rack of cutlery by the till. She moved the last few posters to make room. 'Is this him?'

'Is this who?' Julie asked, given that any reference on the posters to Mid Wales Police was hidden under Julie's arm.

'The man you're looking for about that murder up the road.'

'We're only trying to eliminate him from our enquiries,' Morgan said.

'How do you know we're looking for him?' Julie asked.

'I was in the gym when you went to the Leisure Centre,' the girl said. 'My sister's on the desk.'

'And have you seen him before?' Julie asked, her impatience less well hidden than she would have liked, judging by Morgan's expression.

'Well you wouldn't forget a face like that, would you?' The girl smiled. 'That body of his wouldn't have put you off either.'

'And he was in here?' Julie handed her a poster.

'Yeah, a week, week and a half ago maybe? I don't know what day, but it was sunny, because he sat at one of the tables outside. He had a burger and a pot of Earl Grey tea.'

'Do you remember all your customers in such detail?'

Julie smiled and the girl became flustered.

'It was the tea. I wouldn't have expected a bloke like that to drink Earl Grey tea.'

'A bloke like what?' Morgan asked.

'You know, athletic like. Oh I don't know. He just looked fit.' She grinned. 'I wouldn't have said no.'

Julie smiled back. 'How was he dressed, can you remember?'

'Jeans, white tee shirt, leather jacket, walking boots.'

'Did he have a bag with him? A rucksack maybe or a suitcase?'

The girl nodded. 'He had a rucksack, a great big one. The sort you'd use if you were camping out.'

Julie and Morgan exchanged a glance. 'Was there a tent, then?' Morgan asked.

The woman behind the counter shouted, 'Burger and chips twice.'

'I'll just get your food, I'll be back now.'

Julie drummed her fingers on the table as she waited.

'Thank God she fancied him,' Morgan observed. 'If he'd been as skinny as the bird on the Monks' Trod, she might not have remembered him.'

'Charming.' Julie glared at him. 'There's every possibility that the bird on the Monks' Trod, as you so delicately put it, was ill.'

'Or a druggie.'

'We don't know that for sure. Most of the track marks are pretty ancient. We know she hadn't been using much at all in the recent past, only one or two of the marks were new ones.'

'Do we?'

'According to Kay Greenhalgh she hadn't. Mind you,' Julie gazed out of the window at the traffic in its incessant waltz around the clock tower, 'if the brother wasn't into drugs either, then there's every chance that this isn't drug-related at all.'

'Burger and chips,' the girl said, plonking down a plate in front of Julie, 'and another burger and chips.' She turned to walk away.

'Thank you,' Julie said. 'The tent?'

'Oh, yeah, he had a tent.' The girl smiled. 'Bright blue it was, just like his eyes.'

*

Swift listened carefully as Morgan described the man and his bright blue tent.

'And there's no sign of him or his tent in Rhayader now?'

'No, Sir. He was at the campsite by the cycle path for a few days, then he paid up in cash and left.' Morgan checked his notebook. 'That was on Wednesday last week.'

'And Mrs Wilkinson says she took the cake up to the men on the Friday,' Julie said. 'So that all fits if he stayed with the lads Wednesday and Thursday nights.'

'So what happened to the tent?' Swift asked. 'Why did he need a proper roof over his head for those two nights?'

Morgan shrugged. 'No idea.'

'How did he get to the campsite?'

'The man at the campsite said he thought he'd hitched a lift.'

'Do we know where from?' Swift asked.

Julie shook her head. 'And why would he stay up in Rhayader if it was Rosa he was talking about? If he did know where she was, why wasn't he staying in Llandrindod too?'

'Of course it could be that he wasn't looking for Rosa at all.' Swift tugged his ear. 'The tattoo could be a complete coincidence. He could have been looking for another woman entirely.' He shook his head and ambled back to his office. Julie followed.

'Sir, I think I might have forgotten to mention this.' She handed him the sheet of paper she had grabbed from the photocopier on her way to his office. 'Kay Greenhalgh has had the tox results back on the hair samples she sent in. They confirm there was no drug usage recently. Rosa's hair was so short they can't go back very far, but she definitely wasn't using regularly.'

Swift nodded. 'You said she thought it wasn't very likely.'

'And they've come back with weed-killer and other stuff on her hair that she picked up from somewhere. The doc thinks probably post mortem, but in these amounts it was nothing to do with her actual death.'

'What's the weed-killer?' Swift asked.

Julie scanned the sheet. 'Paraquat, according to the National Poisons Information Service.'

'Dear God, that's evil stuff. A woman in Essex poisoned her husband's steak and kidney pie with it while I was still a probationer. They banned it about ten years ago.' Swift whistled softly. 'Is the doc sure this stuff didn't kill Rosa?'

'She said it's more likely she came into contact with it after death.'

'Well, let's hope so. Apparently it's not a good way to go.' Swift sighed. 'What was the other stuff?'

'Sir?'

'You said weed-killer and other stuff.'

'Er, there were traces of red diesel.' She scanned the e-mail again. 'And creosote, Sir. Old creosote.'

Swift bolted from his chair, straight past her and through the door. 'With me, Sergeant!'

CHAPTER FIFTEEN

Day Four

They were both in the yard, Mal and Sarah. Mal was attempting to kick-start the quad and Sarah had an armful of washing and a peg bag. Julie thought they could have been subjects in an oil painting or one of those old black-and-white photographs of country folk in the 1930s. Sarah wore a wraparound floral pinny over beige slacks and a pale pink turtle neck. Mal wore oil-stained Fred Dibnah overalls, a flat cap, and boots that made his feet look far too big for his body. Behind them the hills soared skywards, dwarfing the two of them and the house and outbuildings.

'Craig.' Sarah tapped Mal on the arm and he looked up and smiled.

'Well, we don't see you for months and now here you are again.' He held out an oily hand, which Swift shook. 'Who's this young lady?'

Julie bristled but managed a smile.

'This is my new sergeant, straight from the mean streets of Manchester she is.' Swift grinned. 'She's getting used to us though.'

'Well you're very welcome, lovely.' Sarah beamed at her. 'It's nice to see a new face up here. We rarely get any visitors at all nowadays. Come on in, I'll put the kettle on.'

Julie went to follow Sarah but Swift shook his head. 'Let's sort out the business side of things first.' He turned to Mal. 'Can you show me where you keep the old creosote you mentioned the other day? Is it in the shed?'

Mal and Sarah exchanged a look. Sarah shook her head. 'He's an old hoarder he is. And he's too tight to pay the council to dispose of it all. I told him I don't like all that stuff in there. What if the sheep or the dogs got in?' She winked at Julie. 'But he's a man, so he's not likely to listen is he?'

Julie laughed. 'You're right there.'

The four of them went into the shed. The dog looked up as they passed, his chain rattling as he put his head back between his paws and closed his eyes.

'The poor old thing's worn out,' Mal said. 'A bit like me, he is.'

'It's that quad.' Sarah still carried her armful of washing and she frowned into it. 'He could keep up with the pony, but he can't run as fast as that blasted bike.'

Mal led them to a door in the furthest corner of the barn. When he pushed at it, it caught on the rough concrete of the barn floor, but it opened in stages, revealing banks of shelving along three sides of a sizeable store room. There were jam jars full of bolts, screws and nails, all neatly labelled with size and potential use. Large swirls of blue polythene piping were held onto the wall by bungee ropes and intricate knots. Ancient tools filled the shelves; an engraved ebony spirit level with metal corners, a wooden mallet, a brace and bit, all in dark brown wood, made long before the advent of colourful plastic tools.

On the ground beneath the shelves were ranks of containers of all shapes and sizes. There were maybe half a dozen blue drums of creosote, which looked remarkably new.

Swift kicked at a barrel of creosote. 'I thought you couldn't buy this stuff anymore?'

'Ah well, you don't know everything then.' Mal chuckled. 'You can still get it, but you have to be an official professional user.'

Julie laughed. 'So what's a professional creosote user?'

'Farmers, builders. But *you* wouldn't be able to buy any, Sergeant.' Mal twinkled back at her and Sarah shook her head.

'But what about this then?' Swift prodded a rusting metal container with his toe. 'This definitely isn't legal, even if you are a professional.'

'Ah,' Mal nodded thoughtfully. 'I have been meaning to get rid of that.' He pressed his lips into a thin line. 'You've got me there, Craig. But I haven't used it. Not for years, it's lethal stuff.'

'You did though, didn't you?' Sarah hitched up the washing basket on her hip. 'He got the wrong tin didn't he, won't wear his specs out here.'

'It only took me three fence posts to notice though.' Mal grinned at her.

'It didn't do the sprayer any good though, did it?' Sarah shook her head. 'I'm going to put the kettle on. Follow me in.'

Swift nodded and Julie followed her out of the barn and across the yard.

'Do you need a hand? I'm a dab hand at folding sheets.'

'Well you can't be any worse than that one.' Sarah's head jerked in the direction of the barn. 'All these years we've been doing it and he still goes the wrong way. I think he does it on purpose.' Sarah smiled, but she was miles away, or maybe just a dozen yards away, thought Julie.

Julie was encouraged by Swift's ability to consume amazing quantities of baked goods. She managed two scones, still warm from the oven and dripping butter onto the tiny china plate.

'Go on, have a piece of sponge cake.' Sarah pushed the plate towards her. 'It's home-made jam.'

'I won't need any tea,' Julie said. 'And that might actually be a blessing.'

'Have you shown Sarah your picture?' Swift asked, wiping his hands on his handkerchief and brushing crumbs from his lap.

Julie fished out a photocopy of the blond man and showed it to Sarah. 'Have you seen this chap up here in the last couple of weeks?'

Sarah shook her head. 'He looks like a film star. Who is it I'm thinking of, Mal?' She shoved the picture across the table. 'Lawrence of Arabia, that Irish chap who played him.'

'He wasn't Irish, he was from Leeds.'

'That's the one.'

'Have you seen him?' Julie asked.

'No, love. I've not seen anyone like that up here, not for a long time.' Sarah smiled at Mal and handed the picture back to Julie. 'Has he got anything to do with that poor girl on the moor?'

'We don't know.' Swift stood up. 'Mal was telling me he's missing a plastic sack from the quad bike. You haven't had a tidy up have you, Sarah?'

'What me, dare to fiddle with his stuff out there?' Sarah wagged her finger at Mal. 'He's the untidiest person I've ever met. Last week he couldn't even remember where he'd parked the quad, never mind where his ratty old plastic sack could be.'

'What day would that have been?' Julie asked 'Can you remember?'

'Of course I can remember. I wanted to use it to nip down to collect the post from the end of the lane. Save getting the truck out and I was waiting for a letter from my sister. It was last Friday morning.'

'And the quad wasn't where you'd left it?' Swift asked Mal.

'I'd left it where I always do, just inside the shed.'

'So where was it?'

'It was down the drive. At a really strange angle, almost in the ditch it was. Like it had rolled down there or something.'

'Had it rolled?' Julie asked. 'Was the handbrake on?'

Mal frowned, his head on one side. 'It was. If it hadn't been, it would have been in the ditch good and proper, but there was no way it rolled down there from the shed. The yard's flat, see.'

'And the plastic bag, could it have blown away?'

'Well I looked everywhere for it. If it did blow away, it must have gone a long old way.'

'He's attached to that sack.' Sarah laughed and refilled Swift's cup from the large brown teapot. 'Says it's the only one that fits his sprayer in properly.'

'Have you washed the quad since then?' Swift asked.

'Don't be daft, Craig. Why would I do that?' Mal chuckled. 'The rain washes most of the muck off it, doesn't it?'

'Would you be able to live without it until I've sent a Scene of Crime Officer out to take some samples? I'll get them to come as soon as they can.'

'What do you think you'll find?' Sarah's smile seemed to have deserted her.

'I've absolutely no idea, Sarah. But it's better that we check everything, just to make sure, isn't it?'

'I suppose you're right. But the thought that someone might have used it for... to do something –.'

'Don't worry, it's just routine. As you say, it's only a thought I've had, it's probably totally wide of the mark. But it's my job to cover all the angles. I don't want you to worry about it. Is that clear?' He wagged a finger at Sarah and she laughed.

'Yes officer,' she said. 'Have another scone.'

*

The phone was ringing when Julie walked through the kitchen door, and she heard Adam pick it up in the lounge. Sid chirruped a greeting and wound himself round her legs.

'Evening, mog, don't suppose you've been fed.' She plonked her bag on the table. 'But you wouldn't admit it if you had, would you?' She reached into the fridge for the remains of a tin of cat food, and the small ginger cat followed her every move. The fridge was stuffed with sweet potatoes, an enormous butternut squash, a marrow and various plastic pots of rice, beans and other unidentifiable and unappetising leftovers. She closed the door and forked the chunks of cat food into the cat bowl. 'Save me a bit of yours, will you?'

The door opened and Adam smiled through the gap. He seemed strangely reticent as he held out the phone. 'You're not to worry, everything's under control. It's your mum.'

Julie took the phone from him and handed him the empty tin. 'Mum, what's happened?'

Her mother's words were calm, but she had never been one to shy away from saying what needed to be said. 'You're not to worry. Everything's being done that needs doing.'

'Just tell me what's happened.'

'I didn't want to mither you with it, but your dad said you need to know.'

'Mum!'

'We've been burgled, love. But you're really not to worry. They didn't take much, not even the money I'd left on the hall table to give to the Christmas Club lady. It's just...'

'What? For God's sake, Mum, just tell me.'

Julie could hear her mother sigh. 'I told him you'd get yourself in a state. Well, we were coming back from your Gran's. She had a bit of a turn in the bread shop this morning. She's fine, Dr Webb says it's probably a reaction to her new tablets, and I'd just taken her a hotpot to warm through because she'd live on toast and sandwiches if you didn't keep an eye on her.'

'Mum, I know all about Gran's bread fetish and I'm imagining all sorts now. Are you both OK?'

'We're fine. Well, we are now. It would have been better if your dad hadn't tackled him, but they've put loads of stitches in and they've said he'll be right as rain in a week or two.'

Julie was more taken aback by her mother's distracted state than the news itself. She was never like this. 'So Dad tackled the burglar and he was hurt?'

'Yes, but not badly. They said it had missed anything important, but he was lucky, and they were lovely at the hospital.'

'I'll come up now.'

'You can't do that, love. Your Adam's just told me you're in the middle of a murder.'

'Give me a few minutes to get things sorted and I'll phone you back.'

'Honestly, love, he's going to be fine and Mr Sanderson's mended the window already.'

'Don't worry, Mum, there's something else I might be able to do while I'm up there.' She smiled at Adam, who was still standing in the doorway with the cat food tin in his hand. 'I'll make a phone call and ring you back in a minute.' She cut the connection and dialled Swift's number.

'Will you be able to get the time off to go up there?' Adam asked.

'If I can clear it with Craig Swift I can kill two birds with one stone.'

CHAPTER SIXTEEN

Day Five

It was barely light when Julie backed the Fiesta into the lane, but Joe was there, watching her. She wound her window down.'

'Morning. Don't you ever sleep?' she asked him.

'I don't need much,' he said. 'You're off on one of them dawn raids are you? Bashing someone's door in on an estate somewhere?' He chuckled. 'Too much excitement for me, that would be.'

'Actually, I'm going back to the big bad city. That would blow your mind, I'm sure.'

'Ah, going for long is it?' He peered into the car, checking the back seats.

'You're not getting rid of me that easily.' She put the car into gear and smiled sweetly at him. 'I'll be back before you know I've even gone.'

Why did she feel as though her every move was being scrutinised? Probably because it was. Whether it was Joe with his fascination for people 'from off' or Morgan Evans questioning her every comment. She sighed. Maybe the only way to solve the Morgan problem was to help him pass his Sergeants' Exam and then he might stop feeling he had to prove himself to her every second of every day. Joe, she decided, was just Joe. He had left the gate open and it felt like a huge bonus, not to have to get out and wrestle with the thing. She had been told more than once to leave gates as she found them, as though Joe thought she'd want to do the opposite, just to be difficult.

There was barely any traffic at all for the first fifty miles of her journey. It still surprised her. Even in the middle of the day it was sometimes as though there had been a nuclear attack with barely a soul on the roads. She negotiated winding roads down into Newtown and on towards Welshpool where there were signs of life around the livestock market. *Marchnad Da Byw y Trallwng* it said on the sign at the gates. Where would you start with that one? Which bit was Welshpool? Was any of it Welshpool? She really ought to get round to learning Welsh, especially in her job. How many nuances and subtleties might she be missing that she didn't even know were there?

It seemed strange to be heading for Chester and the motorway in this direction. Strange and painfully slow. The rush hour had finally begun and the A483 had obviously been built with horses and carts in mind, not cars which might want to overtake each other occasionally. As, finally, she queued to get onto the roundabout which would take her onto the motorway, she watched the other drivers. In the car alongside her, a woman made a shape with her mouth, which could only mean that the application of lipstick was imminent. In front of her, a little boy in a maroon blazer and gold-tasselled cap pulled faces through the back window of a huge Mercedes, obviously not strapped into his car seat. People flouted the law every minute of every day, and in reality, there was little she could do about it. She couldn't even protect her parents or, for the moment, find out who snuffed out Rosa's life up there on that desolate moorland.

Someone behind her beeped. The traffic lights were green, and she slammed the car into gear and followed the little boy in the Merc across the roundabout and onto the slip road. This was what she was used to. Head-down flat-out drivers who steadfastly refused to acknowledge the presence of an interloper waiting to join the motorway. She barged her way into the inside lane between a bus with a huge and smiling cartoon driver on the back and a black Subaru, whose owner seemed less than pleased at her advanced driving skills, judging by the arrangement of fingers she could see in her mirror. This was what she was used to.

The euphoria didn't last long. By the time she had queued on the M60 and sat in stop-start traffic for twenty minutes on the way into Manchester, she was missing the empty tarmac of the A470.

*

She drove down her parents' street and viewed it with the eyes of a stranger. Old-fashioned concrete lamp posts and intermittent wheelie bins stood sentry. Cars were everywhere, parked on either side of the road and planted in twos and threes in what used to be front gardens but were now concrete and tarmac. It was one huge car park, from one end of the street to the other. Apart from number 45. She smiled as she pulled into the drive. Her dad's car would be tucked up in the garage and his garden still was a garden, with precision flowerbeds around a tiny central pond, a little oasis of colour. She was amazed at her relief on seeing grass there and not concrete. Maybe this country living was getting to her. Her mother opened the front door before Julie had even switched off the engine.

'You shouldn't have come.' She squeezed Julie's arm through the open window and stepped back to let her out of the car. 'But I'm glad you did.' She threw her arms round her daughter and Julie caught the familiar waft of Simple Soap and a touch of hairspray.

'So what's been going on here then?' Julie held her mother at arms' length and studied her face. 'Hey, that's not like you.'

'It's just a bit of a shock, that's all. I'm being daft.' She sniffed and dabbed her eyes with a tissue pulled from her sleeve. 'It could have been much worse, but it just makes you feel a bit wary, as though everything's just a bit dirty, if you know what I mean.'

Julie did know what her mother meant. She had lost count of how many times she had heard those exact words from victims of burglary. That sense of violation, that someone could walk into your life and take away some of its security. How much worse would that be for the family of a murder victim? 'How's Dad?'

'Oh you know your dad. He's determined to play it down. He's changed all the locks already, and as far as he's concerned that's an end to it.'

'What about his injuries?'

'They're hardly blooming injuries.' Julie's father was on the doorstep. His left hand and forearm was heavily bandaged, but otherwise he looked just the same as he always did, but desperately tired. 'I was unlucky. He walloped me with a picture frame. It broke the glass, that's all. It'll be right as rain in a couple of days.' He hugged her with his good arm. 'So it takes a bashing by a burglar to get you back here, then?'

Julie blushed. 'I know. I'm sorry, I should have been back sooner, but it's been one thing and another, and I don't know where the time's gone.'

'I was joking, lass. You've got your new life to sort out down there. That's not to say I'm not chuffed to bits to see you.' He stepped inside the hallway to let her in. It didn't look any different, but when she looked down the hall and through the kitchen window, she was struck by how close the houses at the back were. She had never noticed before. She had always thought of the area where her parents lived as being almost suburban, leafy and spacious, but now she was aware of the narrow garden, the fences and walls which chopped the space into tiny, bite-sized parcels of highly-coveted land.

The house was as tidy as ever, surfaces polished, carpets vacuumed, everything in its place. Nobody would ever know that anything had happened.

'What's missing?'

'Nothing much,' Julie's father nodded towards the living room. 'Just your mother's mobile phone. We disturbed him, caught him in the act.' He grinned. 'That's what you say, isn't it?'

'You're certain it was a male then?'

'I'd have said so. It's difficult to say, it all happened right fast. One minute he was in the doorway and then he'd gone. It was only when I reached out to try to grab him that he clobbered me with the picture frame. It was stupid, really, if I hadn't tried to stop him then I wouldn't have ended up with this.'

'What sort of height do you think he was?'

'Don't worry, Julie love, the local police have been wonderful. They've asked all the same questions and they're pretty certain it was just kids, trying their luck.'

Julie nodded. 'Probably. But make sure you lock everything properly. Put the chain on the door.'

Yes, Miss.' Her dad put his good arm round her shoulder. 'Don't you worry about us. We're pretty good at looking after ourselves by now you know. We've had a bit of practice. Now, tell us all about where you're living and what the people are like where you work.'

*

Julie glanced at her watch. Two hours had flown. 'I really must get going,' she said.

Her father smiled. 'You could stay a bit longer, you'll not get back in time.'

'For what?'

'To get back to work. I know you, you'd work twenty-four hours a day if they let you.' He checked the clock. 'You wouldn't be back in time for much, even if you left now.'

'I've got one of those steak and kidney pies you like from Booths in the freezer. And I could do chips.' Her mother certainly knew how to get round her. 'It wouldn't take long.'

Julie grimaced. 'Now that's just not fair, Mum.' She stood up resolutely and slung her bag over her shoulder. 'I don't suppose the pie would be all right tonight if I took it with me?'

Her mother tutted. 'I'll go and get it,' she said, but she was smiling as she left the room.

'You got something else planned for today then?' her father asked.

'Well I have, but it's important.'

'Work then, is it?'

'God, am I so predictable?'

'You are, love. Are you allowed to tell me about it?'

'Not really, but it's about the body of a young woman who was found not far from where I'm living. She's got connections in Preston and possibly Blackpool, so I thought...'

'You thought you'd fit in a trip to the old folks.'

'You're not old. No, it was the other way round. The most important thing was coming to see you and Mum. The other stuff was just an idea I had. I thought it would help to see where she was from and maybe ask the neighbours if they remembered her.'

'I know, love. I was pulling your leg.' Julie's father stood up slowly and shepherded her towards the door. 'Just promise your mother you'll come and see us again soon.'

'You could come and stay with us, both of you. It would be great to show you round the Green Desert of Wales.'

'Sounds tempting.' He lowered his voice. 'I'm not sure your mother would leave the house empty just at the minute. Give her a few weeks and she'll be back to normal, but it's left her a bit wobbly, all this burglar business.'

Julie's mother bustled back in with an oblong package wrapped in newspaper. 'I've put two in there, it's all I had in the freezer. Just make sure you heat them up properly.'

'I do know what I'm doing with an oven, Mum.'

'When did that happen?'

'Yeah, OK, so Adam does most of the cooking.'

'He is a good cook, I'll have to give him that much.' Julie's mother glanced sideways at her. 'You have to be good at something, don't you?'

Julie returned the oblique glance, perfectly aware what her mother meant. 'He's more reliable in most other departments these days, Mum, but the worrying thing is he's decided he's vegan.'

'Vegan?' Julie's dad burst out laughing. 'I've heard it all now. Does he think he's saving the planet?'

'Nope. He says it's the healthiest way to eat and we should all embrace it.'

Her father snorted. 'He has some rum ideas, that lad. And you've embraced this healthy lifestyle, have you?'

Julie waved the packaged pies under his nose. 'Obviously. I'll have my steak and kidney with air-fried sweet potato chips and falafels on the side.'

'Twit.' He hugged her. 'I do miss your sense of humour.'

'You will be all right, won't you?' she asked. 'If you want me to stay, I can.'

'Thank you,' her father said. 'But you have your own life in Wales now. You can't keep worrying about us up here, can you?'

'Just like you don't worry about me down there?'

'Fair point.' He rubbed her shoulder. 'But we're not so far away, are we? Not really. I promise we'll call if we're worried about anything.'

'And you're always welcome to stay here, you know you are. You and Adam,' her mother said. Julie knew that she meant it, even though her faith in Adam's ability to look after her daughter wasn't as solid as it had once been.

'Thank you, that means a lot,' Julie said. 'And you're welcome to stay with us. We have a spare room that's small but perfectly formed. And you will let me know if you hear anything about your... visitor?'

They both hugged her as they said their goodbyes and waved as she reversed the little Fiesta into the road. As soon as she got round the corner and into the next street she had to pull over to blow her nose and wipe her eyes. When did they get to look so old? They weren't old. Of course they weren't. Her dad wasn't quite sixty and her mother a good couple of years behind him, but suddenly they looked as though they were verging on old age. It would be the shock, she thought. They probably weren't sleeping. That would be it. They'd soon be back to normal.

CHAPTER SEVENTEEN

Day Five

When was the last time she had driven this road? Blackpool Illuminations? Sally's hen party in Fleetwood? She overtook a black Range Rover with black tinted windows, which was weaving badly in the middle lane. The driver wore dark sunglasses and copious amounts of chunky bling and was talking on his mobile phone. She glared at him, but he flicked his finger at her and looked away. She had no intention of doing anything about it, and much as it annoyed the hell out of her, she attempted to ignore him.

The last time she had been on this road was with Helen Mitchell, her partner in crime, or rather in attempting to solve it, in her former life in Manchester Metropolitan Police. They had been called to give evidence at Preston Crown Court, in a case involving luxury cars stolen to order for export. Even Preston had seemed small and foreign to her then, let alone the depths of mid Wales. Funny how things turn out sometimes. She cut across the Range Rover into the inside lane, to make a minor point. The Range Rover swerved into the inside lane and sat just inches from her bumper. She wasn't about to pick a fight in a Fiesta with a car the size of a small tank up her rear end, was she? She indicated left, drove down the slip road and joined the frantic junction by the Tickled Trout Hotel. The Range Rover didn't follow. She pulled into the petrol station, parked away from the pumps and phoned Goronwy.

'Oh, it's you. Where are you, the boss said you had things to do up north. You on the trail of the Blackpool connection, is it?'

'I'm just outside Preston. Do you know if Rosa's parents have been informed yet? I thought I'd go and have a nosy round theirs and see if any of the neighbours are of the blabbing variety.'

'They're on their way to us, apparently. The local lads went to inform the parents this morning, once we got final confirmation from Dr Greenhalgh. She confirmed that Rosa probably died on the Thursday or, at a push, early on the Friday morning before she was found. She says that's definite, but that she can't be any more specific than that. The parents are pretty certain it's her from what they were told, but they'd not seen her for quite a while. Her father agreed to identify her and they insisted on driving themselves down, there and then.'

'I can't imagine how that must feel.' Julie watched a father and a little girl with blonde bunches giggle their way from the shop, across the forecourt to their car. 'That must be the worst feeling on earth.'

'Yes, Sarge, it must.' Goronwy sounded as though he genuinely meant it, and Julie smiled to herself. She worked with such a small group of people now, in comparison to the hectic office in Manchester, and yet they were all so different.'

'Did you pin down that address in Blackpool, by any chance?'

'We did. Well, Rhys did, to tell the truth. The house is on Eighth Avenue. We've had a look on Google Street View, and it just looks like an ordinary street.'

'Well what were you expecting? Something with a sign outside saying *Drugs Are Us?*'

'No, Sarge, but it's really respectable. You just don't think that Blackpool would be like that do you?'

'Don't you?' She laughed. 'Not everywhere outside Powys is a den of iniquity, Goronwy. Give us the number and I'll go and have a look there too, it's only about twenty miles from where I am now. It would be a shame not to.'

'Right you are, Sarge. It's number eleven.' There was a pause, then Goronwy added, 'You will be careful, won't you?'

'I will, Goronwy, I will, and thanks for the info. See you tomorrow.' She laughed as she cut the connection. They all thought she was totally reckless after the episode up on the Epynt, which had left her alone and looking down the business end of a loaded rifle.

*

The house in Preston was large and well cared for. An estate agent would have referred to it as an Executive Detached with ample well-stocked and mature gardens. It was as good a place to start as anywhere. At least she'd get a feel for the place and what the family was like. She walked up the drive and pushed the doorbell, always a good move before peering through windows, even though she knew that Rosa's parents were on their way to Wales. She had her warrant card in her hand, and as the door opened, it was a reflex action to show it to the man.

'Detective Sergeant Julie Kite, Mid –,' Her jaw dropped and she scrabbled in her bag. 'You might be just the person I'm looking for.' She looked from her photocopied drawing to an identical face, looking down at her from the step.

The man took the drawing from her and studied it carefully, then he whistled. 'Wow, somebody has a talent for faces. Where did you get this?'

'It is you, then?' She handed him the smaller drawing with the detail of the rose tattoo.

He pulled up the sleeve of his sweater. 'I guess this would give the game away.' He gazed at the picture again. 'Can I keep this?'

'You can,' Julie said. 'We've got a couple of hundred of them.'

'So I'm a wanted man?' He held the door open for her. 'I'm guessing this is about Caroline?' Julie nodded. 'Then you'd better come in.'

Inside, the house was minimalist. Pale wool carpet and doors with heavy brushed steel handles gave way to the black marble tiles and granite of the spacious kitchen. The man held up the kettle. 'Coffee?'

Julie nodded. 'Yes, please.' She clambered onto a red leather stool by the breakfast bar. 'What's your name?'

'I'm Ardal. Stupid name, really, but my mother's Irish. It was her father's name.' He took two white china mugs from the cupboard above the kettle. 'I'm Ardal Patrick Harding. Caroline's brother.'

'She didn't call herself Caroline though, did she?'

'She used to. Well, Caro to her friends.' He smiled. 'She was a great kid. Full of what she was going to do. She was going to be the best small animal vet in Lancashire.' He looked away, just for a second. 'She'd have done it too. If she hadn't got herself mixed up with that bastard.'

'That bastard wouldn't happen to be called Quigley, would he?'

Ardal stared at her. 'How would you know that? Is he wanted in Wales too?'

'Would you accept a lucky guess?' Julie shrugged. 'It seems as though Caroline was calling herself Rosa Quigley, although we haven't found any record of their marriage. Were they married?'

'To be honest, I've absolutely no idea. She didn't mention it when I saw her.'

'Would she have told you?'

'She'd have told me if she thought it would have upset Mum and Dad, so maybe they weren't married.'

'It must be difficult for you, and for your parents.' Julie got up and walked over to where Ardal was spooning coffee into a cafétière, so she could see his reaction in close-up. 'But you found her, didn't you? You know where she was.'

Ardal shook his head. 'I wasn't looking for her. I thought she would still be in Blackpool somewhere, just staying out of the way, keeping her head down. I never thought for a minute that –.' He sniffed, cleared his throat and splashed boiling water onto the ground coffee. 'I had no idea what had happened to her. I was looking for her little boy.'

Julie frowned. 'So you were in Wales looking for Caroline's child?

Ardal nodded. 'Sean. His name's Sean.'

'Why did you think he might be there? Did Caroline tell you she knew where he was?'

Ardal pulled a piece of kitchen roll from the dispenser and blew his nose. 'I hadn't spoken to Caro for months. She told me before Christmas that Sean had gone away, but she didn't know where he was. The next time I saw her was in March, but that was only by sitting in my car outside her house in Blackpool for three days and nights until she couldn't avoid me any longer. She'd made it clear she didn't want anything to do with the family, me included, that she didn't want finding or bringing home but that she was happy that Sean was safe.'

'Did she know where he was?'

'I got the impression that she didn't.'

'And your parents know where Caro was?'

Ardal sighed and shook his head. 'She made me promise not to tell them that I'd found her.'

'Had they fallen out about the baby?'

'It all went very wrong way before that. She met Quigley while she was still at school. He was working at the Pleasure Beach in Blackpool, Jack the Lad on one of the rides. Caro was there on a day out with friends from school. She thought he was exciting and dangerous. Turns out he was just dangerous and an utter bastard to boot.' Ardal stirred the coffee and flung the spoon into the sink.

'So how did you know the boy might be in Wales?' Julie accepted the proffered cup and declined milk.

Ardal hesitated. 'I don't want to get involved with the whys and wherefores.'

'Or the boyfriend?'

'Definitely not with him. And he's seriously into drugs, for what it's worth.' He gripped the edge of the work surface, whether for support or to control his temper, Julie couldn't tell, but his face was as white as his knuckles when he looked up. 'I just want to keep Se away from him. If he went the same way as Caro with the drugs never forgive myself.'

'So when did you come back north?'

'Friday last week. I set off from there at dawn. I had to sort out a job for a client in Ribchester.' Ardal looked up at her suddenly. 'You're going to tell me she was already dead up in those blasted hills, while I was searching for Sean, aren't you?'

Julie shook her head. 'We don't think so.'

Ardal closed his eyes. 'I could have stopped this happening to her. If I'd found her, she might still be alive.'

'Mr Harding, how did you get back from Wales to Preston?'

'I'm being accused of something here, am I?'

'Not at all, but we have to cover every possible combination of facts.'

'I've never heard it described like that before.'

'So how did you get back here? We believe you didn't have a vehicle with you when you were in Wales.'

Ardal looked at her. 'No I didn't. My vehicle has my name plastered across both sides. I didn't think it would be helpful when I was trying to keep a low profile. I got the train from Llandrindod Wells, changed at Crewe and a mate picked me up from Preston Station.'

'Do you still have the ticket?'

'I don't know. I didn't realise it would come in useful.'

'Could you check?'

Ardal scowled but left her sitting there and ran upstairs. He came back triumphantly clutching two tickets. 'It's been clipped too, look,' he said, thrusting the tickets under Julie's nose. 'So whatever you were thinking, you were barking up the wrong tree, weren't you?'

Julie busied herself with her notebook, and eventually Ardal sat facing her across the counter. 'How did you know Sean was in Wales, Ardal?'

He gave a mirthless half smile and looked up at her. 'You'll think I'm a control freak, but I was only trying to help Caro. She couldn't think straight half the time and I thought if I could get Sean back, bring him here, then she might come home.' His words petered out and he sighed again.

'And you're sure Caro didn't tell you where Sean was? Could she have taken him to Wales herself?'

'I don't know the ins and outs. All I know is he was up there somewhere, and it definitely wasn't Caro who took him. I'd worked out he was somewhere near Rhayader, but that was all. I didn't find him.'

'So she didn't tell you where he was?'

Ardal looked down and picked at a fleck of mica deep within the worktop. 'No she didn't. But I only did it for her and for Sean. I wasn't really breaking the law. Not really.'

'What did you do, Ardal? Tell me.'

He didn't look at her, just continued to circle the glittery mineral in the granite. 'I broke into her house in Blackpool. I'd been trying to find him since November and she wasn't telling me anything. So I waited until Caro and the lunatic were both out and went looking for clues.'

'And did you find any?'

'I found a few addresses that might have been possibles. I started with the local ones and worked my way south.'

'How have you got the time to do all this sleuthing?' Julie asked. She realised it was the wrong word as soon as she'd said it. Ardal recovered his colour immediately in response. 'Sorry, I didn't mean anything, it was just... Where do you work?'

'I'm a landscape gardener, freelance. So I've been able to take time away from it.'

'But this must be your busiest time? Aren't you losing money?'

'And clients, but this is too important. I'll just have to work a bit harder once I've found him, won't I? As soon as I've pacified the old dear in Ribchester I'll be back in Wales.'

'What happened to your tent?' Julie asked. 'The blue tent you had at the campsite in Rhayader.'

'Nothing happened to it, it's here in the garage.'

'But when you went to stay with the army lads and the marauding alpacas, they said you hadn't got anywhere to stay.'

'You don't miss anything do you, Sergeant. I just needed to be up there, in that valley. I was tired of the jollity of the campsite, of people on holiday. One day, I thought I'd seen a woman with a child who looked like Sean up above the reservoirs, but she vanished before I could get to her. I spent hours walking the hills up there and then I met one of the lads out on the hill and we got talking. He invited me to go and stay at their place for a couple of nights. Was it one of them who did the drawing of me?'

Julie nodded. 'He said you were desperate to find the little boy. I think he really thought it must have been your own son you were looking for.'

'If we find him, then I'll find a way of adopting him. I've got to keep him safe from his lunatic father.'

'So you're sure Quigley is Sean's father?'

'He has to be. They've been together for years. From the very little she told me about him, he'd never have let her look at anyone else.'

'Ardal, we might be able to help you find Sean. If you could give me more details about Caro's home life and what might have happened to Sean, then we can take it from there.'

Ardal got down from the stool and walked over to the sink. He stood with his back to her. 'I've given you all the clues I can.'

Julie put her mug in the sink and stood next to him.

'Ardal, you were here this morning when your parents left to identify the body?'

Ardal nodded slowly, his face crumpling as the reality of what Julie was saying sank in. 'You really think it's her, don't you? But you could be wrong, couldn't you?'

'Is there anyone who you want to be with you? Can I phone them for you?'

'Just tell me.' Ardal's eyes flashed, anger suddenly mixed with despair.

Julie automatically went into formal mode. 'The body of a young woman was found in the Elan Valley and we have reason to believe that it is the body of your sister, Caroline Harding, also known as Rosa Quigley.' Julie sighed. 'Ardal, we're 99% certain that it *is* Caro.'

He turned to look at her, and it was all she could do not to put her arms round him and give him a huge hug. He looked like a little boy himself, despite the muscular, sun-tanned frame.

'Ardal, I'm so sorry to have to tell you this. We will do everything we can to find Sean, but we haven't found him and we need more help. What was the address you were looking for in Powys?'

Ardal sniffed and wiped his eyes with the cuff of his sweater. 'I don't have the address, just a fragment I found in the bin at Caro's. The house name is *B-a-c-h* and the town is Rhayader, but that's all there was. It was a return address on the back of an envelope, but it was smudged.' He managed a small smile. 'It was under one of her girly teabags, rose hip or something. The ink had run, and there was a chunk missing where the envelope had been opened.'

'And you found this fragment of an address when you broke into the house and found the other addresses?'

From the way Ardal looked at her, Julie knew there was more to come.

'Not exactly.'

'So you've been there more than once?'

Ardal nodded.

'And this fragment with the Rhayader address on it. When did you find that, Ardal?'

He shrugged. 'I don't know the exact date.'

'You're not making this easy, Ardal. When did you find the address in Wales?'

'Two, maybe three weeks ago.'

'You've been making yourself quite at home in Blackpool then?'

'I only went twice, I swear. What would you have done, Sergeant, if your sister had been in trouble?' His face showed true anguish, and Julie was sorry for her glib comment.

She handed him her card. 'Look, I know you're worried, and this isn't the time, not today, but will you call me soon? We can discuss whether you'd like us to bring charges against Caro's husband or boyfriend or whatever he is, for anything at all. It may help us to locate him.'

'What sort of charges?'

Julie hesitated, but then said, 'Did you know she had coeliac disease, Ardal?' She could see something in his eyes, until he closed them against her.

'I knew there was something. All through school she kept saying there was something wrong with her, that she had stomach pains most of the time. She decided milk didn't agree with her, so everything had to be dairy-free. Mum wasn't best pleased.' He smiled then and she was struck with the blueness of his eyes. The waitress in Rhayader had been right. 'I don't know if this has anything to do with it or whether it was just hormones, but she had an absolutely evil temper sometimes, too. That's why the GP put her on anti-depressants.'

'How old was she when that happened?'

'She was doing her GCSEs. The doctor said it was probably the stress of the exams and being a teenage girl. It was meant to be temporary, just until she'd finished the exams.'

'But it wasn't temporary?'

Ardal shook his head. 'She started losing weight, shedloads of it, and she needed more and more of the tablets.' He shook his head. 'Dad thought she was just after attention, but she wasn't, was she? Oh, Caro, you poor little bugger.' He was crying now, not even bothering to hide his tears. 'How did you know she had coeliac disease?'

Julie hesitated. 'From our investigations after she was found.'

The truth dawned and Ardal's whole frame shuddered with a sob. 'You mean a post mortem, don't you?'

Julie nodded and Ardal swallowed hard.

'And why would you be able to charge Quigley with anything relating to that?'

'Well,' Julie paused.

'Go on.'

'Well perhaps we should wait for the inquest, when everything has been finalised. You might not need to know all this.'

'Just tell me, Sergeant. Please.'

Julie wondered what Swift would do in this situation. She hoped she was right as she cleared her throat and read from her notes. '*Coeliac disease causes poor absorption of vitamins and minerals, and if it's not spotted early enough it can lead to osteoporosis, making the bones more liable to breakage.*' She looked up at his face, which had begun to crumple as though he was six years old and had grazed his knee. 'We have absolutely no information about whether Quigley was involved, but you have confirmed that their relationship might not have been entirely amicable. There were several fractures on her body and...'

Defying protocol again, she held him while huge man-sobs rocked his whole body.

Slowly, Ardal became quiet and Julie stepped away, awkward now.

'I'd like you to go to the local police station today and make a statement to them, as soon as you can. Everything you've told me.'

'Why?'

'You're a key witness to Rosa's life and her disappearance. We need to have it all in writing. I can take you there now.'

'There's no need. I'll go as soon as you leave.'

'I will check.'

Ardal nodded. 'I won't be running away anywhere, Sergeant. All I want to do now is make sure that Sean is safe.' He stared at the worktop and back up at her. 'Although I won't be responsible for my actions if I do see Quigley.'

'In that case, unless you let me take you into Preston police station myself, right now, to make your statement, I'll have to arrest you.'

Ardal shook his head. 'You people,' he said. 'You really are the lowest of the low.'

CHAPTER EIGHTEEN

Day Five

The unmistakable shape of Blackpool Tower dominated the skyline for miles. Julie smiled at her first glimpse of it. It might not be as stylish as the Eiffel Tower, but it was definitely a lot more fun. A gang of the girls from work had been to a tea dance in the Tower Ballroom once; afternoon tea with long frocks and the Wurlitzer, all beneath crystal chandeliers and acres of gilt and red velvet. Where would you go for a tea dance in Wales, she wondered. There was plenty of line dancing, though. Maybe she could get a gang from work to go for a night out. Nerys in the canteen would definitely be up for it, and Maggie from IT could always be persuaded, but what about the others? She could always ask, couldn't she?

She parked on a side street behind the Pleasure Beach. Even today, before the school holidays had begun, there were shrieks and screams from The Big One and Revolution, Avalanche and the Big Dipper. Helen had been a nightmare on The Big One. The others put it down to a dodgy burger, but Julie knew Helen was still horribly hung over from the night before. It was a wonder she'd lived to be thirty-two at all, the way she looked after herself. She laughed out loud as she locked the car. God, was she turning into a vegan, triathlete history teacher by association?

Eighth Avenue was just as Goronwy had said, very respectable and also surprisingly quiet, considering its location. Rosa's house was the left hand half of a semi-detached house, red brick and bow-windowed with pale stone windowsills and a little arch picked out in white over the stained glass front door. Julie checked the address. If this was Quigley's property, he didn't bring his work home. The right hand house was identical, even down to the vertical blinds. A hanging basket was placed centrally between the two bay windows. They must have got on then, Rosa, Quigley and the neighbours, Julie thought. No dispute over the placing of the bracket. She'd seen wars over less.

There was no reply to Julie's knock on Quigley's front door. She peered through the letterbox, but could see nothing out of the ordinary in the hallway. She had that feeling, as though the house was holding its breath, that there could be someone inside, but nobody showed themselves. She checked the untidy back garden and looked through the grimy windows of the shed. There was nothing out of the ordinary in there, just a battered lawnmower and a shrivelled paddling pool, the odd paint can, a couple of tatty deckchairs.

The neighbours to the front and back of the house tried their best to be helpful. They gave her as many details as they could. It soon became obvious that Quigley wasn't exactly a model neighbour, and they were appreciating the opportunity to make sure Julie knew just how awful he was. Every one of them was far less scathing though, when it came to Rosa. She was under his influence, they said. He treated her like a slave. The poor girl was terrified of him.

Nobody had any idea what Quigley did for a living or where he got his money from. Suggestions ranged from benefit scrounger to drug dealer and worse, but there was nothing that amounted to hard evidence. There was nothing concrete at all. Even so, Quigley now had to be the prime suspect in Sean's disappearance.

Finally, Julie returned to Quigley's semi, chose the right hand front door this time and let the brass knocker drop hard. A deep voice from behind her made her jump.

'Can I help you?'

Julie turned. The man was maybe late thirties and slim, immaculate in a charcoal suit, white shirt and purple tie. He carried a black leather pilot's bag, and the weight of the world on his shoulders. He looked as though he'd forgotten how to sleep.

'I wonder if I could have a private word with you?' Julie flashed her warrant card. 'Sergeant Kite.'

'And might I ask what this is about?'

'Would you mind if we went indoors?'

The man gave her a long and weary stare. 'Come on in.' He bent down to pick up the post, threw it and his keys onto a shelf by the door, dumped his bag and loosened his tie. 'This is the perfect end to a perfect week. Now, what can I help you with, Sergeant?'

'I just wanted to ask you about the woman who lives next door.'

'What's she done?'

'She's not done anything. What would you imagine she'd have done?' She raised an eyebrow. 'Could I just have your name for my notes?'

The man sighed. 'John Slaithwaite. I'm a solicitor. Put my reaction down to me having a suspicious mind.'

'That goes with the territory, I think. Maybe that's not such a bad thing. What can you tell me about her?'

'I think, Sergeant Kite, that I need a rather large whisky. Can I get you one?'

'Much as I'm tempted, I need to drive back to mid Wales.'

'That's not an easy one from here.'

'It's not an easy one from anywhere, to be honest.'

John Slaithwaite poured himself a large Glen Garioch and sank into a chair. 'I knew this would happen. Originally I was sure she'd come back, but then when she'd been gone for over a week, I realised something must have happened to her.'

'What makes you say that?'

Slaithwaite considered his words. 'It wasn't a happy household next door. There was a time when Rosa and my wife were great friends, but Quigley was very controlling. He didn't like her to even talk over the fence with Lizzie.'

'Lizzie's your wife?'

A shrug and a slug of whisky. 'On paper we're still man and wife.'

'That doesn't sound very definite, Mr Slaithwaite, could you elaborate at all?'

'She left me.' He drained his glass and got up for a refill. 'Last autumn. I came home from work one sunny Thursday afternoon and she'd gone. Left a note telling me not to worry, that it was for the best and she'd be in touch when she could.'

'And you haven't seen her since?'

Slaithwaite shook his head. 'Not even a text or a phone call.'

'Did you report it to the local police?'

'She said it would be better if I didn't try to find her. If somebody says that to you, then you don't rush off and tell the police, do you?'

'And you had no idea that she was planning to go?'

'None at all.'

Julie nodded slowly. 'That must be difficult for you.'

'I just wish I knew what I'd done. I miss her so much.' Slaithwaite sat down again. 'I don't suppose you can help me find her?'

'You'd have to get in touch with Lancashire Constabulary. As the case started here, it would be better to make contact with them first. I'm here because I need to gather some background information on Rosa, who is very much within our jurisdiction.'

'What's she done?'

'We found a body on moorland in Powys. We believe it is Rosa, but it has still to be confirmed. I was given the house next door as her address.'

'Dear God.' Slaithwaite put the glass down on the coffee table with a shaking hand. 'She wasn't exactly your average girl next door, but she wasn't really a bad kid.' He put his head in his hands. 'You don't think there's any connection with Lizzie, do you?'

'Do you?'

'I don't know. They had nothing in common, apart from Sean, Rosa's little boy. Lizzie would look after him when things got heated next door.' He stood up and walked to the window. 'They went to the park a couple of times a week, Lizzie took charge of the pushchair and she looked as though she had two kids.' He smiled. 'There's only about eight or nine years between them, Lizzie and Rosa, but you'd have thought Rosa was Sean's teenage sister if you saw them together.'

'Did Rosa and Lizzie disappear at the same time?'

'No. Lizzie left in the autumn. October. Rosa was definitely still in the house until probably two or three weeks ago. The last time I saw both her and Quigley together was on New Year's Eve. He was off his face and Rosa looked straight through me.' He turned back to her then, realising the additional, unspoken question. 'You have got to be joking, Sergeant. You can't think there's a link between Lizzie leaving and what may have happened to Rosa.'

'I'm just exploring possibilities, Mr Slaithwaite, you know how it goes.'

'My Lizzie is the kindest, sweetest person on the face of the planet. She wouldn't do anything to harm anyone. Just the opposite, in fact.' He smiled to himself. 'Which is probably just as well, given that she's extremely fond of the martial arts.'

Julie's eyebrows disappeared into her fringe. That was unexpected. 'So she can take care of herself?'Slaithwaite pondered for a moment before shaking his head. He frowned. 'She's very strong physically, but she can be quite fragile.'

'Fragile?'

Slaithwaite frowned again and looked more than a little uncomfortable. 'She had a little bout of depression,' he offered, grudgingly.

'Have Lizzie's parents heard from her since she left?' Julie's stare was as expressionless as she could manage. Slaithwaite shook his head.

'There's nobody left, now. She only had her mother, and to be honest, they didn't really get on. She died well over a year ago, but there wasn't much love lost between the two of them.'

'What about friends?'

'She hasn't got any really close friends, apart from Rosa. I asked a couple of people who worked for her in the shop, but nobody knows where she is. They've been brilliant. They kept the shop going for her, but they phoned just after the New Year and said they were struggling to drum up business and could they take on someone to replace her, to do the marketing.' Slaithwaite gazed past Julie, out of the window. 'I should have said yes. Then at least Lizzie would have something to come back to.'

'What happened to it?'

'It closed in March. One of the girls got a job somewhere else and then it wasn't really viable to keep it open any longer.'

'Have you still got the shop?'

'It's all in Lizzie's name and I can't do anything with it. It's just standing empty.'

'And what about the boy, Sean. When was the last time you saw him?'

'I've no idea. I'm not what you'd call the neighbourly type.' Slaithwaite frowned. 'He wasn't with them when I saw them both on New Year's Eve, thank God, but I didn't see him very often to be honest. I usually work ridiculously long hours.' Slaithwaite gave her a rueful smile. 'I'm sure you know all about that, Sergeant.' He shrugged. 'I can only assume Rosa finally came to her senses and got the child away out of Quigley's grasp.'

'And Quigley, is he still here?'

'Most of the time, unfortunately, but to be honest, I've not seen him for a week or so either.'

Julie stood up and held out her hand. 'I'm sorry about Lizzie, Mr Slaithwaite. I'm sure my colleagues from Lancashire Constabulary would do all they could, if you ever changed your mind about wanting to formally report her missing.' Slaithwaite opened and closed his mouth, before giving her a curt nod. 'If you can remember any more about next door, any of them, will you phone me?' She handed Slaithwaite her card, which he took and studied carefully.

'I will, Sergeant. And I'm sorry to be so...'

'I can understand why I'm not exactly the person you'd want to see on your doorstep.' Julie smiled. 'I don't suppose you have a business card I could have?'

Slaithwaite walked out into the hall and rummaged in his briefcase. He passed a card to Julie.

'Could I just ask you, Mr Slaithwaite, do you remember talking to a man, this man, about Rosa, maybe six months ago?' She held up Mick's drawing of Ardal. John Slaithwaite nodded.

'He was concerned about Sean. You don't think he's involved in what happened to Rosa?'

'What did you make of him?'

Slaithwaite shrugged. 'He seemed sound enough. Said he was Rosa's brother, although he called her by another name. Karen maybe, or Cara?'

'Thank you, Mr Slaithwaite, you've been incredibly helpful.'

The door closed behind her. Julie glanced at her watch and walked slowly back to her car. She had dallied long enough. It was time to head for home.

CHAPTER NINETEEN

Day Five

The Friday night motorway traffic was horrendous – nose to tail for miles – and Julie was relieved to get back to the single carriageway A-road which led her into Wales. She grinned to herself. She *was* turning into a bumpkin. The further south she drove, the more the traffic petered out. She phoned Swift and gave him the bare details of what she'd discovered. He seemed happy enough and it relieved the boredom for a few minutes. It didn't feel like driving when all you had to do was point your car between the white lines and the grass verge.

By the time she was south of Welshpool it was as though she had gone back in time to one of those old tinted photographs that Adam loved so much, of Morris Minors and Wolseleys and barely any traffic on the roads. Maybe that was what made mid Wales different. What was that quote Adam liked? *The past is a foreign country: they do things differently there.* He used it to explain his love of history, not just a series of hard facts, but how it had actually felt to live in those days. Julie thought it would apply just as well to mid Wales, definitely a foreign country, different and clinging on to decent values her mum and dad would recognise from their childhoods.

Julie frowned. She should have been there when they were burgled. They were too far away for her to be able to dash back to see how they were doing. What would happen if it were a matter of life and death? What if one of them had an accident or a heart attack and she got there too late? She shook her head. 'Come on, Jules, switch off that over-active imagination.' It went with the job, imagining, thinking about what people could do to each other and then some. Her phone rang and she glanced at the screen. It was Helen.

'Hiya, how are things in the back of beyond?'

'I've just been up there in the shitty city.'

'Woo you've changed your tune. Why didn't you say? We could have met for lunch or something.'

'It was a flying visit, sorry. Mum and Dad had their house burgled and I had to go and make sure they were OK.'

'Oh God, Jules, I'm so sorry. Are they OK, was much taken?'

'They're fine. There wasn't a huge amount taken, but Dad ended up with a million stitches in his arm. He tackled the little sod and was clobbered with a picture frame.'

'That's awful. And you're worrying now about them being up here and you being down there.'

'You know me too well. It's nearly three and a half hours door to door.'

'Ah, the joys of being an only child, eh, Julie? But they do have a pretty good police force up here you know.'

'Very funny.'

'How are things in Wales then? Have you found out what happened to your body on the moors?'

'I wish. But we have found out it was a woman, which was a bit moot for a while.'

Helen snorted with laughter. 'Not very up to date with pathology techniques over there then?'

'Actually, our Dr Greenhalgh has a mind like a steel trap. You'd like her. But the poor lass was so emaciated, she looked like a young lad.'

'Dear God. Was she anorexic, poor bugger?'

'No, we don't think so. She did do drugs, which can't have helped on the nutritional front, but they think it was coeliac disease that caused most of it.'

'I had no idea it could do that.'

'Well you're not likely to be an undiagnosed case, are you? Adam was asking what you were eating for breakfast these days.'

'Cheeky mare. I'll have you know I had porridge and fruit this morning.'

It was Julie's turn to laugh. 'So that was all he had in the cupboard, was it?'

Helen was uncharacteristically silent, for a second or two. 'Yes,' she said. 'Actually it was.'

'No way. Go on then, tell me all about him. Who is he, where does he live, what does he do, is it serious? Does he really eat porridge for breakfast?'

'Steady, I can tell you've not had much excitement lately. His name is Damian Cartwright. He lives in Didsbury, he's an architect, I hope to God it's serious and yes, the huge downside is that he's a healthy eater.'

'What are the chances of that, both of us being lumbered with lentil addicts?'

'Adam's getting worse then?'

'He is. How old is your Damian? Is he from Manchester?'

'He's forty, and yes, he's a Manc.'

'I'm going to have to meet him. Give him the once over.'

'You can stay right away from him, Sergeant Kite. I know all about your interrogation techniques. I'm doing the ignorance is bliss thing and not asking too many questions.'

'Helen Cartwright. It's got a very distinguished ring to it. You could hyphenate it, too, Mitchell-Cartwright sounds very Alderley Edge. You'd better get down to Boodles in the morning, lady and earmark a diamond.'

'I'm not counting chickens, not with my track record. Speaking of which, how's that husband of yours?'

'You are hilarious. He's decided he's vegan.'

'Oh for God's sake. He's pushing his luck. I thought he was on his best behaviour.'

'He is, but not because we had to move away from the temptation of the umpteenth other woman. This time, it's only a would-be other woman, or rather a *not convinced it's over but goes back a while* other woman.'

'Bloody hell, Jules. Are you sure?

'Am I sure of what?'

'Are you sure it's just a would-be and not an actual, still ongoing type of scenario?'

'Am I sure? That's a leading question. He says nothing ever happened between them and that he's the innocent victim. She's still in Manchester, a supply teacher at his old school, one Tiffany bloody Sanderson. He says she's stalking him by phone.'

Helen made a sound between a snort and the trumpeting of a small elephant as she tried to contain herself. 'Who's doing the stalking?' she managed, at last.

'Do I get the feeling you don't rate the explanation?'

'Do you?'

'I think so. He's very plausible.' Julie waited for Helen to answer. She didn't. 'Are you still there?'

'Yep, I'm here. So what's she been doing?'

'Phoning his mobile, sending texts. And someone slashed his bike tyres.'

'She's not going to traipse all the way from Manchester to Llanwotsit just to have a go at his bike tyres, surely?'

'I don't know. I've never been obsessed with anyone.'

'Do you think she is, really?'

'He got a blank piece of paper through the post in a jiffy bag, addressed to where he works.'

'You can't know that was her then?'

'But what if...'

'Go on.'

'This burglary at Mum and Dad's. Dad said he thought it was a bloke, but what if that was her too?'

'Oh come on, Jules, that's a reach even for your vivid imagination. How would she know where they lived?' Helen tutted. 'You're making connections that aren't there.'

'Do you think?'

'I do. The main thing is, what's he going to do about the phone calls? If I were you I'd confiscate his ruddy phone and when she calls again you'll get an idea yourself of what's going on.'

'How do I do that, he's not some fourteen year old who's been grounded for not doing his homework.'

'Just nick it. You're a copper, use your initiative. Anyway, it'll frighten her off if you answer the phone.'

'Maybe. Anyway, what are you doing tonight?'

'We're off to a posh wine bar in Alderley Edge, as coincidence would have it. How the other half lives, eh? What about you, home to a nut cutlet?'

'How dare you speak about my husband in those terms, Helen Mitchell-Cartwright? Go and have a fab evening and think of me when you're ordering your pork chop in Alderley Edge.'

CHAPTER TWENTY

Day Six

'Bacon butty, is it, love?' Nerys already had two pieces of white sliced out of the wrapper.

'How did you guess?' Julie smiled, sipped the strong black coffee that was waiting for her on the counter and sighed contentedly. 'Perfect.'

'You look as though you've not slept a wink,' Nerys said, adding slices of bacon to a sizzling frying pan. 'What have you been up to?'

'Probably not what you think,' Julie set the mug back on the counter. 'Driving round the north-west of England and worrying for most of the night about my parents.'

Nerys pressed the bacon flat with a fish slice. 'It must be difficult living a way away from them. I've never been more than three streets away from mine. They're right next door now.'

'That was lucky.'

'Not really, my uncle passed away and they moved into his house.'

'Oh God, Nerys that was thoughtless of me.'

'You're all right, lovely, he was ninety-seven and he was tired.' She put the bacon and bread together and cut it into triangles. 'There you go.'

'Nerys, you are a lifesaver.' Julie picked up her plate and her mug and headed for her favourite seat in the far corner of the canteen. From here she could see the steep spire of a church and hills beyond. She was still surprised by how rural it was, even in the centre of town.

'Great minds.' Rhys Williams plonked his mug of tea and two slices of golden toast onto the table. He sat down and applied enough butter to leave teeth marks in as he took his first bite. 'How are things going? The boss said you had to go back up north yesterday. Everything OK?'

Julie nodded and applied a serviette to the trickle of grease on her chin. 'A break-in at my parents.'

'Oh that's bad news. Are they all right?'

'They're fine. My dad's a bit battered, but they're good. And I did manage to find out some more about Rosa and the man who was roaming out on the hill.'

'The boss will be pleased. We haven't got any more that I know of. How can someone go missing and have nobody looking for them? If I'm not back from work on time my Rhian gets on the phone within twenty minutes.'

'We spoke to a woman in Llandrindod the other day whose husband walked out in December, and she's not reported him. He cleared out the bank accounts and he could be anywhere. And yesterday I spoke to a man whose wife left in the autumn and told him not to look for her. And he didn't. I can't imagine doing that.'

'But then you're a copper, Sarge. You wouldn't be able to just leave it alone, would you?'

Swift was whistling 'Bread of Heaven' when Julie and Rhys arrived in the office together.

'You had a good day yesterday then, Julie. Can you fill us in with more detail?'

Julie dropped her bag on her desk and joined Swift at the board. 'I spoke to Rosa's brother. She was known as Caroline or Caro until she left home. She fell out with her parents after she got in with the wrong crowd while she was still at school, particularly an extremely nasty piece of work called Quigley. Nobody I spoke to knew his first name, but he shouldn't be too hard to trace, as he seems to own a house on Eighth Avenue in Blackpool. She hadn't had any contact with her parents for at least four or five years.'

'And is the child Quigley's?'

'That's the speculation, although nobody really knows for sure. Maggie's checking to see if we've got him on record.' Julie pinned a photograph she'd taken of the houses in Blackpool on the board. 'Rosa, Quigley and Rosa's son, Sean, lived at this one. The next-door neighbours are John and Lizzie Slaithwaite. He's a solicitor. She's gone missing. She's been away from home since November.'

'What is it with people running away willy nilly these days?' Swift tugged at his ear. 'He has no idea where she's gone?'

Julie shook her head. 'Said something about having to find herself.'

'Oh, good God.' Swift sat down on the edge of Julie's desk. 'And he's not tried to find her?'

'He said she left a note which said not to look for her.'

'What about the man on the hill?' Rhys asked. 'You said you had some information about him.'

'The man seen at the café in Rhayader was definitely the same man who stayed up at the farm with the soldiers. It was Rosa's brother, Ardal.'

Swift stood up again and peered at the information on the board. 'So we've got the body of a girl from Preston who was living in Blackpool and was found dead up in the Elan Valley, and Rosa's brother, also from Preston was up there too, looking for her.'

'No sir, he thought she was still in Blackpool somewhere. He was looking for the little boy, Rosa's son.'

'Right, so we can assume he thought the boy was here somewhere. And there's another woman missing from Blackpool who lived next door to Rosa?'

'That's about it, Sir.'

'So is this Lizzie Slaithwaite connected to the child's disappearance do we think?'

'Her husband said she used to go to the park with the child and Rosa, and that Lizzie used to be in charge of the pushchair.'

'So why would she want to take a toddler away from his mother?' Goronwy shook his head. 'That's terrible, that is.'

‘Is it though?’ Julie asked. ‘Both Rosa’s brother, Ardal, and John Slaithwaite, and all the other neighbours said Quigley’s a head case. Maybe she and Rosa hatched a plan together to get the child away from him.’

‘I like that,’ Swift said. ‘Julie, could you contact Slaithwaite and ask him for a description of his wife, and a recent photo if he’s got one. Get him to e-mail it.’

‘There’s something else, Sir. The reason Ardal thought the child was here. He said he’d come across an envelope with a partial address of a property in Rhayader, in Rosa’s house in Blackpool.’

‘How did he do that?’ Goronwy asked. ‘I thought you said she hadn’t had any contact with her family for years.’

‘He did speak to her now and again, apparently, but on this occasion he broke in. He said he was worried about his sister’s welfare as well as Sean’s. He said he’d sat in his car and watched the house. I get the feeling he’d been doing it for a very long time, not just the couple of times he mentioned. He said the house name on the envelope he found is *Bach*, although even I know it must be something-*Bach* and it looks as though it has a Rhayader postal address.’

‘Morgan, you’re very quiet. Get on to the sorting office, see how many places there are with *Bach* in the name within the Rhayader postal district. Google is absolutely useless for the outlying farms.’ Swift was fired up for the first time in the investigation. ‘Rhys, find out whether the parents are still here. They said they were staying locally overnight, Brian Hughes will know where. I got the impression they didn’t want to leave Rosa… Caroline… here on her own. Get them to come in to see me as soon as they can this morning and I’ll see if they can give us any more information about Quigley and the boy. Goronwy, I’d like you to get onto GPs within a thirty-mile radius and see if the child was registered with them between last November and now. You and Rhys can try nurseries and reception classes too, if he’s three or four years old, the chances are he’d be going to school somewhere by now.’

'So do we assume that Rosa knew where the boy was?' Morgan asked.

'Well, with the envelope Ardal found in her house, it looks that way,' Julie said. 'I suppose she could have got the boy away on her own. Lizzie Slaithwaite might not even be connected with this in any way.'

'Right, people, let's get to it.' Swift turned towards his office. 'Julie, have you got that map of Rhayader with you?'

'Yes, Sir. It's in the car.'

'I'll see you in the car park in five minutes.'

CHAPTER TWENTY-ONE

Day Six

'So where am I looking?' Julie unfolded the map as Swift hung his jacket in the back of the Volvo. When he dropped into the driver's seat, she noticed beads of perspiration on his forehead.

'It's going to be a hot one today.'

'Do you promise?' Julie laughed. 'That would be a first.'

'Anyone would think you came from the sultry south-east and not the rain capital of England.'

'Actually, Sir, Manchester's the sixth soggiest city in England. Funnily enough, Preston's the dampest and Blackpool's about fourth.'

'Very appropriate. No wonder they're all leaving there and heading over here. It must feel like home.'

'Trust me, Sir. It won't.' She grinned. 'So where are we going?'

'See if you can find anything with *bach* in the name, starting from the Wilkinson place and working outwards.'

Julie folded the map into an oblong with the alpaca farm at the centre. 'Well, there are only two, one spelt with an *f* though.'

'And it was definitely *bach* on the envelope, was it?'

'What's the difference?'

'Well *fach* would come after a feminine noun, see, like Ffynnon Fach. *Bach* would be after a masculine noun. So you'd have Tŷ Bach.'

'Seriously, there are different genders for nouns?'

Swift smiled. 'There are. And the *b* changes to an *f* because of it. There are dozens of those rules. Mutations, they're called.'

'And you want to send me on a course to learn Welsh?'

'It's not as bad as it sounds. Trust me, you'd enjoy it.'

'I'll take your word for it.'

'So there's just the one contender, then?'

'Yep, Pull Bach, but it's closer to Mal's farm than the Wilkinsons' place.'

Swift hooted with laughter. '*Pwll,*' he said, ending the word with a flourish and a sound Julie had never heard in her life. 'Pwll Bach.'

'So much spitting in two tiny words, Sir.'

'Right then, let's go and see if we can find it.'

'There's no road to it on the map. It looks as though you'd have to go through Mal's yard and then across the fields.'

'Is it within walking distance of Mal's?'

Julie nodded. 'It looks steep but it's just a couple of fields from his place, according to this.'

'Then I might leave you to check it out while I have another word with Mal and Sarah.'

*

Sarah was wrestling a large white sheet onto the washing line as they drove into the yard. She stuffed the sheet back into the laundry basket and waited for them to get out of the car.

'We've had no visitors at all save the lads with the shearing, and then we see you three times in a week.'

'I know, I'm sorry, Sarah. It's the nature of the enquiry.'

'Don't apologise, Craig *bach*, it's lovely to have company. Shall I go and fetch Mal from the shed?'

'It's all right, I'll go and find him. How would Julie here get to Pwll Bach? Is there a track?'

Sarah pointed a gnarled forefinger in the direction of a metal gate, perched on the hillside above the back of the farm. 'It's straight up there but it's been empty for a couple of years now haven't it, since old Miss Davies passed.'

Julie smiled at Sarah's use of 'old'. She wondered what age you had to be to qualify.

'So there's nobody living up there now?'

Sarah frowned. 'We think there's a woman up there, maybe with a little boy, but we've barely seen them. We did go up, or Mal did, a couple of times to see if they needed anything, but nobody answers the door.

'Right then, Julie. Off you go. I'll be in the shed if you need me.'

'But you'll come in for a cup of tea and a scone, Craig, won't you?'

'Well, if you put it like that, it would be rude not to.'

The field was even steeper than the contours had suggested. Julie struggled to hold onto the heavy metal gate as gravity took hold and it swung out into space. She managed to close it and replace the plait of baler twine which held it shut and she set off again, up the hill. Good grief, Miss Davies must have been a ruddy mountain goat. As she got to the top of the slope, she paused to catch her breath and looked back, down to the farm. It looked like a toy farmyard from here. A couple of miles in the distance, water glistened in the sunlight. She looked at her map. The River Elan curved its way into Craig Goch Reservoir and, from there, down into three others, Penygarreg, Garreg-Ddu and Caban Coch. It looked exactly as it did on the map from up here, much easier to understand the vastness of it all than it had been in the car. So much water. She smiled. At least there was something to show for all the rain.

It was a false summit. The field rose steeply to a second gate and beyond. How would you get a vehicle up here at all? Why would you want to be this far away from civilisation with a small child? That had to be noteworthy in itself.

Finally, just when Julie thought she would never get there, a chimney and then a slate roof appeared, followed by windows and finally two more windows and a door. The little house was perched on the edge of a hollow, gazing out over the spectacular valley beneath it. Like Mal's house, there were no electricity or telephone wires, but a small windmill whirred and there were four solar panels planted on the hillside next to it.

The path led between tall stone gateposts supporting the weathered wooden gate, and up to the glass-fronted porch. It was fronded with tiny yellow flowers and grasping, serrated leaves. Julie poked a piece of white plastic with her toe and a tiny unicorn with rainbow mane and tail tumbled free from the weeds and onto the dark bricks. She picked it up and smiled at its serious little face and ridiculously blue, slightly crossed eyes. She stood the unicorn on the edge of the path and tapped on the glass in the porch door. The door and the glass rattled independently. Small chunks of putty were missing, leaving irregular oblong gaps like missing teeth. There was no reply, but as Julie turned to walk away, a curtain moved, as though a draught had lifted it and let it fall. She knocked again, harder, more insistently. She tried the handle and the porch door opened wearily, allowing her to check and memorise the contents of the porch. Chest freezer, coat hooks with drab, damp-smelling jackets, and boots – wellingtons, green and insubstantial. No boots belonging to the small owner of the unicorn.

She bent to peer through the letterbox and, along with the slit of stone-flagged hallway, she caught the suspicion of urgent whispering. A door snicked shut and a woman walked slowly towards where Julie was waiting. Julie let the letterbox close and stood up as the door was opened.

'Can I help you?' The woman looked around thirty-two or thirty-three years old, Julie guessed. She had long red hair, held in place with tortoiseshell combs, and her clothes buried her slender figure. Folds of floor-length skirt and tunic with a pale green scarf enveloped her.

'Sergeant Julie Kite, Mid Wales Police.' Julie held up her warrant card, but the woman didn't even glance at it. Instead, she kept her gaze fixed on a point somewhere behind Julie's right elbow. She stepped down into the porch and closed the front door behind her.

'How can I help you?' The accent was definitely not local, not even Welsh. She was well-spoken, but the slightly raised inflection at the end of the sentence was familiar to Julie.

'You sound as though you're from my neck of the woods.'

The woman said nothing. 'Lancashire,' added Julie. 'Am I right?' The woman gave the tiniest of nods. 'Have you been here long?'

'Not very long, no.'

'We're asking everyone if they may have seen or heard anything that could help us with our enquiries. You must have heard by now that a woman was found down there,' Julie jerked her head, indicating the valley behind her. 'We need to trace her movements in the time leading up to her death.'

'I haven't seen anyone up here for months.'

'How many months?'

The woman shrugged. 'As I said, I've not been here very long. Nobody ever comes up here. It's what I like about it.'

'And you don't mind being so alone?' Julie glanced at the woman's hands. 'Could I just have your name for my records, just to say I've spoken to you, Mrs...?'

'Jenkins.'

Julie wrote in her notebook. 'And your first name, Mrs Jenkins?'

'Vanessa.'

'And do you live here on your own, Mrs Jenkins, or are there other members of the family here?'

'I'm alone.'

Julie made a show of looking around her, slowly taking in the panorama, the near-vertical ground covered in fern, the flock of small mountain sheep and the tiny fenced-in garden.

'How do you get in and out? You can't possibly walk up that hill with shopping.' She smiled 'It's nearly killed me even without bags. Do you have a car?'

Vanessa Jenkins shook her head. 'I don't drive, but there's a sort of sheep track that runs down from the back of the house, towards the back lane between Rhayader and Llangurig, then it's easy walking into town.'

Julie smiled at the definition of 'town' which was so different to her own. 'So you don't ever get any visitors up here?'

Vanessa smiled a private little smile. 'No, Sergeant, fortunately not.' She opened the door a crack, stepped backwards onto the step and said, 'I'm sorry I couldn't help you,' slid back inside the house like a pickpocket melting into a crowd and closed the door behind her. Julie was left in the porch wondering what was so very wrong with the explanations she had been given. She stood for a moment or two and listened but apart from the odd bleat and the munching of grass behind her, there was total silence. Not even the sound of footsteps receding down the stone-flagged hallway.

*

When she got back to Mal's, the teapot was being refilled and Swift, it seemed, had been busy, judging by the collection of crumbs on his tiny china plate.

'Tea, Sergeant?' Sarah was pouring tea the colour of leather into Mal's cup.

'I don't suppose you have any coffee, do you? I could do with caffeine after that climb.'

Sarah laughed. 'I do, but I can't vouch for what it tastes like, it's been here a while.' She reached into a cupboard for a jar and dug a teaspoon into the contents. 'It just needs a bit of persuading into the cup.'

'You young 'uns,' Mal said, spooning sugar into his tea. 'No stamina have you?'

'You don't climb up there to the cottage do you?' Julie took the cup and saucer from Sarah. 'It's vertical.'

'I used to run up and down there twice a day to check on old Miss Davies,' Sarah said. 'And carry her shopping up there too. It's only in the last year that I've slowed down.'

Julie shook her head. 'Well, respect to you for that. You must be fitter than me.' She sipped her coffee and put it down on the table. 'Do you know anything about the woman who lives up there now?'

Mal slurped tea thoughtfully. 'She's not very friendly with us, really. We did try to chat to her when she first arrived, but we think she's keeping out of our way.'

'What makes you say that?' Swift drained his cup.

'Well she doesn't come through the yard now. We think she must have a car parked on the old road, down the other side of the hill somewhere. Either that or she has her shopping delivered by helicopter.' Mal laughed. 'People can be a little bit strange, can't they?'

'There's nowt so queer as folk, my dad says.' Julie smiled. 'But that's not very politically correct these days.'

Mal laughed. 'You're right there, aren't you.'

Swift stood up. 'Thank you, Sarah for the tea, and you too, Mal, for the samples.' Swift picked up a carrier bag and whatever was inside clinked. 'I'll be back if we need any more information.'

'Or more scones, is it, Craig?' Sarah grinned. 'You're welcome any time, you know that.'

They were almost back in Rhayader before there was a signal on Swift's phone. He handed it to Julie.

'It's an e-mail from Goronwy, Sir. He says John Slaithwaite has sent a photo of Lizzie. Shall I open it now?'

'If the signal's strong enough, you can give it a bash.'

Julie pressed the pdf symbol and waited. They were past the clock tower and on their way out of Rhayader on South Street before the face of a woman appeared on the screen. Her long red hair was held away from her face by tortoiseshell combs.

'Oh my God, it's her!' Julie showed Swift the screen. 'It's 'Vanessa Jenkins', the woman in Pwll Bach.'

Swift checked his mirror, stood on his brakes, pulled the Volvo into a tiny layby and twirled out onto the road, heading back towards Rhayader.

'Which road do you think, Sir?'

'From what she said to you, I've an idea about where she's parking a vehicle. Let's try the other route, just in case she's decided to go out.' Swift indicated left into West Street once again. 'Besides,' he glanced across at her and smiled, 'from what I remember, that hill's not as steep from the other side.'

The road was narrow and tree-lined where it flirted with the River Wye, and the valley rose like a wall from the flat land beside the river. Julie groaned.

'Not as steep? You're joking, aren't you?'

'If I remember rightly, it's just round this bend. Ah, here we are.' The road widened just enough to provide a passing place which, judging by the rutted surface of the grass, was also used as a permanent parking spot.

'I think this is the place.' Swift pulled the Volvo in close to the side and rocked himself out of the drivers' seat. 'It's up there.' He pointed at a lichened wooden footpath sign which marked the way up the hill. Julie gazed at the soil- and leaf-covered path which wound through slender pale green stems of bramble.

'Do you think this path is used much by walkers, Sir?'

'What are you thinking, Julie?'

'Well, it's definitely been used by someone recently, and on a regular basis, I'd have said.'

'You're thinking mud, are you?'

'I am. And I'm also thinking I'm going to give up on shoes altogether and just live in hiking boots.'

'Not a bad idea, Julie.'

She could never tell whether Swift was joking. His deadpan expression was a real asset to his chosen career. She grinned anyway, and pushed through fronds of bracken, some of which were still curled, like little green seahorses. The path curled its way through the tail end of a small wood and out onto the hill, in a vertical direction.

'So much for your memory then, Sir.' Julie laughed and turned back towards Swift. He was sixty feet behind her, only his broad navy-suited shoulders and the top of his head with its thinning crown visible from where she was. 'You all right, Sir?' she shouted down at him.

'I'll catch you up now,' he said, his voice barely reaching her. She turned back and side-stepped down towards him.

'It doesn't need two of us up there, does it? Besides, if she does a runner you can catch her at the bottom.' She grinned and he shook his head.

'I really must do something about getting fitter.'

Julie nodded. 'I can recommend a gym buddy, Sir. Relentless, he is.' She set off up the hill again, casting surreptitious glances back at Swift. It took him a long time to move. Julie wondered for a second whether she should abandon the Lizzie Slaithwaite idea and make sure Swift was all right, but he began to clamber back down the hill and out of sight. There was nothing wrong with his memory, though. After that first initial lung-splitting pull, the hill levelled out and she could already see the back of the cottage ahead of her. From this side, the view was down to the Wye Valley and across the main road to two soaring peaks, either side of yet another deep-sided valley. It was like being hundreds of miles from civilisation and yet she could see the little white Celtic Travel bus wending its way from Llangurig. Apart from the bus and the tiny cars behind it, that view must have been the same for... how long? Centuries, millennia? Since the rocks had been thrust upwards and contorted. She shivered. Talk about feeling like a dot on the landscape.

This time, when Julie knocked on the door of the cottage, 'Vanessa Jenkins' was much less timid.

'Sergeant. Back again so soon?' There was an air of triumph about the woman, as though, somehow, she'd won something important.

'Yes, I'm so sorry, there was just one question I forgot to ask you.' Julie looked down at her notebook and back up at the woman with a smile. 'Is it true that your real name is Lizzie Slaithwaite?'

The small smile on the woman's face disappeared instantly, along with all traces of colour. 'I... it's not what it –' She pushed the door open. 'You'd better come in.'

Julie followed Lizzie down the dark hall and into the small kitchen at the back of the cottage. Even on this bright July day, the lights were on. Lizzie leaned against the Belfast sink and gazed out of the window, her back to Julie.

'How did you find me?'

'You *are* Lizzie Slaithwaite?'

Lizzie nodded but still didn't turn around.

'And you lived until October last year with your husband in a house on Eighth Avenue in Blackpool?'

'Yes.'

'Lizzie, I need you to come to the police station with me and make a statement.' Julie walked over to the sink and stood beside her. The view of the twin hills and their jagged valley was so stunning she was lost for words herself for a second.

'Is this about Rosa?' When Lizzie turned to Julie, her face was ashen.

Julie nodded. 'It is. And about her little boy.'

'It's about Sean?' Lizzie's breath caught in her throat and she closed her eyes tight. 'I'll come with you.'

'Would it be all right if I have a quick look round the house?'

'What are you looking for?' Lizzie turned to face Julie and suspicion was etched onto her pale face.

'It's just routine. In a suspected murder case we have to be sure we cover every possibility.'

'And you think I'm a possibility, do you?' Lizzie's green eyes were suddenly alive.

'If you wouldn't mind leading the way.'

Lizzie showed Julie the tiny parlour and the sitting room, which wasn't much bigger. Both were furnished with what Julie thought were probably antique but fairly basic items.

'Have you bought this place or is it rented?'

'It belonged to a... relative.'

'Oh I'm sorry, were you very close?'

'Do you want to see upstairs?' Lizzie paused with her hand on the bannister. 'It's pretty much like down here.'

'If you wouldn't mind, just for the record.' Julie followed a reluctant Lizzie up the stairs and into what must have been the main bedroom. There was a double bed, two small tables, a wardrobe and a chest of drawers. There wasn't an item out of place. Not even a book beside the bed. The low window had the same glorious view as the kitchen.

The second bedroom was even smaller, with just one narrow bed and a chest of drawers. The lamp beside the bed was the only thing that brought any colour into this little sepia cottage. The base was tall and bright blue with a huge, smiley sun in glorious yellow and the shade was crimson. The bed with its brightly-patterned bedding also seemed to be new.

'Do you have children, Lizzie?'

There was no response, and when Julie turned to look at Lizzie she was disconcerted to see that she was crying.

'I'm so sorry, I didn't mean to upset you.'

Lizzie shook her head. 'It's not your fault.' She sniffed. 'It's my fault. All my fault.'

Julie peeped round the bathroom door. There was only one toothbrush in the mug on the shelf above the sink. 'Come on,' she said. 'Let's wander down to the car.'

CHAPTER TWENTY-TWO

Day Six

Swift motioned for Lizzie to sit opposite him and busied himself with the recording equipment. Julie placed a small folder in front of her on the desk and sat down next to Swift.

'You are not under arrest, Lizzie. You are free to leave at any time you wish.' Julie smiled but Lizzie looked away. Once Swift had pressed record and introduced himself and Julie for the tape, it was Lizzie's turn.

'Could you tell us who you are – who you really are?' Julie asked her.

Lizzie sighed. 'I'm Elizabeth Slaithwaite.'

'And you live at Pwll Bach, between the Elan and Wye valleys?' Swift asked.

'I do.'

'But you lived at a house on Eighth Avenue in Blackpool with your husband, John Slaithwaite, until October of last year?' Julie said.

Lizzie looked up at Julie. 'How is he?'

'He's worried, Lizzie. He doesn't know what he's done and why you left.'

'Did he send you to look for me?'

Julie couldn't decide from Lizzie's face whether that would be a good thing or a bad thing in her eyes. 'He said you left him a note to say he shouldn't look for you.'

She nodded. 'I did say that.'

'But you didn't mean it?' Swift asked. He sounded like a concerned relative, even in those few words.

'I did. At the time, I did. It's just too complicated to explain. I've made such a mess of everything, and I was only trying to do the right thing.'

'We've got all day, Lizzie, just take your time.' Swift smiled at her and Julie thought she could see Lizzie relax before her eyes. How did he do that?

'It was Rosa. She begged me to help her. She was at her wits' end. Quigley was getting more and more violent and she didn't know what to do. I told her to go to her parents, to just take Sean and run, but she was too afraid.'

'What was she afraid of?' Swift asked.

'Jason.'

'Jason?' Julie frowned. 'Who's Jason?'

'Quigley. He's such a nasty piece of work. He used to hit her, he was always hitting her. You could hear him shouting and her crying through the wall sometimes. He was careful though, just like a bully. They don't leave any marks where anyone could see them. He never touched her face, so there was nothing to see, but you could tell that she was in pain just by the way she walked or when she couldn't pick Sean up sometimes.'

'Do you know why he hit her?' Julie asked.

Lizzie shrugged. 'There didn't have to be a reason. He had a dog, a lovely bull terrier called Sam. Sean loved that dog to pieces. Then one day Quigley shot it through the head with a crossbow while Sean watched. Just because he could. That was when Rosa decided she had to do something, otherwise Sean could have been next.' Lizzie stared up at the two of them. 'I can't begin to describe how brutal that man is.'

'Did anyone think of reporting him to the police?' Julie asked.

Lizzie shook her head. 'We were all too stupid. Too scared.

Rosa's desperate to keep on the right side of him, scared to do anything to upset him and I was the same. I didn't want to make things any worse for her.'

'What about your husband, what does he think about Quigley?'

'They rarely saw each other. Quigley was out most nights when John was at home. Besides,' she clenched her fist in her lap, 'Quigley wouldn't dare cross a man. He saves his temper for women and defenceless animals.'

'So your husband wasn't aware of any of this?' Swift asked.

'I once told him I thought Quigley was beating Rosa.' She laughed a mirthless, brittle laugh. 'John isn't good at confrontation. That's how I knew he wouldn't try to find me. I might have caused a scene and that would never do.' Lizzie looked up at them both. 'He has a certain reputation to uphold within the community you see.'

'Did you not think he'd be worried about you though?' Julie asked.

'To be honest, I really don't know any more. We'd been through what John referred to as a bit of a bad patch. Actually, we'd got to the point where we were arguing more than we were talking properly.'

'Was this to do with Rosa's situation?' Julie asked.

Lizzie shook her head and looked down at her fists, balled in her lap. 'It was to do with the fact that, according to him, I got obsessed about not being able to have a child. John said we had to move on, that we were lucky we had each other and that it wasn't the end of the world.'

'I'm sorry.' Julie said. 'That must be a horrible situation to be in.'

Lizzie nodded but said nothing.

'Especially when you could see that little boy next door and were worried about what his father might do to him.'

'If Rosa had just run away from him, everything would have been perfect. Her brother would have gone to the ends of the earth to protect her and his nephew. She knew that. They could have started again anywhere.'

'But instead you took the boy and ran away with him yourself, isn't that right? You see a boy in possible mortal danger, and you would desperately love to have a child.' Julie's question was delivered sharply and Swift raised an eyebrow.

Two pale patches of pink began to rise in Lizzie's cheeks. When the answer came, it was clear that Lizzie had far more fight in her than Julie had thought.

'Yes, Sergeant, I did think the boy's life might be in danger. I saw how badly poor Rosa was treated, terrified of that bullying bastard of a man and yes, the one thing I want in the world is a child of my own to love and to nurture.' She thumped the table with her fist, but only gently, and it was clear to Julie that she was controlling her fury, but only with the greatest amount of effort.

'So did you run away with Sean? Did you take him away from his mother?' Julie's voice was softer now. 'Did you rescue him?'

Lizzie nodded. 'Although I wasn't brave enough to actually take the initiative myself. I had thought about it, believe me, but it wasn't until Rosa arrived on my doorstep holding Sean's hand one afternoon and begged me to take him away that I decided I really had to do it.'

'What tipped the balance? Why did you decide on that day that you would leave your husband and run away with a neighbour's child?' Swift asked.

'Rosa said Quigley had just arranged to have one of his dealers disposed of. She heard him making arrangements on the phone, as casually as ordering a takeaway pizza.' Lizzie looked up at Swift. 'He was going to be executed, shot by a hitman. You can't imagine the state Rosa was in. This was a whole new level of violence. I asked her why she didn't take Sean herself and just go, but she said Sean would be harder to find if she wasn't with him, that nobody would be looking for me, but if she were to run, she would be found in no time. Quigley has contacts in all sorts of places you wouldn't even imagine and he controlled every aspect of her life.'

'So you just decided to leave home and take Sean with you?' Julie asked.

'We planned it, Rosa and me. We had to make sure John and Quigley didn't suspect anything. John can be horribly naïve about some things, even for a solicitor. If he'd been party to the plans and

Quigley threatened him, well, who knows what he would have done, or said. It could have ruined everything.'

'It sounds as though you have a fair idea.' Julie smiled. 'But then John would only have been thinking about your safety, surely.'

'I know,' Lizzie conceded. 'But he doesn't believe how evil Quigley is. Not really.'

'So where is the boy now?' Swift asked.

Lizzie shrugged.

'You're not telling me you don't know where Sean is,' Julie leaned forward until her face was only inches from Lizzie's. 'I don't believe you.'

'He's safe. That's all I can tell you.'

'All you *can* tell us, or all you're prepared to tell us?'

'If there's any chance at all that Quigley is looking for Sean, if he has any idea that Sean is in this area, then I can't take the risk of letting people know where he is.'

'We're not people though are we, Lizzie, we're the police.' Swift still sounded like a concerned uncle and Julie was irritated but she stayed quiet. 'We can help protect Sean from Quigley. We can protect you too, if you'll let us,' Swift said.

'What would he do to you, Lizzie, if he found out you'd kidnapped his son?' Julie asked.

'He's capable of anything.'

'Capable of murdering Rosa?'

'He wouldn't have thought twice about it.' Lizzie stared at Julie. 'So you really think Rosa might have been murdered. You think it could have been her body out there on the path?'

'We were hoping you would be able to tell us whether it might be Rosa. I assume you'd you been in contact with her recently, kept her in touch with how her son was doing during his exile.'

If Lizzie heard the judgemental tone in Julie's question she didn't react. 'I haven't spoken to Rosa for months.'

'But you're convinced that Quigley could have murdered Rosa, even all this way from home?'

Lizzie shrugged. 'If I thought for a minute that Quigley knew where she was, then I'd say it was definite.'

'What makes you think he didn't know?'

'We were very careful. There's no way he could have worked it out for himself.'

'We?'

'Me and Rosa.'

'So Rosa knew where Sean was then?'

'Of course she did. But nobody else did, nobody at all.'

Julie raised an eyebrow. 'You're wrong, Lizzie. Rosa's brother, Ardal, managed to work it out. From an address on the back of an envelope which we assume was presumably sent by you and addressed to Rosa. He found this address in a bin in her kitchen.'

Lizzie's eyes widened and her mouth contorted into the strangest shape. She reminded Julie of a painting she'd seen on Adam's computer. He said that's how he always felt on the first morning of term.

'No, no, no-no-no.' It started quietly, barely audible, but Lizzie almost screamed the last repetition. 'Please tell me you're lying. He can't know where Sean is. He can't have been there.'

'So Sean is at the cottage?' Julie asked.

Lizzie put her head in her hands and began rocking gently. 'No. He can't have been there. He can't. I won't believe it.'

Swift waited until Lizzie was still. 'Where is the boy?'

She sat bolt upright then and stared at the wall above Swift's head. 'I want a solicitor. I'm not prepared to say anything else until I've seen a solicitor.'

'What about your husband,' Julie asked. 'Do you want to see him?'

Lizzie nodded. 'Do you think he will want to see me?' she said, through sobs which rocked her slender frame.

It took John Slaithwaite less than three hours to reach his wife. He must have broken every speed limit between Blackpool and

Boughrood. When Julie went to meet him in reception, Brian Hughes beckoned her over to the desk.

'He's absolutely beside himself, Julie. It might be an idea to take him for a cuppa or something and see if you can calm him down before he sees her.'

Julie nodded. 'Will do. Thanks, Brian. Has he said anything?'

'Nothing other than asking for his wife. You can feel the tension from here, poor bugger.'

Julie approached Slaithwaite, who immediately grabbed her by the arm. Brian Hughes started to run round the counter, but Julie shook her head and he retreated.

'Let's just calm down, Mr Slaithwaite. You don't want your wife to see you in this state, do you? She needs you to be strong, to give her as much support as you can.'

Slaithwaite let go of Julie as though she was suddenly on fire. 'God, I'm so sorry. I can't think what I was doing.'

'It's fine. Don't worry. This must all be very surreal for you. We've just got the doctor in with her now, to give her the once over, but you can see her in a few minutes. Can I get you a coffee? I'm afraid we don't run to whisky in the canteen.'

Slaithwaite managed a small smile which made him look as though he was curling his lip. 'Is she all right?'

'She's fine. She's just a bit stressed out.'

Slaithwaite laughed. 'God, I know that feeling.' He ran his fingers through his hair. 'Yes please, coffee would be perfect.'

Nerys could always be relied upon to cheer anyone up. Julie was even more grateful than usual today for her sunny, no-nonsense delivery.

'There you are, lovely. You look as though you could do with something a bit stronger, you do. But don't worry, our Sergeant Kite here will look after you.' She passed Slaithwaite a mug of frothy coffee and pushed a black coffee towards Julie. 'Bet you could do with this too.'

Julie led him to her usual table, in the far corner of the canteen, away from the raucous jokes and laughter.

'Thank you, Sergeant. I was in a bit of a state back there.'

'I know you were. It's hard when you're a long way from where you need to be in circumstances like this. But she's fine. Lizzie's going to be fine.'

'But are you sure she'll see me?'

'She asked for you.'

'I won't be much use to her though, will I?'

'You're a solicitor, you'll be a great help.' Julie smiled. 'But not in the interview, of course.'

Slaithwaite gave a little half-smile. 'Not unless she wants to buy a house, I won't. I specialise in conveyancing.'

'Well, she needs a friend, and you qualify in that department.' Julie sipped her coffee and could feel the caffeine making its way to the vital places.

'Will she be charged with anything?'

'It's still way too early to be thinking about that. This case is getting more complicated by the minute. But so far, if what she's telling us is true, then she might be all right.'

'At least I know she's safe. That's the main thing.' Slaithwaite pulled the froth on his coffee into little peaks with his teaspoon. 'I thought she might have been... that something awful could have happened to her.'

That, thought Julie, had probably been a lot more likely than even Slaithwaite was thinking right now.

CHAPTER TWENTY-THREE

Day Six

'She was adamant,' Swift said, and poked at the waste bin with his toe. Rhys was bringing the board up to date with his painstaking colour-coded notes. Morgan Evans seemed, finally, to have engaged with the case. Julie watched them all interact and wondered still, what she was missing. There was definitely a link that was eluding her. What the hell was it? She sighed and forced herself to concentrate on Swift's final meeting of the day.

'Maybe Lizzie's telling the truth.' Rhys stopped writing and turned to Swift. 'Maybe the little boy was never at the house in the Elan Valley at all. She could have spirited him away from Blackpool and taken him somewhere else entirely. He might not even be here now.'

'Good point.' Swift knocked the bin over and climbed wearily from the desk to pick it up. 'Or he could have been at the cottage but isn't any longer, now she knows we know about Sean.'

'But she must have had an accomplice, surely.' Julie said. 'I was convinced there was someone else in the house when I went up there the first time. I could swear she wasn't on her own. She even kept the door closed, whereas the second time she seemed extremely keen for me to see that there was nobody there.'

'Did you ask her about Rosa again, after she'd seen her husband?' Goronwy asked. 'Was she any more cooperative then?'

'No.' Swift tugged his ear. 'She really is frightened of this Jason Quigley character. He sounds like a total shit.'

Julie's eyebrows disappeared into her fringe. She'd never heard the boss be quite so forthright about anyone. Well, apart from the creep from hell, Stephen Collins. She shivered. Thank God that one was safely under lock and key.

'So where are we up to, then?' Morgan sauntered over to stand by Julie. 'We know Lizzie Slaithwaite took the child from Blackpool and probably to the house in the Elan Valley. We know that Jason Quigley is a total headbanging nutter and that Rosa was terrified of him. We don't know where he is, and we don't know where the child is, but we can hope the two aren't in the same place.'

'So far you're spot on.' Julie smiled. 'And then there's the little matter of what happened to Rosa Quigley. Was she murdered or was it an accident?'

'Ah,' Goronwy peered over the top of his laptop in the corner of the office. 'Did I not tell you?'

'Tell us what, boyo?' Rhys instinctively reached for his red marker.

'The doc phoned this morning. She says the body was definitely moved post mortem, hundred percent. She says there's a very very small chance it could have been an accident, the actual death, like, but in that case someone still knew about it and they didn't tell us, did they? And she thinks it's more likely, from the pattern of splintering of the fragment of skull into the brain, that Rosa was battered very hard with something very solid, and at least twice.'

'Which makes it nigh on impossible for it to have been done in a fall.' Swift sighed. 'So we need to know where it happened and how she ended up where she did.'

'There's more, Sir.' Goronwy was enjoying being the bearer of important news for once. 'The results of the samples taken from Mal's quad show that it's likely it was used to transport Rosa to where she was found. There are soil traces on the tyres, which don't match his farmland, but do match the soil around the Monks' Trod. And there are traces of exactly the same chemicals that were found on Rosa's hair all over the bike. Creosote, oil, you name it. The doc says it's as good as a fingerprint. Which is just as well, because we don't have any of those so far.'

'But those chemicals would be found on any number of quads in the area. Are there any traces of blood or fibre we can track to the body?' Swift asked.

'No, Sir. Not a thing. Doctor Greenhalgh says it's quite likely that she was wrapped in something that prevented the transfer of evidence from the body to the bike.'

'And that exchange principle, Morgan, is known as what?' Swift asked. 'Seeing as you're gearing up for your Sergeants' Exam again.'

Morgan looked like a rabbit in headlights and Julie could see from his expression the exact moment the relevant information slotted into place. 'It's Locard's principle, Sir. Every contact leaves a trace.'

'Correct, Morgan. Unless, that is, the person you're trying to implicate is one step ahead.'

Swift wandered over to Goronwy's desk and looked over the younger officer's shoulder at the computer screen. 'They haven't found any sign of anything at the farm that could have been used to wrap up the body, have they?'

'No, Sir. They did say they'd need several years and a following wind to go through everything in that shed though.'

'Well that's a bit of a relief in one way,' Swift said.

'But what about the bag, the one Mal said he'd lost?' Julie said.

'You don't think it could be them, surely?' Rhys stared at Julie.

'No, I know there's no way it was Mal or Sarah. Besides, they wouldn't have told us about the quad being moved if they'd used it themselves to move the body, would they?'

'That is also a good point, Julie,' Swift said.

'The obvious candidate for using the bike would be Lizzie, though, wouldn't it? She was right on the doorstep and she would know that there was a quad down there in the shed. They don't lock the shed do they?' Julie asked.

'They don't lock anything at all, car, house, quad. They never go anywhere apart from down to Rhayader for a bit of shopping or to the market. They'll have left the keys in the quad. I bet if you went up there now the keys would be in the ignition of both that and the truck.' Swift took off his glasses and rubbed his eyes.

'So Lizzie could have borrowed the quad.' Morgan Evans gazed at her photograph on the board. 'But she doesn't look the type to smack someone on the head and calmly remove the body.'

'Ah, but wouldn't it make our life boring if you could just look at someone and know what they were capable of,' Swift said.

'To be fair to Morgan, I know what he means. I can't see it either.' Morgan Evans flashed a small smile in Julie's direction.

'Besides,' Julie continued, 'if it was Lizzie, and the deed happened up at the cottage, then how did she get the body all that way down to Mal's yard on her own?'

'There was nothing of Rosa, though, was there?' Goronwy said. He paged through the information on his computer. 'It says in the post mortem report that she weighed just over forty kilos.'

'And what's that in stones and pounds?' Swift said. 'For those of us who went to school in the olden days.'

'It's about six stone four,' Julie said. 'Give or take.' She examined the contours on the map that Rhys had just stuck to the board. 'I'd say it's still too heavy for Lizzie to carry her all that way, especially given the slope on that land and two really awkward gates. It's a fair way down to the yard and she's not exactly huge herself.'

'What are we doing with Lizzie? Can we keep hold of her on kidnap charges?' Morgan asked.

'I don't think that's going to work,' Swift said. 'We need to get all our ducks in a row before we start talking of arrests. I've been on to the magistrates for an urgent warrant to search Pwll Bach, and I've asked that the Slaithwaites both stay in town for a day or two, while we give the cottage a going over and to keep an eye on her, just in case Quigley might be looking for her. The husband's keen to get her back home, but I'm not sure that's going to happen any time soon.'

'So where are we up to then, Sir?' Rhys asked, his pen still poised.

'So, we're back to square one, looking for Rosa's killer,' Swift said. 'But at least we're almost certain it is a killer we're looking for.'

'And it's more than likely Jason Quigley.' Morgan Evans tapped the board. 'He's got to be the link in all this.'

'So where are we up to with locating him?' Swift tugged his ear and sighed. 'Have we got anywhere on mobile phone networks or credit card usage? Are we any nearer tracing where his vehicle might be? Is there anything else we should be doing that isn't being covered already?'

Julie checked her notebook. 'Lancashire Police have searched the house in Blackpool. They're looking for his car and they'll let us know as soon as they find anything useful. There's nothing in the house that would lead us to him,' she said. 'I've also asked the neighbours to get in touch if they see him or any signs of him at the house.' She grinned. 'They're only too keen to dob him in apparently.'

'He's disappeared off the face of the planet,' Goronwy said, breaking the silence which followed.

'Let's just hope he's not taken his son with him.'

'Quite, Julie.' Swift took off his glasses and rubbed his eyes.

'We have had some information on a mobile phone registered to Rosa, though,' Goronwy said. 'They've come up with incoming calls from what they think is a pay as you go mobile, and several texts between them. They're sort of in code, or shorthand.' Goronwy picked up a wodge of paper from his desk. 'They say things like *with you?* and *out Thurs, call me.* One the other way, to Rosa, says *not safe* and another *it's 4 the best, trust me.*'

'They could be between Quigley and Rosa though, couldn't they? She could be involved with the shady dealings we've heard so much about?' Morgan Evans said.

'Or it could be someone who lured Rosa to the Elan Valley maybe?' Julie tapped her teeth with her pen.

Swift looked weary as he climbed off the desk. 'Go home, people, but don't stop thinking about this. Not for a second.'

CHAPTER TWENTY-FOUR

Day Six

Julie parked her car beside the little bridge over the infant Chwefri River and switched off the engine. Thanks to Adam she now knew this was an Irish bridge. She smiled. He was such a know-all. She was only yards from home but she needed to clear her head. Seven ewes in a single-file procession wandered down through the bracken and past the car, peering quizzically at her before meandering across the road and down onto the flat parcel of grass beside the river. Julie grinned. The sauntering sheep were a great metaphor for how things were at work right now. They were all following each other from one place to another, with no significant advantage in having done so. Why was this case so difficult? She opened the car door and climbed out. The evening sun still had warmth in it and way above, high over the slopes of Craig Chwefri, two kites soared on the thermals.

There had to be an accomplice. Someone who had spirited the child away from Pwll Bach before Julie went back the second time. The child and all his worldly goods, assuming he had any. Lizzie must have thought Sean was safe in their hands, that there was still no chance of Quigley finding the boy, otherwise she would be telling them everything she knew, in the hope that they could find him before anything happened to him.

Every check on Quigley had come back negative. Despite his reputation, there was nothing on record. No DNA, no prints, no convictions, and Lancashire Police had done no better with their local enquiries, had they? He must have led a charmed life, or been very clever. Or used other people to do his dirty work for him. Could he have arranged for someone else to follow Rosa?

And what about the burglary back in Manchester? What was that all about? Was there any way at all that could be Tiffany-related? Still, as Helen said, how would Tiffany have known where Julie's parents lived? It was a huge leap from nuisance phone calls and slashed tyres to burglary. The woman was a teacher for God's sake. She wouldn't be so stupid. Would she? Julie leaned back against the car and closed her eyes. Amid the faint bleating of sheep, from high above her she could hear the song of a skylark. How did they breathe while they were doing all that non-stop singing? She smiled and opened her eyes. That thought had never crossed her mind in Manchester.

Adam was outside in the front garden, prodding life into the soil with a trowel. That was another first.

'What are you going to plant in there then?' Julie's shadow loomed over the flowerbed, and Adam looked round with a start.

'I didn't hear your car.' He pulled his earphones out and grinned. 'What do you think? I thought I might have a bash at planting veggies.'

'And there was me thinking you'd decided on roses round the door.'

'Not much point in flowers, is there.' Adam handed her a brown paper bag. 'I've got broccoli, red and yellow peppers and cabbage. And I've ordered some spuds and sweet potatoes.'

'And what are the chances of those growing up here? You'd need a greenhouse or a poly-tunnel wouldn't you?'

'Cheers for your vote of confidence. Actually, you can grow all sorts of things round here. I might even have a bash at something illegal. Nobody would know would they?'

'Over my dead body.' Julie glared at him and thrust the paper bag back at him.

'Joke, Jules.' Adam laughed and stood up, brushing grass from his knees. 'But it has been done round here in the past, and in mega fashion too.'

'What, cannabis?'

'Yep. Operation Julie.'

'Oh very funny.'

'I'm serious. I've been trying to find something that's local and fairly recent for next term's history project and this leapt out at me. It's forty years since the police smashed a huge drugs ring near Tregaron, LSD worth £100 million and somewhere near a million in cash.'

'In Tregaron? Are you sure?'

'Completely. One of the undercover officers infiltrated the gang and lived with them. It sounds as though he was as high as a kite a lot of the time, so he didn't blow his cover.'

'That sounds distinctly above and beyond the call of duty. And Tregaron's just a sleepy little town in the middle of nowhere.'

'That's just the whole point. It was so remote it took eleven police forces well over two years to get to the bottom of it.'

'I can understand where they were coming from. This case is feeling a bit like that at the moment. It's centred round a tiny cottage, also in the middle of nowhere, and we have absolutely no clues whatsoever.'

'I have every confidence you'll get there. Now, what do you fancy for tea? I've got cauliflower korma or lentil dhal.'

'Oh dear God, I'm spoilt for choice.'

'Oh, or you can have cheeseburger and chips if you want to be a total heathen.'

'Seriously?'

'Yep.'

'Oh my God, Adam Kite, you are a hero.' She threw her arms round him and recoiled instantly. 'What on earth is that smell?'

'Ah, that'll be the manure. Joe asked if I wanted any. He was clearing out his sheds and said it would be good for the veg plot. I helped him unload it.'

'Aye well, not even aroma of... no, don't tell me. Not even that can put me off cheeseburger and chips.' She followed him to the kitchen door. 'What's brought about this change of heart as far as my dietary requirements are concerned?'

'If you must know, I had a call from Helen. She told me you'd been sitting in car parks all over the place scoffing Chinese from the carton.'

'It was only once, and I didn't think she'd tell you, the dozy mare. I'll flatten her.'

'I think she only had your best interests at heart.' Adam grinned. 'I suppose I've been a bit single-minded about nutrition just lately.'

'Just a bit.' Julie bent down to stroke the cat and asked her question without looking at Adam. 'I don't want you to over-react to this, Adam, but is there any way at all Tiffany would know where my mum and dad live?'

'Tiffany? What's she got to do with anything.'

'Well, the burglary, but of course I don't know that she has got anything to do with it. It's just been nagging at me all day. Dad said he couldn't see whether it was a male or a female running away, but it was probably a kid, judging by the size. And Tiffany isn't exactly a model for those Beryl Cook prints your mum likes, is she?'

'Don't be daft, Julie. That's a ridiculous thing to say. How the hell would she know where your parents live? Why would she have been –,' Adam closed his eyes. When he opened them, Julie was standing right in front of him, her face inches from his.

'Go on.'

'Honest, Jules, she probably didn't even know whose house it was, I'm sure I wouldn't have mentioned it. I left her in the car while I dropped off that poncho thing you borrowed from your mum for the fancy dress party.'

'The fancy dress party last Christmas?'

Adam nodded. 'We were only going out for an almost the end of term drink. We were meeting the others from school at the Swan in town. Tiff had forgotten we were going and had walked into work, so she needed a lift.'

'I bet she did. And you fell for it?'

'It wasn't like that.'

'And Tiffany, she realised it wasn't like that too, did she?'

'Nothing happened. You have my word.' Adam did the puppy dog look that came so easily to him. Julie resisted.

'There we are then.'

Adam grinned. 'You've gone native, Jules.'

'Don't change the subject,' Julie said, but she could feel the corners of her mouth twitching in an involuntary smile. How did he do it? 'But you're saying you left her in the car outside Mum and Dad's and you still think I'm making connections that aren't there?'

'She wouldn't. She might be obsessed, but she's just not like that.'

'I hope you're right, Adam Kite.'

Adam had insisted on washing up and Julie was watching television with a glass of wine in one hand and a bowl of crisps by the other. When the phone rang, he rushed through to answer it.

'Yes, she's here. How are things up there?' There was a pause and Julie held her breath. 'That's great news,' Adam said. 'I'll just get her.' He held the phone out for her. 'It's your mum.'

'Hiya. How's Dad? Has he been back to the hospital?'

'No love, he's fine. They say most of it's superficial, he was just unlucky. It looks far worse than it is.'

'Has he had any stitches out?'

'No, not yet, love, but the practice nurse saw him today and she's really pleased with the way it's looking.'

'Have you heard anything from the local police?'

'We're not really expecting to, to be honest. We know how much work they have and this really didn't amount to much at all, did it?'

'Even so, it would be nice to know who it was.'

'I'm sure it was random. We've not got much worth stealing, have we? Pity about that picture frame though.'

'Which picture was it?'

'It was that wedding photograph of you and Adam, the one on the steps outside the hotel with Lesley's little boy.'

'Our wedding photograph?' Julie could feel her face reddening. Why would anyone break in to steal a wedding photograph of her and Adam, unless there was some sort of ulterior motive?

'You still there, love?'

'Was that the only photograph he took?'

'Oh he didn't take it, your dad picked it up off the hall table to thump him with as he ran past. The lad grabbed it and hit your dad with it and his arm went through the glass. He says it was his own fault, he should have just let him go. He was really upset that he got blood all over the photo, but it was the nearest thing to hand. I'm just glad he didn't pick up the blinking doorstop, otherwise he'd have been in serious bother one way or the other.' She chuckled down the phone. 'I don't know, the pair of you are as bad as each other for wanting justice to be done. Are you there, love, you've gone quiet again.'

'I'm here, Mum.' She glanced up at Adam, who at least had the decency to have turned as white as a sheet.

CHAPTER TWENTY-FIVE

Day Six

The receptionist was far too polite to comment on John Slaithwaite's nervousness or Lizzie's puffy, red-rimmed eyes and her unwillingness to approach the desk.

'Is it just for tonight?' she asked, handing John a registration card and a biro, which he promptly dropped onto the carpet.

'We're not really sure. It depends on how things go.'

The receptionist smiled. 'Of course. That shouldn't be a problem, but would you mind leaving your credit card details with me?'

Damn. John groaned silently. She probably thought they were having an affair, that they'd had a row and would do a runner at three in the morning. He handed back the registration card and the pen and opened his wallet.

'Use my card.' Lizzie slapped her own credit card on the desk. 'Mrs Lizzie Slaithwaite.'

John laughed. She was still the same old Lizzie under all that angst after all. He turned to her and she was actually smiling. The little lines at the corners of her eyes did that wrinkly thing they'd always done. He moved her hair away from her face and let his hand rest in her hair, his thumb on her cheek. She reached up and covered his hand with hers. The receptionist coughed politely.

'Your card, Mrs Slaithwaite. Would you like an early morning call?'

The room was large and light, with a king-size bed draped in chintzy linen. Lizzie perched on the corner.

'I hope you don't mind... I didn't know whether you'd want to...

I can change it for a twin room if you'd prefer it.' John twisted the button on his shirt cuff.

'It'll fall off.' Lizzie smiled at John's confusion. 'Your button. It will fall off if you don't stop.'

John perched next to her on the bed. 'I packed you some things. From home. I didn't know if you would be... whether you would want to come back.'

Lizzie stood up and walked to the window. She rested an elbow on the high ledge and watched a man and a woman swing a child of about six years old between them. All three of them were laughing.

'I've made such a mess of things, haven't I?'

'We can sort it out, Lizzie.'

'You didn't try to find me.'

'You asked me not to. I didn't want to scare you off.' John walked over to stand beside her, but his gaze never left her face as she watched the outside world pass by. 'I thought you'd only be gone a couple of days and then you'd come home, I could apologise for being an insensitive prat and we could try to sort out our options.'

'I didn't leave because of you.'

'I was wrong. I realise that now. I never understood how badly you wanted a baby.' He put his hands on her shoulders and turned her, gently, to face him. 'I have never felt so alone in my life as I have since last October.'

'It seems like a lifetime ago.' Lizzie smiled up at him.

'It's been nine months, three days and,' he looked at his watch, 'almost eight hours.' John shook his head. 'Why couldn't you tell me how you felt, Lizzie, you could have made me understand.'

'I'm not sure you'll ever do that. I'm not sure I understand why I did it, not really. I thought it would all be over in a few days, maybe a week at most, just until Rosa had managed to go to the police about Quigley. I thought she would come and get Sean and we'd all come home.'

John was frowning now. 'What did Rosa have to do with it?'

Lizzie's eyes were wide. 'I thought she would have told you. She promised me she would tell you where we were.' She put both hands up to her face and leaned forward and let her hair cover them.

John took one of her hands and held it tight. 'Whatever's happened, Lizzie, it's going to be all right.'

Lizzie shook her head. 'It isn't, John. It's never going to be all right again.'

John took her by the hand and led her back to the bed and sat her down. He pulled up a chair and sat facing her. 'Right, let's have the whole story. You're going to have to tell the police in the morning and I think I should hear it first. I think you owe me that much.'

Lizzie nodded, blew her nose, ran a hand through her hair and took a deep breath.

'I *was* upset with you that day, you know I was. But that wasn't the reason I left. It was Quigley's fault. If it hadn't been for him and the way he treated Rosa, then none of this would have happened.'

'Quigley? You ran away from Quigley?'

'Sort of. Just let me tell you and then you can decide what you think.'

John nodded, walked over to the mini bar, emptied a miniature bottle of Scotch into a glass tumbler, and sat back down. 'Right then. Let's have the full sordid details.'

Lizzie sighed. 'Quigley came home livid about something someone had done. Rosa wouldn't tell me what it was, but I'd never seen her in such a state before.'

'And we've seen her in some states.'

'We have. Anyway, he'd battered her right arm with the iron, she said, and he'd told her that next time it would be the brat that got it.'

'Sean? He said that about Sean?'

Lizzie nodded. 'Rosa said he meant it too. She was absolutely beside herself. He'd obviously broken her arm, but she didn't dare leave Sean with him to go and get it sorted out. He told her he'd kill her if she went to hospital and told anyone about how the accident had happened.'

'So she didn't go?'

'What could she do? She'd put up with it all for so long that she just got to the end of her rope that day. She asked me if I could take Sean somewhere, anywhere, and hide him.'

'And you said you could?'

'Well what was I supposed to do? She was absolutely terrified that Quigley would actually kill him.'

'He wouldn't have done that, though, would he?'

'We didn't think it was worth waiting to find out. Rosa brought Sean and a little suitcase round to the house, dumped both and fled back to Quigley.'

John sipped his whisky and frowned. 'But how did you end up here? What made you think of mid Wales?'

Lizzie looked away. 'It's a long story. But Rosa said she would tell you where I was.'

'So why did you leave the note, asking me not to look for you?

'I was paranoid that Quigley would track you down if you tried to follow me. It wasn't meant to be for more than a few days. When I didn't hear from you, I just thought you were angry with me for getting involved with them.' She looked up at him. 'With your job and your reputation in the community.' She tried out a small smile, which he returned. 'I know it was a stupid thing to do. I should have taken Sean straight to the police, and Rosa too.'

John gazed into what was left of the amber liquid in his glass and considered. 'And it would have been her word against his, all of it.'

'That's what she said. When she went to report him over the poor dog, they said there was nothing they could do. Quigley found out and broke two of her ribs.'

'You could have told me.'

'And then you'd have been in the same mess I'm in now, frightened to death of Quigley and still desperately worried about Sean. Except that maybe Rosa might not have ended up with a broken arm that day I left.'

'You can't blame yourself for that.'

'Can't I? I should have stopped him, stood up to him and protected her.'

'You did what you thought was right. I can see that.' John put the glass down on the small table and went to sit beside Lizzie on the bed. 'Was it Quigley who killed her?'

Lizzie nodded and the tears started again. 'Who else would it have been? That poor girl. How she ended up with him, God knows. She deserved so much better.' Lizzie gulped.

'She could have walked away from him herself though, couldn't she? She had family not too far away, didn't she?'

'Are you saying I was wrong to take Sean away from that animal?' Lizzie's voice rose to dangerously shrill levels. The last thing Slaithwaite wanted now was to alert other guests or the nosy receptionist.

'It's all right, Lizzie. Let's just think about this. Where is Sean now?'

'I don't know.'

'You don't think he's with Quigley?'

Lizzie shook her head. 'He's not with Quigley.'

'How can you be sure of that?'

'He just can't be.' Lizzie's chin quivered ominously and John backed off immediately.

'It's all right, I'm sure you're right. But you're absolutely sure that Sean's safe?'

Lizzie nodded.

'You don't want to tell me where he is?'

'No. There's no need for you to know where he is.'

'So you don't trust me?'

'Of course I trust you.'

'Well it doesn't feel that way, Lizzie. Not from where I'm sitting.'

'Then I'm sorry, but it's safer for you if you don't know anything about it.'

'Quigley isn't going to know that you've not told me though, is he?' John stood up. 'I'm in it up to my neck now, aren't I?' He walked over to the mini bar and opened the door, peered inside and found no more whisky. He closed the door and walked back to the bed. 'But you're going to tell the police everything in the morning, aren't you?'

Lizzie neither spoke nor moved a muscle, just sat, staring at the swirls of pattern on the carpet.

'I need another drink. And you look as though you've not eaten properly for weeks.' John crouched down to look at her face. 'Come on, Lizzie, let's go and find the restaurant.'

Lizzie stood up. 'I'm sorry,' she said, in a voice hardly more than a whisper. 'I'm so sorry.'

John held onto her so tightly that she gasped. 'I thought I'd lost you. We can work this out, Lizzie; whatever happens, we'll work it out together.' He held her at arms' length and examined her face. 'I promise you, everything will be all right.'

Lizzie Slaithwaite clung to her husband with every ounce of strength she could muster and wept as she never had before.

CHAPTER TWENTY-SIX

Day Seven

It was still dark when Julie woke, but by the time she had fed the cat, dressed and swallowed a cup of coffee, the sky was turning pink and the pine trees on the hill were a jet-black serrated line against the wisps of colour. Despite the promise of another hot and sunny day, there was still a chill in the air, and Julie zipped up her jacket as she closed the door and stepped out onto the drive. She thrust her hands into her pockets and set off up the lane.

Lizzie was going to be interesting, later on. That poor husband of hers looked like a small and insistent dog who had been kicked very hard, and she wasn't going to be a pushover herself, despite the tears. Julie kicked at a loose stone and sent it skittering into the grass verge. What was she doing up there in that cottage? Was there someone else up there with her, if so who? And where had they gone?

The black and white horse was still asleep, but he stirred when he heard her voice, anticipating a breakfast of carrot, if he was lucky. He was. He crunched his way through a carrot the size of Julie's wrist and snorted, spraying her face with a damp mist.

'Oi, Cam, you great dollop, there's no need for that.' Julie stroked his nose. 'Someone ought to teach you a few table manners.'

'Well, you could do that yourself, the offer's still there,' came a voice from behind her. 'When you've finished faffing about up the Elan Valley, we're going out for a ride.'

Julie turned and saw Menna, grinning like a Cheshire cat.

'You're turning into an early bird. It must be the country air,' Menna said.

'It's more like too much stuff whirling around my tiny brain.' Julie laughed. 'Couldn't you sleep either?'

'Gwyn likes to get up with the sun. The theory is that we go to bed early and get up early, but it never quite works like that. It comes from his days up at his parents' place. No electricity see, and his dad was a tight old bugger. He hated running the generator, so they went to bed when it went dark.'

'Bet that was fun in December.'

'It was never what I'd call fun up there. It's a wonder Gwyn ever got the hang of electricity and the telly.'

Julie laughed. 'I just can't imagine life without lights, especially not here. I've never been anywhere so dark in my life.'

'You're not wrong there. They have a saying in Welsh, *fel bol buwch*. As black as a cow's stomach. That says it all.'

'There are some delightful sayings in Welsh, not. It sounds so poetic and then you get the translation.'

'How are you doing with the poor girl on the Monks' Trod?'

'Don't ask.'

'That good?' Menna laughed. 'Well, I'll be round once it's all solved. You've put off taking this lad out for too long already.'

'I might hold you to that.' Julie smiled, but as she turned to set off back down the lane, the smile faded. What had happened to Rosa? Who knew she was staying at the B&B in Llandrindod? Was it just chance she was there? She stopped walking. What had the manager at the Met said? Had Rosa been looking for any B&B, or was she actually looking for that one, for Mrs Pritchard? Or Mr Pritchard, for that matter. She smiled at the thought of Rosa and the upright Mr Pritchard being an item but the smile drained from her face almost immediately. What if James Pritchard was involved in this, somehow? Was that why he had gone missing? The timing wasn't exact, but it might fit. She started to walk, then jog in her rush to get home.

*

Adam was wheeling his bike down the drive when she got back.

'I wondered where you were.'

'You know me, case-related insomnia.'

'And has the horse come up with anything useful?'

'More than you know. Do you want breakfast?'

'I'm going to go for a quick spin round the block. I've got to be in early this morning. Lots of end of term shenanigans to sort out.' Adam clicked a cleat into his pedal. 'Will you have gone when I get back?'

Julie nodded. 'I think it has the makings of one of those days. I'll let you know if I'm going to be late.'

'Have fun.' It took less than half a minute for Adam to disappear round the bend and into the folds of the hill.

*

Swift was in reception as Julie arrived at work.

'You're early, Sir.'

'You too, Julie, but you've still missed the Slaithwaites.' He waved several pieces of paper full of neat, handwritten notes. 'We've arranged that they'll come back later on, once we've had a chance to read this lot. Mrs Slaithwaite is nothing if not reticent.'

'Oh fabulous, just what we need. Why is she being difficult, do you think? Do you think she had anything to do with Rosa's death?'

Swift shook his head. 'Unlikely, I'd have said. But I'd love to know who else might have been involved.'

'I might just be able to help you there. Can I go back and see Mrs Pritchard in Llandrindod this morning?'

'You don't think she's involved?'

'No, but I think the errant Mr Pritchard might be able to tell us a thing or two though and I have a feeling he might just have been in touch.' Julie waved at Brian Hughes and followed Swift through the doors and down the corridor. 'Shall I take Morgan with me?' Swift hesitated and she knew he was itching to join her himself. 'We need to do a bit of bonding, Sir, I think he's in danger of getting up to his old tricks where I'm concerned.'

Swift nodded. 'He does seem a bit out of sorts, just lately. Do you think a trip out with you will help?'

'Well it might help us to talk a bit more.'

'Point taken.' Swift laughed. 'I'm not very good at sitting in the office. But make sure you're back by half eleven. I want you in on the Lizzie Slaithwaite interview. You can get her on side, you being a woman and a northerner at that.'

'I think I'll take that as a compliment, Sir.'

*

If Morgan Evans was pleased at being allowed out of the office again, he was hiding it extremely well. It took until they were passing the primary school in Llanelwedd before Julie managed to illicit more than a grunt in response to her cheery questioning.

'How's the revision for your exam coming on?'

Morgan hesitated, but finally took it in the spirit in which it was meant. He grimaced. 'Oh God, Sarge, how do you remember it all? It goes straight through and out the other side, with me, it does. Nothing of it sticks at all.'

'How are you revising? Have you got a plan?'

'Nothing so organised. I just keep looking and looking at it.'

Julie glanced across at him. He did seem genuinely concerned.

'Well I can never remember anything unless I write it down. I had packets and packets of those little coloured cards, one colour for each major subject. If I could remember what colour card it was likely to be written on, it made it easier to recall the facts.'

Morgan laughed. 'Has anyone ever told you, you're really weird, Sarge?'

'Only all the time. Helen, the DC I used to work with in Manchester, she thought I was totally bonkers. I didn't even tell her about the flip chart paper in strategic places in the flat.'

'I get the feeling this is going to be a little bit scary. What did you do with that?'

'I had three sheets for each colour of card and I wrote everything from the cards on the flip chart paper as bullet points, in tiny writing, so the three huge pieces of paper had everything I had to know about that subject that was also on the little cards I could take out with me.' Julie was aware that Morgan was staring at her with his mouth open.

'How long did it take you to do all that, do you think?'

'In total? Hours and hours. And then Adam would fire questions at me from all over the flat too. Evidence and Procedure from the living room, Crime from the kitchen...'

'Isn't there an easier way of doing it?'

'You could probably do a lot less than I did, but passing the exam isn't really the point, is it?'

'Isn't it?'

'It's having all that information in your head, knowing as much as you can.'

Morgan sighed. 'You really are a perfectionist. I bet you buy the new editions of the manuals every year.' He laughed at his own joke.

'Actually, Morgan, I do.'

'God, Julie, I wasn't serious.' Morgan shook his head. 'Your old partner might have been right.'

'Helen is right about a lot of things, Morgan. Trust me.'

*

The manager at the Metropole was absolutely definite. Rosa hadn't asked for Mrs Pritchard by name, or the name of the B&B. It had definitely been at his suggestion that she had gone to Bryn Awel. He'd only mentioned it to her because he thought Mrs Pritchard might do Rosa a cheaper deal, given the circumstances. Thank goodness for people with wonderful memories, thought Julie, even if it did blow a huge hole in her theory. Or did it? They left Julie's car in the hotel car park and walked from there to the row of impressive houses where Rosa had stayed.

Mrs Pritchard seemed different this time. She still wore the pristine uniform of lambs' wool turtleneck and pearls, but today she looked completely exhausted. Her eyes, above pale grey circles, seemed deeper set and less alert. Running a B&B must have been harder work than she'd thought. Julie introduced Morgan Evans.

'What can I do for you, Sergeant?' Mrs Pritchard made no move to let them into the tasteful grey and cream hallway.

'I've just a couple more questions about your husband's disappearance, if you wouldn't mind.'

'I don't know any more than I told you last time. I don't know what more I can add.'

'Were you getting on well before he left?'

'Well,' Mrs Pritchard looked down at the toes of her shoes, 'James was tired. Things at work were getting on top of him, he said.'

'But you were happy enough at home?'

'We were happy, yes. Or he was.'

'And you weren't so happy, perhaps?' Julie cringed at Morgan's tone, but Mrs Pritchard appeared not to have noticed. She shook her head.

'Who knows what that even means, Constable?'

'And you're absolutely positive you'd never seen Rosa before, either here in Llandrindod or anywhere else in the area?' Julie asked.

'Totally sure.'

The door behind her opened slightly, and despite Mrs Pritchard's desperate attempt to pull it shut, the face of a small boy appeared in the gap. The boy's skin was horribly pale, his eyes dark and doe-like above the prominent cheekbones. Julie almost gasped out loud.

'He's a guest,' Mrs Pritchard said, ushering the child back into the hall and closing the door behind her. 'His grandfather can't keep up with him.'

'Is he all right?' Julie asked.

'I'm sure he's fine,' Mrs Pritchard smiled.

'Quite,' said Morgan.

'Is there anything else I can help you with, Sergeant?'

'Not for the moment,' Julie said. 'Thank you for your time.'

Morgan and Julie walked down the path and onto the pavement. Mrs Pritchard was still standing on the doorstep, watching them go.

'That all seems fairly plausible, Sarge.'

'I'm not so sure. Did you think she was desperate to get the child out of our way?'

'Probably just didn't want him running onto the road.'

'Mmm. Maybe.' Julie glanced over her shoulder one last time before they turned the corner. Mrs Pritchard was still there, watching.

They were almost back at the car when Julie's mobile rang. It was Swift.

'Are you still in Llandod?'

'Yes, why, what's up?'

'Can you get yourselves up to the Elan Valley?'

'Now, Sir?'

'As soon as you can. I've just had a cryptic phone call from Mal.'

'That sounds intriguing.'

'It is. He says he's found something unexpected in his cess pit.'

'Oh God, that's all I need. Is that something connected with Rosa's death?

'I would say that's probably highly likely.' Swift cleared his throat. 'I've asked Dr Greenhalgh to get there as a matter of urgency.'

'Ah, are we talking another body here, do you think?'

'That was my first thought from Mal's painstaking technicolour description.'

Julie grimaced. 'Understood, Sir.'

'Thank you, Julie. I'll be there as soon as I can.'

*

The tractor was parked in the centre of the yard, its bucket at just above head height. Between the large oblong teeth, an arm dangled. What skin was visible appeared discoloured and was covered in small amounts of what Morgan referred to in his notebook as 'matter'. As they crossed the yard, Julie could hear the low rumble of Dr Greenhalgh's Alfa, which slowed only to rattle across the cattle grid before speeding into the yard and stopping in a cloud of dust.

'I didn't know what to do with it.' Mal was standing beside the tractor, his cap in his hands. I thought it would be better to bring it down here, but I left the bucket as it was. I didn't want to dislodge anything.'

'Quite right.' Kay Greenhalgh nodded her approval. 'I wonder if you would be kind enough to lower the bucket for me, so I can see exactly what I'm dealing with.'

Mal climbed into the tractor and started the engine. He lowered the bucket very gently. Even so, foul-smelling fluid slopped onto the concrete, forming puddles from the dark splashes. He switched off the engine but it was several moments before he climbed down from the cab.

'Is he dead?' he asked Dr Greenhalgh, who by now was clad in a white paper suit, blue overshoes, gloves and a mask. She nodded.

'Very definitely. And from the state of him, I'd say he's been in there a few days, at least.' She leaned forward to get a better look and Morgan retched. 'Are you all right there, Constable?'

Morgan nodded. 'Sorry.'

'No need to apologise. He is particularly fragrant, I'll grant you that.' She turned to Mal. 'Now, could you tell me exactly how you found him?'

'I was digging out the pit, see. It all gets a bit backed up so I went and gave it a bit of a poke. He was my second bucketful. I didn't even notice him until that arm flopped over the edge of the bucket. It gave me a bit of a moment, it did.'

'I can imagine. And how often do you have to poke your cess pit?'

'Just now and again.'

'So, you've no idea how long he's been in there?'

Mal shook his head.

'Could it have been accidental?' Julie asked. 'Could he just have fallen in?'

'Well,' Dr Greenhalgh lifted the end of a thick piece of twine and held it aloft, 'it's possible. I'd have said that this might have made him more than a little unsteady on his feet.'

'Ah,' Morgan said. 'So he was strangled?'

'He's been garrotted. The twine is attached to this piece of excruciatingly sharp wire. I've never seen anything quite so vicious. It's a wonder his head's still attached. See here, where it's sliced through his windpipe.'

Morgan had the good sense to move away before revisiting his breakfast.

'So it's not suicide then?' Julie asked.

'Oh hilarious, Sergeant. No, definitely not suicide. I can't give you any timings yet, because of the increased temperature brewing in the cess pit, but I'd be surprised if he hadn't been here for about five days or so.'

'Anything else you can tell us?'

'I'd say he must have been killed here, rather than just dumped.'

Morgan wiped his mouth with the back of his hand. 'What makes you say that?'

'Well, he couldn't have walked here, could he, not with that neck wound.' She pointed down at the dark stains on skin and clothing, still visible despite their immersion in the fetid liquid of the cess pit.

'He could have been carried, though, couldn't he?'

'I don't see how you could do that successfully.' Dr Greenhalgh traced the wire round to the right hand side of the corpse's head with a single finger. 'Not without the head becoming detached.' There was a squelching sound as the head moved away from the neck under the slight pressure, breaking the temporary seal.

Julie tried not to smile as Morgan once more departed across the concrete. Poor Morgan. He really wasn't cut out for the visceral side of policing. 'Any clues as to who he is, Kay?'

Dr Greenhalgh shook her head. 'I'd rather get him back to the table before I start rummaging for ID. Everything's a bit precarious, but I'll get onto it as soon as I get him back to the office.'

*

It took more than three hours before Kay Greenhalgh was satisfied with her notes. Julie took photographs and made her own notes for Swift. Where was he? This was so unlike him.

'It looks as though his transport's arrived,' Julie said. A large black van with tinted windows slid into the yard and three dark-suited men sloped out. If they were concerned at the heinous state of their client, it didn't show as they worked silently and methodically, aided by the three Scene of Crime officers.

The van had already left by the time Swift arrived. Dr Greenhalgh was back in civvies and getting into her car. When she saw him she climbed out again. 'Craig! Where the hell have you been? You've been hours. You've missed all the action.'

Swift wrinkled his nose, looked at the digger and the latest pile of vomit, which Sarah was scrubbing with the aid of a yard brush and hose, and nodded. 'Thank heaven for small mercies then, is it, Doctor?'

'Are you alright? It's not like you to be late to an investigation. I know you always like to see the deceased in situ.'

Swift glanced at her. 'I had an urgent appointment. It took longer than expected.' He looked away, down the drive. 'I might have to ask your professional advice at some point.'

He stopped abruptly and turned away as Julie reached them.

'Everything in hand, Sergeant?'

'It is, Sir. We've got loads of videos and photographs.' She showed Swift a photograph on her phone and he grimaced.

Kay Greenhalgh twinkled at him. 'You lads, you've no blinking stamina.' She got back into her car and slid the window down. 'Julie's got everything under control, and I'll get back to you as soon as I can with first impressions.' She put the car into gear. 'Phone me,' she said to Swift, then she whirled the Alfa round, waved and set off down the long drive like a guided missile.

Swift watched her go, and turned to Julie. 'Did she beat you to it?'

'Not quite, but she wasn't far behind us.'

'It's a wonder she's not been banned. She was at the hospital when I phoned her. You must have had a twenty mile head start.'

'Well fortunately, she does everything at top speed. She's promised an update by the end of the afternoon.'

'Do we know who he is?'

'No. But I know who I think it might be.'

'Quigley?'

'He'd be top of my list, Sir.'

'Mine too. What's happened to Morgan?'

'He's getting cleaned up. He was a bit overwhelmed. Several times. To be fair, it was pretty gruesome.'

'I think I'm glad I was late.'

'Did you speak to Rosa's parents, Sir?'

Swift nodded. 'They confirmed the ID beyond a shadow of a doubt from a scar on her knee. She fell off her bike on a gravel path after her dad decided it was time to take the stabilisers off.' He looked away from her, up to the hill. 'They're absolutely destroyed by her death.'

'Maybe they feel guilty?'

'Maybe they do, Julie, but we don't know what Rosa put them through, do we?' Swift sighed. 'Come on, let's go and see what Mal and Sarah have to say.'

Sarah was close to tears. She insisted on putting the kettle on and filling plates with food, but she was obviously very shaken. Julie helped her with mugs and teaspoons.

'Thank you, *cariad*. I wouldn't trust myself with the china, not today.'

'Are you all right?

'Do you know, I don't think I am. How do you manage to do this every day?'

'It's not every day, Sarah, thank goodness. This sort of thing is pretty rare, even where I'm from.' Julie took the teapot from her, which stopped the quiet rattling of its lid. 'I don't suppose you know who he is?'

Sarah shook her head. 'You wouldn't even recognise anyone you knew really well if they were in that condition, would you?'

'Has there been anyone hanging round the farm in the past few days?'

'Nobody. We had a new fish man come up the day before yesterday. He seemed very nice, but the freezer's full of lamb, so we didn't buy anything. Apart from him, the postman and the lads who come up to help with the sheep, there's been nobody here.'

Mal came in from the scullery, wiping his hands on a large loop of towelling, rubbing carefully between his fingers.

'I've never seen anything like that in my life,' he said. He put the towel on the side and lowered himself into a chair. 'And I don't ever want to see anything like it again.'

'Was he floating in the pit?' Swift asked. Sarah retreated to the sink and Julie went to stand with her.

'He must have been. I hadn't got very far, just scraping at the surface I was. I should have seen him.' Mal rubbed his eyes. 'Do you think I did him any damage?'

'I don't think there's any doubt that he'd been dead for quite some time,' Swift said.

'Even so, I wouldn't like to think I hurt him.'

Swift put his hand on Mal's arm. 'Don't worry,' he said. 'He was way past that.'

CHAPTER TWENTY-SEVEN

Day Seven

John and Lizzie Slaithwaite were sitting in reception when Julie, Morgan and Swift arrived back at the station. Lizzie looked far less fraught than she had been the previous evening, and fences were obviously in the process of being mended as the pair sat holding hands.

'Love's young dream,' Brian Hughes said, raising an eyebrow. 'I don't know that I'd be so willing to forgive my wife if she'd run away for eight months.'

'Maybe he didn't notice.' Julie grinned. 'He seems to be a bit of a workaholic.'

'Aren't we all?' Brian shook his head. 'People never cease to amaze me. What time do you want them?'

'Give us five minutes for a sandwich and a *panad*, and we'll come and get them,' Swift said. 'They don't look as though they're in a rush.'

Lizzie looked totally different today. Even John looked as though the weight of the world had been lifted from his shoulders. Would Lizzie be so relaxed if she had been involved in either of the deaths by the Monks' Trod? As Julie approached, the Slaithwaites looked up in unison.

'I'm so sorry for keeping you waiting for so long,' Julie said. 'We were unavoidably detained.'

John Slaithwaite laughed. 'Makes a change for you to be the one being detained, I'd imagine.'

Lizzie frowned. 'You've read my statement?' I thought it might save some time so we can finally get home.' She looked at her husband. 'John helped me.'

'Thank you, that will be helpful,' Julie said, 'but we will still want to interview you, just to make sure we cover every eventuality.' She smiled at John Slaithwaite. 'I'm sure you'll understand that we have to follow procedure.'

'Of course, Sergeant, but Lizzie isn't under arrest. Even the statement is above and beyond what she is actually required to provide.'

'Mr Slaithwaite, we are as keen as you are to bring this matter to a speedy conclusion.'

Slaithwaite offered a curt nod. 'Don't worry, Lizzie. Everything will be fine. If you want me to be with you, then I'm sure there will be no objections.'

'I'll be fine, John. I want to do this.' Lizzie stood up and smiled down at her husband. 'I'm sure they won't keep me for long.'

Swift was at his most reassuring, but Julie kept replaying the conversation on the doorstep of the cottage. Who else had been in the house? Where did they go? It was time to throw some doubt into the pleasant little chat between Lizzie and Swift.

'So, Lizzie, you've told us that you kidnapped Sean.'

'I didn't kidnap him, Sergeant. Rosa asked me to get him away from Quigley.'

'So you had her permission to take her child and bring him to Wales?'

'Yes, I had her permission to take him. She begged me to take him.'

'And did you have permission to bring him to Wales? Did she know where he was?'

Lizzie looked down at the table. 'No she didn't. Not at first.'

'So, how long was it before you let her know where her son was?'

Lizzie looked at Swift, but he busied himself with her statement. She sighed. 'You don't understand what Quigley is like. He's an animal. Rosa wouldn't have asked me to get involved if she hadn't been desperate.'

'But you told her where you were eventually.'

Lizzie nodded. 'She kept texting me and leaving messages. I didn't know if it really was her or Quigley using the phone so I didn't dare reply. I thought it would be safer to write to her with the address. That way he wouldn't necessarily have known anything about it.'

'And how do you work that one out?' Julie asked. 'Exactly why would that have been any safer?'

'I sent it to my own home address but with Rosa's name on it. I knew John wouldn't hand it to Quigley if it was addressed to her.'

'So you wrote to her at your own address, knowing your husband would deliver it to her, but you didn't have the decency to tell him where you were and what you were doing?' Julie's voice was rising and Swift interjected with a cough.

'That was very clever of you, Lizzie.' Swift tugged his ear. 'But how could you make sure that Quigley wouldn't find the letter once it was in Rosa's possession?'

'She wouldn't be so stupid as to leave it lying around, would she? She was absolutely terrified he would find Sean.'

'But someone did find it, Lizzie.' Swift stared at her. 'Someone who then tracked her down to the Elan Valley.'

Lizzie's mouth opened and closed, but no words came out.

Julie relented. 'We don't know if that's how Quigley knew where she was.'

'What do you mean? Are you trying to tell me that Quigley could have followed her?' Lizzie was speaking quickly now, frantic to get her words out. 'But just because you're assuming that Rosa came here after she got my letter doesn't make it true, does it?'

'But we know she was here, Lizzie, that maybe she had come for Sean. And we know that at least one person worked out your location.'

'I don't believe you. She would have told me if she was planning to come. She didn't come to the cottage, she didn't even phone me for directions. There's no way she would have found us.' Lizzie was rocking now, very gently and rhythmically. 'It's not true.'

'We've just received this from the police in Lancashire. Could you confirm whether this is Jason Quigley?' Julie slid a black and white photograph across the table. The name across the top was Donal Quinlan.

Lizzie picked it up and frowned. 'Yes. That's Jason Quigley.' She dropped the photograph onto the table. 'I don't understand.'

'Then we know that the man you know as Jason Quigley probably did know where both you and Sean were. We also believe that he may have brought Rosa with him to persuade you to hand over the child.'

Swift turned to look at Julie but Julie's gaze never wavered from Lizzie's face.

'Oh God, you're really sure he's here? I need to go.' Lizzie darted out of her seat and was at the door before they could stop her.

'Lizzie, we need to talk to you.' Swift's plea was met with a sneer.

'And you can protect Sean from Quigley, can you?'

Julie and Swift exchanged a glance. 'My husband tells me that if you aren't going to arrest me, then I'm free to go at any time.'

'That's true, but we can help you.' Swift's tone was desperate now.

'I doubt that very much, Inspector.'

'Where is he, Lizzie, where is Sean?' Julie asked.

Lizzie turned on her heel and scurried down the corridor. Julie followed close behind, with Swift bringing up the rear. Lizzie crashed through the doors into reception and, without stopping for the automatic doors to open fully, she jinked through the gap and was outside and gone. John Slaithwaite looked up from his phone and glared at Swift.

'I'm letting her go for now, Mr Slaithwaite, but I need you both to go back to the hotel and wait for my call. If you can't guarantee that, then I will have to arrest her and bring her back. Is that understood?'

Slaithwaite nodded. 'For today, Inspector, and only for today, I will make sure she stays in the hotel. If we hear nothing from you by the end of the day then we will be making arrangements to leave first thing tomorrow, and I will instruct a colleague who is better-placed than I am to assist my wife.' He turned and hurried after Lizzie. Julie went to follow him, but Swift put his hand on her arm.

'There's nothing we can do, Julie. We don't want to arrest her for kidnap because she says she removed Sean with Rosa's permission. We've absolutely nothing that links her to either Quigley's death or Rosa's. If we arrest her now, we'll show our hand too soon.'

'I wish I thought we had a hand to show, Sir.' Julie opened the folder and Quigley's face glared back at her. 'Should we not keep an eye on where she is, just for now?'

'She's been hiding since November, she's in the habit of being careful and suspicious. There's no way she'll lead us to that child.' Swift watched John Slaithwaite weave through the traffic and disappear, just as his wife had done.

'Why didn't you tell her about the body we found at Mal's?'

'We don't know yet if it *is* Quigley, do we?' Swift said. 'I noticed you didn't categorically confirm that Rosa is dead either.'

'Fair point,' Julie conceded. 'There's something about her that I don't trust, Sir. I can't tell you what, but I think she has more information than we have at the moment.'

'Agreed. If you're right, though, it'll have to come out soon or she'll be on her way back to Blackpool.'

'That's another thing. That map bothers me. Why would you have part of an Ordnance Survey map in your bag with your own house circled on it? Did Rosa put it there, or did someone else? Did they want us to find it?'

'Now you're into the realms of female logic, Sergeant. I'll leave that one to you. We need to know who the body in the cess pit is and quickly, before John Slaithwaite spirits his wife away.'

'I'll get back onto Kay Greenhalgh and see if she's any more to tell us.'

'Go and have a coffee first, Julie. You look as though you could do with five minutes to yourself.'

Julie succumbed to a warm scone. Nerys was wasted in the canteen. She could persuade anyone to do anything. Maybe she should have been the one in there with Lizzie Slaithwaite. She couldn't have done a worse job on her, could she?

'I've got some strawberry jam for that, brought it in special. Mam made too much, we've got jars and jars of the stuff and I don't want to offend her by not taking it do I?'

'Go on then, I could do with a dollop of sugar.'

'You look shattered, lovely. Are you all right?' Nerys pushed a mug across the counter. 'I don't know how you cope with all the blood and guts you come across. I've just had Morgan in here, white as a sheet he was. He said you don't seem bothered by it all.'

Julie shrugged. 'It's just a machine really, the body.' She counted out change into Nerys's hand. 'If you don't teach yourself to think of it like that then you can't be objective.'

Nerys counted the change into the till. She didn't look convinced. 'But all that mess you have to see, and then knowing what horrible things people can do to each other. You can't unsee it, can you?' She grimaced. 'I'd never sleep again if I had your job.'

'I'm not very good at sleeping to be honest.' Julie gave a small smile. 'But in my case, it's usually trying to work out how things fit together that keeps me awake.'

Julie took her mug and her plate and went to sit down. If only she could *see* it, whatever it was, never mind unseeing anything. She took a bite of scone and a blob of bright red strawberry jam landed on her blouse. That made a bad day slightly worse. She dabbed at the jam with a serviette and transferred crumbs to accompany the preserve. Scone crumbs. She frowned. Would someone else's crumbs left on the table be enough to make someone with coeliac disease ill? She stared at the remains of the scone on her plate. And was there a way of passing coeliac disease on to someone else? She gulped down her coffee and left the canteen at a trot.

Would it even be possible? Kay Greenhalgh would be bound to know.

CHAPTER TWENTY-EIGHT

Day Seven

'Well you've excelled yourself with this one, lady.' Julie could hear the smile in Kay Greenhalgh's voice. 'What a mess.'

'I don't envy you the smell, let alone anything else.'

'I'm not talking about the detritus. That is pretty grim, but this one's a real beauty in the live fast and die young department. He's got the body of an eighty-year old.'

'That's just how I feel.'

'Well, unless you've got a perforated ulcer, lecture-noteworthy sclerosis of the liver and a suspected brain tumour, you're not even trying.'

'Blimey. That's quite a selection. Would he have known about any of it?'

'Well, there's a chance he'd have known about the ulcer. It was pretty nasty and had left him with raging anaemia. As for the rest, it's anyone's guess. He was PhD level in terms of substance abuse, so he probably wouldn't have felt a thing. He had virtually no septum left. I can't decide whether that would make snorting the stuff impossible or twice as efficient. Then there was the empyema.'

'That's a new one on me.'

'Lucky you. Trust me, the smell was worse than anything in that cess pit. It's where pockets of pus collect in body cavities. In this chap's case, it was mostly in the space between the lung and the chest wall.'

'And that was caused by the drugs?'

'It was. As was the knackered heart valve. He was a walking time bomb. It was a wonder he'd lasted as long as he did.'

Julie whistled softly. 'Is it wrong of me to suggest he would have done several people a favour if he hadn't?'

'It would be completely unprofessional of you, Sergeant Kite. But on this occasion I'd have to agree with you.'

'And the garrotte was the cause of death?'

'Partially. He would have bled to death almost instantly, with that amount of trauma to the throat.'

'I'm sensing there's a but coming next.'

'But there was also a huge amount of fluid in his lungs.'

'Fluid from the pit? So he drowned?'

'It's difficult to tell the absolute order of things, but there's no way that amount of fluid would have reached his lungs if his throat had been sliced open before he hit the water. Conversely, he could have still been alive when the garrotte was applied, but only just. There was some blood on the clothing, but not enough for his heart to have been pumping efficiently when his neck was sliced. I thought initially that there had been more blood and it had been washed off, but now I'm inclined to think he was more or less deceased from drowning before the wire was used.'

'Someone wanted to make sure.'

'Well, either that or the garrotte was more of a prop, to make the death more theatrical perhaps, or to leave a warning.'

'Bloody hell, this case just gets more and more bizarre.'

'By the way, that cess pit is illegal. Building Regulations state it should be covered.'

'Mal said he was doing a bit of maintenance on it at the time.'

'Even so, he was breaking the law leaving it unattended and uncovered.'

'You're a hard woman, Dr Greenhalgh.'

'Just a stickler, Sergeant Kite. And wait for it, you'll like this bit... the blood we found on Rosa's clothes was Quigley's. His blood was also on that knapsack of hers you sent Morgan back with this morning.'

Julie closed her eyes. 'So he had to have died, or at least bled onto

Rosa's clothes while she was still alive. Rosa could have fought with Quigley, she ended up with a head injury and he ended up drowning with a severed head. This is turning into an episode of *Midsomer Murders.* All we need now is a trebuchet and we've got the full set. Does he have any other wounds?'

'Nice try, but that's the only one. But there's more. We did find Rosa's blood on the gatepost at the cottage.'

'So she made it all the way up there? But then Lizzie must have seen her there, surely?'

'I'm glad the speculation is your department, Sergeant. I'm much happier with hard facts.' Greenhalgh smiled. 'Good luck with that one.'

'Thank you so much.' Julie sighed. 'Do you think Rosa would have been strong enough to apply the wire to Quigley's neck?'

'Not a chance, I'd say. Even if she'd had the strength to do it, that arm of hers would have meant a much more one-sided wound. This was someone with two working arms.'

'So we're looking for a man, do you think?'

Kay paused. 'Not necessarily. There are a number of ways he could have ended up in the pit, and that wire was absolutely lethal. It wouldn't have taken a ridiculous amount of force to slice through the victim's windpipe with it.'

Julie groaned and put her head on her desk.

'Are you still there?' Dr Greenhalgh asked.

'I'm still here. But suddenly I'm wishing I was on a beach in Lanzarote.'

'Tell you what, make it Tuscany and I'll come with you.'

'You're on. And I might do a Lizzie Slaithwaite and just not come back.'

'You don't mean that, Julie. You love it really.'

'Sometimes I love it.' Julie laughed. 'But today I'm having my doubts. I wanted to ask you something about coeliac disease. It's just a thought and I might be barking up the wrong tree entirely, but is it hereditary, by any chance?'

'It is, well, there's more chance of having it if a parent has it. You need the right genes to be susceptible. Why, what have you found?'

'You know we're looking for Rosa's little boy, well, I saw a lad about the same age in Llandrindod today. He was as skinny as Rosa and like a little ghost he was so pale.'

'That might be a needle in a haystack thing. Are you adding two and two and coming up with eleventy-seven?'

Julie laughed. 'It's quite possible, although there might be a connection. Granted it's a tenuous connection.'

'Well, failure to thrive is a sign, and sometimes an evil temper, but I wouldn't know the difference. I don't do kids very well.'

'Neither do I. Do you think we're missing something?'

'Speak for yourself, Julie. I intend to go straight from motorbikes and fast cars to the adults-only retirement village.'

Julie was still smiling as she put the phone down. Swift sauntered over to her desk.

'What's making you so happy?'

'Dr Greenhalgh. She's a star.'

'She did really well to get those fingerprints back to us so quickly. It turns out Jason Quigley is only one of half a dozen aliases. It's no wonder we couldn't pin him down. He must have been pretty bright to keep up with all the different names and contacts. Rhys and Goronwy are going to be checking that little lot for days.'

'She's done better than that.' Julie explained the latest findings and watched Swift's smile grow wider with every revelation.

'I think, Sergeant Kite, that it's about time we asked Lizzie Slaithwaite to stop lying.'

'I'll phone the hotel and get them to come back in.'

'Don't worry about it, Sergeant, follow me. I feel an imminent arrest coming on.'

The girl on the desk had no hesitation in directing Swift and Julie to the Slaithwaite's room on the first floor.

'There's something a bit odd about those two, if you know what I mean,' she said, as they hurried past her.

John Slaithwaite opened the door and closed his eyes. When he opened them, Swift and Julie were still there.

'Oh come on, this is bordering on harassment, Inspector.'

'We've come to speak to your wife, Mr Slaithwaite,' Swift replied. 'I'd be grateful if you would let us in.'

Lizzie was gazing out of the window, apparently oblivious to their arrival.'

'Elizabeth Slaithwaite,' Swift said, 'I would be obliged if you could come with us. We would like to talk to you in connection with the kidnap of Sean Quigley and the disappearance of Jason Quigley.' Lizzie turned to face them and for a second she stared at Swift before crumpling into a tidy heap on the plush carpet.

*

'The doctor says Lizzie's fit to be interviewed.' Julie leaned on Swift's door and smiled. 'And, despite assurances that Lizzie hasn't been arrested yet, Mr Slaithwaite has insisted on the assistance of the duty solicitor until he can instruct his own brief.'

'And who is the duty solicitor?'

'It's Eurig Powell.'

Swift nodded. 'Good. He'll help her.'

Julie smiled. 'I'm not sure that's how you're supposed to think about a possible suspect, Sir.'

'I'm still not convinced she is a suspect, but I do think she holds the key to this whole thing, and I really don't want her to run away back to Blackpool. And don't forget, we still don't know where the child is.'

'I'm not so sure about that, Sir.'

'Well let's see if we can sort that one out while we're at it, shall we? Are you ready?'

'I'm ready.'

Eurig was fussing, making sure Lizzie had water, that she was feeling well enough to proceed. Swift readied the tape and each of them announced their presence. Swift reminded Lizzie that she was not under arrest and was free to leave at any time.

'You know why you're here,' Swift said. Lizzie nodded.

'You have to say it out loud for the recording,' Eurig smiled. 'Don't worry, Lizzie, it's just a formality.'

'Yes. I know why I'm here. But I had nothing to do with Quigley's disappearance. Not that I hadn't wished him all sorts of bad luck. I used to pray every night that he would overdose on the crap he used to sell to kids and poor sad losers, pray that he just wouldn't wake up in the morning.'

'But he did,' Julie said. 'He just kept on waking up, and you were worried for Rosa and for Sean.'

'Of course I was. Who wouldn't be?'

'Worried enough to do something about it?' Julie asked.

'What could I do? I couldn't tackle Quigley. The man was vicious. I did the only thing I could do.' Lizzie shuddered. 'Rosa arrived on my doorstep one afternoon out of the blue. She said Sean had been whingeing all day, yet again. Quigley had hit her because she couldn't get him to stop. She was convinced he'd start on Sean, so she asked me to take Sean away and hide him. I begged her to come with us, but she was too terrified to leave him, too petrified of what he might do to her.'

'Was Rosa a drug user, Lizzie?'

Lizzie nodded. 'She'd tried so hard to stop, but Quigley forced her. She said he even injected it when she was asleep. That kept her dependent on him didn't it? She could never have afforded to buy the stuff, so she had to stay with him.'

'So you took Sean and you ran away.'

Lizzie nodded again. 'Yes. I took Sean away.'

'And you took him to the cottage in the Elan Valley, Pwll Bach?'

'Yes.'

'And how did you know about the cottage, Lizzie? It wasn't

advertised for rent anywhere, we checked. It wasn't in newspapers, on the internet or with an estate agent. How did you know, all the way from Blackpool, that this cottage was available, and that its isolation suited your purposes so beautifully?'

Lizzie glanced at Eurig, who nodded. 'I know the person who owns it. They told me about it.'

'And who would that be, Lizzie?'

Lizzie looked at Eurig again and he bent towards her and whispered something to her behind his hand. She shook her head.

Julie sighed. 'Come on, Lizzie, help us out here. Was it Mrs Pritchard from Bryn Awel Bed and Breakfast in Llandrindod who helped you?'

Lizzie shook her head. 'No. I don't know Mrs Pritchard. I've never met her.' She looked down and her hair drifted across her face.

Julie leaned forward across the table, so she could see Lizzie's eyes as she asked the next question. 'But you do know *Mr* Pritchard, don't you, Lizzie?'

The effect was more than Julie could have hoped for. Lizzie burst into spectacular snot-laden sobs which streaked mascara down her cheeks and caused both Swift and Eurig to shift uncomfortably in their seats.

'Do I take that as a positive, Lizzie?' Julie's voice was uncharacteristically soft and Swift raised an eyebrow.

Lizzie nodded. 'I only found him last summer.' She dabbed at her wrecked makeup and blew her nose, leaving a black smudge. 'I never knew I had a dad until last year. Thirty-eight years old and suddenly I had a father.'

'That must have been quite a shock. How did you find him?' Julie was calm, as if nothing had just happened.

'My mum died a year ago last Christmas. She never spoke of my father. It was always a taboo subject. All the years I was growing up, all through school when all the other kids used to talk about their dads, I was the one who'd never known her father. She told me he was dead. She actually said he died before I was born.' She managed a small, private smile, and blew her nose. 'She told me he died in a trawler accident off the coast of Fleetwood.'

'So how did you find out about your father? Did he contact you?'

Another shake of the head. 'He didn't know I existed. When Mum went into a hospice I had to go through all her things. I didn't have long to linger about it. The council wanted the house back within seven days. There were boxes and boxes of paperwork going back to when I was born.' Lizzie frowned. 'I hadn't seen any of it before. There was a name and address scrawled on a piece of paper in the bottom of a shoebox. That's all I had to go on.'

'That must have given you a moment, finding out you did have a dad after all that time.'

'I think it gave Dad more of a moment than me, Sergeant. He's married with grown up kids.'

'So you had a ready-made step-family too.' Julie frowned. 'Why was it that you could tell your father about running away with Sean, but you didn't tell your husband?'

'It's not like it sounds.'

'And how does it sound, Lizzie?' Julie's voice was sympathetic, and she was surprised to find that she actually meant it. That was a worry.

'I didn't want to get my husband involved in any way with Quigley.'

'And that's all it was?'

'Honestly, Sergeant? I'm not sure any more. John is very concerned about the integrity of his position in the community. He couldn't handle the fact that I succumbed to depression over the little matter of being unable to conceive a child.'

'But your father was more understanding?'

'He doesn't know about that... side of things. I just didn't know who else to turn to when Sean and I were in that car, heading out of Blackpool. Rosa didn't plan any of it, she was absolutely desperate that day, and I didn't have time to think too hard about it either. I just flung a few clothes in a suitcase and left. Sean and I spent the first few nights in a Travelodge in Chester, but he was so distraught he was making himself poorly and we were drawing attention to ourselves. I had to find somewhere else, somewhere Quigley would never find us.'

'Did you take him to a doctor?'

'He was fine. And I couldn't risk anyone finding out where we were.'

'Has he seen a doctor at all, since you left Blackpool?'

Lizzie shook her head. 'It comes and goes, the tummy problem.' She looked at Julie and then Swift. 'It's the anger I can't cope with.'

'Sean's anger?' Swift was suddenly interested. 'How old is he?'

'He's four, nearly five. But he has these uncontrollable rages. He can be quite terrifying sometimes. Maybe there's something of his father in him.'

'And what about you, Lizzie? You must have been more than angry with Quigley. And you were terrified of what he would do to Sean.' Julie's voice was calm.

'What are you saying?' Lizzie's eyes narrowed and Eurig raised an eyebrow.

'Did Rosa bring Quigley to Pwll Bach? Did they come for Sean?'

'Quigley at the cottage? Forgive me for pointing out the obvious, Sergeant, but the last I heard, Quigley was doing his nasty trade in Blackpool. It's not far enough away, not by a long shot, but at least he doesn't know where we are.'

'Jason Quigley is in the mortuary at our local hospital,' Swift said. 'Didn't you know?'

The look on Lizzie's face told them everything. Her hand flew to her mouth, her eyes as wide as Julie thought it was possible for eyes to go. But when she put both hands over her face and started to shake, Swift exchanged a glance with Eurig.

'Are you all right, Lizzie? Do you want to stop?' Swift asked. Lizzie could not reply and Eurig got to his feet. But when Lizzie removed her hands, she was laughing, her shoulders shaking with apparent mirth.

'Quigley is dead? Are you really sure?' She giggled. 'I thought you were making it up.'

Swift nodded. Julie thought he was as perplexed by Lizzie's response as she was.

'Has anyone told Rosa?' Suddenly Lizzie stopped laughing. 'Rosa needs to know.'

Julie looked at Swift, who was betraying no emotion whatsoever. What the hell was this all about? Lizzie must have known Rosa was dead already. Surely the rumours about the identity of the body on the Monks' Trod would have reached her by now. Was she in denial or was there something more sinister in the diversionary tactic?

It was Eurig who actually broke the news. From underneath the fringe, which flopped into his eyes, he told her.

'Lizzie, Rosa is dead too. Her identity has been confirmed by her parents.'

'No!' It was a scream which was feral in its intensity. Within a few minutes, Lizzie had experienced the whole range of emotions, and now she sobbed once again.

'Oh, come on, Lizzie, you must already know that it was Rosa's body out there on the Monks' Trod,' Julie said. Lizzie blew her nose and shook her head. 'Are you saying you didn't see her at the cottage at any time and more specifically on the night of the fifth of July?'

Lizzie's breath still caught in tiny sobs. 'Rosa? At Pwll Bach? You must be mistaken.'

'There's no mistake, Lizzie. The pathologist found Rosa's blood on the gatepost.'

'I didn't see her. I haven't seen her since that afternoon in my kitchen at home.' The tears started again. 'I have this vision of her trying to carry Sean's little case and shepherd him through the door. She was in so much pain with her poor arm.'

'But what about Sean? Where is he?' Swift asked.

'He's safe.'

'We've got past that now, Lizzie, this is serious.' Swift's voice was a perfect mix of steel and sympathy.

'And he's at Bryn Awel B&B in Llandrindod with what Mrs Pritchard describes as his grandfather, isn't he?' Julie was already standing.

Lizzie closed her eyes and shrank into her chair. Then, slowly, she nodded. 'I haven't told John about my dad.' She looked up at Julie. 'Does he have to know?'

'First things first, Lizzie,' Swift said. 'Interview suspended at 14.35.' He switched off the tape and stood up. 'We would like you to stay in town for the time being. We will want to speak to you again.'

Julie and Swift hurried from the interview room.

'Why didn't you arrest her, Sir? What if she does a runner? She's obviously making it up as she goes along. What was all the performance about not knowing Rosa was dead?'

'We still haven't got any evidence that she was involved in anything other than taking Sean.' Swift wheezed and slowed down. 'You know we've not got nearly enough to make it stick and we're nowhere near confident of wrapping this mess up imminently. We can get her back in once we've got James Pritchard in custody and we're sure the boy's safe.'

'I do hope you're right, Sir.'

*

Mrs Pritchard was still wary, although she did seem to be slightly mollified by Swift's presence in place of Morgan's.

'May we come in, Mrs Pritchard?' Swift beamed and managed to insinuate himself into the tiny gap between Mrs Pritchard and the door. She had no option but to take a step backwards and they followed her into the hall. Julie marvelled at how someone of Swift's rotundity could do that so effortlessly.

'Do you think we could have another look at the room Rosa was staying in?' he asked.

'Why?'

'Oh it's just routine.'

'I'm afraid that won't be possible, Inspector. I have guests staying in that room.'

'Could we have a look at your register, do you think?' Julie asked, walking towards the dining room.

'It's not up to date, Sergeant. It was mislaid for a little while and I haven't caught up with myself yet.' Mrs Pritchard dithered between the stairs and the dining room door, attempting to prevent either of them from achieving their goal.

'Have you heard any more from Mr Pritchard since we last spoke to you?' Julie asked.

Mrs Pritchard was like a rabbit in headlights. It was several seconds before she replied and when she did, it was unconvincing.

'No, nothing at all I'm afraid. Wherever he is, he's not going to tell me now.'

'Have you stopped looking for him then?' Swift smiled. 'It must be tempting to draw a line under it all and concentrate on your new life.'

'It is.' Mrs Pritchard nodded. 'I'm getting used to my own company.'

'I saw a small child when I was here this morning,' Julie said. 'Is he one of your guests?'

'Yes, I er, he's staying here with his grandfather.'

'So he's not staying here as a favour to anyone? Perhaps because of Rosa's connection with this house?' Julie said.

'Certainly not.' Mrs Pritchard's reply was too rapid. At the sound of a wail from the next room, Swift pushed past Mrs Pritchard and into the kitchen. At the table sat a small, pale child and a well-dressed man of maybe fifty, fifty-five years old, who appeared to have lost the will to live. His face was almost as pale as the child's, his hair was lank and uncombed and every shriek of the child's made him flinch as though the noise caused him physical pain. He stood as Swift and Julie entered.

'Mid Wales Police. Detective Inspector Swift.' Swift showed his warrant card. 'Are you Mr James Pritchard?' The man nodded, his expression immediately a mixture of concern and relief.

'And this must be Sean Quigley,' Julie said, walking round the table to the boy.

'So it's over.' James Pritchard put his head in his hands and rested his forehead on the table. Slowly he sat up, looked from Swift to Julie and finally at the child who was still scowling at him.

After a nod from Swift, Julie recited the caution.

'James Pritchard, I am arresting you in connection with the murder of Jason Quigley. You do not have to say anything. But it may harm your defence if you do not mention when questioned something which you later rely on in court. Anything you do say may be given in evidence. Do you understand?'

'No.'

'No, you don't understand?'

Pritchard shook his head. 'No. I can't believe that creature is dead. How do I know you're telling me the truth?'

'Why would we lie about it?' Swift asked. 'What could we hope to gain?'

'Inspector, I haven't slept properly for months. I've deceived my wife and my children. I've caused people no end of worry and all because of that man. He has pursued us across the country. I have no doubt that he killed his poor wife, and I am convinced that he will not rest until he finds this child.'

'Believe me, Mr Pritchard, he's resting now.' Julie said. 'Mrs Pritchard, we will be taking your husband into custody and Sean will be examined by a doctor as soon as we can arrange it. You are welcome to come with us. There is a uniformed police officer outside. She will stay with Sean until we can contact social services who will make arrangements for his care.'

Mrs Pritchard fingered the pearls at her throat. 'Thank you, Sergeant. I will stay here. I have guests arriving shortly. I would be obliged if you could keep me up to date with what is happening.'

Swift took Pritchard's arm and guided him towards the door into the hall.

'Just one more question, Mrs Pritchard, if you don't mind,' Julie said.

Mrs Pritchard gave a small nod of consent.

'Did you change the locks when your husband left?'

'No, Sergeant, I didn't.'

She didn't look at her husband or the child who stood half-hidden behind Swift. Sean's little face looked even paler now, with his huge dark eyes and pale purple semicircles beneath them. He watched her as she walked out of the kitchen. They could hear the stair treads creaking as she climbed.

CHAPTER TWENTY-NINE

Day Seven

John Slaithwaite was pacing the reception area when they arrived back at the station.

'I need to take my wife home, Inspector. She's beside herself, she needs to see her own doctor.'

'I'm sorry you're having to wait so long, Mr Slaithwaite, but things aren't straightforward. Our doctor says she had a panic attack, but that she'll be fine. It might be better if you were to take her back to the hotel and try to keep her calm. I'll come and fetch you both if there are any developments.'

Slaithwaite sighed. 'Thank you, Inspector. I'm sorry, it's just all been such a shock and we need to get back to Blackpool as soon as we can and attempt to sort a few things out.'

'I understand, Mr Slaithwaite. Try not to worry.' Julie knew as soon as the words had left her lips how ridiculous they sounded. She offered him a small grimace, which he accepted.

While Swift waited for Pritchard to be processed, Julie made her way to the office. Rhys and Goronwy were on the phone, and Morgan Evans was standing by the board with its maps, photos and carefully scribed capital letters and arrows.

'What's new?' he asked her.

Julie stood beside him. 'I've only got a few minutes, but I'll fill you in once we've interviewed James Pritchard. The boss has got him downstairs.' She gazed at the board. Rhys had added a photograph of Lizzie. All that red hair she had, with the perfect pale skin and green eyes. She tapped Morgan on the arm. 'Could you see if you can trace Lizzie Slaithwaite's date and place of birth, mother's name, whether the father's named – all the usual.'

'But why, Sarge, we know who she is.'

'I'm not sure we do, Morgan. Julie smiled. 'OK, it might be bonkers, but humour me. I think she's lying about her age.

'Whatever you say, oh weird one.' Morgan smiled at her. That was a rare state of affairs. 'And what's Pritchard supposed to have done?'

'We're still flying on instruments, but I have a feeling things are about to become slightly clearer.' Julie rummaged in her desk drawer and emerged triumphant, bearing a Twix. 'Sustenance,' she said, unwrapping it as she ran back out of the office.

James Pritchard wouldn't look at them. When Swift asked him to identify himself for the tape, he spoke quietly, his gaze fixed firmly on the table.

'You have been cautioned, so you know why you're here, Mr Pritchard?' Swift asked. Pritchard nodded. 'For the tape, Mr Pritchard.'

'Yes. I know why I'm here.'

'We are investigating the death of Rosa Quigley, on or about the fifth of July in an area between the cottage, Pwll Bach, and the farm, Sŵn y Coed. What can you tell us about that?'

Pritchard shrugged. 'I can't help you.'

'Are you saying you weren't involved in that death?' Julie asked.

'The death was nothing to do with me.'

Julie frowned. 'Do you also deny that you were staying at Pwll Bach with your daughter, Lizzie Slaithwaite, and Sean Quigley, Rosa Quigley's child?'

'That's not a crime, not as far as I know.'

'And while you were staying there, did anyone come looking for you?'

'For me? Who would come looking for me?'

'Your wife perhaps? You left her not knowing where you were for months. She says you just disappeared, last December, without a word,' Swift said.

Pritchard looked up. 'I couldn't tell anyone what I was doing. It would have been far too dangerous for the boy if anyone knew where we were.'

'Did Lizzie tell you that?' Julie asked.

Pritchard nodded and Julie pointed at the tape deck. 'Yes,' he said, 'Lizzie told me about the things that despicable excuse for a human being did to Rosa. I was terrified he would do the same to Lizzie.'

'And why would he do that, Mr Pritchard?' Swift asked.

Pritchard looked at Swift in disbelief. 'Because she had taken his son away from him.'

'You haven't known Lizzie very long, have you?' Julie asked. 'And yet you believe every word she tells you?'

'She was telling the truth. I've done my own research on Quigley.'

'And how did you manage that? We haven't found it easy, discovering what made Quigley tick. How were you able to do it?'

'Well, Lizzie gave me a lot of the information.' Pritchard was blushing now.

'And you would have done anything for your daughter, a daughter you had nothing to do with for thirty-odd years?' Julie raised an eyebrow and leaned back in her chair. 'I can understand why you wouldn't want to rock the boat in your fledgling relationship.'

'You don't know anything, Sergeant.' Pritchard's lips disappeared in a grim line. 'I had been denied any knowledge of my daughter for decades.'

'And yet, knowing how that feels, you colluded to keep a small boy from his father.' Swift's face was similarly grim.

'That wasn't the same thing at all.' Pritchard had finally found his voice. 'You have no idea what you're talking about. Quigley didn't want his child, he just couldn't bear not to be in control.'

'So you killed him?' Julie asked.

'If I'd seen him I would have done. He would have had no hesitation in murdering my daughter to get at Sean.'

The duty solicitor put a hand on Pritchard's arm and gave a slight shake of the head. 'I think my client is over-wrought, Inspector. I'm sure he didn't mean his last comment.'

'Did you, Mr Pritchard? Would you have killed Quigley if he'd threatened Lizzie?'

Pritchard shook his head. 'Only in my mind, Inspector. I'm far too pathetic to have actually done anything about that bastard.'

'What about Lizzie, would she have done absolutely anything to protect Sean from Quigley?' Julie asked.

'Don't be so ridiculous. You have no idea what Lizzie is like. She's the kindest, most patient person in the world. She could never hurt anyone.'

'She hurt her husband, Mr Pritchard. When she disappeared into the hills with you.'

'Don't make it sound so sordid, Sergeant. How does your smutty little mind work?'

Julie smiled. 'Do you deny you were living at the cottage with Sean and Lizzie?'

Pritchard rolled his eyes. 'No, I don't deny we were living there. But I slept on the sofa, just in case that's what you're thinking. I was only there to keep them both safe.' He frowned at her. 'Like a guard dog.'

'You left your wife in December, without telling her where you were going. She's searched to find you and struggled financially on her own for eight months. And all this for a woman who merely claims to be your daughter and who had kidnapped a neighbour's child.' Julie looked up from her notes. 'That seems rather naïve, Mr Pritchard, wouldn't you say?'

'I couldn't tell Marilyn. She wouldn't have been able to keep it to herself.' Pritchard rubbed his eyes. 'I should have told her something, but I left it too long. After a while it's just not possible to go back, is it?'

'Does she know that Lizzie is your daughter?'

Pritchard nodded. 'She does now. That went down like a lead balloon, as you'd expect. But I was seventeen years old when I had a fling with Lizzie's mother. She was working at a fairground, on the rifle range. A gang of us from Sixth Form had gone over to Blackpool for the weekend. We'd been in a debating competition with Kirkham Grammar School on the Friday, which we lost, and then we went out on the town. I got so drunk and the others thought it would be hysterically funny to set me up with her. I didn't even remember anything about it the next morning.'

'Not a great start for Lizzie then?' Julie asked.

'No, Sergeant, I'm aware of that. I didn't know she even existed until last autumn. Lizzie had been going through her mother's things. Apparently, I had left her with my name and address. I had no recollection of it.' He shrugged. Lizzie tracked me down and dropped her bombshell.'

'Did Lizzie leave the cottage at all while you were there?'

Pritchard shook his head. 'Neither of them did. She said that before I moved in she had only been able to go out to buy food now and again. She'd had to leave Sean at home. She said she couldn't risk him being seen.'

'And with him not being well, it would have drawn attention to them?' Julie asked.

'What do you mean, not well? He's hard work but we put it down to the things he's seen, the people he came into contact with. There's nothing wrong with him.'

'So he wasn't registered with a doctor or a dentist? He should have been going to school. Did Lizzie intend to live like that for ever?'

'It wasn't a well thought-out plan. It was a spur of the moment decision. When she did think about it, she realised it wasn't an ideal situation.'

'So why didn't she come to us? We could have protected the child,' Swift said.

'She was worried that she would be arrested for kidnapping Sean. Who else would be able to tell Sean about his mother, her dreams and hopes, what she was like and what she wanted to be.'

'Rosa had a brother, Mr Pritchard. He is desperate to know where Sean is too. I don't suppose that occurred to either of you?'

'No, Inspector, it didn't. Lizzie said Rosa had told her she had no family.'

Swift nodded slowly. 'Why would anyone need to tell Sean about his mother, Mr Pritchard? Surely Lizzie's plan was to reunite them?'

Pritchard didn't reply, but it was obvious that this potential outcome had escaped him until now.

'So how did you get Rosa's body from the cottage down onto the Monks' Trod?' Julie's face gave nothing away, but Pritchard's demeanour switched instantly from cautiously self-assured to totally wrong-footed.

'I... it...' He glanced at the solicitor.

Swift's voice had lost all trace of understanding. 'Do you know Mal and Sarah Preese?'

'I don't think so.' The shimmer of sweat on Pritchard's forehead contradicted the steadiness of his gaze.

'You know of the property Sŵn y Coed?'

'I... yes of course. I know where the farm is. I've spent a lot of time in the Elan Valley over the years.'

Swift raised an eyebrow. 'And have you ever used the quad bike belonging to Mal Preese?'

'No.'

'And you're quite sure about that, are you?'

Pritchard nodded. 'I'm sure, Inspector'.

Have you ever moved anything in any of the outbuildings at Sŵn y Coed?'

'Of course not. Why would I?'

'So is there any reason why we might find your fingerprints at Sŵn y Coed or on Mal Preese's quad bike?'

Pritchard sighed. 'I've told you. I have never been there.'

'We have found fingerprints on Mal's quad bike, which we are confident will match yours. We have also, this afternoon, found a heavy-duty plastic sack which we believe was used to cover the victim's head. We believe that similar prints will be found on that too.' Swift leaned forward. 'Did you kill Rosa Quigley, Mr Pritchard?'

'No!' Pritchard was on his feet. 'You've got it all wrong.'

'Sit down, Mr Pritchard.' Swift barked the instruction. 'Now!'

The duty solicitor was suddenly animated, towering over Swift. 'I must protest at your aggressive and oppressive behaviour towards my client, Inspector.'

'I apologise,' Swift said, offering Pritchard a small smile.

Pritchard and the solicitor sat down, Pritchard slumping into the chair with his right hand clamped over his mouth. Swift waited.

'I didn't kill her.' It came out as a whimper and Julie almost felt sorry for him. Almost.

'But you moved her body away from the cottage and lied to the police,' she said. 'Did Lizzie help you?'

Pritchard shook his head. 'She doesn't know Rosa was even up there.'

'Did she tell you that too?'

Pritchard nodded.

'So where was Lizzie while all this was going on?'

'She was in the house with Sean. He'd been doing the usual all morning. I just had to get out for a walk, get away from it. I don't have the patience I used to have, and Sean never stops. I had to get out of the house before...'

'Before what, Mr Pritchard, before you did something you'd regret?'

'I would never have touched him.'

Julie gave a half nod. 'So you left the cottage. Did Lizzie suggest you should go for a walk?'

Pritchard looked at her and Julie was sure she had seen something change in his face. 'Yes, Sergeant, she suggested I could do with some fresh air.'

'And then what happened?'

'She was there, Rosa. Just lying there below the gate. I didn't know it *was* Rosa, not then. She'd obviously been close to the cottage, I saw blood on the gatepost. But I swear we didn't know she was there. The way Sean was carrying on, we wouldn't have heard her even if she'd knocked on the door.'

'Was she dead?'

Pritchard shook his head and shuddered. 'Almost. To be honest, I thought she *was* already dead, but as I leaned over her, she reached out and grabbed my jacket. I nearly died of fright. She looked horrendous, her face was plastered in blood.'

'Did she say anything?' Swift asked.

'I asked her what had happened to her. She only managed one word before she died.' He shook his head as though he could erase the picture in his mind.

'What was that word?' Swift said. Julie could tell he was beginning to lose patience with Mr Pritchard.

'She was so weak, I could barely hear her. She just whispered his name. Quigley.'

'What did you take that to mean, Mr Pritchard?' Julie asked.

'Well obviously, I thought Quigley had hit her, and that he must still have been there somewhere. I didn't know what to do. I couldn't do anything to help her.'

'Why would she have called him Quigley? Why not Jason?

Pritchard shrugged and stared down at his hands. 'As I stood there trying to think how to help her, she made a horrible gurgling sound and I knew then that she was dead. There was nothing I could do.' He closed his eyes again.

'Could it have been *Lizzie,* Mr Pritchard? Could Rosa have said Lizzie's name with her last breath?'

'No!' Pritchard's stare was furious, then bewildered. His mouth moved silently as he tried out the two names. He glanced away, refusing to meet Julie's gaze.

'I've told you, I had to move her away from the cottage, otherwise Lizzie's hideaway would have been useless. She could have staggered there, trying to get help and there would have been attention from

Quigley and if not him, then the authorities, but I had to leave Lizzie and the child to move what I had to assume was Rosa's body. I didn't know what to do.'

'Why didn't you contact us, Mr Pritchard? You found a dying woman on a hillside and your first thought was to move the body?' Julie asked.

'Only half an hour before, Lizzie had reminded me that Quigley might be out there. My imagination was working overtime. I even thought he might have left Rosa there as a decoy to get me away from the house. So I just picked her up and ran down the hill. I didn't know what I was going to do, but I saw the quad bike by the shed at the farm and I put her on it. I couldn't bear to look at her face, her eyes were still open and she looked as though she was watching me.'

The tears, which had been blinked away for several minutes finally began to roll down Pritchard's face. 'There was a plastic sack in the box on the bike, so I put it over her head.' Pritchard screwed his eyes shut. 'It felt less like a person then, when I couldn't see her face. Stupid.' He opened his eyes, but he wasn't focussing on anything in the room. 'Then I drove her down the farm track and out onto the moorland, just above the path.'

'And nobody saw you?'

'You've been up there, Sergeant. There isn't anyone there. I would have been unlucky to see anyone on that day.'

'So when you got to the Monks' Trod, then what did you do?'

'I didn't know what to do with her. But it felt as though it would be sacrilegious to just dump her there.'

'So you arranged her against the rock as though she was just sitting there?' Swift asked.

Pritchard nodded. 'I see her every time I close my eyes. Why I didn't just keep driving and bring her to you, I'll never know. But I had to get back to the cottage in case Quigley was roaming around.'

'We think that wasn't very likely,' Julie said.

'Have you caught him?' Pritchard's eyes widened. 'Have you got the bastard?'

'You took Rosa's bag back to her room at the B&B, at your home in Llandrindod, didn't you?' Julie asked. 'How did you know she was staying there?'

Pritchard frowned. 'Lizzie must have told me.' Julie thought he wasn't convinced about this angle. He put his head on one side and stared up at the ceiling. 'No, that's probably not right. She can't have known that, can she? That wouldn't make any sort of sense.'

'But what was the point of taking it all the way back to Llandrindod?' Julie waited until he was looking at her, before adding, 'Did Lizzie tell you to do that too?'

Pritchard closed his eyes. 'I forgot to take it with me when I took Rosa away. I had to get it away from the cottage and I chickened out of going back to the body to leave the bag with it... her. So I took it home, to Bryn Awel. I wasn't thinking straight, or I'd have just stuffed it in a bin somewhere. I phoned Lizzie and told her I had things to do in Llandrindod. I told her to stay inside and keep the doors and windows shut tight. When I got down to the car, I thought I'd better check what was in the bag. I thought there might be something in it with Lizzie's address on it.'

'And was there?'

Pritchard shook his head. 'But there was a key for Bryn Awel B&B in the bag. I had no idea whether it was my home or another Bryn Awel, but I didn't want to leave it to chance. I didn't know Marilyn had turned it into a B&B. I didn't even know if she had changed the locks, but I had to get rid of the bag somewhere safe.' He looked up at Julie. 'I know it sounds ridiculous now, but it made perfect sense at the time. I waited outside in the street that night for Marilyn to go to bed, and tried the front door key. I crept into the house and left the bag with the rest of what must have been Rosa's stuff in what is now Room 3, not that she had much.' He frowned. 'How did you know I took the bag back?'

'There was blood on the bag which could only have come from the area between the cottage and the farm on a certain day,' Julie said. 'How many people would have known that Rosa was staying there? Did you know, before Lizzie told you? How did Rosa know about your wife's B&B? Did Lizzie tell her about it, about you?' Julie stared at Pritchard.

'I can't remember Lizzie telling me anything.'

'So you find a dying woman on the doorstep, you get her down the hill to the farm, put her on a quad bike, drive her to the Monks' Trod and dump her body. Then you take the quad back to the farm and tell Lizzie you have to go out. Then you wait until it goes dark, deliver Rosa's handbag to your own house, just on the off chance that she might be staying there and you saunter back to the cottage at bedtime?' Julie shook her head. 'And you thought a madman was on the loose out there, ready to attack your daughter? I'm not buying that, Mr Pritchard, any of it.' Swift shook his head. Pritchard shrugged. 'And surely you must have been covered in blood and all sorts of other noxious substances from that bike? Not to mention the peat and the mud from the moorland.'

'I had intended to go straight back to the cottage after I parked the quad in the yard. I'd walked halfway up the hill before I realised what a state I was in. I picked up Rosa's bag, bypassed the cottage and walked down the other side of the hill to my car.'

'So you'd taken your car keys with you?' Julie asked.

'I'd been out to Llanidloes in the morning for supplies. We go to different places so we aren't building a routine, just in case anyone is watching. I had my keys in my pocket. I drove to one of the charity shops in Newtown and replaced my clothes. I got changed in the toilets by the bus station and dumped my old stuff in a wheelie bin outside the library.'

'Anyone would think you'd done this sort of thing before. How did you keep calm enough to do all of that?' Swift asked.

'I was on automatic pilot somehow. I couldn't get my head round what had happened and why I'd done what I did. It wasn't rational, leaving the poor girl out there like that.'

'So you went from not being able to leave the cottage long enough to inform us that you'd found a body, to being able to take a run out all the way to Newtown to kit yourself out in new clothes?' Julie raised an eyebrow. 'Did you really think Quigley was still a threat?'

'Of course I did.' Pritchard's eyebrows knitted into one and his nostrils flared and Julie had to supress a smile at his righteous indignation.

'Jason Quigley was found murdered a few hundred yards away from the cottage, Mr Pritchard. And forensic evidence suggests that it was his blood on the bag you took back to your home in Llandrindod.' Swift's delivery was slow and musical, but it hit Pritchard like a lump hammer.

'You're not suggesting… Quigley is dead? Are you sure?'

'Oh yes, we're sure.' In her mind, Julie could still hear the squelch as his head had moved under Kay's tender care. 'What were Lizzie's movements in the hours before you left the cottage to go shopping early that morning?'

'She was with Sean while I went up to Llanidloes.'

'And then, when you got back.'

Pritchard looked up at the ceiling. 'She made us sandwiches for lunch, and then about an hour or so after that Sean started playing up again. She said she needed some air, so she went for a walk.'

'How long was she out of the house?'

Pritchard shrugged. 'I'm not sure. An hour, maybe two?'

'You've told us she wasn't averse to leaving Sean in the cottage on his own while she went out,' Swift said.

'That was different.'

'How was it different?'

'She had no choice before, when they were in the cottage on their own.'

'Before you arrived and rescued them?' Julie asked.

Pritchard glared at her. 'It's not like that.'

'And how did she seem when she got back?'

'If she had seen anything happen she would have told me, Sergeant.'

'That wasn't what I asked you, Mr Pritchard. How was Lizzie behaving when she got back to the cottage after her walk?' Pritchard looked down at the table. 'James, what happened when Lizzie got back?'

'Nothing happened. She was just hot and bothered from her walk, that's all.'

'So she was agitated?'

'Well, we were both agitated. It's not easy living a life in hiding, especially with a child who seems to think that yelling is a twenty-four hour a day occupation.'

'Was she more hot and bothered than usual?' Julie asked.

'No, well, only that she came back without her coat and seemed annoyed that I'd asked her where it was. I don't know why I made such a fuss, it was only an old work coat. She grabbed all sorts of useless stuff in her rush to get Sean away from Blackpool.'

'And what line of work is she in?'

'She's a florist,' Pritchard said.

'Is there a possibility that she lost the coat on purpose, do you think?' Swift said.

'And why would she do that?' Pritchard smirked, and Julie had an inkling of what his wife had meant about him.

'If it had blood on it, for example?' Julie watched his face closely.

Pritchard sighed, a raw shuddering sigh of desperation. One hand was clamped over his mouth; the other gripped his forehead, pushing his fringe away from his face. Slowly he looked up at Julie, drooped his shoulders and let his hands drop into his lap. 'I don't think I should say any more, Sergeant.'

'Why is that, Mr Pritchard?' Swift leaned across the table. 'Is there something in Lizzie's behaviour that you now realise may have been suspicious?'

'I killed him, Inspector. It was me who killed Jason Quigley.'

Swift and Kite exchanged glances.

'But you said a few moments ago that you had no idea he was dead. You convinced me that you were telling the truth,' Julie said.

'I killed Jason Quigley. I have absolutely nothing else to say on the matter.' Pritchard folded his arms and looked up at the ceiling. His solicitor attempted to attract his attention, but Pritchard ignored him.

'I really don't understand, Mr Pritchard.'

'What don't you understand, Inspector?'

'Why is it that you were prepared to take the word of a total stranger when she said you were her father, as though it were gospel truth? Why would you do all of this for such a tenuous, uncertain connection?'

'There's nothing tenuous about it. Lizzie's mother wrote to me four months after our school visit to Blackpool. She sent the letter to the address I had left her, and my mother opened it. The letter told me that she was pregnant and that I was the father. I went back to Blackpool and met her, challenged her, said she had no proof of that, and she told me she would go to the police and report it as rape.'

'But if you weren't responsible, why would you be worried? If you can't remember anything about that night, how do you know you were even capable of fathering a child in those circumstances?' Julie asked.

Pritchard blushed. 'It was the first time I had been alone with a woman,' he said. 'And that was the problem. She wasn't actually a woman yet.' He leaned back in his chair and stared at the ceiling. 'She told me she was fourteen years old.'

Swift tutted. 'So a girl of fourteen tells you she's expecting your child. What did you do? Did you tell your parents?'

Pritchard looked back at him. 'Well obviously my mother knew.'

'And what happened then?'

'Nothing happened. Well, I'm not totally sure what my mother did. I know she went over to Blackpool but she didn't tell me what the outcome of her visit was. She decided we should do nothing and wait and see what happened. My mother was, and still is, formidable, but she is also terrified of my father.'

'But what about your father, did he not have something to say about it?' Julie asked.

Pritchard looked down at his fingernails. 'My father is the reason for my mother's reticence. He was a Methodist minister. Of the fire and brimstone variety. He made her life an absolute misery – he still does. If he had found out about my Blackpool problem, then there was no telling what could have happened. If he were to find out now, then I would fear for my mother's life.'

'Are you serious?' Swift asked.

'Oh yes, Inspector, deadly serious.'

'And you just ignored the poor girl, your "Blackpool problem", and carried on with your life?' Swift could barely conceal his contempt for Pritchard.

'She never contacted me again. We lived in fear for three or four months, mother and me, and nothing ever happened. Then I went off to university and tried to forget about her.' Pritchard ran his hand through his hair. 'I was unsuccessful, Inspector. I've spent the last few decades looking over my shoulder, waiting for the knock at the door, or the phone call that would unravel everything. When it came, it was less terrifying than I had imagined. Until now.'

Julie frowned. 'Lizzie's very well-preserved for someone who says she's approaching her forties, wouldn't you say, Mr Pritchard?'

Pritchard shrugged, but the frown was obvious. 'What do you want me to say?'

Julie didn't reply immediately, but as she watched the full implication of her question hit home, she leaned back in her chair. 'This confession, is it out of a sense of duty? Do you feel that you owe Lizzie or her mother something?' Julie asked.

'Not at all. I would like to reiterate, that I am responsible for the death of Jason Quigley. I will answer no further questions.'

'How did you kill Jason Quigley, Mr Pritchard?'

'No comment.'

'Then I have to remind you that you are still under caution. This interview will be suspended now, Mr Pritchard. You need to discuss this matter further with your solicitor. You will be escorted to the cells and we will recommence the interview later this afternoon.'

CHAPTER THIRTY

Day Seven

Swift sent Julie running across the road to the Slaithwaites' hotel as he followed at a considerably slower speed. She waved her warrant card at the receptionist and took the stairs two at a time. She hammered on the door of the room and heard John Slaithwaite shouting back.

'Good God, Lizzie, what's the matter? Did you forget your key? There's no need to make such a spectacle of yourself.' He flung the door open.'

'Where is she?' Julie panted.

'But why...'

'Where is Lizzie?'

'I... er, she's gone for a walk. She said she needed to go and buy something from the newsagents.' He glanced at his watch.

'How long ago was that?'

'She's been gone well over an hour. I must have fallen asleep.'

'What frame of mind was she in before she left?'

Slaithwaite shrugged. 'I'm not sure I know what she's thinking any more, to be honest. Obviously, she was still extremely upset about Rosa.'

'I can imagine. Did she say anything?'

'Nothing you've not already heard. But it must be so hard for her to get that image out of her mind.'

'Sorry, I'm not quite with you there. Are you saying she told you she saw Rosa after she was injured?'

Slaithwaite looked like a rabbit in the headlights.

'So she knew that Rosa was dead?' Julie stared at him and Slaithwaite squirmed.

'I, er,' Slaithwaite pressed his lips together, 'I may have misunderstood.'

'And maybe you didn't, Mr Slaithwaite.' Julie tried not to glare at Slaithwaite. 'Is she on foot?'

'What's happened? Is it Quigley, is he here?'

'Not in an absolute sense,' Julie said. 'Mr Slaithwaite, has she taken the car?'

'No, she can't drive my car. She's only got a licence for an automatic. It's there, in the car park.' Slaithwaite stepped over to the window and pointed to the space where his Audi had been parked.

'Shit. She can't drive it, she's dangerous even in her Smart Car.' He patted his pockets and ruffled the debris on the dressing table. 'The keys are gone.'

'Do you have any idea where she would be? Would she have gone home?'

He shook his head. 'God knows. I don't think I know who she is any more, if I'm honest.'

'Give me the registration number of the Audi.'

Pritchard closed his eyes and recited the number.

'Colour?'

'It's an A5, Matador Red.'

Julie turned to go, just as Swift appeared in the doorway, breathing heavily, and they both hurried from the room.

'Stay here, Mr Slaithwaite, in case she phones,' Julie said.

'If you find her, please be patient with her,' Slaithwaite shouted after them. 'She's not normally like this, really she isn't.'

*

Swift was not used to driving at speed and the Volvo wallowed disconcertingly. Julie hung onto the door handle and braced her feet against the footwell.

'Why the great haste, Sir? Do you think she is likely to do something stupid?'

'Don't you?' Swift changed from fifth to third gear and hurled the car round a crawling livestock lorry. 'You were right, we should have arrested her sooner.'

Julie looked in her door mirror at the irate flashing from the driver of the lorry. It probably meant something in Morse code.

'But you were right too, we didn't have any evidence at all. Have we now?'

'Only in as much as her father, or purported father, has just incriminated himself by confessing to Quigley's murder. There's no way he did it. He's far too wet for that.'

'Sir, that's not like you. You always see the best in people.'

'He walked out on his wife without a word, didn't he? He left her short of money and worried to death that something had happened to him, so he could help a woman claiming to be his daughter who had kidnapped a neighbour's child and run away.'

'If you put it like that.' Julie laughed at his grim expression. 'But do you believe her about Rosa wanting her to take Sean away from Quigley?'

'Only because of the drug-related damage and the fractures we've found on Rosa's body. Otherwise I wouldn't even be sure of that.'

Swift squealed the Volvo round a double bend over a narrow bridge and Julie closed her eyes. 'I would have taken my Kwells if I'd known, Sir.'

'Try the PC who's with Sean, Cara Davies. They should be back at the station by now. Have you got a signal?'

Julie nodded. 'Yes, but it's just ringing out.'

'Then phone Brian Hughes and make sure they've arrived.'

Julie punched numbers into her phone and immediately heard Hughes' reassuring tones. 'Brian, Julie Kite. Has Cara Davies pitched up at the station yet, with a little boy?' She put the phone on loudspeaker.

'No. We're still waiting for transport for them. There's been some sort of major incident in Carmarthen and we haven't had a car available.'

'Then get onto Mrs Pritchard. Just ask her if they've seen Lizzie,' Swift said.

Julie cut the connection to Brian Hughes and let go of the door handle to reach into her bag and retrieve Mrs Pritchard's number. As she bent down, Swift swerved round a cyclist and Julie had to put a hand on the dashboard to save herself. 'Steady on, Sir, you'll set the air bags off.'

'I'm sorry, *cariad*. But I have a horrible feeling in my bones that I got this one really wrong.'

'There's no reply. Didn't she say she was waiting for guests to arrive?'

*

The front door was open when they got there.

'That's Slaithwaite's Audi.' Julie pointed at a deep red convertible. Swift double-parked beside it, effectively blocking the road, and the two of them hared into Mrs Pritchard's hallway. There was no sign of anyone at all. They checked the dining room, and Swift headed for the stairs. Julie went on into the kitchen and skidded on something.

'Sir, you'd better see this.'

The black and white tiles in the kitchen doorway were covered in small off-white pearls.

'Shit.' Swift bent down to pick one up.

'Sir, listen.'

There was muffled banging from somewhere beneath the back of the kitchen, then shouting. A woman's voice.

'Where are you?' Swift bellowed, the urgent tone of his sing-song baritone making the hairs on the back of Julie's neck stand up.

'In the cellar. Mrs Pritchard is here, too, but she's badly injured. A woman took Sean.'

'I'll phone for backup and get them out,' Swift shouted. He turned to Julie. 'I'll get Morgan and Rhys to check on the railway station and taxi companies. You run and see if you can see any sign of Sean and Lizzie.'

'They could be anywhere, Sir.'

'I'm aware of that, Sergeant, just go.'

'But you know the area far better than I do. Shouldn't you go and I'll stay here?'

Swift looked at her. It took a moment before the words came out. 'I can't, Julie.'

'Is there something wrong?'

'No, it's... nothing. Just doctor's orders, Julie, now go!'

Julie ran from the B&B towards the centre of town. Nobody she asked had seen a woman with a small pale child. She ran the length of Middleton Street, peering into shops. She sped down the hill past the Metropole and the Cycle Museum, and at a signpost she had to make a decision. *The Lake* or *Rock Park*. Either sounded as though it could be fraught with danger for a small child and a distressed woman. She chose the lake and walk-jogged up the steep hill. The little playground was empty, the swings and slide and climbing frames stood idle. Down the slope, the lake was spread out in front of her. She could see swans and coots, moorhens and ducks and huge Canada geese with their striking black and white heads. In the centre, a dragon rose from the water, its body coiling round itself, its mouth spouting water. Julie ran through families, mums and dads, children of all ages, feeding the swans.

In the kitchen, Swift flung open doors, which hid high, old-fashioned cupboards and the pantry, but there was no sign of the way into the cellar.

'Where are you?' he bellowed. 'I can't find the door.'

A frantic knocking on the water pipes made him spin round. The muffled voice of PC Cara Davies floated up to him.

'Over here, Sir. The door's in the dining room. I've no signal. Please phone the ambulance. It's really urgent.' Swift hurried back into the hallway, punching numbers into his phone and skidding on the fallen pearls. At the back of the dining room, almost hidden by a huge, dark dresser, was another door. It didn't budge when Swift tried it.

'Inspector Swift, Mid Wales Police. I need an ambulance now, please.' Swift attempted a shoulder-charge, but the door failed to budge and the manoeuvre left him nursing his shoulder.

'I don't know what sort of state the casualties are in.' He scrabbled on the carpet by the door for the key, checked on the dresser and, in desperation, kicked hard at the bottom of the door. It creaked open slowly towards him.

'It's Llandrindod, Bryn Awel, near the park.' Steep stone steps led down into gloom. He felt around the doorway and found an old-fashioned Bakelite switch, which operated a forty-watt bulb on a twisted cord. Hurrying down the steps, he could hear Cara's voice.

'Stay with me, Mrs Pritchard, please don't go to sleep on me.'

There was another groan, deep and feral, and Swift's heartbeat began to pound in his ears.

'As fast as you can please,' he shouted into his phone, just before the signal faded.

As the path wound its way round the lake, there were dog walkers and fishermen, but very few of either. Julie was getting nowhere. She turned and retraced her steps. She sped back down the hill and crossed the main road, towards Rock Park. Why had she never really looked at Llandrindod before? And why was she exploring it now? In Manchester there would have been enough local PCs to search the area, she wouldn't be running around blind. There'd be sirens and mayhem and she'd feel right at home.

The path led downhill over a stream. This park and the lake reminded her of holidays she'd had as a child in Scarborough, playing in Peasholme Park – the Chinese lanterns, the pagoda on the lake, the little dragon-shaped boats. The funny thing was, it felt here as though it had all those years ago in Yorkshire. Was this why people retired here, to recapture times past? Better times maybe?

The path led into a wooded area now, rising steeply to the right of the path and presumably giving the place its name. To the left, there was a small gorge, through which a stream tinkled under a wooden bridge.

There were a few people in the park, more dog-walkers, a couple of red-faced ladies jogging slowly uphill in matching bright pink vests, but no sign of a pale-faced child and a would-be mother. Julie was running hard by now. This was pointless. If she didn't find them in the next few minutes she would have to go back to the house and tell Swift she'd made the wrong choice. Shit, where would Lizzie run to and why?

PC Cara Davies was sitting on the floor, her legs straight out in front of her, cradling Mrs Pritchard's head in her lap. Her uniform trousers were soaked in blood, which looked horribly vivid to Swift, even in the dim light and against the dark fabric. Mrs Pritchard was conscious, but only just.

'Oh God, no. Where's the child?'

'A woman arrived about fifteen minutes ago. We could see her fists battering the patterned glass. She kicked at the door so hard I don't know how she didn't break it. I advised Mrs Pritchard not to open the door.'

'She obviously didn't listen.'

Cara shook her head. 'We didn't know who she was or what she wanted, she came screaming at us. The boy was playing in the dining room. The cellar door was open.' She nodded down at the injured woman. 'She had been looking for jam for Sean's tea. Mrs Pritchard managed to put herself between the boy and the woman, but the woman began screaming like a banshee. She kept battering Mrs Pritchard with her fists and pushed her so hard that she fell all the way down the steps.'

Swift dabbed his handkerchief over his lip. 'The ambulance is on its way. Are you OK?'

Cara nodded dismally.

'And how did you come to be down here with her?'

Cara looked up at him. 'I didn't know she was going to take the child, Sir, did I? My orders were just to wait with the two of them.' Tears began to well in her right eye and she looked away from him. 'I'm so sorry. I thought it was Mrs Pritchard she was after. If you'd heard the sound of her head hitting the steps... I had to make sure she was all right. I ran down here and then I heard the woman slam the door above us. When I ran up the stairs and tried the door, I couldn't open it. It was locked.'

Swift looked down on them as Cara stroked Mrs Pritchard's shoulder. He didn't tell her that the door had only been stuck and not locked. That could wait until another time.

'I'm so sorry. I know what you're thinking. I just didn't think it through.' Cara's voice wobbled to a stop.

'Let's not worry about that now, Cara. What can I do here?'

'I don't want to move her, Sir. Why don't you go and wait outside for the ambulance, show them where we are?'

'Will you be all right?' With a final look at the tableau at his feet, Swift scurried away, up the steps, through the dining room, down the hall and out into the fresh air. He stood on the doorstep, breathed in the clear air and dialled Morgan Evans.

'Where's the backup? What about the station or the Cardiff bus? Has anyone thought to ask taxi drivers or look at CCTV footage? Where the bloody hell are the troops?' He cut the call and bent down. By his foot on the black and white tiles lay a scruffy toy dog.

Julie ran the whole way down the narrow path, which ran under the perfect arch of a railway bridge and alongside a stream, which rushed over rocks, twisting and turning as it went. The path led down to a wooden bridge with the glass-roofed Pump Room beyond. Which way? To the right, the path sloped up towards the high red brick edifice she recognised as The Gwalia; to the left another slope, towards tidy bungalows and the Bowling Club. She followed the path to the left, which led out of the houses and back into woodland. She was still running, gasping for breath, picking her way through tree roots and rocks. This was hopeless. She took her phone out of her pocket to phone Swift. As she dialled his number, she heard a child screaming way ahead of her. This was no petulant toddler, this child was terrified.

Julie ran on, stumbling on the uneven track between the ancient trees. Swift answered his phone. 'Thank God.'

'Sir. I'm in the woods... beyond the Bowling Club... there's a child, he's screaming and it's bloody terrifying.'

'Slow down, Julie. Do you think it could be them?'

'Yes, Sir.'

'I'm on my way. Rhys has just reached me and I'll send him on ahead. Be careful, Julie, don't put yourself in any danger, and don't cut this call.'

She knew he was worried about her, but she couldn't help thinking, after her near miss in April, that he was also concerned about what might happen if she rushed into things. The open phone channel felt like an invisible tether. Behind her, in the far distance she could hear a siren.

Between the trees to her right there were glimpses of water. Not the tumbling stream now, but a wide, meandering river. As she ran, the track rose steeply in front of her and the chasm between her and the river began to look increasingly worrying. All the time, the child ahead of her wailed for all he was worth. The path divided: one fork carried on ahead up the hill, and to the right, wooden-edged steps began to descend towards the sheer drop above the river. Julie hurled herself down the steps. Ahead of her, Lizzie was running too, dragging Sean by the hand. The toes of the little boy's shoes scuffed the rough path as he was almost lifted off his feet as Lizzie ran.

'Lizzie, stop. We can sort this out.' Julie knew her voice was being muffled by the thick foliage, but Lizzie had heard. She glanced over her shoulder and Sean tripped, loosened his grip and backed out of her grasp.

'You ungrateful little...' Lizzie grabbed him around the waist,

Sean kicked out again and again, but Lizzie seemed oblivious to the thrashing limbs.'

'Lizzie!' Julie shouted again.

'Stay away from me.' Lizzie took a step off the path and towards the steep bank. 'If you get any nearer we're both going over the edge.'

Julie could hear Swift's voice, shouting urgently from her phone. She had one chance to get this one right. She edged towards Lizzie and the boy who had quietened. He was looking over Lizzie's shoulder and down into the eddying water, which must have been forty feet below them, maybe more. Julie watched him hide his face in Lizzie's shoulder.

'If you come any nearer I promise I'll jump.'

'I'm staying here, Lizzie.' Julie held her hands out as if to concede. 'I just want you to put Sean down on the path. He's terrified.'

'Don't you dare tell me how to look after Sean.'

'I know you only want the best for him, but he's frightened. Please put him down.' Julie was fighting hard to keep the desperation out of her voice. 'Put him down and we'll talk.'

'I've done enough talking. To you, to my father, to my useless bloody husband. Nobody was there when I needed them.' Lizzie took another step towards the precipice. 'There's no way out now, is there? Apart from this.'

'Please, Lizzie, just come away from the edge and we can sort this out.'

'It's too late.' Lizzie took a step further and the ground gave way beneath her foot. She screamed, Sean wailed and Julie lunged forward.

'Stay away!' Lizzie had grabbed a slender branch with her free hand, which stopped her from falling, but the tiny tree was beginning to move, its shallow roots nowhere near solid enough for Lizzie and Sean's joint weight.

'You don't want to hurt Sean, Lizzie, I know that. Move towards me and give me your hand.' Julie was only a couple of metres from Lizzie now, but she didn't dare move any closer.

'Get away. There's no reason for me not to jump and take him with me. We've been through too much together for me to just walk away. He'd be better off dead than without me.'

'Come away from the edge and we can talk about this. We can sort things out. You can't do this to Sean. After all he's been through. He doesn't deserve it. We need to get you both sorted out.'

Suddenly Julie could see a dog, a black and white collie, heading straight towards Lizzie, and two women walking some distance behind it. She signalled to the women to stop, but they waved back and carried on talking and walking towards her.

'Police! Stay where you are,' Julie screamed at them. Oh God, please don't let Lizzie jump. She could hear Swift shouting her name over and over on the phone. The women kept coming.

Sean heard the dog and twisted round in Lizzie's arms to look at it. Lizzie stumbled with the shift in weight and Sean cried out. He began to kick at Lizzie. The collie barked and jumped up, catching Lizzie off balance. She wobbled and lurched, pitching to her left, towards the edge. Julie leaped forward and grabbed Sean from Lizzie's grasp. The two women were suddenly either side of Lizzie, each grasping an arm in a no-nonsense grip.

'Let's get you down.' The younger woman reached up and put her arm round Lizzie's shoulder. 'The dog won't hurt you,' she said. 'I'm so sorry he frightened you.' She guided Lizzie back to the path while the other woman held out her hand to Lizzie. 'Come on, lovely, you shouldn't be over there, it's not safe, is it?' Julie lowered Sean onto the path and he wrapped himself round her leg, watching Lizzie.

Lizzie took the older woman's hand just as a little girl would, but without warning, she dropped to her knees and began sobbing, taking in huge, noisy gulps of air. The collie licked her face; the more she cried, the harder the dog tried to help. Sean squealed with delight and reached out for the dog and in a second, Lizzie was on her feet and had snatched him once more. As she did, her foot slipped away from her and the pair of them lurched down the bank. Both women screamed, the dog barked and Rhys Williams galloped over the horizon like the hero in a western. Lizzie was once again leaning out, over the river with Sean in her arms.

'If you don't back off, I'll let go of him.'

'But you wouldn't do that, would you, Lizzie?' Julie crouched as close to Lizzie as she dared. 'You wouldn't go through all you've been through, just to let Sean drop now. Not when you've risked your life to make sure he had a future.'

Rhys tried to shepherd the two women away, but they were engrossed.

'Come on, Lizzie, pass him to me.' Rhys smiled at her. 'He's being such a brave boy, isn't he?'

Lizzie looked down at Sean's pale little face. He was absolutely still, his eyes wide and terrified. Then the dog barked. Sean laughed, a deep, dirty chuckle. Lizzie's shoulders slumped and Rhys leapt forward and grasped Sean just as Julie reached for Lizzie's arm and dragged her up and back out onto the path.

'Well, that was a close one. Well done.' The younger of the dog walkers fussed around Lizzie while Julie rummaged in her pocket with her free hand. When she slapped her handcuffs on Lizzie's wrist, the women were outraged.

'What's the poor girl supposed to have done?'

'It's a very long story,' Julie said. 'Thank you for your help.'

'But there's no harm done.' The younger woman clipped the dog's lead onto its collar. 'The little boy's fine. You can't do that to his mother while he's watching.'

'There we are, ladies.' Rhys smiled at them. 'We'll take it from here.'

The women were tight-lipped as they walked away, but they looked back several times before they disappeared over the brow of the hill. Julie couldn't tell what they were saying, now they were out of earshot, but it was all too easy to imagine.

Julie guided Lizzie by the elbow while Rhys looked after the little boy. There was nothing of him, his arms and legs were stick-thin. Rhys jiggled him on one hip and smiled.

'Well, you gave us a bit of a fright, boyo. Let's go and see if that nice Mr Swift has managed to rescue your doggy, shall we.'

Julie laughed. 'You're a natural, you should have kids of your own.'

Rhys' face clouded, but only for a second as he looked down at Sean. 'It'll happen one day, I know it will.' He moved away, towards where Swift was puffing up the hill with the battered toy dog in his hand, before Julie could question him any further.

Swift handed the toy dog to Rhys. Lizzie kicked Julie hard in the shin and the surprise caused her to let go of Lizzie's arm. Lizzie turned and Julie fully expected to be head-butted, but instead – and despite the handcuffs – Lizzie began to run back towards the precipice. Two uniformed officers appeared, their radios buzzing, but it was Swift who brought her down inches from the sheer drop. He apologised profusely as he helped Lizzie back to her feet.

'Well done, Sir. That was one hell of a rugby tackle,' Rhys said.

'You never forget it, see. All that training hones your body,' Swift replied.

Julie laughed and Swift looked crestfallen. 'It does, Sir. Muscle memory and all that.'

The two uniformed PCs were leading Lizzie towards their car. All the fight seemed to have left her now. She looked to Julie as though, without their support on either side of her, she would just fade away. The strange little party, of three plain-clothed police officers and a small boy clutching a toy dog, followed on behind.

'Will we interview her tonight, Sir?'

Swift watched Lizzie fold into the police car. 'Maybe just the basics tonight, if the doc thinks she's fit to be questioned.'

'Do you ever think you're too kind?'

'Maybe. But I don't think we'll get much sense out of her in that state, do you?'

'I don't know. Might it not be better to strike while the iron's hot?'

'Let's see how things are when we get her back to the station.' Swift smiled. 'I think we're going to have trouble prising the poor child from Rhys.'

Rhys was making Sean's little dog walk up and down Sean's arm and wag its tail, and he was barking little yappy barks.

'Sam!' Sean squealed, and Julie had a vision of a bull terrier and a crossbow bolt.

'I think the lad's broody.' Swift smiled.

'What will happen to Sean?' Julie suddenly felt strangely maternal herself, despite her best efforts.

'Social services will find him somewhere temporary, and after that, who knows?'

'Do you think Rosa's family will be allowed to adopt him?'

Swift shrugged. 'I don't know. They're pretty rigorous about it these days.'

'But Ardal would be so keen.'

'You need a little bit more than that to be able to take on a child I think, Julie.'

Julie blushed. 'I know. It's just that he was so desperate to find Sean.'

'Wherever he ends up, Julie *fach*, it will be better than where he was.'

'But Rosa couldn't do anything about it, could she? She was terrified of Quigley.'

'Slaithwaite told you that Sean and Rosa used to go to the park with Lizzie, didn't he?' Julie nodded. 'So how much time would she have needed to get on a train or a bus and get him to her parents?'

'But Ardal said they didn't get on with each other, not for years.'

'I think, Julie, if my daughter turned up on my doorstep in the state she obviously was, with a small child in tow and told me they were both being mentally and physically abused, I would do something about it, whether we'd fallen out or not.'

And that, thought Julie, was Swift's last word on the matter.

CHAPTER THIRTY-ONE

Day Seven

'What have we here?' The doctor was jovial, ruddy and ancient. 'This lad looks as though he could do with a square meal. I think he'd be better off with Nerys than with me.' Julie thought he might be right.

'This is Sean, he's nearly five. He's been having some tummy troubles, and I wondered whether he could be coeliac. His mother has... *had* coeliac disease.'

'It's not likely, Sergeant. It's pretty rare, you know.

'But it does run in families, and his mother has a confirmed diagnosis.'

'Well there's not much I can do about that. He'll need to be referred by his GP. I can check him over for bumps or breaks, but otherwise he seems fine to me.'

After the most perfunctory check, the doctor pronounced Sean fit.

'The trouble with you detectives is that you think you can solve everything at the drop of a hat. There's nothing wrong with this lad that a decent meal wouldn't sort out.'

'Thank you, Doctor, for your help,' Julie said. But as she walked down the corridor with Sean, away from the doctor's room, she was already on the phone, talking to Kay Greenhalgh.

'You need to get him signed up with a GP. The only way to make sure is by blood test, and I'm not usually involved with blood tests on living subjects. Far too tricky.'

'I can't even begin to work out where he'll end up, or who will be responsible for finding him a GP.' Julie looked down at Sean and sighed. 'Poor little thing. I guess he'll go to social services now. Should we tell them to keep him off gluten?'

'No, that's the last thing you should do. It would alter the bloods for the test. But make sure you tell them they must get it sorted as soon as they can. It's not right to keep him in that state for longer than he needs to be.'

'Thanks anyway, Kay. It's appreciated.'

There was a pause and Julie held her breath.

'I do know a rather lovely GP in Llandrindod. If Sean is going to be staying in the area for a little while, I could have a word with him, just to speed things up a bit.'

Julie punched the air silently. 'Sometimes you can forgive people for being from Yorkshire.'

'That, Sergeant Kite, I will take as the highest form of compliment.'

*

The doctor also declared Lizzie fit enough to be questioned. Julie had no problem with that opinion, but she knew Swift wouldn't want her to go in too hard. She sighed and pushed open the door of the interview room. Lizzie was already there with Eurig, and Swift was preparing the tape. Formalities completed, he leaned forward in his chair.

'Elizabeth Slaithwaite, you have been arrested in connection with the murder of Jason Quigley and with a possible connection to Rosa Quigley's murder, along with the kidnap of Sean Quigley.' He paused, his elbows on the desk and fingers steepled in front of him. Lizzie said nothing.

'So what happened that day, Lizzie, the day that Rosa died?' Julie asked. Lizzie shrugged. 'OK, let's go back a little bit then, shall we? You've said that Rosa begged you to take Sean away, to keep him safe from Quigley. Did she ask you to bring him to Wales?' Julie smiled encouragingly.

'Not exactly. We didn't discuss where I'd take him. Rosa just wanted him out of the way.'

'And was that meant to be on a temporary basis? Did she expect you to bring him back, or was she happy that you took him away for over eight months?'

'I told her where we were.'

'Lancashire Police have found a letter from you to Rosa Quigley addressed to her at her home in Blackpool. According to information contained in this letter, you only wrote to her for the first time three weeks before her death. The letter was posted in Llangurig, and included directions to Pwll Bach. It's pretty clear from the contents of that letter that Rosa didn't know where you or Sean were until that time.'

'I phoned her and told her.'

'We have traced records for Rosa's phone at the house in Blackpool, and for her mobile. The call logs show no record of a phone call to the landline or to Rosa's mobile from your own mobile until just over two weeks ago. But the call log from the pay as you go phone we took off you shows plenty of attempted landline calls recently from Rosa to your mobile, and texts and messages from her mobile number, asking where you were.'

Lizzie sighed. 'That was a complete misunderstanding. I knew she didn't want Quigley to know where we were. It was just easier not to call her. I couldn't text because I couldn't be sure Quigley wasn't reading her messages.'

'So it's only your word against Rosa's that you took Sean away at her request.'

Lizzie treated Julie to a long stare. 'She's not in a position to argue, is she?'

Julie had to fight hard not to reach across the table and slap her. Instead, she glanced at Swift then back to Lizzie. He'd know from that look that something more direct was coming. 'Could it be that you simply decided you wanted Sean for yourself? Your husband told us how much you wanted a child.'

Lizzie shook her head. 'What gives you the right to sit there in judgment on me? You don't know what it's like, trying and trying for a baby, the prodding and poking, the indignities of IVF, the absolute crushing depression when it hasn't worked for a third time. How dare you sit there and condemn me. I sat there day in and day out, listening to what was happening on the other side of the wall, how that child cried when he saw his mother beaten, watching him become a shadow of the child he should have been.' Lizzie's breath caught in her throat, but it was anger on her face, sheer furious anger.

'We have to ask these questions, Lizzie. We need to find out exactly what happened up there.' Swift's voice was soothing.

'I just wanted to help. I thought I was helping.' Lizzie dissolved into tears of which, Julie thought, Audrey Hepburn would have been proud.

'So you wrote and told Rosa where you both were, and she came over to Wales to find you?'

'I don't know anything about Rosa having been here. I wrote and said everything was fine. Yes, I sent the address, but I left it vague. If she'd really wanted Sean back she would have come to find him.'

'Which of course is exactly what she did. Funnily enough, your husband happened to mention to me this afternoon that you told him you found Rosa in the garden of the cottage on the day of her death.' Julie held Lizzie's petulant stare, attempting not to match it.

'He must have got it wrong. My father must have found the body. I don't know what he did with it, I wasn't involved.'

'So you didn't ask him how he disposed of the body of one of your closest friends?' Swift was beginning to harden his line. Lizzie did not answer him. Julie riffled through her notes and Lizzie leaned back in her chair. There was a knock on the door, and it opened slowly, revealing Rhys, making urgent thumb-and-little-finger phone signals to Julie.

'DS Kite is leaving the room,' Swift said as the door closed behind her.

'It's Dr Greenhalgh, she wanted to speak to you. I explained you were in an interview with Lizzie Slaithwaite.'

'What did she say?'

'Good. She just said good.' Rhys shook his head. 'I haven't a clue what she means.'

'I think I do.' Julie increased her speed and bolted into the office, ran to her desk and picked up the phone. 'Kay?'

'Did I ever tell you how blooming marvellous our police dogs are?'

'You didn't,' Julie said, breathlessly. But you're going to tell me why, I can tell.'

'One rather fabulous springer spaniel by the name of Spud came across a discarded jacket earlier today. It was found in a dense thicket of brambles mere yards from the fragrant cess pit where Jason Quigley breathed his last.'

'Go on.'

'The sleeves and one side of the jacket were covered in blood and faecal matter. I've just matched that blood to our friend Quigley.'

'And I don't suppose there are any clues to the owner of said garment?'

'One or two. It's definitely a woman's, approximately a size ten. There's no label in it. It's well worn, probably a work garment. There are crumbs of a green substance we've identified as oasis in the pockets and in the fabric itself, and there are small lengths of ribbon and a spool of thick wire in one of the pockets, along with a pair of wire cutters. I would say with absolute certainty that this coat belonged to a florist.'

'That's unlike you, to be so categorically definite.'

'Ah well, that would be the business cards lodged in the lining, along with the fact that young Rhys has just provided me with the final clue.'

'And?' Julie sighed with impatience and Kay laughed.

'Think of your blood pressure, Julie. And, the name of the business on said cards is *Busy Lizzie's*. That's *impatiens walleriana* I think, also known as *patience*, strangely enough, although I'm assuming it's a play on words and refers to the owner of the business, one Lizzie Slaithwaite.'

Julie shrieked, Goronwy and Morgan turned to look at her, Rhys laughed and Kay Greenhalgh swore down the phone.

'Sorry, Kay. How soon can you let me have the jacket?'

'Sorry, I can't hear a word. I seem to have been rendered hard of hearing.'

'Very funny. Could we have it tonight?'

'I'm just waiting for a couple of test results. Could we make it first thing in the morning? I'll be here at seven and I'll know then whether I need more samples. Can someone pick it up?'

'I'll be there at five to.' Julie put the phone down and gave Rhys a thumbs-up as she scurried away.

Julie was delighted to see the look of bewilderment on Lizzie's face as she burst back into the interview room and failed, quite spectacularly, to hide the enormous smile on her face. She bent to whisper in Swift's ear. Swift managed not to smile, but both eyebrows appeared over his glasses, marring the otherwise deadpan expression.

'I am suspending this interview at 16.37 hours. We will recommence at 9am tomorrow.'

CHAPTER THIRTY-TWO

Day Seven

Julie stopped the car on the Epynt in her usual parking space, looking out over the fields and woodland of Garth and Llanafan, and the foothills of the Cambrian Mountains rising behind them. When she'd first arrived, this view had made her almost agoraphobic, all that space with scarcely a building or a road in sight. Now it was comforting to know that in this vast expanse of land, she was making a difference. Julie knew Swift didn't believe that Pritchard was the killer, but she still wasn't certain that he agreed with her completely about Lizzie. She sighed and dialled Helen's number.

'I was just about to phone you,' Helen said.

'You always say that.'

'It's true.'

'How's the love-life?'

'Amazing, thank you. I get to go to all the best places.'

'Such as?'

'Well, last night I was at a black tie dinner at Mottram Hall.'

'Oh my, we are going up in the world. Any particular reason?'

'Some sort of awards dinner for Damian's firm.'

'Architectural back-slapping?'

'Yeah, something like that. They can certainly put on a good bash though.'

'And that's what you were going to tell me?'

'Well sort of. I don't suppose you've seen *Lancashire Life* this month?'

'Oh, now let me see, I think my copy must have got lost in the post. Of course I haven't, you daft bat. *Border Life* though, now that's a different matter.'

'Do you want to know what I've discovered or not?'

'Sorry, I'm just not used to this new you.'

'Cheeky mare. Well, that Tiffany Sanderson who was pursuing your Adam is in there.'

'Arrested for stalking? Sending dodgy correspondence?'

'Nope. Not even close. She was on the arm of Edmund Hales, wearing a dress that left absolutely nothing to the imagination, and more bling than you could shake a stick at.'

'Who's Edmund Hales?'

'Oh bloody hell, Julie, how long have you been living over there? You can't have forgotten Edmund Hales. The rower? Cambridge blue, all round good egg, runs Daddy's restaurant chain. One of those places offering larks egg on a soupçon of lightly toasted spelt bread and feta frittata.'

'Are you sure it's her?'

'Not only that, my dear, she also appeared to be wearing a diamond the size of a small lark's egg herself.'

'They're engaged?'

'That's the point. It was their engagement party at The Principal on Oxford Street.'

'Oh my, there's posh.'

'You've gone native, lady.'

Julie snorted. 'You've made my day. I can still rely on you to make me laugh. I do miss you.'

'And I miss you too. Parky's all right, but you can't have a natter in the loo with him, and he's no bloody use if you forget your lippy.'

'Well, that's going to be interesting, explaining that to Adam.'

'So what's up over there then? Did you find your killer?'

'I'm positive I know what happened, it's just going to be a challenge proving it. The person I think is the murderer is completely denying it and someone else has sworn that they did it.'

'Are they both going to end up denying it so you won't be able to pin it on either of them?'

'No, I don't think so.'

'So you'll get someone for it, at least.'

'But...'

'Yeah, I know. Where's the fun in that?'

'How about you, what's happening there?'

'I'm going to be paired up with Sophie from next week, the new girl who took your job.'

Julie sighed.

'What's up?' Helen sounded muffled and Julie laughed.

'You're lighting a fag.'

'Don't tell your Adam.' Helen let out a long breath. 'That's better. What's up,' she said, clearly.

'I don't know. Daft really, but it feels as though it's the end of something, you joining forces with Sophie.'

'I've told you before, we need to get you back here a couple of times a month. You need to hang onto that Manc sense of humour and rhetorical sarcasm.'

'I know, and I will. But will you have time to come out and play now that you're with Damian.'

'Try stopping me. Where do you fancy going then?'

'You'll laugh.'

'Go on.'

'Castlefield. I really fancy walking along the canal, round St Ann's Square and along Deansgate. And I really miss the John Rylands.'

Helen snorted. 'I can't think of anyone else who would be missing a library. I blame Adam. It's all that education, it's rubbing off on you.'

'Don't laugh, but the pathologist we've got here makes me wish I'd gone to uni and done forensic pathology. She's an absolute ruddy genius.'

'Well, it's never too late, is it? That's what you used to say to me all the time. If you want to do it, what's stopping you? Listen, kid, I've got to run. Damian's taking me out to the Palace tonight.'

'Buck House?'

'Sarky git. It's a play.'

'I'm not jealous, hardly at all.'

'Get your Adam to take you to Cardiff. They've got a brilliant theatre down there. Mam went to see *Les Mis* on a bus trip just after it opened. It's donkeys' ago but she still talks about it.'

'I know. It's just that everything takes so long from here.'

'Join the wrinklies and do a matinee while he's on his summer holidays.'

'Yeah, could do.'

'I'm off for my evening of culture... but, Jules –.'

'What?'

'Just don't get boring, eh?'

Adam was cooking and she had to admit it smelt gorgeous – warm spices and potatoes baking in their jackets. He grinned when she walked into the kitchen.

'How are you doing? Had a good day?'

Julie yawned and nodded. 'We're getting there.'

'Glass of wine?'

'Oh my, are you sure? I thought wine was the spawn of Satan.' She plonked in a chair and yawned again. Adam stirred the pan, put the spoon on the draining board and retrieved a glass from the cupboard.

'I think you might need a glass yourself, Adam.'

'I've told you, I'm not drinking any more. It dulls the intellect.'

'Oh don't be so boring.' Julie smiled, thinking of Helen's words. She always had been a bad influence. 'Anyway, a small celebration is in order.'

'Oh aye?' He poured her a glass of wine from the fridge and put the bottle back.

'Trust me, this little gem of a story's a good one.'

Adam sat down and waited for her to sip her wine. 'Go on then.'

'Your Tiffany has got herself engaged. It was in *Lancashire Life*.'

Adam's eyebrows rose but he wasn't consumed with as much alacrity as she'd thought he would be. 'Who to?'

'Oh, some rower. Cambridge blue apparently, pots of money.' Julie sipped her wine and watched him. 'So are you going to join me?'

Adam smiled, but it wasn't one of his best. 'Yeah, go on then.' He retrieved a glass and poured, but he was frowning.

'What's the matter, are you jealous?' Julie laughed, but only until she realised she might possibly be right. 'You *are* jealous.'

'No I'm not. It's just... I thought she might have told me.'

'Why should she? You told her to sod off, according to you, why would she keep you up to date with her love life? Although maybe that's just what she was doing. What if she was phoning you to tell you about her upmarket engagement?' Julie smiled, but her stomach was doing that old familiar thing it had always done when she suspected there was more to what Adam was saying than she knew. 'Well I think it's cause for celebration, anyway.'

Adam left his wine untouched and turned his back, as he checked the pan. When he turned back to her, he was smiling. Proper smiling, she thought. He picked up his glass and raised it towards her. 'Cheers, here's to a Tiffany-free future.'

'Thank God for that, I thought you were going to go and scratch his eyes out.'

'I'm sorry. I've just been so worried about her and then she goes and does this. I knew there were other boyfriends, but she said she only wanted to make me jealous.'

'Why were you worried?' Julie put her glass on the table and stared at him.

Adam looked away. 'Because in the last phone message she left, she threatened to kill herself, even though when I'd phoned her to tell her to leave me alone, she must have already been going out with him. It wasn't me she wanted at all.'

'Well she's got over it remarkably quickly. That's emotional blackmail that is, and... oh my God.'

'What? Are you all right? Tell me.' Adam was round the table faster than she'd ever seen him move.

'I'm fine, sorry. I shouldn't have overreacted like that, it's just work. I've just realised that something's been staring me in the face.'

Adam let out a long breath. 'Sometimes, do you think we're better matched than we think?'

'Sometimes.' Julie smiled. 'Always. I've got to make a phone call.'

CHAPTER THIRTY-THREE

Day Eight

The day hadn't started well. Kay Greenhalgh phoned her mobile at 6.30am to tell Julie one of the tests needed to be re-run and she had two urgent meetings and an inquest, all before 11am. When they finally got the coat and the relevant information from Kay, Lizzie was just as intractable as she had been the previous afternoon. The night in the cells hadn't made any difference; she denied everything and answered nothing. Julie could tell Swift was losing patience, and the PACE clock was still ticking.

'We have evidence that you were instrumental in the murder of Jason Quigley,' he said. Lizzie shook her head and smiled. 'Our evidence places you at the scene of Quigley's murder. There is no other way that this evidence could be interpreted.'

Eurig raised an eyebrow. 'And are you going to tell us what this evidence is, Inspector?'

'I think your client is already well aware of what it is.'

From under the table, Julie retrieved a large evidence bag and slapped it on the table. Lizzie jumped and Eurig flicked his fringe back from his face to get a better look.

'We believe this is your coat.' Julie pushed the bag closer to Lizzie. 'In the pockets there are traces of what I'm reliably informed is oasis.' Julie looked up from her notes. 'There is also a small roll of very heavy gauge wire, used in flower arranging.'

Lizzie smiled again. 'That could be anybody's coat, Sergeant. And flower arranging isn't a minority activity.'

'There are also these business cards which were lodged in the lining of the inside pocket. James Pritchard told us you are a florist.'

Julie read from the card. '*Busy Lizzie's Flowers for all Occasions.* Are you asking me to believe that a florist's in Blackpool with a name like that is nothing to do with you, Lizzie? Especially as your name and e-mail address are handily printed on the other side.'

There wasn't even a pause. 'I lost it. I went out for a walk and I got too hot. I took it off and left it in the field. I was going to pick it up on the way back, but it had gone.'

'You lost it?' Swift shook his head.

'And these wire cutters,' Julie flourished a second evidence bag. 'These are nothing to do with you either?'

'Anyone could have found that coat.'

'That's true, of course, but our forensic specialists have discovered that, on a microscopic level, the wire that was used to garrotte Jason Quigley was cut from this roll, with these wire cutters.'

'But you can't say it was me who cut the wire or used it to kill Quigley.'

'Well, actually, Lizzie, we can. The prints which you very kindly provided yesterday are the only ones on the cutters and the spool of the wire itself. The fact that there was baler twine attached to each end of the wire garrotte, which would have enabled its use without cutting the user's hands to shreds, would suggest that this weapon was prepared in advance.'

'I might have tied the string onto the wire, but I didn't kill him.'

'So who did?' Julie asked.

'James Pritchard.'

'You're saying your father murdered Jason Quigley?'

'Isn't that what he's told you?' Lizzie smiled.

'Is that what you told him to say, Mrs Slaithwaite?' Swift managed to spit the name.

'I've told you, Inspector, none of this is anything to do with me.'

'I am well aware what you told us,' Swift glared at her. 'And I don't believe a word of it.'

'Inspector –,' Eurig was helping Swift out, puncturing the growing tension, and Swift recognised the fact with a nod.

'Perhaps you can tell us why, if your father killed Jason Quigley, there were no traces of florists' oasis on Rosa's body, not on her clothes or in her hair?' Julie asked.

Eurig looked up at her and then at his client.

'Why would there be?' Lizzie managed to look wide-eyed.

'Because if, as you claim, your father had killed Jason Quigley with wire that had been in your pocket, he would have been covered in the stuff, and then, when he moved Rosa's body, surely there would have been traces of it on her too.' Julie's face was all innocence. 'Apparently it gets absolutely everywhere.'

Lizzie smiled. 'You really are clutching at straws, aren't you, Sergeant? You don't have a shred of evidence against me and you know it. How could you have? It was nothing to do with me, none of it. My father killed Quigley.'

'Why would he do that?' Julie tapped her pen on her teeth.

'To protect me and Sean.'

Swift shook his head. 'And Rosa? Are you telling me that your father killed Rosa too?'

'I have no idea.' Lizzie shrugged. 'You'd better ask him.'

Julie's phone buzzed quietly and Swift glared at her.

'Sorry, I need to get this. Could we have a break for a few minutes?' There were nods all round, and Julie hurried from the room. If this was what she thought it was, Lizzie Slaithwaite might have even more explaining to do.

'Hello, Mr Slaithwaite?'

'You were right about the photograph, Sergeant. I turned the whole house upside down looking for it. Then I had a small brainwave. It was pinned on her noticeboard in the back room at the shop.'

'Fantastic, could you take a photo of it, and the back, if there's anything written on it?'

'There was a press cutting too, which might be of help. Should I send that too?'

'That would be brilliant. Would you be able to send it now?'

'Yes, Sergeant, I would.'

'I don't suppose you found the certificates I asked you for?'

Slaithwaite hesitated. 'I did. You'll want those too will you?'

Julie heard the change in Slaithwaite's voice. He knew.

'Thank you, Mr Slaithwaite, you've been more than helpful.'

'That, Sergeant, is what worries me.'

Julie ran back to the office and waited, tapping her phone on her teeth as she did so. When the photograph arrived, complete with the four names written on the back, she printed both out, along with the third photo and the certificates, and returned to the interview room.

'Sorry to keep you waiting.' Julie smiled and sat down, placing the copies face down on the table. 'Your husband told me yesterday that he was nipping back to Blackpool to pick up more clothes for you both and check his work mail.'

'God forbid that anything as trivial as the wrongful arrest of his wife would stop him keeping up with his work mail,' Lizzie said with a smirk.

'I asked him if he would mind looking for this.' Julie turned over the copy of the photograph with a flourish. Four fresh-faced lads with long hair and huge collars fastened with fat ties smiled out at them. Lizzie's smirk evaporated. 'There's a date on the back too, twenty-third of June 1979. Given that you claim your date of birth is the fifteenth of March 1980, I'd say there's more than an outside chance that these are the lads who met your mother when she was working on the rifle range at the fairground in Blackpool.'

Swift suddenly sat a little straighter in his chair. 'One of these boys could be your father?'

'So?' Lizzie folded her arms.

'So it bothered me, how you found out which of them it was.' Julie turned over the second piece of paper and looked at the names. 'But you didn't, did you?' She put the paper on the table and looked up at Lizzie. 'How did you decide which one to go for? Ah yes, it says here, on the back of the photograph.' She pointed to the list:

Colin Hughes – moved from Hereford to Arizona, 2001

Gary Brough – died August 1981, car accident near Aberystwyth

James Pritchard – Llandrindod Wells, Powys, Engineer at Dilwyn & Morris Ltd, Newtown

Anthony Jackson – Prison Officer, HMP Swansea

Lizzie looked down at the list and looked away.

'But that list on its own doesn't mean very much, does it?' Eurig was clutching at straws and was aware that Julie knew it.

'This might help, though?' Julie turned over the final copy. It was an article from the *Blackpool Gazette*. 'This is dated the same week. It says these same boys were enjoying a weekend in Blackpool after attending a debating competition at a local school.'

Julie shook her head. 'Is this how you did it, Lizzie? Is this how you decided which of these boys was your father? The only one who was still in a position to be blackmailed into helping you?'

'That's a very strong accusation, Sergeant.' Eurig pushed his fringe away from his eyes and stared at her.

'Is it? Is it not emotional blackmail to tell a man that he's your father, without any real proof, just so that you can use him for your own schemes?' Julie frowned. 'That's quite a number to do on someone.'

'He could be.' Lizzie shrugged again. 'One of them was. Mum couldn't remember. She was drunk, apparently, which was no great surprise.'

'How did you persuade James Pritchard that he was your father?' Swift asked. Julie noticed he had clenched his fists, which were resting in his lap.

'I didn't have to persuade him, he *is* my father. My mother contacted him when she found out she was pregnant.'

'Did he not need evidence?' Julie asked. 'I'm not sure I'd take the word of a total stranger about something as important as this.'

'That's his problem, surely?' Lizzie turned to Eurig. 'If he chose to believe that he was my father, what crime have I committed?'

'That,' said Swift, 'is irrelevant to this case.'

'It's not though, is it?' Julie said. 'The only reason James Pritchard left his wife and emptied his bank account was to help you buy that cottage. The cottage is in your name, Lizzie, isn't it?'

Lizzie shrugged.

'And the only reason he moved Rosa's body from outside your cottage was because you persuaded him that Quigley was after you and the boy. If he'd already killed Quigley, why would he have needed to move Rosa away from your hiding place?' Swift asked.

'Well he couldn't just leave her there, could he?'

'I think you killed Quigley. You saw what he had done to your friend over the years and you were terrified he would come for you next.'

'You've got it all wrong, Inspector. Quigley must have killed Rosa and my father killed Quigley to protect me.'

'So how was it that Quigley and Rosa were both there, on the hillside outside your cottage,' Julie asked. 'That's one hell of a coincidence.'

'Rosa obviously decided she wanted to come and see Sean. Quigley must have followed her.'

'Or you arranged the whole thing. We're running a check on a pay as you go phone we found in the lining of your coat, along with your business cards.' Julie smiled. 'And if we find that you contacted both Rosa and Quigley recently, that would put a different light on your story, wouldn't it, Lizzie?'

'And that coat, your coat, was also covered in Quigley's blood. How do you account for that?' Swift asked.

'My father must have found it and worn it when he killed Quigley.'

Julie laughed. 'Lizzie, you are a size ten after a bad week on the diet front and James Pritchard is six foot two and well built. He wouldn't even get his arms into that coat.'

Julie turned over the remaining copies. One was a marriage certificate, the other a birth certificate.

'Your husband very kindly supplied us with these.' She turned them round so that Lizzie could read them. 'You weren't born in 1980, were you, Lizzie?' Julie watched with satisfaction as the colour drained from Lizzie's face. 'You were born in 1988.'

'So?'

'So James Pritchard was married and living in Llandrindod by 1988. And it will be easy enough for us to establish who your real father is.'

Lizzie shrugged. 'Well, you'll have to prove it, won't you?' She laughed. 'Good luck with that one.'

'I'm suspending this interview.' The three of them looked at Swift. 'Take her back to the cells.' Swift signed off and stormed from the room.

'What was all that about, Sir? Are you all right?'

'I know. It was unprofessional.' Swift was leaning on the wall by the door to the office when she caught up with him. 'I just couldn't bear to listen to her. Let her sweat for half an hour.'

'Do you want me to continue the interview? Morgan could sit in?'

Swift shook his head. 'She's right. We can't prove it yet, especially as long as James Pritchard insists he killed Quigley.'

'But Pritchard can't even tell us how Quigley died.' Julie frowned. 'So what would happen if we told him there's absolutely no chance he's Lizzie's father?'

Swift punched her on the arm. 'Julie Kite, you're very bad. Thank goodness.' He looked at his watch. 'Well, we have to do something, and soon. The clock is ticking down merrily.'

'Have I got time for coffee?'

'Definitely. Fetch me one, would you?'

wift pushed the door open and Rhys dashed through, phone in l.

's the woman at the alpaca farm, Mrs Wilkinson. She wants to to you, Julie. It's urgent.'

s Wilkinson? It's Julie Kite.'

'Oh, thank God you're there. I was going to phone for an ambulance but he said he wouldn't go with them. He'll only speak to you.'

'Who? Slow down and start again. What's happened?'

'It's Mick. He's cut himself.'

'I don't see –.'

'He's slashed his wrist, pretty badly too from what I can see from the window. He won't come out of his flat, he's locked himself in. He wants to speak to you. He says he should have done something to stop it. I've no idea what that means.'

'OK. I'll organise an ambulance. See if you can persuade him to let you in. Do you know any first aid?'

'Yes, but I don't know how bad it is.'

'Just do your best. I'm on my way.'

This time, Julie was glad of Swift's driving. Why was everywhere so far away? Wherever you needed to be took forever, even with a blue light on the roof and an advanced driver.

'What do you think he saw?' Swift asked.

'I'm guessing he knows what happened to Quigley, but we might never know now.'

'Sometimes I hate this job.' Swift swung left into West Street once again and roared past parked cars, forcing oncoming traffic to dive into the side. 'Sorry,' he mouthed to each one as he sped past them.

Over the bridge in Cwm Deuddwr, right along the wooded lane, it just went on and on. How good were Mrs Wilkinson's first aid skills? Had she even been able to get into the flat? Julie crossed everything and found herself praying. She never prayed. This case had hurt so many people, people who had nothing to do with the main players.

She was out of the car before Swift had stopped. Two paramedics, a man and a woman stood by the open back doors of their ambulance.

Julie showed them her ID and the woman shrugged and pointed

towards the stable block. 'He won't let us anywhere near him,' she said. 'Hope you have more luck, he looks pretty bloody from what we could see.'

Julie flung the gate open, ran down the path and into the yard while Swift was still climbing out of the car. The first door stood open, its handle hanging by one screw. Splinters of bright red wood lay on the ground, along with a large screwdriver. Julie slowed and peeped round the door.

'Mick? Mrs Wilkinson?'

'Come in, Sergeant.' Mrs Wilkinson was standing behind the sofa, holding Mick's arm aloft with both hands, squeezing the arm for all she was worth. The sofa, Mick and Mrs Wilkinson were covered in blood to varying degrees and Mick was conscious, but as pale as young Sean had been. His arm was wrapped in a towel and a linen tea-towel, and Mrs Wilkinson's knuckles were white from the pressure she was exerting.

'We found him, the man you drew.' Julie sat down on the sofa next to him. 'You helped us so much, we wouldn't be as far as we are without you.' Mick smiled a slow smile and gave a little nod. 'I need you to tell me what's bothering you, what you saw, and how I can help you.'

With great effort, Mick raised his undamaged hand and pointed to the dresser, then slumped back into the sofa, his head resting on Mrs Wilkinson. She stood like a rock as the big man leaned into her.

'Are you OK there for a minute longer?' Julie asked. Mrs Wilkinson nodded. Julie ran to the dresser and opened the doors. Twenty, maybe thirty sketches tumbled to the floor.

'These?' she asked Mick. He nodded, causing Mrs Wilkinson to
ble. Julie picked them up and flicked through them. They were
tory of Jason Quigley's death, in beautifully drawn sketches.
knelt in front of him. 'This is why you've hurt yourself?'
e nodded again.

'Mick, I don't want you to worry about anything. We've got the information you wanted to give us and it will help us such a lot, but I need you to get yourself put back together so you and I can talk about it all. Do you understand?'

Mick's eyes began to close, and Mrs Wilkinson whimpered with the pain of holding up his arm. Swift appeared in the doorway.

'Sir, could you go and get the paramedics in here now. Knife wound, plenty of blood loss.'

Swift turned around and they could hear his uneven jog receding across the concrete.

'We've let him down.' Mrs Wilkinson looked down on Mick. She was unable to wipe away her tears, which dripped off her chin and into Mick's matted hair. Julie stood and took hold of Mick's damaged arm, releasing Mrs Wilkinson. The smell of iron was overpowering.

'You've not let him down. Far from it.'

'If he could only have come and told us.' Mrs Wilkinson pulled a tissue from her pocket and blew her nose. The paper stuck to her bloodied fingers. 'He was terrified of my husband.'

'Still am.' Mick's words were barely audible, but he looked across at Mrs Wilkinson and winked. 'Not your fault,' he said.

CHAPTER THIRTY-FOUR

Day Eight

The sketches were spread out across two desks in the office. It was all there, the whole story. They were even numbered, so there was no doubt at all about the sequence of gruesome events.

'That's the first time I've ever had a storyboard of a crime.' Swift tugged his ear. 'Do we know how Mick is?'

'The hospital think Mrs W saved his life. She did all the right things,' Julie said.

'She must be the only person in this case who has.'

'He lost a fair bit of blood, but he's going to be fine.'

'In a manner of speaking.' Swift looked down at the drawings. 'These must have taken him hours and hours to do. Why didn't he just come and talk to us?'

'He's still wary of being interviewed. Mrs W thinks he was tortured when he was captured in Afghanistan. He won't tell her, but she does know that he hates being questioned.'

'So he drew it instead.' Rhys picked up the first picture. 'He's got a real talent. So this is Rosa?'

Julie nodded. 'And that's Quigley, and this is the scaffolding pole he smashed her head with.'

Rhys sighed. 'I'll never get over how people can do things like that to each other.'

'So, what if he didn't hit her twice?' Julie picked up the fourth picture, where Quigley had the pole raised above his head. 'What if he hit her once, she tottered to the cottage to find Lizzie for help, and Lizzie caused the second injury?'

'But why would Lizzie do that?' Rhys picked up the fifth picture,

Rosa on her knees, holding her head with her left hand 'Does she look as though she's crawling away?'

'I'd have said so.' Julie took the picture from him.

'And this is lovely Lizzie.' Swift handed her the next. 'Standing in the bushes by the cess pit, watching. And look, she's wearing her coat.'

'So she didn't help Rosa then?' Julie asked. 'Oh God, I hope Mick's able to talk soon. The gaps between these pictures could tell a different story.'

Swift walked down the line of remaining drawings. 'Quigley being caught off balance, being pushed into the cess pit by Lizzie, Quigley attempting to crawl out of the pit and being garrotted by none other than Lizzie Slaithwaite.'

'God, this is gruesome.' Morgan shuddered and Rhys passed him the wastepaper bin. 'Who told him?' Morgan frowned at Julie.

'Don't look at me,' Julie laughed. 'It's happened to all of us.'

I bet it hasn't happened to you,' Morgan said. 'Mrs Iron Guts.'

'Just give me empty eye sockets and a kite or two circling overhead and I'll be with you. Now, concentrate, is there any sign of James Pritchard in these pictures?'

'No, Sarge, just Rosa, Quigley and Lizzie.'

'Right,' Swift said. 'I'm going in. Are you ready for this, Julie?'

'I certainly am. Shall I bring these with me?'

Swift nodded. 'Bring a selection. Rhys, you go and get James Pritchard and see if you can raise Eurig will you? Let's start by telling Pritchard the good news that he's almost certainly not related to Lizzie Slaithwaite, shall we, before we see what she's got to say?'

Pritchard was shaking. It was only slight, but Julie could see a tremor in his fingers. He sat down in the orange plastic chair and looked down at the table.

'How are you doing?' Swift asked him.

'I'm just wishing I never got involved in any of this, wishing I'd come to you instead of being persuaded to move poor Rosa. What was I thinking? When I think what I gave up.' He shook his head. 'I must have been mad.'

'Maybe not as mad as you think,' Julie said. 'We think you have been manipulated, that you would have confessed to anything, if it kept Lizzie Slaithwaite happy.'

Pritchard raised his head and looked at her. He couldn't have slept a wink. His hair was lank, and the stubble on his face included a surprising amount of grey. Already he looked like a different man to the one who had walked with them into the station yesterday. He didn't speak.

'We have some news for you about Lizzie Slaithwaite.' Julie waited but there was no response. 'We have received information which makes it less likely that she is in fact your daughter.'

Pritchard closed his eyes.

'Apparently her mother couldn't remember which of the four of you she slept with. She kept a newspaper cutting with a photograph of your debating team. Lizzie had worked out who you all were and what had happened to you. She knew that one member of the team had emigrated to Arizona, another had been killed in a car accident. The third is a prison officer in Swansea, and then there was you, slap bang in the middle of rural Wales, the only one who she could use to achieve her goal.' Julie shook her head. 'Of course, it might not have been any one of the four of you at all. It could have been someone else entirely. Especially given the fact that Lizzie's actually eight years younger than she has been claiming.'

Pritchard looked at his solicitor. 'What do I say?' His face was white now. This would be the moment he remembered, Julie thought, the moment he realised that he had allowed a total stranger to systematically unravel his life.

'I think the best policy now would be to tell the truth, James,' the solicitor said.

Swift waited until Pritchard raised his head from his hands. 'Mr Pritchard, new evidence has come to light which suggests you were not involved in the murder of Jason Quigley. We also think that you had absolutely nothing to do with Rosa Quigley's death. We think you were persuaded by Lizzie to move Rosa's body, which implicated you beautifully for Rosa's murder.'

'Lizzie wouldn't do that.'

Swift laughed a totally mirthless laugh. 'Ha. You think so? After all you now know, you would still lie for her? What makes you think this wasn't her plan all along? We now think what she wanted was Sean. That was always the case. Even if she had to kill his parents to make sure she got him permanently.'

'No. It can't be true. She told me. She only took Sean because she was afraid for his life.'

'And nobody can corroborate that now, can they, Mr Pritchard?' Pritchard suddenly looked totally defeated and Julie felt so sorry for him. His world had been turned upside down twice in under a year. She very rarely felt sorry for anyone who was guilty of wrong-doing, but this man had lost everything because of Lizzie Slaithwaite.

'Did you kill Jason Quigley or Rosa Quigley?' Swift was business-like, sharp even. 'Please answer the question.'

'No.' It was whispered, barely there.

'You'll need to speak up for the tape.' Pritchard's solicitor smiled at his client. 'It won't be heard otherwise.'

Pritchard paused. 'No. I didn't kill either of them. I moved Rosa's body away from the cottage because Lizzie and Sean were in danger from Quigley.

'But they weren't, Mr Pritchard. Jason Quigley died before Rosa did,' Julie said.

'That can't be right. Lizzie told me he was out there somewhere, looking for them both.'

'Lizzie told you that?'

'She was terrified, she couldn't have known he was already dead.'

'Mr Pritchard, we believe that Lizzie Slaithwaite murdered Jason Quigley. We also suspect that Rosa, having been seriously assaulted and badly injured by Quigley, crawled as far as the gateway to the cottage and that Lizzie inflicted a second, fatal head injury on Rosa,' Swift said. 'We think she planned the whole thing.'

Julie had never enjoyed seeing grown men weep. She knew that Pritchard cried for the damage he had done to his real family, for the daughter he thought he had finally found and lost again and for his own stupidity.

'You will want to make a new statement.' Swift was still clipped, much to Julie's puzzlement. Pritchard nodded.

'Can we just have a few moments for Mr Pritchard to gather his thoughts?' the solicitor asked.

'I'll send another officer in to take Mr Pritchard's statement, Swift said. He signed off from the tape and stood up. 'I can only hope you never realise how much damage you've done to so many people with your blind faith in that woman.' He swept out, leaving Julie with the two men.

'I'll give you twenty minutes before I send in someone to take your new statement. I'll arrange for coffee to be sent in.' She stood up and opened the door.

'Thank you.' Pritchard's voice was hoarse. 'I'm so sorry.'

CHAPTER THIRTY-FIVE

Day Eight

Lizzie was in far better shape than James Pritchard. That didn't make Swift's mood any better, Julie noted. She had appointed a new solicitor, recommended by a colleague of her husband's and he was city-smart in a tight, dark suit, white shirt and crimson tie. His pilot's bag contained colour-coded files. He withdrew a red one for Lizzie. With some satisfaction, Julie noted that it was Rhys's colour coding for both murdered and murderer on the board in the office.

'My client is concerned at the lack of suitable representation to date,' the solicitor said. Swift did not respond, nor did Julie.

'Perhaps we could get on with the matter in hand,' Swift said. 'Namely, that your client is accused of the murders of both Jason Quigley and Rosa Quigley, on or about the fifth of July.'

'These are charges which she most strenuously denies.'

Swift stared at the solicitor before applying his gaze to Lizzie. 'The man you say is your father now denies any involvement in the two deaths.'

'The man I *say* is my father? Have you any real evidence to suggest otherwise?' Lizzie blinked slowly. 'And what did you do to him to make him change his mind?'

'It wouldn't be in anyone's interest for us to do anything that would prejudice the outcome of this case, Lizzie.' Julie smiled.

'Sergeant, I would tread carefully if I were you.' The solicitor stroked a gold signet ring on the third finger of his left hand with long, slender fingers.

'We also have new evidence which puts you at the scene of Jason Quigley's death.'

For the first time, Lizzie seemed wrong-footed. 'What new evidence?'

'We have a witness who saw the whole thing and recorded it for posterity.' Julie smiled.

'I don't believe you.' Lizzie glowered at them both. 'You're lying.'

'We're not lying.' Swift turned over the drawing of Lizzie standing in the bushes, watching.' Lizzie gasped and the solicitor scribbled notes in a leather-backed book. 'How do you explain this?'

'That could have been anywhere. And who was spying on me?'

'Nobody was spying on you, they were just unfortunate enough to see what happened that day,' Julie said.

'This is probably a better indication of location, wouldn't you say?' Swift placed another drawing in front of Lizzie. This one showed her pushing Quigley and him toppling into the cess pit, the next showed him crawling out and the third showed what sharpened florists' wire can do to a man's throat. Mick had even captured the glint of the wire along with the blood and 'matter'. The last pictures Swift turned over showed Lizzie leaving her coat behind in the scrub, and then running away from the scene of her gruesome crime.

'You've just got a police artist to draw out what your vivid imaginations have come up with,' Lizzie said.

Julie shook her head. 'Unfortunately for you, we have a witness who drew these and a good many more from the images he saw on that day.'

'I think, perhaps, this might be a good moment for me to speak to my client,' the solicitor said. 'I wonder if you would be kind enough to leave us.'

Swift signed off, collected the drawings and with one last long, withering look at the pair opposite, he stood and left the interview room.

'There will be an officer outside if you need anything.' Julie addressed the solicitor. She wasn't altogether happy at leaving him with this disturbed woman.

Swift was still out of sorts when she caught up with him in the office.

'But we've cracked it, Sir. She's not coming back from this one.'

'We need to speak to that soldier, we need to make sure he'll testify to what he saw in court.'

'How likely is that, do you think?' Morgan Evans asked. 'I thought he was a basket case.'

'Evans, my office. Now.' Swift spoke quietly but everyone heard. Morgan trotted after Swift, who closed his door rather too firmly. The glass in the windows of all three small offices rattled.

'Why does he do that?' Goronwy shook his head. 'That boy's got a death wish.'

They could hear Swift's voice booming through the glass, could see Morgan's shoulders sag further and further. When Morgan was dismissed and slunk out of the office, everyone was suddenly very busy. He walked through the middle of them and out onto the corridor. Swift followed, but stopped by the board.

'Right, we need to get to the hospital and interview Mick. Julie, you can do that. I want to know if Mick told the other two lads up at the alpaca farm anything about this. Rhys, take Goronwy and go and ask all of them, the lads and the Wilkinsons. I'm going to go and ask Mal and Sarah if there's anything else they remember. Evans is staying here and manning the phones. Are we clear?'

'Yes, Sir.' Swift strode out of the office. Julie grabbed her bag and ran after him.

'What?'

'Aren't you letting this get to you just a bit, Sir?' Julie closed one eye as she trotted behind him, waiting for the retort. Instead, Swift stopped suddenly and Julie walked into him. 'Sorry, Sir.'

'No, Julie, you're right. I'm sorry. I over-reacted to what Morgan said too. I just can't believe what that blasted woman has done, how many people she has affected with her scheming, the fact that she was prepared to let Pritchard take the blame for everything, that Mick is so disturbed by what he saw that he tried to kill himself. How can one person wreak so much havoc and think they can get away with it?' Swift tugged his ear. His face was flushed and damp with sweat. What if he was about to keel over on her?

'What about we both go to the hospital and let Morgan go and have a word with Mal and Sarah?' Julie said. 'He can't help himself, he just opens his mouth and words come out, they bypass his brain completely.' She waited to be shot down, but Swift just laughed. 'Where's he gone? Shall I go and tell him he can go up to Mal's?'

'He's in the canteen. I told him to go and calm down,' Swift smiled. 'Yes, tell him the good news. I'll have to go back to the office anyway.'

'Why, Sir?'

'I bounced out without my car keys.'

CHAPTER THIRTY-SIX

Day Eight

They approached the A&E reception desk in the usual formation. Julie in front, breathing in the sights and smells of the hospital, wishing she had applied herself and gone to medical school and Swift following behind her, trying not to breathe at all and keeping his gaze steadfastly away from the potential horrors of the screened areas. Julie showed her warrant card to the nurse behind the desk.

'Detective Sergeant Julie Kite, Mid Wales Police. You had a chap called Mick brought in a couple of hours ago by ambulance. Knife wound to the wrist. Would it be possible to see him?'

The nurse tapped the keyboard and ran a finger down the crowded screen. 'He's still pretty poorly to be honest.'

'Will he recover?' Swift asked.

'Oh yes, the doctor has done a lovely job on his arm. He didn't need to go to surgery, it was a nice clean cut, just a bit deep.'

Swift's clean white handkerchief was out of his pocket and he dabbed his mouth. 'When can we speak to him?'

'Well it's more his mood that's causing us a bit of worry, you see. We want him to see a psychiatrist, but given how weak he is after the loss of blood he was surprisingly and very loudly rude at that suggestion.'

'I think he's had his fair share of help in that department already,' Julie said. 'Would it be possible to see if he would talk to me?'

'Well, I don't know. Usually we wouldn't let him, not until he's been evaluated. Do you know him?'

'I have spoken to him before. He will know who I am. He asked for me when he cut himself.'

'Well just let me have a word with doctor. I'll be back now.' The nurse hurried off.

'I hate these places,' Swift said.

'I know you do.'

'You should have let me go to Mal's.'

'I'm keeping you away from scones.'

'That's very thoughtful of you, Sergeant.'

'Seriously, Sir, you need to look after yourself. Your blood pressure must have been through the roof earlier. With Morgan.'

Swift shot her a glance and looked away. 'The older I get, the more I seem to let certain people wind me up.'

'You don't have to be older for that, Sir, trust me.'

Swift turned to her and laughed. 'That's what I like about you, Sergeant, you say it as it is.'

'Gobby you mean?'

'Not at all. And thank you.'

'What for, scone avoidance?'

'No, for not letting me blow Morgan's comment completely out of all proportion.'

'You're welcome, Sir. Marginally out of proportion was just about spot on I'd say.'

The nurse beckoned from a door just behind the desk. 'You can see him now, but I've to stay with you.'

'It's a bit delicate, to be honest, Sister,' Swift said. The nurse smiled. Her name badge made no mention of the exalted rank. 'Could you stay outside and we promise to call you immediately if we need your help?'

'Well, I shouldn't, but go on then. Just don't let me down.'

'We won't,' Julie said, wishing she had that much confidence in her abilities to calm a suicidal ex-soldier while discussing a brutal murder.

Mick was pale, heavily bandaged and staring into the distance.

'Hello.' Julie approached the bed while Swift stayed by the door. 'How are you feeling?'

'I'm glad you've come. I wanted to thank you.' He looked down at his bandaged arm. There was blood still encrusted under his fingernails. 'I didn't think you'd come all that way out to the farm just for me being a prat. I honestly thought I was done for. Stupid.'

'Why would I not have come?'

'People let you down.'

'I hope I haven't let you down. Did my questions about Ardal worry you?'

Mick shook his head. 'It's me that worries me, nobody else. You were straight with us that night. I knew I could trust you.'

'You still can, you know.'

'I should have stopped her. It was all my fault that man died. I could have prevented it. I just froze. It was like I was watching something that wasn't real, as though it was a film.' He tried to hitch himself further up the bed and winced.

Julie shook her head. 'I'm not sure I would have been able to stop her either. I don't think anyone could. She was a woman on a mission that day.'

'I spent hours on those drawings and every time I looked at them it reminded me of the dead and the dying, all of them, every single one I've ever seen. It brought it all back, all the mindless killing, all those wasted lives.'

'I'm sure it did. I can't begin to imagine what you've seen, how you feel. I wish I could.'

'Believe me, you don't want to know.' Mick pulled the sheet up towards his chin and held it there in one balled fist. 'I dream death so often, I spend most of my nights just walking on the hill, out in the open.'

'Could you tell me what you saw that day? Would it help or would it make things worse for you?'

Mick glanced at Swift, hovering by the door. 'Who's he?'

'That's Detective Inspector Swift, my boss.' She leaned forward and whispered to Mick. 'He hates hospitals.'

'I know the feeling.'

'Are you up to talking?'

'I can try.'

'Tell me if it gets too much.'

'Oh believe me, Sergeant, you'll know if it gets too much.'

Julie pulled up the chair and sat down. 'Just take your time and tell me what happened up there.'

Mick took a deep breath in and let it out again, slowly. 'Well, I was looking for two of the alpacas. The Major thought they'd strayed, so I volunteered like a shot when he wanted someone to find them. I like being by myself up on the hill.' The faintest of smiles, then it was gone. 'I was checking the scrub, the little buggers like to get tangled up in the brambles by Preese's boundary. I hadn't even seen her at first, the woman.'

'The one in the coat?'

Mick nodded. 'There was another woman, well, she was so skinny maybe she was just a girl, but from the shouting she was doing at the man, she was definitely female.' He smiled. 'My wife used to shriek like that when she got mad. And she got mad a lot. I don't blame her, I wasn't easy to live with, not after I got back.'

'What happened to the woman, Mick?'

'The woman in the green coat was goading them, especially the man. She was like a ringmaster, cracking the whip. Then, once they were really arguing and the skinny woman was hurling abuse at the man, she backed away and let them fight. The skinny woman yelled something at the bloke, which made him really mad. She turned her back on him, started to walk away. I saw him pick something up, a piece of wood or a pole, I don't know. She never saw it coming. He smacked her hard on the back of the head and she went down. Then he was running, towards where I was hiding in the scrub. He didn't get as far as me. As he got alongside the pit, the woman in the coat came from nowhere. She hurled herself on him, lashed out at him and he went in.'

'When you say she lashed out at him, what do you mean?'

'She was like something possessed, kicking and punching him. She must have caught him off balance and he went backwards.'

'So he fell into the cess pit?'

'Aye, went arse over... base over apex, straight into the –. He went straight in, under the surface. I thought he'd drowned, and all the time, she was standing there, waiting for him. I couldn't do anything to help him. I couldn't move.' Mick looked up at her, and Julie could see how hard this memory was for him. It was as though the scene was replaying right in front of his eyes. 'Somehow, he got himself half out of the pit. Came out of there like a monster from the deep and just lay there with his head and shoulders on the concrete.' Mick pinched the bridge of his nose. 'She took something out of her pocket, wrapped it round his neck and pulled.' He sniffed hard. 'That obviously didn't do what she wanted it to do, because she had another go then. She rammed her knee into his shoulder to give her a bit of leverage. It was as vicious as anything I've ever seen in combat. Even from where I was, I thought his head would come off.' Mick shivered. 'Then she just shoved him back into the cess pit.' Mick's breath began to come in short rapid bursts.

'Are you OK? Should I call someone?'

Mick shook his head. He pulled the sheet down and Julie could see that the damaged arm was oozing blood. The bandage was saturated, and deep red blood dripped from the elbow onto the sheet. Swift flung the door open and the nurse almost fell into the room.

'Will you sign a statement for me?' Julie asked.

'You'll have to leave now.' The nurse pressed a buzzer in the wall and attached Mick's arm temporarily by its bandage to a drip stand, which she manoeuvred into position with her foot. Julie stood up and walked round the bed towards the door.

'Sergeant,' Mick said. 'Yes, I'll do it. I'll do anything it takes if it will help put that woman behind bars.'

'It will, Mick. Believe me, it's about the only thing that will.'

Swift relaxed as soon as they were out in the car park. They leaned on the Volvo in the sunshine.

'You did well in there with him.'

'He's a good bloke. He wanted to help when we were trying to identify Ardal.'

'Do you think he will testify, from what you've seen of him?'

Julie considered. 'I think he would. But to be honest, Sir, with a full statement and his drawings, then maybe that will be enough. I'm not sure how he'd cope with a courtroom. There's plenty of forensic evidence for Quigley's murder.'

'But not for Rosa's, is there?'

'Kay said there were two injuries to Rosa's head. Maybe it wasn't the first one that killed her, though how even Kay would sort that out, I don't know.' Julie flicked through her notebook. 'She's still working on it. They're both in the same area, on the back of the head.'

'Maybe Mick just didn't see the first blow and Quigley did hit her twice,' Swift said.

'Or maybe Quigley did only hit her once and the second injury was actually from the gatepost at the cottage, where the blood was found.'

'Did we get the new results on Rosa's bag back yet?'

'Not that I know of. Shall I run down and see if Dr Greenhalgh is there?'

Swift turned his face to the sun. 'You do that, Sergeant. I'll just wait here for you.'

Kay Greenhalgh was in her office. She reached for the kettle as Julie poked her head round the door.

'Brew?'

'I can't stop, the boss is outside, and we've got someone on the PACE clock.' Julie said. 'We were just about to charge her and we were called over here.'

'He won't mind waiting for five minutes,' Kay said, spooning coffee into two mugs. 'He's happier out there than he is in here.'

'Did you get the results back on that bag?'

'I did, they're... here.' Kay retrieved a sheet of paper from her post tray. 'And we've been lucky. I don't know how it happened or how we missed it the first time, but I can tell you that there are microscopic flecks of plagioclase feldspar crystals in the fabric of the bag which match the stone gatepost at Pwll Bach.'

'And that tells us what?' Julie took the mug from Kay and sipped the strong black liquid.

'That tells us that the bag was up there, actually at the cottage, and that it contacted the gatepost with some force.'

'But surely there are lots of places with – what was it – feldspar?'

'There are, but this particular one is from the Carneddau Volcanic Formation which is from the other side of the Llanelwedd Quarry in Builth. Large lumps of that type of rock aren't normally seen in the Elan Valley; they would have been much more inclined to use the local stone for building purposes.' Kay sipped her coffee. 'And the best is yet to come. The same feldspar crystals are in Rosa's head wound. They're well embedded, and deep, deeper than the extent of the first head wound.'

'Could they be from the rock she was propped up against though?'

'No. That rock is a completely different composition. It's a conglomerate, formed from turbidite activity.'

Julie whistled quietly. 'How do you know all this stuff?'

'I have to hold my hands up to that one, I'm afraid. I haven't the vaguest idea about rocks. But I do know a man who has.'

'Why doesn't that surprise me? Is it enough to make it absolutely certain that she was up there?'

'Well the rock chemistry and the indigenous soil traces are enough to make it certain that her bag was up there, and that her head came into contact with the same type of rock.'

'And if her bag was with her in the pictures that Mick drew, when they were down by the cess pit...'

'Now you've lost me.'

'Sorry. It's all coming together, but just from random sources.'

Julie put her mug down and stood up. 'Thank you so much for your help. I'd better go and drag the boss back to the nick.' She opened the door, but turned back.

'OK, this is probably going to sound like a ridiculous question, but how would you go about learning about forensics properly? Not that I want to do the medical school thing, but I would like to know more about it.' She blushed. 'Daft idea.'

'Not at all.' Kay grinned. 'I'd say it just confirms what I've always thought.'

'What's that?'

'You're wasted as a copper. Get yourself a proper job.'

'Thank you, Doctor, for that vote of confidence.'

'Seriously though, there are courses you could go on. Would you fancy specialising within the police force?'

'Oh, I don't know. I've not really thought about it. It's just that every time I speak to you, I realise how little I know, stuff that would be really useful.'

'I can find you some information if you like?' Greenhalgh smiled. 'And believe me, Julie, I would be absolutely useless at what you do.'

'A perfectionist like you, Dr Greenhalgh?'

Kay laughed out loud, a huge hooting chuckle. 'Bagged. Now bugger off and let me get some work done.'

CHAPTER THIRTY-SEVEN

Day Eight

Back at the station, Morgan Evans gave Swift a thorough and comprehensive report on his visit to Mal's. No, there was nothing else they'd remembered, but Mal had picked up a scaffolding pole he'd found in the field, which must have been moved from outside the shed, and not by him. He definitely didn't remember taking it up the field. Fortunately, on the day he found it, he had been side-tracked by a huge delivery of hay and the pole was still where he'd left it when the lorry had arrived, just by the shed door. Morgan had already sent it to the lab. Julie could tell Swift was impressed. Maybe he'd discovered the key to getting the best out of DC Evans.

Goronwy and Rhys had spoken to the other two soldiers.

'Did Mick tell them anything about what he had seen?' Swift asked.

'Baz said Mick never speaks to anyone about anything, not really,' Rhys said.

'So they didn't know anything about what happened up there?' Julie asked.

Goronwy shook his head. 'Nope. But he did tell him that Ardal bloke had been inside Lizzie's cottage on one of the days Mick was doing his solitary thing up on the hill. He saw him. Mick told him Ardal had waited for the woman who lived there to leave with her son, he said. I think Baz was really shaken about what happened to Mick. They thought he was past that self-harming stage.'

'Has he tried to cut himself before?' Swift asked.

'It was a long time ago, they said, before either of them arrived.'

'So why didn't Ardal tell you about his visit to the cottage, I wonder?' Swift tugged his ear. 'That was a bit of an oversight on his part, I'd say.'

'Oh no, Ardal. We haven't told him that Sean's safe. I'll phone him, Sir, shall I?' Julie said.

'Do that, and then we'll get back to our guests downstairs. Maybe Morgan would like to come and help me finish off the interview with James Pritchard?'

Morgan smiled, and followed Swift from the room. Julie grinned. If only he wasn't so ruddy prickly, Morgan would be a completely different person. Her phone was ringing. It was Brian Hughes from the front desk.

'I've had a message just now from Mrs Wilkinson about Mick. She said to say he's fine, the doctor hadn't spotted that Mick had nicked a blood vessel but he's sorted now and will be back home tomorrow. Apparently he's keen to do everything he can. She says to say thank you, and that you must have made an impression on him, Sergeant.' Julie could hear the question in his voice.

'Long story, Brian. Let's just say he was a lot more forthcoming than we'd imagined. Thank God.'

She dialled Ardal's number. This one hadn't done quite so well in that department, had he?

'It's Julie Kite, Mid Wales Police.'

'Ah, right.'

'So I don't suppose you'll have heard the news about what happened to Jason Quigley?'

'I haven't. I truly hope it's something absolutely horrible.'

'It is, Ardal. Like you wouldn't believe. Jason Quigley has been murdered in a particularly gruesome manner.'

She could almost hear a smile spreading over Ardal's face. 'That's the best news I've heard for a very long time. What a pity someone didn't do that to him years ago, before he murdered my sister.'

'We're still investigating Rosa's death, Ardal. I can't talk to you about that. What I really want to know is was Lizzie in her cottage in the Elan Valley when you went calling?'

'I don't know what you mean.'

'You said you were looking for Rosa – Caroline. You didn't mention that you'd found the cottage where her neighbour was staying with Sean.'

'I must have mentioned it.'

'Was she there when you paid a visit?' There was a pause. She could hear Ardal's brain working. 'Was Lizzie at home when you went to her cottage? You were seen, Ardal.'

'No, all right. She was out.'

'And did you know she was out when you went inside?'

'I didn't go inside. I knocked on the door and there was no reply.'

'Again, you were seen, Ardal, coming out of the cottage. Was it just the once you were there?'

'Yes. I came home the following day.'

'So did you get up to your little party piece while you were in there?'

'What do you mean?'

'What were you looking for, Ardal?'

'I told you, I was looking for Sean.'

'The information we have says that you waited until the cottage was empty before you went in. You must have seen Lizzie leaving with Sean.'

'I didn't want to scare her off.'

'So what were you looking for? I thought you said you wanted to find Sean.'

'I was trying to be too clever about it, Sergeant. I thought she might be trying to take Sean out of the country, out of Quigley's way, or for her own reasons, who knows. I certainly don't any more.'

'And?'

'I was looking for travel documents, passports. Anything that would tell me what she was planning to do with Sean, and when.

She couldn't be planning to live there forever, could she? I couldn't just steal Sean from her, could I?'

'So what were you planning to do?'

'I thought if I could work it all out, I could persuade the police to be there, to catch her in the act.'

'It doesn't work like it does on television, Ardal. The chances of that happening would have been slim.'

'I know that now. I wasn't thinking straight.'

'Burglary is an offence, Ardal. You seem to be making a habit of it.'

'I didn't do any damage.'

'Ardal, you made a statement to Lancashire Police which was blatantly untrue.'

'It wasn't untrue. I just didn't mention the fact that I went to the cottage. I didn't find Rosa, which is exactly what I said.'

'What did you take from the cottage, Ardal.'

'I didn't take anything, Sergeant.'

'So you didn't find passports or travel documents?'

'No, Sergeant, I didn't.'

'I'm very glad to hear it,' Julie said. 'Now, do you want to hear some good news?'

*

James Pritchard looked terrible. What would he look like after a few years behind bars, wondered Swift. Poor sod. If he hadn't got involved with Lizzie Slaithwaite, then none of this would have happened. He'd still be living in his nice Victorian house with his doting wife, and his grown up kids pitching up for Christmas dinner and birthday lunches, blissfully unaware of the scheming woman from Blackpool.

'Mr Pritchard, you are still under caution, do you understand?' Pritchard nodded. He didn't look at Swift. 'We know that you did not murder Jason Quigley. We also know that it's unlikely that you murdered Rosa Quigley. Is there anything you can tell us about that?'

Pritchard looked up at the solicitor and then at the two officers. 'I didn't murder anyone, Inspector.'

'So why did you confess to the murder of Jason Quigley, Mr Pritchard?'

'For Lizzie. I thought I could protect Lizzie and Sean. The boy deserves a decent life.'

'And now that you know that Lizzie isn't your daughter?'

Pritchard nodded. 'I wish to God I'd known that before. But it doesn't matter anymore, does it, Inspector? That woman is evil. I want nothing more to do with her. I can't think how I ended up in this wretched situation. I'm usually far too sensible for my own good.' Pritchard attempted a smile. 'Conservative, my wife calls me. What she means is, I'm bloody boring.'

'How did Lizzie contact you in the first instance?' Morgan asked.

'She wrote to me. This was a few months before she left Blackpool with the boy. She sent a letter to my office.'

'How did she find out where you worked?' Swift said. 'Was she stalking you?'

'I have absolutely no idea.'

'So how did Lizzie get in touch with you?' Swift asked.

'Through one of those business link sites. I'm pretty useless at it, but I was looking for a new job and Marilyn said it would be a good way of making new contacts.' Pritchard closed his eyes. 'How is Marilyn, Inspector?'

Swift stared at him. 'She's in an induced coma, which they hope will allow the swelling in her brain to reduce. The doctors tell us the next twenty-four hours will be critical.'

'I don't suppose I would be allowed...'

'You want to see her?' Swift's expression was softening.

'Would it be possible?'

Swift cleared his throat. 'Well, we may be able to organise something. In the circumstances.'

Pritchard looked up at the ceiling and blinked back tears, before holding out his hand to Swift, who shook it.

'Yes, well, when did Lizzie tell you she was your daughter?' Swift removed his hand from Pritchard's grasp and tugged his ear.

'Straight away. She said she thought we ought to meet. I was a bit reticent. I thought she might have been a scammer or whatever they're called.'

'But you agreed?' Swift asked.

Pritchard looked up at the ceiling again, and then down at his hands. 'She said she would tell my wife we were having an affair if I didn't meet her.'

'And alarm bells didn't start ringing?' Morgan looked at Pritchard as though he were quite mad. Swift coughed and Morgan rearranged his features.

'Some of us aren't quite so clued up about social media, Constable. I panicked. I thought it wouldn't hurt to meet the woman and tell her to leave me alone.'

'What happened when you met her?' Swift asked.

'She told me her mother had been looking for me. That she had died of a broken heart. She said all her mother had ever wanted to do was to find me and that there was no doubt that she was my daughter and she had paperwork to prove it.'

'And did she have paperwork?'

Pritchard nodded. 'She showed me a birth certificate which named me as the father.'

'I don't suppose you checked up on it at all?' Morgan was trying his best to keep his tone of voice neutral.

'Not at the time.'

'But you've checked since?' Swift asked.

'I was going to do it when I got back to Bryn Awel, but I didn't get round to it, in the circumstances. I'm guessing you must already know that there's no record of the birth with me as the father.'

Swift nodded. 'So you never confronted her, or asked her for proper proof?'

'I didn't.'

Morgan shook his head, but kept quiet at a warning sideways stare from Swift.

'So how long do you think you would have stayed with her, Mr Pritchard?' Swift asked.

'Honestly? I have absolutely no idea. I was getting to the point where I had to get away from her. She is so totally controlling. And the boy – I was never very good at kids, Marilyn dealt with all that, but he's something else. He never stops crying and yelling. I'm way too old for all that.'

'Why didn't you just leave? Why did you stay with her?' Morgan asked.

'I felt responsible. She'd persuaded me I owed her.'

'And the cottage, did you buy the cottage for her?'

'Yes, Inspector, I bought the cottage.'

'And that's why you consolidated your assets.'

'Yes.'

'Do you still own the cottage?' Swift asked.

Pritchard exhaled slowly and deeply. 'No. I transferred it into Lizzie's name.'

'She asked you to?' Morgan asked. Pritchard nodded. 'The most worrying thing, as far as we're concerned, is that you moved Rosa's body. Where was she originally, when you found her?'

'Not far from the gate.'

'The gate at the cottage?'

Pritchard nodded.

'For the tape, please, Mr Pritchard,' Morgan said.

'Yes, the gate at the cottage.'

'Where *exactly* was she?' Swift said.

'Four or five yards away, if that.'

'And you just took it upon yourself to move her? You told us earlier that Lizzie was in the cottage. So there was no discussion with her about whether to move Rosa or not?'

Pritchard looked weary. He folded his arms and lowered his chin onto his chest like a small boy who had been ticked off by his teacher. 'I wanted to phone you. I did dial 999 on my mobile and then Lizzie came screeching out of the house like a wailing bloody banshee and stamped on my phone.'

'She smashed your phone?' Morgan asked. 'What did you do?'

'I didn't get much of a chance to do anything. Lizzie demanded I move the body. She told me it was Rosa, that Rosa was Sean's mother and that Quigley must be following her. She said if Quigley found her and Sean, the same thing would happen to them.'

'And you –?' Morgan's question and his incredulous expression were cut short by Pritchard's shout.

'Yes, I bloody well did believe her. She had me terrified of my own shadow. Can you believe I used to sit crouched in the back seat of the car for ten minutes when I got back from going anywhere and parked in that lane below the cottage, just to make sure nobody had followed me? I was *that* stupid.'

'Lizzie must have been very persuasive,' Swift said, his voice visibly soothing Pritchard's ruffled feathers.

There was a knock at the door and Swift motioned for Morgan to answer it. A muffled conversation followed, then Morgan sat back down.

'It seems Lizzie Slaithwaite had made plans for all of this long before she ever contacted you, Mr Pritchard. She stopped financing her florist business last August, without telling her husband or the people who worked for her.'

Swift's eyebrows shot up. 'Did you know anything about this, Mr Pritchard?'

'No I did not. What a scheming, conniving, bad-minded, manipulative bitch she is.'

Swift suppressed a smile. At last, some backbone.

'You will definitely be charged with your part in moving the body, Mr Pritchard. It will depend on the Crown Prosecution Service whether there will be any charges relating to the murders. I assume you will be wanting to withdraw your confession?'

CHAPTER THIRTY-EIGHT

Day Eight

'What will happen to Sean?' Tears coursed down Lizzie Slaithwaite's cheeks, gathering on her chin and plinking onto the table. Julie still couldn't decide whether she was a very good actress or whether she really wasn't totally sane.

'We don't know yet what will happen to Sean. He is being looked after by social services. As you are neither parent nor guardian, I'm afraid we are unable to tell you any more about his care.'

'You bitch. You're enjoying this, aren't you? I've looked after that child almost all of his life. That no-good mother of his was always off her head on smack, coke, legal highs, whatever she could get her grubby little hands on. She was no bloody use at all. She shouldn't have been allowed to have a child in the first place.'

'Was that what this was all about, Lizzie? You saw the boy living in what you considered to be an unsuitable home and decided you would take him for yourself?' Julie stared hard at Lizzie, who was easily a match for her.

'Those two were scum. They gave up any rights to him the day I found them both crashed out in the garden, off their heads. Sean was inches from a lit barbecue. They'd left him strapped in a high chair next to an open fire and then shot up with God knows what. It was criminal negligence.'

'And you couldn't have children of your own?' Julie took no pleasure in this question, but Lizzie had made no allowances.

'Have you got children, Sergeant? Do you know what it's like to try for months, years to get pregnant? There was no justice in it. They had a gorgeous baby boy and half the time they didn't even know he was there. And then there was me, watching the sparkle go out of his eyes with the treatment they doled out.'

'We know you lured James Pritchard, blackmailed him to look after the two of you, or you would have told his wife you were having an affair. Did you think he really was your father?'

'Of course I did. Why would my mother lie to me?'

'We only have your word for that of course. Although you did lie about your age to Mr Pritchard, didn't you?' Julie ignored Lizzie's smirk. 'And a colleague of mine has been very thorough in his searches,' Julie said.

'I'm so pleased for him.'

'He tells me that the *Lancashire Evening Post* is a mine of useful information.' Lizzie's smug smile faded, but she said nothing. Julie unfolded a sheet of A3 paper. 'He's found an edition dated 1998. This is a photocopy. It concerns the tragic death of the entire crew of a fishing trawler, off the coast of Fleetwood. Among the crew was a man called Eifion Jenkins.'

'What do you want me to say?' Lizzie was petulant now, rocking her chair to and fro.

'Eifion Jenkins was your father, Lizzie.'

Lizzie shrugged. 'You must be mistaken, Sergeant.'

'But you persuaded James Pritchard that *he* was your father. You made him buy you a property to hide out in, made him give up his job to keep guard for you, when all the time you were pulling everyone's strings.'

'What do you mean?'

'You intended to take Sean abroad, didn't you?'

Lizzie shrugged. 'Did I?'

'Had you got this all mapped out before you even contacted James Pritchard?'

Lizzie shrugged again and a slow smile crossed her face. 'You don't know anything, do you?'

'And the map of Blackpool, with Rosa's house circled. You put that in her bag, didn't you? It was important that we found out who she was, so that we would know Sean's parents were dead. If anyone ever traced you, that is. Was that it? Was it just a game?'

Lizzie said nothing, just held the sarcastic smile.

'What about your husband? You left him without telling him where you were and just disappeared into the Welsh countryside with a kidnapped child and no intention of ever contacting him again.' Swift was as disapproving as Julie had ever seen him.

'John's a nice man. He loves his work and he's very good at it. But he didn't understand.' The smile was gone.

'What didn't he understand, Lizzie?' Swift asked.

'He didn't understand me, Inspector. He didn't even try.'

'So you planned the escape to God knows where, and Sean's kidnapping, then you decided to hook James Pritchard and persuade him to buy you the house in Wales. What made you change your plans?' Swift asked. 'Why didn't you just start a new life? Why did you need James Pritchard to help you? Why did you need to dispose of Sean's parents?'

'I don't think I want to talk to you any more, Inspector.'

Julie frowned. 'You wrote to Rosa, telling her where you were living. I don't believe she had ever asked you to take Sean away. No doubt her life was even more of a misery after that, with Quigley taking the boy's disappearance out on her. Did you not care about Rosa at all?'

Lizzie shrugged again. 'They deserved each other. They were scum, the pair of them. People like that don't deserve to have children.'

'So did she ask you to take Sean?' Swift's voice had a hard edge. Julie could see he was beginning to lose patience with this self-obsessed woman.

'Would I lie to you, Inspector?'

'And you contacted both Rosa and Quigley, telling them where you were and where they could find the boy, giving them a date and a time.'

'You can't prove that.'

'We may well be able to prove that very soon. So what happened when they turned up on Mal's land? Did you guide them to the exact spot? Did you cause an argument between Rosa and Quigley? Did you think he would do your job for you, and murder Rosa?' Swift asked.

Lizzie shrugged. 'I can't remember.'

'He didn't though, did he, Lizzie? He hit her, but that didn't kill her. She managed to get herself to your cottage and once you'd dispatched Quigley with your florists' garrotte, you completed the set piece by smashing Rosa's head against the gatepost.'

'It's your word against mine, though, isn't it? I've told you, it's nothing to do with me. It's James Pritchard you need to be talking to.'

'That's what you think, is it?' Swift tugged his ear. 'Then I think you're forgetting that we have a witness.' Swift gave the smallest of smiles. It looked almost sympathetic, but Julie knew better.

'Your cartoonist? He could have made the whole thing up.'

'The game's up, Lizzie. All that planning and deception. All those lives ruined and for what? You'll never see Sean again.' Julie leaned back in her chair. Suddenly she felt the need to put as much distance as possible between Lizzie and herself.

'You'll never prove it, any of it. I'm the victim here. And once you've worked that out, then Sean and I can go abroad and start a new life.'

'I hate to disillusion you, Lizzie, but the CPS are confident that you are definitely not the victim,' Swift said.

Lizzie's solicitor looked at Swift and then at Julie. 'I think I'd like a word with my client now, if that's all right.'

CHAPTER THIRTY-NINE

Day Eight

The others were going for an early drink after work, but somehow, Julie couldn't stomach the celebration. She sat in the empty office, looking at the photographs, maps and drawings on the board. Followed Rhys's arrows and colour-coding to the obvious conclusion. Except that it would never be concluded, not for her. This would be added to the long list of cases she went back to night after night, the ghosts of murdered and murderer and others caught in the crossfire. What a bloody job. What was the betting Lizzie would plead diminished responsibility, if she ever stopped accusing James Pritchard. Julie collected up Mick's drawings and locked them in her drawer and, with a last look round the office, she walked slowly out of the door.

Brian Hughes was still on the desk in reception. 'Good result there, Julie. You must be pleased.'

She nodded. 'I am, Brian, but nobody wins in this one, do they?'

'You mean the little boy?'

'Yes, and James Pritchard and his wife and family, John Slaithwaite, they've all been damaged by that woman.' Julie sighed. 'And her mother had a hand in it too. It turns out that she was eighteen when Pritchard had the misfortune to stumble across her in Blackpool.'

'But what about the little lad? He'll thank you for all your efforts, in years to come. He's got the chance of a better life now. You must feel good about that bit.'

'I do. Oh I don't know. Maybe I'm just never satisfied.'

'I think that goes with the job though, Julie. Don't you?'

Suddenly Swift burst through the door and Julie and Brian stared at him.

'Have you finished down the boozer already?' Julie asked.

'I'm glad you're still here,' Swift said. 'I'm going up to Mal's. Morgan has just told me that when he went to see them they were talking about moving away from the valley.'

'Because of this?'

Swift nodded. 'I'm so bloody angry. I can't believe the damage that woman has done. I'm going to see if I can reassure them. Will you come with me?'

'Actually, Sir, if we're going up that way, I'd quite like to have another look in that cottage of Lizzie's.'

'What for?'

'Well,' Julie frowned. 'If we could prove that Lizzie had this all planned beforehand, as Ardal thinks, then it would help Pritchard's case, wouldn't it? We could do with some proof that he was targeted by Lizzie.'

'Well, I don't suppose it would hurt,' Swift conceded. 'They won't have missed anything though, but we can still go back and have another look, if you think it's important. And I'm guessing there's more to it than that?'

'I've been here too long. You can already tell what I'm thinking.'

'I wouldn't go that far, Julie. Not by any stretch, but I just know there's something else bothering you.'

Julie grinned. 'You're right. It's Mick. If we can fill in a few more of the gaps ourselves then he might not have to go through the ordeal of giving evidence. It doesn't feel right that he has to get dragged into this.'

'But what are you expecting to find?'

Julie shrugged. 'I'm positive Lizzie had this organised to the letter. It must have been meticulously planned, to get everyone in the right place at the right time. We've been through the B&B from top to bottom and there was nothing. There must be some clue, somewhere.'

Swift shook his head. 'You're sure you want to do this now? Wouldn't you rather go to the pub with the others?'

'Ordinarily, Sir, I'd be there like a shot.'

'If they were all as keen as this one eh, Craig?' Brian Hughes laughed. 'You don't like loose ends, do you, Sergeant.'

Mal was sitting on a bench in a still-sunny spot on the yard, under the kitchen window of the farmhouse, with his collie at his feet. He had his wellingtons on, despite the dryness of the soil. He raised a hand as the two cars appeared on the yard, and Sarah came out of the front door, wiping her hands on her wrap-around apron. They both looked weary, and Swift shot Julie a look, which she understood immediately. That bloody woman.

'Mal, Sarah, evening both, how are you doing now the excitement has quietened down?' Swift took the hand Mal offered and shook it, then sat down on the bench next to him. 'A little bird tells me you're feeling a bit unsettled by everything that went on up there.' He pointed, with his forehead, to the hill above the house.

Sarah sighed. 'He thinks we should move away now, get a bungalow down in Rhayader.'

'Is that true, Mal?' Swift asked.

Mal sighed. 'I always thought this place was special, Craig. As perfect a place as you could ever find anywhere in the world, but now I'm not so sure. Not sure at all.'

'What about you, Sarah?' Julie asked. 'Are you worried by what happened?'

'Well it's not likely to happen again, is it? Not here. I'd say we were just unlucky that it happened at all.' Sarah sat on the arm of the bench next to Mal and put her hand on his shoulder. 'This daft old thing says he can't keep me safe now.'

Mal reached up and covered Sarah's hand with his. 'It's important to me.'

'Well you've managed so far, *cariad*, haven't you?' Sarah looked down at him and smiled. Julie felt as though she and Swift were intruding.

'What would you do with yourself all day down in town?' Julie asked. 'Would it make life easier for you, being close to the shops and other people?'

'You can tell she's a townie, can't you?' Swift grinned. 'But she might have a point. Do you *want* to move?'

Mal stared at his boots and Sarah nudged him. 'Well I don't want to move,' she said. 'What would we do with Chip? He can't live in a house can he?' She stroked the collie's head. 'We're both a bit too used to spending all our time outside.'

'But it's not safe anymore, *cariad*.' Mal looked up at the hill. 'Nothing will be the same here now.'

'If you want to stay,' Swift said, 'then I'll do my best to make sure we look after you.' He bent to stroke the dog's head. 'You need a mobile phone, now that they've put that new mast up. That would help you feel a bit more in touch with the rest of us.' He smiled. 'And you could do worse than let the Wilkinsons help you. They're actually quite normal, and the men they have working for them are good lads.'

'See,' Sarah said. 'I told you we'd be all right.'

Slowly Mal took in the panorama, from the hill, around the yard and down the lane to the distant sparkle of water, then back at Sarah's troubled face.

'So you don't think we're past it, then?' he said.

Sarah laughed. 'Speak for yourself.' She stood up. 'Anyway, if you can't cope with having neighbours quarter of a mile away, how would you get on in town?'

Mal nodded once. Then he stood up and thrust out his hand to Craig Swift. 'Thank you,' he said. 'You've cleared a few things up for me.'

'When you choose to move down to Rhayader, because you think the time is right, then that will be different,' Swift said. 'But moving before you're ready, just because of what happened up there, well, you'd never forgive yourself.'

Mal put his arm round Sarah and smiled. 'You're sensible people, ›ou policemen.'

Swift smiled. 'Sometimes, Mal, we are. And now, if it's OK with you, we just need one last look up at the cottage, just to draw a line under everything, once and for all.'

Despite the search carried out by the forensic team, the cottage was still tidy. They started in the bedrooms, checking under the mattresses and in every drawer and wardrobe. Julie checked the panel on the bath and the laundry basket. There was nothing at all. The house was kitted out like a holiday cottage, minimalist and short on belongings. In the kitchen, Swift opened and closed cupboards and checked underneath drawers. Julie leaned against the sink and gazed at the view.

'It's in a fabulous spot.'

'You really are getting used to all this, aren't you?' Swift closed the cutlery drawer and crossed the kitchen to stand beside her.

'Where would you hide something in here? There's hardly any storage space at all,' Julie said.

'Do we know what we're looking for?'

'Not a clue, but if Ardal's instinct is right, if she was going to take Sean abroad, then there might just be tickets here somewhere. John Slaithwaite swears there's nothing else at Eighth Avenue or Lizzie's shop, and we've had the B&B upside down ourselves and found nothing, so they have to be here.' Julie pushed herself back from the sink and crawled under the small dining table.'

'Clutching at straws, Julie?'

Julie bumped her head on the table as she got up and she stifled both the exasperation and the expletive. 'No, Sir, there's nothing. Absolutely bugger all.' She brushed dust from her knees and looked down at the uneven stone floor. 'This could do with a bit of a clean.'

'So Lizzie's not much of a domestic goddess then?' Swift chuckled. 'Come on, Julie. Let's go home.'

'Hang on, Sir. What would cause those marks?

Swift bent down to look at the scuff marks on the uneven flags. 'Chair maybe? Would that do it?'

'Unless...' Julie walked over to the sink and paced out an arc between the edge of the fitted unit and the marks by the table. Swift watched her with one eyebrow raised.

'Go on, Sergeant, I can hear your brain working overtime from here.

'It's like that door in Mal's shed, the one that sticks. It left marks like this on the floor.' Julie was on her hands and knees now, feeling the kickboard. 'Is there no other light in here? I can't see anything.'

'Will this do?' Swift flashed his mobile phone at her.

'Perfect.' Julie located two screws hidden under tiny pieces of insulating tape and worked her way along the kickboard. 'Ha, you beauty.' She rummaged in her bag and applied the blade of a small penknife to the first two screws, then the next two. Slowly, the screws were worked free and the kickboard fell forward, onto the flags. Swift knelt beside her and shone his phone into the gap.

'Nice try, Julie.' He stood up. 'But there's nothing there.'

Julie stood up too, trying not to show her disappointment. 'Bugger, I really thought I was onto something there.'

Swift was frowning, his head on one side. 'I don't suppose you have a tape measure in that bag of yours, Mary Poppins?'

Julie laughed. 'No, Sir. What are you thinking?'

'What if there's another piece of board at the back? This gap under here isn't deep enough to go all the way back to the wall, is it?'

'Oh, Sir, that's bloody genius.'

'I do my best, Sergeant.' Swift laughed. 'So what do we think?'

'It could just be pipes though, couldn't it, blocked in before the units were put in?' Julie was already lying on the floor, feeling her way round the narrow space. 'I just can't see anything.' She sat up. 'It's like being down a pit in this kitchen.'

'I'll take your word for that.'

'*Fel bol buwch*, wouldn't you say, Sir.'

Swift laughed. 'It's no good, Julie, this isn't going to move.' He knelt down and poked at the board in frustration. There was a faint click and, almost in slow motion, the board toppled forward and lay flat on the stone flags under the pipework for the sink. Swift reached into the space and stood up slowly.

'Look, Julie.' He handed her a small package wrapped in white-spotted cellophane and tied with a piece of green raffia.

'Go on,' Swift said, handing her a pair of blue latex gloves. 'You were the one who brought us here.'

Carefully, she untied the raffia bow and unfastened the thick cellophane. It was like opening a present, wondering whether what she would find inside was what she'd been hoping for.

'Oh my, look.' She pulled out two passports. The first one she opened was for Sean. The photograph was Sean, but the name was Kieran Jenkins. Swift picked up the other.

'This one's for Lizzie, but she's calling herself...' Swift had opened the other passport and he flicked to the third page.'

'Vanessa Jenkins?' Julie asked.

'How do you do that?'

'That's the name she gave when I first met her up here. She must have panicked and given me the first name that came into her head.' Julie leaned over to look at the photograph. Even the tiny thumbnail photo showed Lizzie Slaithwaite with the same supercilious stare to which they had been treated so recently. 'How does she do that?'

'What?'

'Manage to look so obnoxious in a regulation passport photograph?'

'It has to be a forgery though, Julie.' Swift nodded at the cellophane parcel. 'What else is in there?'

'There's a ferry ticket from Fishguard to Rosslare for Tuesday next week, which was booked last August.' Julie checked back to the passports. 'The passports are dated August last year too.'

'So what's this,' Swift said, handing her a package wrapped in black plastic.

Carefully, Julie sliced the package open and whistled. 'Oh you beauty.' She held it out to Swift. 'It's yet another mobile phone.'

CHAPTER FORTY

Day Nine

Adam was in the kitchen when she came downstairs the next morning, reading something on the worktop. Suddenly she felt weary, despite ten hours' sleep. God, please don't let him be looking for a recipe for anything with lentils in it. Not tonight. Just for once.

'Come and sign this,' he said, holding out a pen.

'What is it?'

'It's an engagement card.'

'Who do we know who's engaged? Oh God, don't tell me Helen's phoned.'

'Nope. This is for Tiffany. I thought we needed closure. All of us. If we both sign it, then we're saying it's over aren't we?'

'Are we? Is it that easy?' She picked up the pen and tapped it on her teeth. *I hope you'll be very happy,* she wrote. She glanced up at Adam, who smiled back. *Best wishes, Julie.*

'You are a star, you know,' he said.

She added three kisses to the bottom of the card.

'Are you being sarky?' Adam asked.

'Possibly.' She put the card in the envelope and handed it to him. 'I forgot to ask you, with all the stuff that's been going on at work. What happened about your bike tyres? Was it one of the kids having a go?'

'You said I was paranoid.'

'Yes, but I was being nice about it. I've just come face to face with the real thing and it's not pretty.'

'Well, I wasn't going to say, because you were right, as usual. I was being paranoid, it turns out it was a manufacturing fault, a dodgy batch. The manufacturers wrote to the bike shop to tell them. When they get warm they can just split at high speeds.'

'Well thank goodness for that. We can put the stalking theories to bed too.' She put her arms round his waist. 'Isn't it easy though, to think something is pointing to one conclusion and to be so certain, when in reality it's something totally different. We were convinced that everything, from the empty envelope to Mum and Dad's burglar, were all Tiffany. It feels very real though, at the time.'

'What's brought this on?'

'Oh, just some poor chap who was totally convinced that he had a long-lost daughter and that said daughter was being pursued by murderous drug-taking psychopaths.'

'And he hadn't, and she wasn't?'

'No he hadn't, and she probably wasn't. But she was absolutely evil.'

'No wonder you look like that.'

'Like what?'

'I'm saying nothing. Get your glad rags on, I'm taking you to The Trout for a steak lunch.'

'And what will you be having? Curried beetroot? Chick peas in a Provençale sauce? Tofu trifle?'

'Life's too short for all that, Julie. Besides, we've got a celebrity engagement and a solved case to celebrate. Well done.'

'Thanks. She kissed him before heading upstairs to get dressed. From the lane she could hear the sound of horses' hooves. She ducked to look out of the low window, and Menna was outside on the drive. She was riding her own horse and leading Cam, who was groomed and tacked up. Julie leaned out of the window and Menna shouted up to her.

'Come on then, Miss Marple, you said you'd come out when the case was finished.' Menna patted Cam's empty saddle.

Julie threw on jeans and a tee shirt and ran downstairs to find Adam on the drive, chatting to Menna and patting Cam carefully on the nose.

'Is it OK if I go?'

'Why not? I'll get the bike out and go out for an hour too. It'll do you good to get out in the fresh air.'

'What about lunch?'

'I'll re-book it. There's always tomorrow, Julie. Isn't there?'

CHAPTER FORTY-ONE

Day Nine

Julie looked at the height of the stirrup from where she stood on the lane. There was no way that was going to happen.

'Just stick your foot in and bounce.' Menna was laughing at her. 'You make it look too difficult.'

'I'll never get my foot in there. You'd have to be double-jointed to even think about it.'

'Stand on the wall then.'

When even the garden wall proved difficult for Julie to scale, Menna leapt off her own horse, looped both sets of reins round her right arm and clasped her hands at knee height.

'I'll give you a bunk up.'

Julie hadn't giggled so much in months. She finally landed in the saddle red-faced, with tears streaming down her face.

'Things can only get better,' she said.

Menna showed her how to hold the reins. 'Keep your heels down and your head up,' she said. 'They told me that in Pony Club. She smiled. 'That was more than a little while ago now.'

'How old were you?'

Menna shrugged. 'About six, I think. You soon get the hang of it, just don't think too hard about it.'

'That's my biggest problem, thinking too hard.'

'Walk on,' Menna said, and Cam ambled on alongside Menna's horse. Julie grabbed the front of the saddle until she was used to the motion.

'Everything moves.'

'Of course it does.'

'I thought the front end would be fixed, like riding a bike.'

Menna laughed. 'I'm going to have my work cut out with you, I can see.'

'I think I may not be a natural in the horse department.'

'From the grapevine, I hear you're due a bit of relaxation. They say you've solved the mystery of the poor girl on the Monks' Trod.'

'Not on my own, I didn't.'

'Well, from what I've heard, you're pretty good at what you do.'

Julie blushed. 'I try.'

Menna nodded. 'Lean forward into the hill, it's a steep one.'

'I know, I've attempted to walk it.'

Cam was as unfit as Julie was unbalanced, but somehow they wheezed and wobbled their way to the top of the hill. Menna guided them through a gate and onto the forestry track.

'Joe tells me you wanted to ride these tracks.' She closed the gate, leaning further out of the saddle than Julie thought possible.

'I get the feeling my ears should be burning at all times.'

Menna laughed. 'It's bound to happen. You and Adam are the most interesting thing to happen up here in a while. A police officer and a sporty history teacher, it's quite a combination.'

Cam tripped and Julie dipped forward with a small shriek.

'Don't worry, you won't go anywhere. Do you want to try a little trot up this hill? He won't manage to keep going for long, he's so unfit. He's not been ridden for years.'

'Why does Joe keep him? I thought animals had to pay their way on farms.'

'Sometimes people surprise you don't they? Cam belonged to an old friend of his, and Joe promised to look after him for her.'

'What happened to her?

'She died.'

Julie raised an eyebrow. 'He doesn't strike me as a soft touch.'

'It's all an act. He's a lovely man under all the gruff stuff. Trot on.' Menna made a clicking sound and both horses broke into a trot.

Julie jiggled and squealed while Menna sat like a gaucho, barely moving in the saddle as though she and the horse were one.

'I think that's enough for him. We don't want to overdo it first time out.'

'Never mind him, I don't think I'll ever be able to walk again after this.'

Menna turned both horses round and they walked slowly down the hill. The views to their right were stunning. A couple of farm buildings nestled into the hill and above them, the land changed from lush green cultivated fields to dense heather, gorse and bracken. They seemed to have reached the boundary of the limit of man's influence over the land.

'What decides where you stop farming and leave the land to its own devices?'

'When it's too steep to get a tractor on it.' Menna leaned forward to open the gate. 'And when it's too boggy to bother. Some things are just too difficult.'

'You can say that again.'

'You'll know all about that I imagine. How do you do that job of yours?'

'I've never thought about doing anything else really.'

'Do you not you have nightmares about the things you see?'

'Sometimes,' Julie admitted. 'Sometimes the people really get to you, the victims mostly.'

'And you must see some sights.'

'You do.'

'So why did you want to do it? Lean back a bit, take the weight off his front end on this hill.'

Julie did as she was told and she could feel Cam lengthening his stride beneath her. 'I suppose it's about right and wrong. Making sure that justice is done.'

'Well, whatever it is, I'm glad you're doing it.'

Julie's phone trilled in her pocket and Menna reached over to take her reins.

'Hello, Sir. Any luck?'

Swift laughed. 'You don't need to worry about Mick giving evidence, Julie. It's that latest phone of Lizzie's. We've got separate text messages from this phone to both Rosa and Quigley, asking them to meet her out on the hill to discuss Sean's future. She arranged the whole thing, date, time, place.'

'But why would she keep it on her phone? Surely if it would incriminate you, you'd erase it, or you'd lose the phone?'

'It's a power thing, surely? She won, she called all the shots and got exactly what she wanted.'

'I thought she was cleverer than that.'

'So did I. Thank goodness her ego was large enough for her to trip over it eh, Sergeant.'

Cam snorted and Julie laughed.

'Where are you, Julie?'

'I'm on a horse on a forestry track with a very patient neighbour.'

'Good for you. I'll let you go then. And well done.'

Julie blushed. 'Thank you, Sir. You too.'

They rode on in companionable silence. By the time they got back to the cottage, Julie was beginning to relax.

'We'll make a rider out of you, yet. Whose is the car?'

'Oh my God, it's Mum and Dad.'

'Go on, you go, I'll sort Cam out.'

'Are you sure? I should help you take his gear off and take him back to the field.'

'No bother, you don't see them every day, do you?'

'Thank you so much, I've really enjoyed this.'

Menna nodded. 'Go on then.'

Julie didn't move. 'Menna, how do you get off?'

'Oh my, you're walking like John Wayne.' Adam hooted with laughter and waved at Menna, who trotted off up the lane.

'Very funny. Did you know they were coming? Are they all right?'

'Yes, I knew they were coming and yes, they're all right.'

'Why didn't you say?'

'And spoil the surprise?' Adam grinned as Julie's mum came rushing down the drive.

'Julie, this is an amazing place. Why didn't you tell me? And you're horse riding!'

'How's Dad? Did they find out who broke in?'

'He's absolutely fine, still a bit sore, but he doesn't say anything, you know what he's like. And he's happier now that we know who it was.'

'Did the police catch him?'

'Not exactly. His mother came round and apologised. She brought my mobile phone back.'

'No way. Who was it?'

'It was young Jason next door. She said he'd been out boozing with his friends from school. Celebrating the end of his exams. Apparently he was so drunk he just got the wrong house.'

'But how can you not recognise your own house?'

'He was tipsy, love.'

'But why did he run, and why did he have to attack Dad?'

'He panicked. He says he didn't recognise your dad.'

'It sounds to me as though he was on more than booze.' Julie's expression made her mum laugh out loud.

Julie's mum shook her head. 'There's no real damage done, is there. Isn't it strange, how you can get yourself completely worked up about something without having all the facts.'

'You don't need to tell me about that after the week I've just had.' Julie laughed. 'Still, it's all sorted now.' She smiled at Adam.

'Did he not know it wasn't his house when his key didn't fit the lock?' Adam asked.

'He was too far gone to even attempt to get his key in the door,' said Julie's dad, who had reached the little group and hugged Julie lopsidedly. 'He broke the little window by the side of the door.'

'Come to think of it, you did mention that when I came up. That window needs proper toughened glass in it, and you need a better lock than that battered old Yale.'

'It's all done. We're sorted.'

'And what about your arm?' Julie said.

'It's grand, love. There's nothing to worry about.' He flexed his fingers. 'Anyway, that's enough of all that. Adam tells us you're due a couple of days off.'

'I am.'

'That's perfect.' He looked around him at the hills and the fields dotted with sheep. 'Then why don't you show me and your mum where you've been hiding all this time.'

'But reprehensible though it is, jealousy is almost rather to be pitied than blamed – its first victims are those who harbour the feeling.' (Arthur Lynch, *Moods of Life*)

ABOUT HONNO

Honno Welsh Women's Press was set up in 1986 by a group of women who felt strongly that women in Wales needed wider opportunities to see their writing in print and to become involved in the publishing process. Our aim is to develop the writing talents of women in Wales, give them new and exciting opportunities to see their work published and often to give them their first 'break' as a writer. Honno is registered as a community co-operative. Any profit that Honno makes is invested in the publishing programme. Women from Wales and around the world have expressed their support for Honno. Each supporter has a vote at the Annual General Meeting. For more information and to buy our publications, please write to Honno at the address below, or visit our website: www.honno.co.uk

Honno, 14 Creative Units, Aberystwyth Arts Centre
Aberystwyth, Ceredigion SY23 3GL

Honno Friends

We are very grateful for the support of the Honno Friends: Jane Aaron, Annette Ecuyere, Audrey Jones, Gwyneth Tyson Roberts, Beryl Roberts, Jenny Sabine.

For more information on how you can become a Honno Friend, see: http://www.honno.co.uk/friends.php